W9-CAH-258

Edwardian England

An era of opulence and hypocrisy, where those with money and status enjoy and those without, serve . . . where pampered aristocrats freely indulge in the most scandalous of pleasures. This is Edward VII's world—frock coats and horse-drawn cabs, secret trysts and tête-à-têtes, luxuriant palms and heavy drapes, coal-fired kitchen ranges and hip baths. A world where one woman, with neither education nor money, but with vision, initiative and beauty, rose to become the owner of a famous exclusive hotel, a celebrated chef, and the confidante of the great. Her name was Louisa Leyton but she was known as . . .

The Duchess
of
Duke Street

The Duchess
of
Duke Street

by Mollie Hardwick

BANTAM BOOKS · TORONTO · LONDON · NEW YORK

*This low-priced Bantam Book
has been completely reset in a type face
designed for easy reading, and was printed
from new plates. It contains the complete
text of the original hard-cover edition.*
NOT ONE WORD HAS BEEN OMITTED.

🚩

THE DUCHESS OF DUKE STREET

*A Bantam Book / published by arrangement with
Holt, Rinehart and Winston*

PRINTING HISTORY

*Holt, Rinehart and Winston edition
published April 1977*

Bantam edition / November 1978

*All rights reserved.
Copyright © 1976 by Egret Productions, Ltd.
This book may not be reproduced in whole or in part, by
mimeograph or any other means, without permission.
For information address: Holt, Rinehart and Winston,
383 Madison Avenue, New York, N.Y. 10017.*

ISBN 0–553–11360–7

*Bantam Books are published by Bantam Books, Inc. Its trade-
mark, consisting of the words "Bantam Books" and the por-
trayal of a bantam, is registered in the United States Patent
Office and in other countries. Marca Registrada. Bantam
Books, Inc., 666 Fifth Avenue, New York, New York 10019.*

PRINTED IN THE UNITED STATES OF AMERICA

ACKNOWLEDGMENT

This novel is based on the BBC Television series "The Duchess of Duke Street," created and produced by John Hawkesworth. The author wishes to thank him and the BBC for their cooperation, and to acknowledge her debt to the following scriptwriters upon whose work she has drawn:

David Butler
John Hawkesworth
Jeremy Paul
Jack Rosenthal
Julian Bond
Bill Craig

The Duchess
of
Duke Street

to go her to eat market and market out thing
yourself. Even a potato."

He beckoned her to follow him
now it to the place. She could see I
get up through the smoky water.

[PART I]

The
Way Up

One

She came out a pace or two from the narrow arched porch of the two-storied, terraced brick house, and looked skyward, assessing the weather. The light of the early spring morning was diffused, bright. The cloud mass was solid, though high. She thought it seemed as if a tent had been put up over London, to keep any rain off for the day. She smiled at the pleasing fancy and turned back to reach for the door-knob.

"Ta-ra!" she called into the recesses of the little house.

Without waiting to listen for any response she shut the door firmly behind her and sailed off down the short street, heels clicking, long skirt swishing about her ankles, chin held high, bright eyes alert to notice any little change in the familiar surroundings of the pretty Essex village, just south of Epping Forest, that was protected by flat open land from the clawing reach of the metropolis.

It was across the broadest of these virgin stretches of grass and low scrub—Wanstead Flats—that the girl walked after leaving the village behind. She was embarking upon a day's voyage of exploration, a sortie from behind those green defenses, which would take her into the heart of the bustling, noisy, grimy,

3

smoky, snobby agglomeration of poverty and luxury, splendor and squalor that was London.

Louisa Leyton was not, however, the sort of person to be deterred, or frightened, or even overawed by this combination of almost wholly alien elements. At twenty-one, she had the moral confidence of having graduated to womanhood. She was healthy and vigorous, almost without experience of lassitude or boredom, and well seasoned in the business of looking after herself. Although she was presently living with her parents, she had been out and about in the world of domestic service since the age of twelve. She had discovered early that while hard work could not be less than hard, it could be made less onerous through efficiency and good organization. If brass were there to be polished, she would polish it as though it were her own, delighting in the result. Fellow servants, watching her, had scoffed and gone on taking shortcuts, making do with the least they could get away with. Louisa had shrugged her shoulders and continued to give of her best, for her own satisfaction as much as for her employers'. She was confident that she would not be doing such work forever. So, meanwhile, what was worth doing was worth doing well; and if something was not worth doing, she was not afraid to say so. Even in the year 1900, there was enough of a servant shortage to enable one so capable to risk being given the sack.

And she was beautiful. Louisa's beauty was not of the lush, exotic kind. Her eyes did not smolder; they were bright-blue and huge, and they twinkled. Her lips were not invitingly full; they were simply in perfect proportion to the oval, clear-complexioned face. Her dark-brown hair shone. Her figure was trim and slender, exactly suited to her five feet five inches.

As she walked on that morning into the busy Stratford High Street and made for the Swan Inn, many men glanced at her and then gazed, openly or furtively. She swept by imperviously, having long since become unselfconscious about her looks. Ambition was the sole preoccupation of Louisa's mind.

The Swan was the starting point of the Bow and Stratford service of the London General Omnibus Company Limited. Every ten minutes, from 8:00 A.M. until 10:40 P.M., there departed one of the green-painted horse-omnibuses, which, for sixpence, would carry one as far as Regent Circus, the heart of the West End of London (and, there were those in distant countries who nostalgically averred, of the British Empire itself).

As she came in sight of the Swan, Louisa hurried a little, for an omnibus stood ready to leave. The burly driver, walrus-mustached and top hatted in the old fashion, already had his rug wrapped about his knees and the four leather strands of the reins in his left hand, while with the right he was lifting the long whip from its socket. The conductor, a much younger man wearing a curly-brimmed bowler and a dusty suit and overcoat, occupied the iron platform at the rear, at the foot of the curving metal stairs. He was reaching for the bellpull. Louisa was still twenty yards away when she heard the sharp *ping-ping* as he jerked it twice.

"Hey!" she yelled, clutching up her skirt and breaking into a sprint. A little cheer went up from a group of loafers propping up the pub wall as she threw herself at the slowly moving vehicle, grasped the stair-rail, and heaved herself aboard, giving a fine display of ankle in the process. Louisa's ankles were well worth seeing, as the young conductor noted, leaning back against the rail and watching her all the way up the stairs.

It never so much as occurred to her that he was looking. It was the pink of sudden effort, not embarrassment, that colored her cheeks as she emerged onto the open top of the swaying omnibus. Most women, especially unaccompanied ones, preferred to travel in the glassed-in downstairs compartment, leaving the outside to the men, with their uninhibited talk and their tobacco. Not so Louisa Leyton. She loved the top of a bus, that tallest of horse-drawn vehicles, with its bird's-eye viewpoint of all that was going on in the street below and behind the windows of the offices and homes it passed.

It was midmorning when she left Stratford and the top of the bus was completely empty. The choice among the banks of seats was hers. Steadying herself with both hands, she lurched forward along the ticket-littered gangway and took her favorite vantage point, just behind the driver, from where she could see forward as well as to the side. The old man sensed her arrival and glanced around briefly. He grinned and winked. She returned a friendly smile and settled herself to enjoy the journey.

A ride into central London was no new experience for her, but she never found it boring. People fascinated her, people of all kinds. And the route from Stratford to Regent Circus offered a more cosmopolitan cross section of them than any other stretch of a few miles in the world could have done.

It took her through the very heart of the East End, along Bow Road, the Mile End Road, the Commercial Road, Whitechapel, Aldgate. Their pavements teemed with folk. Idling groups of men leaned against public-house walls, smoking and spitting. Respectable, working-class housewives and artisans hurried past them about more purposeful pursuits, carrying baskets, bundles, tools, laden sacks; passing in and out of shops whose signboards bore such names as SMITH, NELSON, HOARE, MIDDLETON, as well as LEVINSKI, TAUB, JAKOBSON, ALVAREZ, WYSZOGRADSKIERSKI and others as exotically complicated, which Louisa tried silently to pronounce and found she couldn't.

And there were people to match such names wherever she looked in this district of the densest immigrant population. She tried to put a nationality to the appearance of a portly man with snow-white hair and intensely sad features who stood on the curb awaiting the chance to cross the road. Was he German, a Pole, a Russian? From what far-off homeland had he come to this overcrowded neighborhood, where poverty, filth, and crime—if not so rampant as Louisa understood them to have been a few years earlier—were still rife? Had he come here willingly, a shrewd man with some capital, tempted by reports of an easy living to be made by taking advantage of the vulnerable poor? Was he some sort of exile, parted from a wife and family—or even one of the anarchists who, rumor had it, had been sent to this part of London to prepare for the revolution, or whatever it was to be?

The omnibus rattled on and the man was lost to her sight, soon to be forgotten. She saw black faces, sallow faces, fat red faces whose owners stumbled and swayed as they progressed; skeletal faces of women with thin, lank hair, who sat motionless on boxes and bundles against garbage-stained walls, so deeply asleep that they might have been dead. And she noticed gaudily dressed and painted girls—children almost, some of them seemed—parading arm in arm, chaffing groups of passing men who were clearly foreign sailors from the docks. Louisa knew that between the stall-lined Commercial Road along which the omnibus was carrying her and the Thames on their left lay the notorious Ratcliff Highway, rechristened St. George's Street and to some degree cleaned up, but still known to sailormen all over the world for its low public houses, its places of unspeakable entertainment, its opium dens, its polyglot—and, to a considerable extent, criminal—population.

The bus stopped frequently and fellow passengers came and went. Louisa was scarcely aware of them, absorbed by the pageant below her. Now the shellfish stalls, the cheap, bright goods of cloth merchants, the darting children, the street musicians and scavenging dogs of the East End gave way to a more orderly, more somber, and, to her, less interesting district. Tall buildings loomed over the neatly dressed men who scurried about the pavements carrying little brown suitcases and wearing preoccupied expressions. Here was the City, where, she knew, life was earnest and grim, too, although in a different way from the East End.

Leadenhall Street, and Cornhill, then out into the congestion of the junction where the imposing Royal Exchange, the Mansion House, and the Bank of England stood, and where the stone Duke of Wellington sat high on his stone horse, oblivious to the live horses of all sizes and conditions that converged from six major thoroughfares, all seeking to cross simultaneously.

"Get back to the bloody bogs!" Louisa heard her driver bellow at a startled little man driving a hooded country cart with the name MURPHY painted on its canvas. The advice was supplemented by cruder suggestions from other drivers obviously more accustomed to London than this interloper. His horse had stopped with fright in the very middle of this broad junction and was impeding the progress of several dozen vehicles, some of which had become locked against one another in trying to squeeze around. Louisa watched with amusement as a huge, bearded City policeman strode fearlessly into the melee, calmly took the petrified animal's head, and proceeded to lead the country wagon across into Poultry, ignoring with dignity the ironic cheers of the other drivers.

They were able to move on again: past the begrimed majesty of St. Paul's; down the steep slope of Ludgate Hill, with the driver's feet bearing hard on the brake. There was a further holdup at Ludgate Circus, where a motor omnibus had broken down, to the derision of the crews of passing horse-trams; but Louisa's veteran driver spied a brief opening, jerked his reins, and took them clattering through, with barely an inch to spare between imprisoned vehicles on either side.

"Well done, driver!" a well-dressed gentleman called out from a seat across the gangway from Louisa. Without turning, the old man raised his whip in acknowledgment. Louisa smiled agreement across at the gentleman, startling him into raising his top hat. By the time they had traversed crowded Fleet Street and the Strand and stopped at Charing Cross, he had gone.

The journey was almost at an end. They negotiated Trafalgar Square, Waterloo Place, with its striking memorial to the Guards dead in the Crimea, and up the short stretch of Lower Regent Street to their destination, Regent Circus, already becoming more widely referred to as Piccadilly Circus.

Clutching her skirts, Louisa went carefully down the steps, to the further gratification of the young conductor, who had stationed himself in readiness. She saw him eyeing her legs and stuck out her tongue.

"Mucky ha'porth!" she told him.

He grinned and made as if to pinch her bottom, but she evaded him with a deft swing of her hips and jumped down to the pavement.

"Ta-ra, ducks," he called. "See you on the way 'ome."

"Like hellers," she answered, and went down into the ladies' conveniences.

Having done what she had been increasingly longing to do ever since they had been somewhere in the neighborhood of St. Paul's, she washed her hands and face and examined herself in a mirror, thankful to note that the white parts of her attire were still white. Fortunately, it was not one of London's grimier days.

When she had climbed the steps again to the street, she stood doubtfully, looking this way and that, staring up at the Eros statue as if it might call down some advice as to the next move she should make. Instead, a female voice at her elbow asked, softly and ingratiatingly, "Are you lost, my dear? Stranger in London, are you?"

She turned to find a plump middle-aged lady, well dressed and wearing jewels, smiling at her. The expression was pleasant, but Louisa didn't fail to observe a certain watchfulness in the eyes, which were not smiling in a way that corresponded to the lips.

"No thanks," she answered politely but firmly. "I'm just wondering which way to take."

"Oh? Where for, my dear?"

"Charles Street, Mayfair."

"Mayfair!" the woman exclaimed. "Oh, that's the other side of town almost. You weren't thinking of walking?"

"I don't mind," Louisa said. The fact that she had walked several miles to catch her bus earlier that morning did not deter her, even though she was wearing her best boots, which were new and still rather stiff.

"I tell you what," the lady said, leaning a little closer. "Come and take a cup of tea with me at the A.B.C. café just across Piccadilly, and I'll draw you a little map of the way. You'd never find it otherwise."

"No you won't, Annie," another voice intervened: a man's, gruff and authoritative. The lady's smile vanished instantly and Louisa looked up to see a tall, grizzled-haired policeman towering over them both.

"You know her, miss?" he asked her, jerking his head at the other.

"No, officer."

"Thought not." He turned to the older woman, who was bridling angrily. "I've warned you once this month, Annie Cork," he told her, "and I'm warning you now for the second and last time. If I catch you accosting any more young women I shall take you straight in. I've had my eye on you the last half-hour, so don't think I shan't know where to watch for you if you try it anywhere else on my beat. Now, buzz off back to Seven Dials and your own kind."

He stared implacably at the woman, almost as if taunting her to insult him and give him the excuse to arrest her. She tossed her head, sneered in Louisa's direction, and flounced away.

"What's all that?" Louisa asked, mystified.

"An old pro. Keeps a couple of places now up Seven Dials way. On the lookout for new talent for her customers. Strangers in London are meat and drink to the likes of her. But," he added more grimly, "she's not finding any on my patch if I can help it. Not her, or any others of her kind. Now, miss, where was it you wanted to be?"

"Charles Street, Mayfair. Is it the other side of town?"

He grinned, showing tobacco-stained teeth.

"Not it. Look, you could go up Regent Street here and cut across Berkeley Square way. You know that?"

"Not really," Louisa admitted. None of her previous visits to London had taken her much farther west than where she stood now.

"Right, then," the policeman said. "See there—Piccadilly? Just you walk along there and keep going ten, fifteen minutes till you get Green Park on your left. Then keep watching the turnings on the opposite side and you'll come to Half Moon Street. All right?"

"Half Moon Street. Yes."

"Go up there and bear left and across into Queen Street. Go up that, and Charles Street runs right across the end, left and right. You can't miss it."

"Half Moon Street and Queen Street," Louisa repeated. "Ta very much."

"Whole way won't take you more than about twenty minutes." He winked. "Not a sprightly young lass like you. But don't go speaking to strange women— or men."

She rewarded him with her warmest smile. The policeman touched the brim of his helmet in salute and stood, watching admiringly the sway of her hips as she went off in the direction he had indicated.

The walk down Piccadilly proved as interesting to her, in a different way, as the bus trip had been. The pavements were again crowded, as was the broad thoroughfare. But now the people she passed among were almost all well dressed, some exceptionally so; and among the omnibuses and trams and cabs moved trim, highly polished private carriages, with glossy horses and liveried drivers, and sometimes a footman standing on a little platform at the rear.

Before long, on the left, as the policeman had instructed, began Green Park, fringed by trees overhanging its tall railings, which in turn were fringed by a long line of hansom cabs awaiting hire. The gleam of water caught her eye beyond the grassy stretches, and flights of white birds wheeled and settled. Louisa's spirits, already exhilarated by so many interesting sights, lifted further at the country-like prospect.

But now she must begin looking out for Half Moon Street. Stratton Street, Bolton Street, Clarges Street . . . Could she have missed it? No, here it was—the next turning. Thankfully, she took it. At its end she found herself in what seemed almost to be a replica of some old-fashioned village, with a cobbled square and small, spruce houses with sash windows, and bow-windowed shops. But there was nothing old-fash-ioned-looking about the many girls who sauntered here or leaned against doorways and corners; unless, Louisa thought, with another of her happy fancies, it was their profession that was old-fashioned. She read a sign, SHEPHERD MARKET, and recalled having heard of the place in some scurrilous connection.

She passed through it, incurring a variety of curious and hostile glances from the girls, and found Charles Street at last. And now she paused, and from her little handbag brought out the letter bearing the precise address she was seeking. Looking left and right, she located the section of the street in which the house number would lie. She read the letter for the last time, checked again the address and the name, then put the paper back into her bag.

For the first and only time her heart gave a little flutter of apprehension. She took a deep breath and swallowed.

"Come on, girl," she admonished herself silently. "Here we are. Let's get on with it."

And, bracing her shoulders back and sticking her chin an inch higher into the air, she strode purposefully toward Lord Henry Norton's town house.

Two

The woman who greeted Louisa in a plain but comfortable room far beyond the front door of the Georgian house could have been no bigger than herself, so far as actual feet and inches went. But her middle age, her long, firm-jawed face, and her black attire made even the spirited girl feel very much the raw junior offering herself up for scrutiny. The instinct irritated her and she consciously fought back at it.

"I am Mrs. Catchpole, Lord Henry Norton's housekeeper," the quietly formidable woman was saying. "And this"—she indicated a heavily built, mournful-eyed man of about her own age, dressed in black morning coat and striped trousers—"this is Monsieur Alex, his lordship's *chef de cuisine*."

Louisa hesitated, unsure whether to offer her hand to either, but since neither made any move she refrained. The heavy man did not so much as nod. He regarded her sadly, as if anticipating her bringing some further burden of sorrow for him to bear.

"Please sit down," Mrs. Catchpole said. It was more order than invitation. Louisa sat on the hard chair indicated, keeping her back straight and her chin up, a pose which, assiduously studied some years before, had now become habitual to her.

Mrs. Catchpole picked up a letter from the table in

front of her. Louisa could recognize it, despite the distance between them.

"We have here your letter applying for the position of assistant cook in Lord Henry Norton's household," the housekeeper went on. "Tell me, Miss Leyton—do you *enjoy* cooking?"

"Oh, yes, ma'am," Louisa could reply honestly.

She heard a rumble as the man cleared his throat, preparing to speak. His accent was, she presumed, French.

"Miss Leyton . . . *why* do you want to come here?"

"I'd like to come and work, and learn things—from a proper French cook like you, sir."

She saw his eyebrows rise at the word *cook* and realized too late that she should have said *chef.* He looked even more sorrowful.

Mrs. Catchpole said, "Your references are good. But it appears you haven't worked before in an establishment such as this one."

"No, ma'am." Louisa put all her ambition into her further words. "But I've always wanted to. Ever so much. For years and years. Ever since Ma . . . my mother took me away from school and put me into service."

"Oh? And how long ago was that?"

"Nearly ten years, ma'am. When I was twelve. I'd learned a bit of cooking at the Board School, you see. They gave you classes when you was older. But I've had to do everything—kitchen maid, scullery maid, tweeny . . . until the last year or two, that is, when I've been cooking."

The chef asked, "What standard of cooking have you reached?"

She turned to face him and answered frankly. "Not too bad. I mean, nothing really fancy or special. That's why I want to come here and learn."

It seemed to do nothing to reassure him. He fell silent again. Mrs. Catchpole went on. "We aim to achieve a very high standard of service in this house.

We maintain a large staff, and there are strict rules."
She watched keenly for Louisa's reaction.

"We do not allow gentlemen followers."

"No, ma'am."

"You yourself . . . are not in any way attached?"

"No, ma'am," Louisa answered, with a firmness which clearly surprised her interrogator. "Nor do I intend to be."

"I see. One half-day off a week is allowed, and every other Sunday. Church attendance is expected. Are you Church of England?"

Louisa hesitated fractionally, then reminded herself that she had been a few times in her life to the beautiful Georgian parish church of St. Mary's at Wanstead.

"Yes, ma'am," she answered. If Mrs. Catchpole noticed the hesitation, she let it go without comment.

"You would have to provide all your own uniform. You would have twenty-six pounds a year and a bedroom to yourself. Do you wish to be considered for the position?"

Louisa's heart leaped.

"Yes, please, ma'am." There was no hesitation at all this time.

"Very well," Mrs. Catchpole said with finality. She rang a little handbell and the young footman who had opened the door to Louisa and escorted her to the housekeeper's room returned for her.

"Then if you have no questions," Mrs. Catchpole said, "you will report with your belongings on Monday morning." She glanced at the letter again. "You have a long way to travel, so not later than ten o'clock will be in order on this occasion."

"I'll try to get the first bus—at eight," Louisa babbled in her excitement. "Only there's a lot of men crowds it out, usually. I won't be late, ma'am. Thank you, ma'am. Sir."

She could feel the cook's hooded eyes on her as she marched smartly away in the footman's wake. No.

Not *cook*. *Chef de cuisine*. As was her habit with anything she knew she must learn, or sensed would be useful to her sometime, Louisa Leyton imprinted the title firmly into her mind. Like everyone else, she admitted, she made mistakes. But it was her proud boast that she never made the same mistake twice.

"Assistant cook!" her mother eehood when Louisa got home, after a journey during which she had sat oblivious to everything except the day's achievement.

"Assistant cook! That's not much to write home about. You were a proper cook in your last place."

"Oh, yeh. To a pipsqueak of a dentist in Muswell Hill. They hadn't no class. Nothing. They even had high tea."

"We have high tea!" Mrs. Leyton bridled. She was in her late forties, handsome about the eyes, with narrow cheeks and large upper teeth which showed prominently when she drew back her lips in a laugh or a sneer. A volatile, emotional woman, she was capable of doing either with little provocation.

"For pity's sake, Ma," Louisa said, "it's nothing to do with high tea. It's with getting on in the world."

"Well, I just don't understand you, Louisa. Cook and now assistant cook . . ." Her tone softened. "Look, you've grown up into a very nice-looking girl. . . ."

Louisa enjoyed baiting her mother.

"Think I should go up the West End, then? If I'd have known, I could've taken me chance today."

"If you talk like that I'll clip you one," her mother threatened. "And you know what I mean. I mean there's at least three or four respectable, hardworking young men round here would marry you like a shot, and you know it. And there's no need to snort like that. Frank Belling's been round to see your dad and me."

"Frank Belling!" The young man was a harmless,

insignificant being, apprenticed to his father's family upholstery business. "You never told me."

"Well, he has. He's a nice boy and not bad-looking. . . ."

"Sort of thing you turn up under a stone. Anyway, I don't want to get married to Frank Belling or anybody else. I want to get on for myself, by working for the best people there is. Rich people. Lords and ladies, with big houses and jewels and lovely clothes. And the best food. I want to see it all. Be part of it."

Her mother rolled her eyes. Louisa insisted. "You know what they say. 'Rub against gold and a bit may stick to you.' "

"Marvelous! Think you're a duchess already, I suppose. And all the time getting less than you had before."

"That's all you worry about, isn't it?" Louisa shouted back, really stung. "It's all you've ever worried about. Well, you'll get your money regular, same as before, so don't you worry."

"That's not fair!" Mrs. Leyton answered indignantly.

"It is fair," she retorted. "You may not like it, but it *is* fair. It's all you've ever worried about with me. It's why you made me into a drudge when I was twelve and wouldn't let me stay on at school and be a teacher, like I wanted. You wanted me off your hands, and that's what you've got. Only, now I'm going to do what I want to do—and no one's going to stop me!"

She stamped away to her little room and began sorting through her limited belongings, deciding which garments would still do and which would have to be replaced from her few pounds' savings.

Her insistence that the accusation she had made against her mother was a fair one was partly justified, partly not. She had been taken from school against her will and sent into service, and she had been made to hand over a proportion of whatever little wages she had earned. She did not know that they were much poorer than she believed.

Both Ernest Leyton and his wife came from respectable origins. His father had been a senior clerk in a mercantile office in the City. Hers had been a craftsman, an engraver and setter of precious stones. Both were now dead.

Louisa's parents had been married nearly twenty-seven years now, living for almost all that time in the southern part of Essex. They had two children only —Louisa and her brother, Gerald, three years her senior. Her father's trade was self-employed clockmaker and repairer, and her recollections of childhood were of a happy atmosphere in the home and less of the pinching and scraping which seemed to have been going on now for almost as long as she could clearly remember.

Gerald had stayed at school until he was fifteen. He had then gone into an insurance office, where he had stayed four years before dismaying the rest of the family by throwing away a job with good prospects because of some apparently petty dispute with his manager and joining the army as a trooper. He was now serving in the South African war with his regiment, but seldom wrote home.

What Louisa didn't know was that her parents had agreed that she, too, should be allowed the benefit of a full school career. She was bright and eager, and her teachers had shared her hope that their own profession would be within her chances of attainment. But when she was twelve her father had sunk his savings into an automatic mechanism for clocks shown to him by a persuasive German traveler who had convinced him that, by taking on the sole British agency, he would make a small fortune. Ernest Leyton had discussed with his wife what sounded like a most favorable gamble, and she had agreed to his taking it.

The traveler never visited Mr. Leyton again, and letters to his German address were returned as undeliverable. Small supplies of the mechanism had, indeed, arrived. It was a good device and well made. Its only defect was that it was copied from someone else's recent patent, and it was not long before Ernest Leyton was being notified of this by lawyer's letter, after he had disposed of six new clocks. The clocks could not be sold over the counter without infringing the patent law. They were returned to Mr. Leyton, who was just able to scrape up enough money to make a full refund. The premium he had paid for the exclusive rights, though, was irrecoverable.

Without money to buy legitimate stock he could carry on business no longer; but he had no source of such money, except the freehold house in which they all lived in Epping. There was nothing to do but sell it and look for something smaller. Nothing suitable had been available in Epping, but the little house in Camden Road, Wanstead, had been brought to their notice. In size it was quite a comedown from what they had been used to. The neighbors were respectable, though, and Wanstead was no less agreeable a place in which to live than Epping. So they had moved. And Louisa, who had sadly expected to be transferred from her happy Board School at Epping to an unfamiliar one at Wanstead, had been shattered to be told instead that her schooldays were over, and she must work for a living.

Her parents could have confided the reasons to her, and she would have understood. They did not. Some false sense of shame and pride prevented Mr. and Mrs. Leyton from explaining what had gone wrong for them. The firm that had discovered Ernest Leyton's unintentional deception had acted harshly against him, implying that he had known perfectly well that the clock mechanism was being used without license, and had accused him of endangering their good name. Since none of the clocks had actually been sold to the public, and full restitution had been made, they had been prepared to let the matter rest without recourse to legal proceedings, they had told him in a severe letter. But there could be no question of future dealings.

This had left the susceptible Mr. Leyton feeling like a reprieved criminal. Together with the self-reproach he had adopted for letting himself be fooled so easily, as he saw it, it had broken his will to work. An embittered ruin of a once-eager craftsman, he now worked at home, taking in what repairs he could get from advertisements in the local newspaper and only occasionally making a clock to order.

So Louisa's small contributions to the household expenses had been of more importance than she had ever known. Her mother had bitten her lip and kept silent when her daughter had reproached her for taking her away from school. Her consolation was that, with such looks and vivacity, the girl would make an early marriage and would soon forget all about wanting to teach.

Oddly enough, though, Louisa had never shown any romantic inclinations. She had openly scoffed at the news that this or that girl in the neighborhood was going to be married, commenting that that was about all they were fit for, anyway. For a while, Mrs. Leyton had believed that this was merely adolescent braggadocio, or even secret envy. In recent years she had become less sure. She still made attempts at matchmaking, but Louisa's response was invariable.

For her part, after getting over the initial shock and the many little humiliations associated with a first experience of menial service, Louisa had felt ambition growing.

Her first visits home from her place of employment had been ones of blissful release. But in time she had come to find the little house less inviting in its cramped atmosphere of gloom. She had struck up some warm belowstairs friendships—although keeping the male servants firmly in their place—and she found herself reluctantly having to admit to feeling relief when the time came for her to end her brief visit home and go back to work.

Not that she had worked in any grand households so far. Her first employment—eight pounds a year and no washing—had been in the home of a manufacturer whose servants included a female cook, a serving man (scarcely grand enough to be termed a butler), a housemaid, a lady's maid, a young man of all work, and herself, as "general help and bottle-washer." It was a modest enough detached suburban house on a couple of acres of ground, but the discipline was strict: up at half-past five for a "spit and a lick" of her face from the cold water in the ewer; then downstairs to clear out the grates and riddle their contents in order to salvage for reuse any fragments of coal; then on to light the fires—kitchen fire first, of course, for preparing tea and bacon for the other servants coming down.

Then cleaning shoes, washing linoleum, dusting, sweeping, running errands, carrying heavy loads up flights of stairs (while pretending to be invisible, should the mistress or her visitors be encountered on the way), and scores of other duties which filled the day to the full, only to be repeated the next and the next, for as far ahead as could be seen.

But she was strong, and she was young, and she was cheerful. It made the most thankless task lighter, she believed, if you convinced yourself that you were contributing to the efficient running of an organization, which in turn was enabling the master to conduct his business efficiently and prosperously, which in turn . . . Louisa's philosophy of work amused her fellow servants, none of whom seemed to share it—except the cook.

This elderly spinster who bore the honorary title *Mrs.* before her name, which was Wilkinson, was a no-nonsense Yorkshirewoman in her mid-sixties

whose plain style of cooking was superbly carried
out. She had been cooking all her life, she told Louisa, and even on the most ordinary dish the girl never
saw her work without care and concentration.

"There's steak and kidney, and there's steak and kidney," Mrs. Wilkinson declared, after being complimented on one of her pies for staff luncheon. "Doesn't
matter a scrap how much tha spends on what goes in
if tha doesn't bother to think on all't time tha's mek-
king it. I say, tha must *think on*."

Louisa had learned a lot from this excellent woman;
not least that cookery was the most creative of all the
domestic crafts, and the one least taken for granted
by those for whom it was done. Nor was it capable
of being done by just anybody. Louisa resolved then
that, if she were to remain a servant, she would become a cook and run someone's grand kitchen the
way she wanted it run, and no more scurrying about
at everyone else's beck and call.

She was many years becoming a cook at all, though.
The domestic ladder was too steep for a child to
climb; and for every cook, there were a dozen other
lesser servants. Her first employer died suddenly
when she had been at his house less than a year. The
widow sold up and the staff was dispersed. Louisa
went down to an agency and found another place.
But it was like starting all over again, in a less agreeable household, among less agreeable servants and
employers. So she tried elsewhere, and then elsewhere again, learning that the atmosphere belowstairs reflected that upstairs, and that hard masters
and mistresses made for tyrannical butlers and dis-
contented cooks who took out their resentment on
their underlings. Her own refusal to be put upon
brought her into several conflicts. In seven years she
had twelve jobs, and her references began to read
less than enthusiastically.

Then she became a cook at last, because she was in
one of those households that only ran to a cook, a

man, and a little maid. She lied her way into the post, the mistress of the house having been called away for a few days and only the master being there to interview her. Luck went her way. He ate out at his club on each of the several days before his wife returned. It gave Louisa time to get herself organized in the kitchen, read up the notes she had taken from Mrs. Wilkinson all those years before, and do some experimenting on herself and the other two servants. They expressed themselves satisfied with what she gave them. She, judging it against her memories of her Yorkshire mentor's products, reassured herself that she'd got the touch, all right. When the household was reassembled she was able to cook for it with confidence; and when, at length, her master's firm moved him away and she had to find yet another situation, she took with her a truly glowing testimonial to her abilities as a "good plain cook."

There had followed the less than fulfilling months with the dentist's family at Muswell Hill. During it, Louisa had given herself a good catechizing one Sunday, as she sat on Hampstead Heath among hundreds of others of her class. It was not long after her twenty-first birthday. She had spent nearly ten years in a sphere of life she hadn't wished to enter at first, but with which she had come to terms. They hadn't been wasted years. She had used them to gain knowledge and experience. All she had lost had been some of the outside pleasures a less confined occupation might have let her enjoy, and she didn't mind about those. (She had also lost, without realizing it, something of the good speaking accent she had once had. Without knowing it, she had let herself be influenced by the prevailing Cockney of most of the servants she had lived among.)

So, nothing had been wasted yet; but from now on, it would be.

"Come on, gel," she said to herself, getting up impatiently and brushing grass from her bottom. "It's time you was making a move, 'cos you've a long way to go."

After a few days of searching the newspapers she had come across the advertisement that had led her to Charles Street, Mayfair, that later morning.

Three

As she traveled in one of the crowded early buses on Monday morning, with her small carpetbag tied to the outside of the stair-rail by the same cocky young conductor, Louisa congratulated herself yet again on having got entry into a great house as helper to a real *chef de cuisine*—she no longer needed to remind herself not to think of him as a cook. She couldn't know how miserably he himself was viewing the prospect of her coming.

Mrs. Catchpole was at that moment defending the awaited newcomer from further despondent speculations. "Nonsense, Monsieur Alex. She seemed tidy and clean, and well mannered."

He gave a Gallic shrug.

"But does she look like a *cook?* More like a chorus girl."

It was Mrs. Catchpole's turn to shrug.

"Her references are very satisfactory. I've spoken on the telephone with her last employer."

"The dentist?" he asked with an edge of sarcasm.

"His wife, of course. An intelligent, educated-sounding woman. She assessed the girl's qualities very candidly."

"But I do not want a woman. Women make cooks, not chefs."

The housekeeper sighed and reminded him yet

again. "There were no male applicants for the post. They all want restaurant work, you know perfectly well, Monsieur Alex. We must simply do our best with her."

He let out a great sigh, whose meaning needed no seeking out.

So, although she didn't know it, Louisa already had the housekeeper as her champion, which was not a bad start.

Louisa's theory that servants reflected masters would have seemed insubstantial—if she had even given it thought at the time—when Mrs. Catchpole introduced her to her colleagues that morning. They seemed to be a mixture of the aloof, the indifferent, the friendly, and, she sensed in two instances, the downright hostile.

The kitchen of Lord Henry Norton's house was larger than any Louisa had yet been in, let alone worked in. It had all the appearance of a small factory, with benches, machines, brass wheels, pulleys, and rack upon rack of the equipment of cooking and serving. The number of servants passing to and fro astonished her.

The dislike she encountered was in the eyes and manner of the two kitchen maids. The elder, Jean, was dark and Scottish, in her late thirties, perhaps. She was neat and prim, and a contrast to the other, Ivy, a much younger blonde girl, grubby and untidy, with a hoarse, coarse voice that seemed to fit perfectly with her appearance. Her accent was a mixture of London and the country.

A third maid, the maid of all work, gave Louisa a warm smile and a decent handshake. She was the youngest of all, and the smallest, still in her teens. Her pretty round face was topped with neat dark hair. She was introduced as Mary, and when she spoke it was with an engaging Welsh lilt.

Louisa sensed accurately that Jean and Ivy were jealous of her appointment as assistant cook. She would soon be giving them orders. Meanwhile, she anticipated that they would put plenty of obstacles in her way, in the hope that she would pack up and go. Well, she'd show them about that! That they were also jealous of her looks never occurred to her.

"Looks a proper little trollop to me," Ivy confided to Jean beyond the glass window of the scullery, not long after Louisa had been set to her first task by Monsieur Alex.

"I've no doubt that's exactly what she is," Jean agreed loftily.

Mary, scrubbing the floor, said, "I think she looks nice."

"No one asked your opinion," Jean reminded her.

"No," Ivy said. "And don't you speak till you're spoke to." She and Jean peered through the glass. "What's she doin'?"

"Making *crème caramel*," Jean answered. "Like he always tests them with."

Ivy snorted. "I bet she 'asn't the first idea. I mean, look at them clothes. Button-up boots in the kitchen! I dunno why you didn't get the job, Jean. Honest, I really don't. I reckon Missyer Alex must've gone soft in the 'ead."

"Nothing to do with him," Jean answered darkly. "He's very upset about it. It was all influence, if you ask me."

"What influence?"

"*Upstairs* influence."

"What! You don't mean 'is lordship . . . ?"

Jean tossed her head and went on with her work, as she saw the chef enter the kitchen and go over to inspect the new girl's progress. He picked up the copper mold containing a set yellow mass, and put it down again without a second glance.

"Who taught you to do this?" he asked in his monotone.

Louisa missed the nuance. She replied proudly, "Oh, I just picked it up. You know, from other cooks."

His response startled her. "It will be *dégoûtant*. Disgusting."

She stared into the heavy features.

"Give us a chance, Monsieur Alex. Wait till it's cool."

"My dear young lady, I do not need to wait until it is cold to say that it will be uneatable. Like leather. Too many whites of egg. Overcooked."

Even his low tones were audible to the girls in the scullery. They nudged one another delightedly, as they heard him add, "For the moment you will please go and help Ivy with the washing-up."

What came next took them completely aback.

"No, I will not!" came the high, ringing response. "I didn't come here to wash up. If you wish it, I'll go. But if I stay, I'll stay as your assistant cook, not as a scullery maid."

The girls stared as Monsieur Alex stared, too. They saw him glance toward the window at them. He turned sharply and walked out of his kitchen, followed, moments later, by the new girl, chin held high.

They giggled together.

"Well, I never did," Ivy said. "Thought she was going to 'it 'im, for a minute."

"She's a real little minx, that one," Jean agreed. "I don't want her coming in here, and I shall tell Monsieur Alex so."

"Don't worry, luv. She'll be out by dinnertime—on the street."

"Aye. And that's where she should have been in the first place."

Louisa had gone straight to her attic room, in obedience to the first instinct that had come to her. She took down her carpetbag from the top of the small wardrobe, opened it, and started to throw things into it from her drawers. After a few minutes there came a knock at the door.

"Yes," she demanded, not caring who it was.

The door opened and the little Welsh maid came

cautiously in, carrying a cup and saucer on a tray, and a plate of biscuits.

"I thought you might like a cup of tea," she said shyly. "As I was making some for the others."

Touched and deflated, Louisa said, "That's very kind of you, Maisie."

"Mary, miss. It's really M-e-r-r-i, you know, only no one knows that name here, so Mary's the easiest way."

"Sorry, Mary," Louisa said, taking the tray. "You been here long?"

"Quite a long time," the girl answered. "At least, it seems so. It will be fourteen weeks next Monday."

"Happy?"

"Well . . . No. Not very happy."

Louisa poured her tea. "Well, that was a silly thing to ask, anyway. How can a maid of all work be happy?"

"But I'm very grateful for the position," came the eager answer. "It's a lot better than nothing."

"You know how to make tea, at least. Was it 'nothing' before?"

"Almost worse. There were so many of us at home, we were nearly sleeping on the roof. They said in our street that every time my father sneezed my mother had another baby. Only, my father died last year. My Aunt Gwynnedd brought me up to London and found me this job. So I was lucky really, wasn't I?"

Louisa smiled sympathetically, pleased to meet a fellow philosopher. Mary continued, "Though, there's some days, with Jean in one of her moods, and Ivy going on at me all the time, I could just run away."

Louisa put down her cup. It rattled sharply against its saucer.

"Don't you run away, Mary. Don't you *ever* run away. Wait till they chuck you out first."

Mary looked doubtfully at the half-packed case and asked, "Have they given you your notice, then, miss?"

"No," Louisa had to admit. She sighed. "It's all my own fault if they do. I can't keep my big mouth shut, Mary. That's my trouble. Never have been able to. I need a clothes-peg. I got a temper, too, and that's not much help."

But Mary was looking at her admiringly.

"I thought it was wonderful, the way you stood up to Monsieur Alex," she said. "He had no right to treat you like that."

" 'Turn the other cheek,' " Louisa quoted. "Fighting back doesn't get you nowhere."

But Mary replied, "I don't know so much. I remember one day when my Uncle Ifor had had a few drinks he came back swearing and saying he'd knock my Aunt Gwyn's block off. And she just stood up to him and gave him what for and spat in his face. And he just sat down in a chair by the fire, quiet as a little dog. And he's a big man, my Uncle Ifor. Played rugby for Neath."

"There you are, then," Louisa said, personally fortified by this. "Next time Ivy gets at you, just remember your aunt."

"Oh, I couldn't do that," the girl smiled wistfully. "It's not in my nature. But I'll remember you, miss. Finished?"

She took the tray, and went quietly away. Louisa sat on for a few minutes, thinking. Then she got up, unpacked the bag, and put the things away. She returned the bag to the wardrobe top. She went to the washstand mirror to check her hair, put her tongue out at her reflection, and went back downstairs.

Monsieur Alex had obviously been waiting for her. He beckoned her to follow him into his little office. Her instinct was to apologize, but he forestalled her.

"Frankly, I do not understand why I should have to waste my valuable time teaching you to do something for which you have no talent. But I am told that I must do what I can with you." At this, all thought of apologizing left her.

"I'm sorry you feel like that," she answered. "All I want is a chance, like I was promised when I was took on."

"*I* never promised anything," he retorted, then lapsed into baleful silence, as if engaged in some inner conflict. At length he let out one of his sighs and continued, "Tell me, Leyton, what do you personally consider is the most important piece of equipment of a cook?"

"Well, I suppose the stove . . ."

"No, no, no." He tapped his nose. "It is this. And after smell, taste—the tongue. And then the eyes."

"I see," she said unconvincingly. He shook his head.

"I don't believe you see at all. You are a good-looking girl. Why don't you try to find something else to do? Why do you want to be a cook?"

She determined, once and for all, to squash these attempts to deter her.

"'Cos I do. I can't say why—not exactly, but I do. I may be a lousy cook now, but I'm willing to learn. I'll work myself to the bone and won't skimp nothing, if you'll teach me. I love cooking. I do really."

Her sincerity was evident to him, and he capitulated to it.

"Please sit down," he said, in an altogether less dispirited tone. Then he began to pace the floor, saying, "The first thing to learn is that cooking is not just *un métier*—a job. It is an art. The kitchen is as important as an artist's studio. To be a cook needs hard work, but it also needs talent. Nothing is worse than to be a bad cook. It is better to wash dishes than to cook badly. So first you have to wipe your mind clean. Forget everything you have learned before. Yes?"

Louisa nodded eagerly. He had put into words exactly what she already felt about cooking.

"*Bon!*" he said. "Now, first principle, everything must be clean, exact, planned. Plain, simple food, well cooked, is always the best. But always the best materials. Michelange always used the best marble. And only one way is possible to be sure of the best. That is to go out to the market and choose everything yourself. Even a potato."

He beckoned her to follow him again and led her back to the kitchen. She could see Ivy and Jean watching hopefully through the scullery window. She fancied their expressions changed when, instead of sending her to her room to pack, as they had confidently expected, he took her to the working table and indicated the objects on it.

"Here is how you must each day lay the table for me, for the *chef de cuisine*. Each item must be exactly in the correct place—salt box, pepper mill, chopping board, knives, cloths, thyme, parsley . . ."

He was interrupted by the arrival down the kitchen steps of a tall, dark-haired man in black. Louisa recognized instantly that he must be the butler. She was surprised by his youthfulness for the high office. He could not be more than thirty-five or so.

"Good morning, Monsieur Alex," he said.

"Good morning, Mr. Trotter. May I introduce my new assistant here? Miss Leyton. Mr. Trotter, the butler."

The butler shook her hand, and granted her a formal little smile. Then he and the chef went away into Monsieur Alex's office, discussing the wines to accompany that evening's dinner, leaving Louisa to wander around the kitchen, familiarizing herself with its layout and equipment.

When the butler had gone back upstairs Monsieur Alex returned to her.

"*Eh bien*," he said. "Now, for the next few weeks you are going to learn how to make pastry. I expect you think you know how to make pastry, eh?"

She had the sense to answer "No, Monsieur Alex." It pleased him.

"Give me your hands," he said, to her surprise. She held them out across the table and he took each in one of his. Louisa noticed Jean crossing the kitchen with a mixing bowl. Her face was a study as she watched the chef's incredible behavior. But his expression had nothing of emotion in it. He released her hands with a nod of satisfaction.

"You have cool hands. That is a good start. For pastry, everything must be cool."

He turned aside for something. Louisa took the opportunity to grin sweetly at Jean, who went on her way with a set face.

Louisa was able to pay Mary back for her kind gesture within a few days. She came into the kitchen one evening to hear crying from the scullery. She went through and found Mary, washing up a great pile of crockery and cutlery and crying helplessly, so that the tears ran down her nose and into the washing-up water.

"What on earth's the matter?" Louisa demanded.

The Welsh girl shook her head.

"Nothing, miss."

"I thought it was your evening off."

"So it is," Mary managed to answer. "Only, I broke another plate breakfast time and Ivy said I was to stay in and do the washing-up tonight. And she's gone out in my place."

"Has she," Louisa remarked grimly. "But that's not enough to cry about, love."

The girl wiped her face with her forearm.

"It's not that, miss. It's my Auntie Gwyn. She lives in London now and she's been took poorly with the failing of the lungs. She's in hospital, and I'd promised to see her tonight."

Louisa made up her mind. "So you shall. I'll finish this."

"Oh, no, miss, that's not your place. Anyway, the

hospital's away the other side of the river. It'd be too late by I got there now."

"Then you must go in a cab," Louisa told her. She got out her little purse and produced some silver coins and held them out to Mary, who shook her head.

"I could never take that from you, miss."

"Course you can. It's not anything valuable. It's only money."

Mary had never in her life heard anyone speak so casually of that most important of all things. She took the four shillings in a soapy hand and said, "You're . . . a saint, miss. You really are."

"No I'm not. Now, you go and get yourself tidy, and just leave all this lot to me."

The girl hurried away to change. Louisa rolled up her sleeves and began a more orderly assault upon the washing-up.

There was a lot of it, and she was still working when Monsieur Alex came into the scullery. He was wearing his coat, ready to go to his regular rendezvous at one of the servant's public houses in the neighborhood. He frowned when he saw Louisa.

"Why are you doing this? We have two girls."

Louisa said quickly, "Ivy had to go out and Mary's a bit poorly. I dunno where Jean is. Anyway, I don't mind. It's here to be done."

He shook his head. "It is a question of dignity. You are a cook. You do not do menial tasks."

"I'm sorry, Monsieur Alex. I won't do it again."

He grunted and went out. Louisa smiled to herself. Only a few days earlier she had risked the sack by refusing his command to go and help with the washing-up.

The irony was rounded off soon afterward when Jean came in and expressed her own resentment of Louisa's doing work that was not rightly hers. This was the very Jean who only the day before had refused Louisa's request to fetch a cooling tray for some cheese straws Louisa had just drawn from the oven.

"You've got two arms and two legs, same as everyone else," had been Jean's response.

"Yes, I have. But I happen to be using all four of 'em, just at this very minute."

"Well, too bad. Let's get one thing clear, Miss Leyton—I'm Monsieur Alex's kitchen maid, and no one else's. If you want someone to fetch and carry for you, ask one of the others."

Louisa had managed to restrain her tongue, for once, in the interests of future relationships. She did so again, in the face of Jean's complaint about the washing-up, merely remarking, "I must say, we get through an awful lot of stuff for a bachelor household."

Jean said in a superior tone, "The fact that Lord Henry is unmarried doesn't mean that he lives like a hermit. There are guests almost every evening."

"So I notice."

"Hello, hello!" A male voice from the doorway surprised Louisa. It was not Mr. Trotter or any of the footmen, but a tall, very well-dressed young man. She noted instantly how handsome he was, with fair hair and smiling gray-green eyes. But it was Jean he was addressing.

"How nice to see you again, my dear Jean. And how *is* the 'fair maid of Perth'?"

"I'm very well, thank you, Mr. Charlie," she replied. It was obvious to Louisa that he had some connection with the family and seemed to be on very free and easy terms with the maid. He glanced at Louisa and smiled, but Jean made no move to introduce her.

"You may have heard I'll be staying with my uncle for a while," he said to Jean. "Just got here in time for dinner. Actually, I came down to say hello to Monsieur Alex and congratulate him on that delicious lemon sorbet."

She said, "I'll tell him when he gets back, Mr. Charlie. I'm sure he'll be pleased."

This was too much for Louisa. She withdrew her hands from the washing-up water and dried them vigorously, saying, "Excuse me, sir. I made the sorbet. I'm Monsieur Alex's assistant, Louisa Leyton."

He glanced from her to the washing-up and back, then smiled and came to shake her hand.

"Did you indeed?" he said. "I'm Charles Tyrrell. So, my compliments to you, then, Miss Leyton."

He smiled at them both and went out again.

"Of all the cheek!" Jean seethed.

"No it wasn't. It was the truth. Anyway, who's he when he's at home?"

" 'He' happens to be the Honorable Charles Tyrrell, Lord Henry's nephew, son and heir of Lord Haslemere."

Louisa was impressed. "Nice-looker, too."

Jean scowled at her. "If you take my advice you won't start trying any of your tricks on Mr. Charlie."

It was the other way around, though. That night Louisa trudged thankfully upstairs for the last time, looking forward to the comfort of her little bed. She opened the door of her attic room. To her surprise the light was on. In the little wicker chair beside her bed sat the Honorable Charles Tyrrell. He was wearing a silk dressing gown over pajamas. At the sight of Louisa's shocked face and open mouth he quickly put a finger to his lips.

"My dear Miss Assistant Cook," he said in a low voice. "I just came to congratulate you on that sorbet —properly."

She had half closed the door, but made no move to close it completely, though she instinctively kept her voice down.

"I'll bet you have," she said. "And to sample some of my other wares, no doubt."

He smiled broadly. He was very handsome indeed.

"What a percipient young lady you are," he said. From his dressing-gown pocket he had withdrawn a long, slender, expensive-looking box. He held it out to her.

"Here is a little token of my admiration for your cooking . . . and your 'other wares.' "

She did not take it, so he opened it and tilted it forward, to reveal a jet necklace. It was attractive, but Louisa said resolutely, "I don't want nothing from you, thank you very much, sir."

He got up, still smiling confidently.

"I'm sure you're a sensible girl. Experienced, I don't doubt. . . ."

"Here!" Louisa retorted indignantly. "What do you take me for? What do you mean by that?"

He was startled into checking his advance toward her. Her voice had risen and he glanced nervously toward the half-open door.

"I . . . I'm sorry," he stammered. "Please forgive me."

"There's nothing to forgive, and there isn't going to be, neither. So push off."

He grinned tentatively and ventured another step toward her. She pointed to the door.

"If you so much as lay a finger on me I'll scream, and I'll go on screaming till Lord Henry himself hears me."

"Sssh! You don't mean it."

"You just try me."

He hesitated, looking as though he were weighing up the risk. Then he gave a shrug of defeat and went out. Louisa went to close the door behind him, not noticing that he had left the necklace in its box on her washstand.

The next day Louisa was too busy to think of him. That night, alone in her room, she prepared for bed, exhausted. She took off her cap, rubbed her tired eyes with the backs of her hands, and then began unfastening her dress. The sight of her bared neck in the mirror reminded her of the necklace Charlie

Tyrrell had offered. Glancing around the room, she spied the box on her washstand. She couldn't resist taking the necklace out of the box and slipping it on. It looked charming. She pulled down the top of her dress, the better to admire the effect of the necklace in conjunction with her slender neck and the fine skin of her shoulders.

"Marvelous!" Charles Tyrrell's quiet voice came from behind her. "You look like a princess."

Louisa jerked her dress back up, pulled off the necklace, and turned to toss it at him.

"Ooh, you are a sneaky devil, you are!" she told him.

He held up his hands.

"I'm not going to touch you. I promise. May I sit down?"

His manner was so disarming that Louisa relented enough not to object when he quietly closed the door and sat down in the wicker chair.

"You seem to do what you like in here," she said. "Liberty Hall."

"I'm disappointed in you, Louisa Leyton," he said, almost seriously.

"And I'm disappointed in you, the Honorable Mister Charlie Tyrrell. You're all the same, aren't you? You think we're here just for your pleasure, like animals. Have you ever thought what happens when a servant gets put in the family way by one of you lot?"

This frank allusion to his unspoken purpose the previous night startled him visibly. He murmured, "Some . . . some arrangement is made . . . as a rule."

She shook her head. "Arrangement my foot. Chucked out with a week's wages, and no reference, and no hope. If she gets over the baby, which a lot of 'em don't, there's only one thing left—the streets. You go out and ask any tart you like. Even money, she'll tell you she started out in service. At my last place but one there'd been a housemaid called Mona had gone with a sailor. They found her body in the river at Wapping."

He said uncomfortably, "I didn't really come here to be lectured on the problems of the . . ."

"I know what you came for. And it's ones like you that causes the problems."

"Look," he persisted, "I want to talk to you. I mean, seriously."

This surprised her. She said suspiciously, "It's a funny time, and a funny place, and in funny clothes, if you ask me."

He had regained the initiative and answered masterfully, "I'm not asking you. You see, I'm at a . . . a bit of a loose end. I thought of going out to the war . . ."

"Good idea. Give you something to do. Take your mind off other things."

He let the rebuke pass and went on. "The trouble is, all the world and his wife's gone dashing off to South Africa. They don't want any more amateur soldiers, except to dance with the generals' daughters. Of course, there's this new Chinese rebellion. That looks quite amusing, but Pekin's a long way to go just for a lark. So the long and the short of it is that I'm thinking of setting up an establishment in London. I can always come and stay here, but there must be a moment when even a favorite nephew outstays his welcome."

He broke off and looked at her earnestly for some moments. She wasn't aware that she was smiling sympathetically at these ingenuous confessions. When he continued, he picked his words with care.

"If I did . . . set myself up . . . I'd need someone to look after the place for me. To look after me, come to that. I was wondering if that . . . that someone might be you?"

Louisa was staring at him now, genuinely astonished and rather bewildered.

"Bit . . . quick, isn't it?" she managed to reply. "You hardly know me."

"Oh, I'm quick at making decisions. Miss Leyton, I'm serious. It would be a little house, somewhere secluded. A carriage at your disposal, clothes, servants . . ."

Some of his excitement transmitted itself to Louisa, despite herself. Suddenly, totally unexpectedly, she was being offered a position which, while not exactly in high society, would bring her into its ambit and could take her who knew where? She had no doubt about the precise nature of what he was proposing to her. It wasn't a "respectable" situation in the conventional, suburban sense. It almost shocked her, but she did know that these things were looked at quite differently in society. She would no doubt be accepted readily by his friends, and she knew she was capable of adapting herself to the new way of life. It was a chance she had never dreamed would come her way and brought her instantaneously in sight of the goal she had vaguely in mind for herself.

He was looking at her hopefully. She had only to say the word. . . . Instead, she said, "Look, don't think I don't see a gentleman like you needs that sort of place. And, of course, you'll need . . . need a lady to . . . well, you know. That is to say, I'm very honored to be asked. . . . But the fact is, I wouldn't be no good for you."

She saw his disappointment, and felt for him, but she had to go on.

"You'll think I'm barmy, I expect. But I know what I want to be. I want to be the best cook in England. That's all I want to be."

She had only realized it herself at that same instant. Either way, it had to be all or nothing, and she had chosen to go along with her strongest instincts. She looked at him, expecting him to persuade, to argue, even perhaps to laugh. But he only said, very quietly, "What a good idea."

He got up and picked up the necklace. He held it out to her.

"Please keep it, Louisa. From one friend to another."

"All right," she said, and took it. "Thanks, Mr. Charlie."

"Goodbye, Louisa," he said, his hand on the doorknob. "Good luck."

He went out, quickly and quietly. He did not see Jean, in the dark corner of the landing, where she had been standing, straining to hear what was going on in Louisa's room.

Left alone, Louisa sat on the bed and looked at herself in the mirror. She held up the necklace again and looked at its effect against her neck.

"Louisa Leyton," she said to the reflection, "you need your head examined. That's what's wrong with you."

And she proceeded to undress and go to bed. But she went to sleep knowing that, whatever had prompted her to make the decision she had, it had been the right one for her.

Four

It was not the custom for Mrs. Catchpole and Monsieur Alex to take their breakfast with the rest of the servants. They were served alone in their respective rooms. Louisa was in charge of all breakfast operations, although most of the actual work was done by Jean and Ivy.

When staff breakfast was over the next day, Louisa set out the kitchen table with Monsieur Alex's equipment and waited for him to appear. Instead, one of the footmen came to her and said she was wanted in Mrs. Catchpole's room. It was not unusual, although most of the instructions she received came from, or by way of, Monsieur Alex.

Today she was surprised to find them both awaiting her, wearing grim faces.

"Morning, ma'am," Louisa unsuspectingly greeted the housekeeper. The greeting was not reciprocated.

"We have a very serious matter to discuss with you, Leyton," Mrs. Catchpole said. Louisa wondered whether her doing the washing-up had been a graver breach of discipline than she had imagined; or whether she had done wrong in giving Mary the money to go to her aunt when she had been ordered to stay in.

"I'm sorry, ma'am," she began, but Mrs. Catchpole waved her silent.

"Do you admit," she asked, "that there was a man in your bedroom last night?"

Louisa felt the shock of the unexpected, but after the initial confusion she managed to pull herself together.

"Oh, yes, ma'am."

The housekeeper seemed surprised by the ready admission.

"You know it is completely forbidden to admit a man to your room."

"I know, ma'am. Only, it wasn't me admitted him. He admitted himself, bold as brass, when I went up to bed. And I chucked him out."

She had not referred to her visitor's identity. She wondered whether they knew it. She wondered, in fact, how they knew any man had been there at all. Mrs. Catchpole's next words made all clear.

"We have heard that Mr. Tyrrell was in your room by your invitation, and that you made the assignation with him when he visited the kitchen. . . ."

It was immediately plain to Louisa who had carried the tale. She let her temper go.

"Well, you heard wrong. You've been told a pack of lies, and I can just guess by who. Creeping and crawling about . . . spying on people. That's what she was doing, wasn't it? Poking her nose in where it doesn't belong. And you believe her."

The vehemence of this outburst had silenced Mrs. Catchpole. She was looking perplexedly at Monsieur Alex, whose customary lugubriousness had changed to an air of keen interest.

"Jean has been with us for some years," he reminded her.

She turned on him savagely. "So it's her word against mine, is it? All right, you can have my notice here and now. Or we'll all go up and see Mr. Tyrrell and ask him the truth, shall we? Yes, and take Jean up with us."

Both her superiors recoiled from this notion. Mrs. Catchpole said quickly, "Now, Leyton, we . . . we mustn't get all hot and bothered about this. As we know, even in the best establishments there are bound to be upsets from time to time. It's up to us to try to settle them in the most sensible way."

Louisa appeared far from appeased, though. The housekeeper went on with difficulty.

"You've done very well here so far. Monsieur Alex was telling me only yesterday that he is quite happy to leave the kitchen in your hands when his lordship's away and he himself is on holiday. In view of the circumstances, then, and in the light of your own honesty, I think the best thing is for us to forget the entire thing."

Louisa said, more calmly, "Thank you, ma'am. I'm quite prepared to forget all about the incident . . . on one condition."

The others looked sharply at one another, but they turned back to listen to her finish.

"On condition that Jean apologizes to me in front of Monsieur Alex."

Mrs. Catchpole was about to reply that this was quite unnecessary and to remind Louisa that it was not for her to dictate terms to her superiors. Monsieur Alex sensed as much, though, and nudged her under the table with his knee. She looked at him and read enough in the almost expressionless face to make her desist.

"Very well," she told Louisa. "I think that would be only right."

Jean was sent for, there and then. After some hedging and protestations that she hadn't meant to accuse Louise outright, but had merely been "doing her duty as she thought fit," she had to capitulate. She turned to Louisa and held out her hand, saying, "I'm sorry I made a mistake about you, Miss Leyton. I wish to apologize."

There was no apology in her eyes; but Louisa took the hand and said, "Do you? That's nice. Thank you, Jean."

When the two girls had gone, the housekeeper and chef breathed sighs of relief. Clearly Louisa Leyton's wrath could be formidable. Each of them made a mental note not to stir it up again without complete justification for taking the risk.

Lord Henry Norton, a bulky, retiring man in his late forties of whom Louisa had seen very little in the few months she had been in his employment, duly went off to Scotland in the summer, taking his nephew with him. Monsieur Alex departed for Spain to visit a sister who had married and settled there. Dust sheets were spread over the furniture in most of the upstairs rooms and the drawing-room chandelier was taken down, dismantled, and sent away for regilding.

Usually, Mr. Augustus Trotter, the butler, traveled with his master, but on this occasion he had not been required to do so. He and Mrs. Catchpole remained to preside over an empty house and a much-depleted staff, with Louisa in full charge of the kitchen.

One afternoon Louisa was summoned again to Mrs. Catchpole's room. This time she found Mr. Trotter there. He held a piece of paper in his hand and both of them regarded her with serious speculation as she entered. She wondered what she had done wrong this time.

"Miss Leyton," Mrs. Catchpole began, to Louisa's relief—it would have been just "Leyton" if there had been trouble coming—"Mr. Trotter has received a telegram from his lordship. He is returning from Scotland earlier than we had expected."

The butler flourished the telegram.

"There is to be an important dinner party for ten on Thursday."

Louisa stammered, "But we haven't got a chef. Could we borrow Lord Haslemere's?"

Mr. Trotter shook his head. "The family have taken him to Yorkshire with them."

Mrs. Catchpole said, "We would like you to cook that dinner, Miss Leyton."

"Me!" was Louisa's reaction. "You . . . you said it was important."

"So it is. Monsieur Alex has expressed every confidence in you. You've a full kitchen staff, so there should be no problems about the number."

Mr. Trotter gave Louisa an encouraging smile.

"You might regard it as your big chance," he said warmly.

Feeling rising excitement, Louisa swallowed and said, "Well, I'll have to, then, won't I? I wouldn't like to let his lordship down."

"Good girl. Now, come with me and we'll discuss the menu in detail."

The butler led her off to his pantry, where they remained a full hour, with paper, pencils, and Mr. Trotter's invaluable pantry book, in which he had written and pasted innumerable scraps of information, garnered over his years in service. The menu they eventually decided on was as follows:

Chicken Broth
Sole with White Wine Sauce
Roast Grouse, Bread Sauce, Game Chips,
Truffles, Mixed Spices
Champagne Water Ice
Pears in Lemon Juice

"So," he said finally, reviewing the list of wines he had needed no list to choose from, "Madeira with the soup, champagne, dry monopole with the fish, Richebourg 'Eighty-four with the grouse, Château d'Yquem 'Seventy-nine with the pears in lemon juice. Should do very nicely."

Louisa said admiringly, "However do you remember all them, Mr. Trotter?"

"Practice . . . experience," he answered proudly. "I think I was almost born with a certain interest in wine. And traveling with his lordship has somewhat sharpened that interest."

"Where have you been mostly?"

"Most years we shoot partridges with the Duc de Noailles near Paris. Then on to Count Metternich for the boar-shooting in the Eiffel. And home of course it's the pheasants mainly, at Sandringham or Chatsworth or Welbeck."

"'We'? D'you mean you're allowed to shoot as well?"

"Yes, indeed. I act as his lordship's loader but I'm often permitted to be one of the guns. I'm a fair shot, come to that. In my opinion, that's an inherited talent, too."

"Oh. Did your father teach you, then?"

Mr. Trotter didn't answer immediately. Then he said portentously, "It, er, is not talked about, but I think it is generally known in this household that my, er, parentage is somewhat veiled in mystery. It is fairly certain that my mother was of noble birth. As to my father . . ." He shrugged eloquently.

Impressed, Louisa said, "Oh, I can see that, Mr. Trotter. I ain't . . . haven't got much to boast about in that line, I'm afraid. Except my mother's dad helped to make some of the Crown Jewels."

"Did he indeed!"

"With his own hands. And he was an engraver, too." He indicated the notes she had been taking.

"Perhaps that accounts for his granddaughter's beautiful handwriting."

"Oh, no. I taught myself that. From one of them copybooks."

"Well," he said. "I'm sure the menus are going to look splendid, then."

"I don't know I can manage it all in French," she said. "I might spell some of it wrong without noticing."

"What's the matter with English, then?" he smiled. "Now, I must go and supervise the opening of the rooms. Good heavens, the chandelier! I've got to get it back urgently."

He hurried out. Louisa gathered up her notes, feeling she had found a friend.

In fact, Augustus Trotter treated Louisa as a true equal just before the arrival of the guests that Thursday evening. She had ventured up to have a look at the dining room, which she had never yet seen in its full array.

She looked at it incredulously. The long, high room was decorated and furnished exactly as it had been in the 1750s. The walls were elegantly paneled and painted in pastel coloring, with gilt linings at the angles. The sideboards were not the heavy Victorian-made affairs she was accustomed to seeing in any room of such size, but delicately proportioned, with galleries and decorations of reeded urns with acorn finials at each end. There were no mirrors in clumsy mahogany frames, but a profusion of portraits, glowing under their high varnish, in carved, gilded frames. Most of them were of men in uniform or hunting costume, with reds and blues predominating.

The great, many-legged table was crowded from end to end. A branched candelabrum dominated its center, with smaller ones to right and left, and silver epergnes, their numerous little dishes filled with savory bits of all kinds. A floral arrangement in a silver vase stood by each place, and each setting consisted of four sets of knives and forks, four gleaming glasses of different shapes, and a starched white napkin, elaborately folded in the shape of a fan.

The footmen, in full livery and powdered white wigs, were applying the finishing touches, under Mr. Trotter's elegant supervision. He smiled at Louisa, who was carrying her menus in a paper cover to keep them pristine.

"Do you approve, Miss Leyton?" he asked.

"Oh, Lor', yes! Yes, I do."

She had noticed that while most of the settings had silver-framed place cards, one or two had not.

"Who's coming?"

"Just one or two of his lordship's more intimate friends," he answered nonchalantly. "By the way, I wanted to ask you something."

"Yes?"

"How do you wish the boiled truffles to be served?"

Delighted to be treated with such deference by the senior servant, Louisa answered, as casually as she could, "Oh, just in a plain white napkin, please, Mr. Trotter."

He gave her a slight bow. "So it shall be done, Miss Leyton."

Supervising the presentation and serving of her first really big dinner was a test of Louisa's nerves and stamina. Fortunately, Jean and Ivy were kept at such full stretch by the sheer press of duties that there was no time for backbiting or sullen slowness. The only fracas was between the two of them, when Ivy, carting dirty plates from the serving lift to the scullery, blundered into Jean, knocking a dish of four grouse to the floor. Louisa firmly and calmly terminated their exchange of abuse and sent Jean back for replacements, which were, luckily, available.

It was only when the dirty savory dishes had come down that Louisa was able to relax, her duty done. She felt drained.

"Didn't leave much, did they?" Jean remarked, in quite a friendly tone for her.

"Must've been hungry," Louisa agreed, gratified to have noted that no dishes had come back down untouched. "They say the proof of the pudding's in the eating. But I suppose Monsieur Alex would've done 'em a bit more proud."

She was surprised to hear Jean say, "He wouldn't have done much better."

At that moment Mr. Trotter came down the steps. He looked strained and serious.

"Miss Leyton, you're wanted in the dining room."

"Me? Oh, Lor', what's gone wrong? Look, whatever it is, I did my best. I only . . ."

His mouth twitched in a smile.

"They want to see whoever cooked the dinner."

He winked.

"Oh, Lor'!" Louisa cried again, partially reassured but stricken with panic. She dashed into Monsieur Alex's room, where there was a good mirror, and tidied herself up quickly. When she emerged Mr. Trotter gave her a comforting nod, and, taking her arm, piloted her up the stairs, watched openmouthed by Jean, Ivy, and Mary.

Outside the dining room Mr. Trotter paused and looked at her. She returned his gaze, smiling tentatively. He seemed to want to say something. But finally he pushed open the double doors, went in first, then turned and beckoned her to follow.

Five men were clustered at the far end of the table, where they had evidently grouped themselves after the ladies had withdrawn. Cigar smoke was heavy in the air, and the light of the many candles twinkled on the ruby color of their port glasses.

Louisa recognized Lord Henry, and Charles Tyrrell, who had turned to smile at her. Two of the other men she did not know. She didn't give them more than a glance, in any case. Her gaze was riveted on the fifth member of the party. He was fat and bearded, with heavy-lidded eyes. A huge cigar protruded from his mouth. Anyone in England would have recognized him at once.

Lord Henry had nodded to his butler, who addressed this lounging figure.

"Your Royal Highness, I beg your pardon. Might I present Miss Leyton, who cooked the dinner tonight?"

Edward, Prince of Wales, withdrew the cigar from

his mouth and exhaled smoke. Louisa correctly interpreted this as an invitation to advance toward him. She curtsied.

The Prince cleared his throat with a rasp and said in a surprisingly guttural voice, "I sent for the chef to congratulate him, and I find it's you. So I must congratulate you instead. And I do congratulate you. Here is my hand on it."

The royal eyes surveyed a woman who was unquestionably no lady, yet who held herself with a natural grace. Her head was tilted at the angle taught to debutantes; her hair, prettily flushed face, and dress were all pleasing to the eye and in the best of taste. Good blood somewhere, perhaps. And she was beautiful, or attractive—it was hard to tell which. It was not Edward's custom to take women of the lower class for his pleasure. Actresses were different—fair game. It had been a young actress who had initiated him into sex, many years before; the shock of it had killed his sainted father, his mother had declared. But Nellie Clifden had been no shock to the inexperienced young prince, only a great and unexpected pleasure. Perhaps he had made a mistake to confine himself to upper-class ladies and the charmers of the stage all these years. Unless his veteran eye was much mistaken, here was a treasure for the taking. She would fit into the social scene, in her particular niche, and for a man who adored food it might be amusing to have a mistress who was also an expert cook.

He held up a pudgy white hand. Louisa took it. It was soft as silk, she thought afterward. He held hers for two or three seconds, gazing steadily into her face. She felt too honored to recognize the thoroughly searching nature of that scrutiny. At length he let her hand go and fished with finger and thumb in one of his tight-stretched jacket pockets. He took out a little case, from which he produced a gold coin.

"Here's something to show how much we liked our

dinner," he said. He placed the coin in her palm. "A present sovereign, from your future sovereign."

The other men murmured appreciation. Mr. Trotter caught Louisa's eye, and his head moved slightly but significantly. With a murmur of thanks and another curtsy she left the room, the butler following to close the doors behind her. He grinned, and took her arm warmly to lead her downstairs.

"Mr. Trotter!" she admonished him, when they were out of sound of the dining room. "Whyever didn't you tell me before?"

"Mrs. Catchpole thought it might put you off your cooking."

Louisa made a face. "It might at that."

When they reached the kitchen she faced her helpers and told them whom they had been unwittingly serving.

"He said," she lied, "to thank you, one and all, for his lovely dinner."

Even Ivy smiled gratefully at her. Poor little Mary was almost in tears.

A slight popping noise sounded behind her. She turned to see Mr. Trotter advancing with an opened bottle of champagne and a little tray with tulip-shaped glasses.

"This'll make you all feel better," he said, pouring deftly. He passed the glasses about and then held up his own. "To Miss Leyton and her staff. May I add my own congratulations to those of His Royal Highness the Prince of Wales?"

They all drank. Mary giggled, spluttering.

"Ooh! It's gone straight up my nose!"

Louisa had sipped carefully. Although she didn't say so, it was her first experience of champagne. She liked the taste.

The memory of it lingered with her as she combed her hair that night. She heard a creak and looked round at the door, half expecting, half hoping, that it would open and Charlie Tyrrell would come in. But nothing happened. She got into bed. Then she got out again, took the sovereign from its resting place, and fondled it for some moments before placing it under her pillow.

She turned out the light and soon fell asleep, to a fantasy of Charlie Tyrrell, the sovereign, and the Prince who had given it to her.

Five

Despite the formal reconciliation between Louisa and
Jean, the latter did not stay much longer in Lord
Henry Norton's employ. Something in her Scottish
pride refused to let her forget the rebuff she had
been given as a result of her own mischief-making. It
was clear to her, as to everyone else, that the newcomer was making an unexpected impression on both
Monsieur Alex and Mrs. Catchpole with her eagerness
to learn and her aptitude for doing so. Jean gave in
her notice and went back to her native heath to live
with and look after a maiden aunt who eventually left
her enough capital to become a maiden aunt herself.

Unknown to Louisa, the impression she had made
had been anything but limited to the members of the
household she served.

A few weeks after the triumphant royal dinner
party, Mr. Trotter announced a caller to his master.
Lord Henry was in the library after breakfast, drinking a final cup of coffee over *The Times*. His visitor
was a sporty, good-looking man in his late thirties,
with dark hair and green eyes. He was a major in
the Grenadier Guards, but now occupied a civilian
post requiring a good deal more finesse than the military calling.

He greeted Lord Henry with the familiarity of an

old friend. "Good morning, Harry. Sorry to burst in so early."

"Not a bit, my dear Johnnie. Matter of fact, I've been expecting you."

"You have?"

"Oh, come on. I know what you're here for, and I apologize. I apologize."

"What on earth for?" Major Farjeon asked, accepting Lord Henry's waved invitation to pour himself coffee and take a chair.

"My behavior," his host explained. "Last night. I dozed off over the baccarat and H.R.H. was offended. You've come in your official capacity to give me a wigging for it, haven't you?"

"My dear Harry, it wasn't even noticed. Except by me, and I was able to nudge you awake for your turn."

Lord Henry said, "Oh, thank God for that. Look here, *can't* you get him to play bridge? Much more civilized game. I mean, baccarat goes on so long. With bridge, at least it's usually over by midnight and some of us poor devils can get home to bed."

Major Farjeon could sympathize all too readily. As equerry to the Prince of Wales he had to endure it all: the tedious, overtaxing meals; the prolonged gaming; the boring ritual conversations; the cold and damp of the field sports; the discreetly organized hide-and-seek after bedtime . . .

He nodded. "As a matter of fact, he's playing bridge tonight. At Lady Savile's. Shall you be there?"

Lord Henry nodded without enthusiasm.

"I expect so. I've been asked. D'you know, I find his energy at the moment astonishing. He's—what—coming up to fifty-nine. That makes me ten years younger and I can't begin to keep pace. Anyway, if you haven't come to wig me, what is it you're after me for?"

Farjeon answered in a slightly uncomfortable fashion which escaped the older man.

"It's a domestic matter, actually. A . . . request for the services of your cook."

"My cook? Oh, you mean my chef. Monsieur Alex."

"No, Henry. Your *cook*. The young woman who cooked for you the other week when H.R.H. dined here."

"What! Miss, er, Leyton?"

"Yes. She is still with you, isn't she?"

"Eh? So far as I know."

"I hope so. The Prince, if you remember, was most impressed, and he'd like to borrow her. He's entertaining the Kaiser, privately, at Mrs. Markham's, next Wednesday. Now, can you spare the girl, do you think?"

Lord Henry wrinkled his brow.

"So long as she's still working here, I'm sure I'd be honored. Some servant or other left, but I'm dashed if I can remember who. Soon find out. But, look here . . . do you think she's up to it? I mean, isn't she inexperienced or something? It's quite an undertaking."

"So was the other night," the younger man reminded him, amused at the aristocratic vagueness.

"Yes, yes," Lord Henry agreed. "But that might have been a bit of a fluke, mightn't it? Is it fair on the girl? That's all I'm asking."

"I'd say so. The brief impression I gained of her was that she's intelligent and rather ambitious." Farjeon paused slightly, before adding, "Capable of handling . . . the situation."

"Oh! Is she? Oh, well, if you're happy about it . . ."

"I am. So I'll get on with the arrangements, may I? Assuming that she's still here, of course."

"Ah, yes. Please do, my dear fellow. Please do."

Major Farjeon sought out Mrs. Catchpole and ascertained that Louisa was still, indeed, a member of the staff. Then he interviewed Monsieur Alex and went away, leaving the chef and the housekeeper to break the news to the girl.

"I congratulate you, Miss Leyton," Monsieur Alex said sincerely. "An honor for you."

Louisa was not unaware of that fact.

"Thanks, Monsieur Alex," she said. "Yes, it is."

"And what will you delight His Royal Highness with this time?"

Mrs. Catchpole interrupted, "That's all taken care of. They're sending the menu round in a day or two."

"I'd want to do my own marketing," Louisa said abruptly. "I want my own vegetables."

"There won't be anything wrong with their vegetables, Miss Leyton," Mrs. Catchpole replied, with a look at Monsieur Alex. He said kindly to Louisa, "When the menu arrives, I think you had better pass it to me. We shall go through it together. I shall instruct you in every detail, and you will have a grand success."

To his considerable surprise, Louisa answered, "Very kind, and I much appreciate it, Monsieur Alex. But I prefer to manage on my own, thank you."

"*Pardon?*" was all the response he could manage.

"Well, there's no point in going, if all I'm going to do is serve it up—is there? I'm sorry, but it was me he asked for. Look, I'm sure if you'd done that dinner for him, he'd have been asking for you now. But you didn't, so . . ."

She looked from one to the other of their incredulous expressions and went out of the housekeeper's room. They shook their heads sadly at each other.

When the day itself came, though, Louisa's sang-froid briefly deserted her.

"All the buttons, Mary," she raved at the little Welsh girl, who was helping her into a simple but elegantly cut white dress. "Don't miss any."

"I won't, Miss Leyton. Oh, do stand still, please."

"Well, hurry up!"

"I'm going as fast as I can. There. That's it."

"Boots. Where's me *boots?*"

"Under the chair."

"Give 'em here. Quick. Oh . . . They're too tight. Me feet must've swelled up with nerves. Push Mary."

"I am."

"*Push!*"

At last she was ready, looking virginally beautiful in her white. All the other servants contrived to see her go to the carriage bearing royal arms, which had been sent for her.

"We all wish you well," Mrs. Catchpole said, with almost a hint of affection in her tone.

"*Bonne chance,*" Monsieur Alex intoned, as gravely as ever. "I take it as a compliment that my *protégé* has been chosen by the Prince of Wales."

"Good luck!" said Mary and Ivy in chorus.

Mr. Trotter winked and said, "You look nice, my dear. No—I'll take your bag."

So, with such civility and honor attending her, Louisa Leyton set off in a royal carriage to cook dinner for a prince.

All the discomposure Louisa had been experiencing left her soon after her arrival at Mrs. Markham's house. The kitchen was smaller and inferior in equipment to Lord Henry Norton's. It was also less than clean. The resident cook, a fat old woman, stayed just long enough to see what Louisa looked like before making her prearranged departure to her room, in long-worked-up umbrage at having her position usurped for the evening by an outsider, and a chit of a girl at that. Louisa felt positively superior and proceeded to throw her authority about right and left.

"No!" she rebuked the elderly butler, Mr. Pritchett, about to place a large floral decoration among the massed dishes on the dining-room sideboard. "I'm putting *this* there." She indicated a dish of pheasants being carried by a young footman accompanying her.

The butler made way for the footman to put down his dish, then handed him the flower vase.

"Far be it from me to make any suggestions, miss," he said, with the weight of years of office, "but it is often the look of a room that contributes to a happy and successful dinner. Elegance might seem old-fashioned to a modern young woman, but I can assure you that His Royal Highness . . ."

Louisa cut him short. "I believe in elegance, too, Mr. Pritchett. Look at me. Aren't I elegant?" She smiled away his surprise. "But I also believe in simplicity and things in their proper place. And the proper place for *that* is a lily pond."

The old man couldn't help smiling, as he said, "In truth, Miss Leyton, you are a most amazingly . . . confident creature. I can only say . . . I can only say . . ." He turned to the waiting footman. "Oh, take the damn thing out!"

When the man had gone, the butler addressed Louisa again, this time in a more ironical tone.

"Will you be requiring me for anything, Miss Leyton?"

She shook her head impatiently, her mind concentrated on the many duties before her. The old butler gave her a little bow and went out, thinking of more orderly times.

Even he had to admit at the evening's end that the dinner had been as successful as any he had ever witnessed. The Prince of Wales had been in his finest fettle, almost throwing himself at every dish, gobbling voraciously as if he had been a starving man instead of a sated old glutton. But the other guests, less greedy, and some of them with appetites affected by nerves in the royal presence, had also done ample justice to the meal.

At the Prince's request, Mrs. Markham had sent for Louisa, and once more she had curtsied before that heavy-lidded appraisal and had her hand held in the pudginess of his.

Now she was on her way back to Charles Street, in the same carriage that had fetched her, again escorted by Major Farjeon, with whom she had begun to feel considerably at ease.

"Always cook the potatoes and the beans and the asparagus yourself," she was pontificating, as they creaked through the gaslit streets. "My rule is not to leave 'em to a scullery maid or anyone else with no brains. I tell you, I take more trouble with the cabbage than most cooks do with the chicken. I take trouble with the chicken, of course, but I won't chop it up and decorate it with all sorts of stuff that's not going to be used. If it's a chicken, you want it tasting like a chicken, don't you?"

Farjeon, quietly amused, confessed that he did.

"No messing things up, that's what I believe," she went on. "Leave things with their natural flavor."

"Did you, er, learn all this from your mother?"

"Her! She's not interested in cooking. You can't be, if you can't afford to buy good food. I mean, it was easy tonight. Anyone could've done it."

"Have you a large family, Miss Leyton?"

"No. Just my father and mother, and a brother. That's all."

"What does your father do?"

"He's a clockmaker and repairer. Only part-time, though. I dunno why. He used to have his business, but he doesn't seem interested anymore."

She smiled at him in the gloom.

"But my mother's side of the family, they're engravers. My grandfather made part of the Queen's coronation crown. Least, I think he did. So, you see? I've got some connection with royalty, haven't I?"

"Oh, yes," he agreed with a grin. "Anyway, you're a . . . royal cook now."

She reflected upon that in silence for some moments. Then he asked, "What about your brother? What does he do?"

"He's a soldier. In South Africa." Then she surprised her companion by adding suddenly, "Wish I'd been a boy."

"You don't really!"

"I do. Wake up every morning hoping for the miracle."

"But why?"

"Well . . . cooking, for one thing. How many women are *maîtres chefs?* I've always thought boys get a better chance in life."

"I don't agree," Farjeon insisted. "Think of all the beautiful women through the ages—loved and pampered and doted on . . ."

Her sharp laugh interrupted him. "Cor! I wouldn't want that. It's not my way of living. You're in the fellers' power, and what happens when they go off and leave you? What's a woman to do then?"

He regarded her speculatively. He seemed about to renew the conversation but turned his head away to look out of the window. They were passing along Park Lane and would be in Charles Street in a few minutes. Louisa decided she must ask a question that had been hovering on her lips for some time.

"Excuse me, sir . . ."

He turned to look at her again.

"Do I . . . get paid anything for this evening?"

To her relief he smiled and said, "My goodness, I'd almost forgotten!" He felt in his breast pocket.

"Sorry for asking, only . . ."

"No, no. Quite right." He had produced an envelope and handed it to her. She thanked him and put it away in her bag without opening it. But he was delving into another pocket, in his overcoat. He brought out a small box and put it into her hands.

"And this is a small token from the Prince. He intended giving it to you personally, but the Kaiser detained him, so he entrusted the pleasant task to me. He sends it with his thanks to you for a most successful and enjoyable dinner."

Louisa had not opened the box. He looked inquiringly at her.

"Another sovereign?" she speculated.

"Look and see."

She did, and gasped aloud to find a small gold pendant on a slender chain. The major helped her loosen her coat and gently pulled down the back of its collar, to enable her to pass the chain around her neck. He fastened its clip for her, then sat back with an admiring smile.

Whatever next? she thought—but she did not say it.

The carriage halted outside the tall, looming house. It was midnight, but she saw that the hall lights were still on. Major Farjeon escorted her to the gate. He shook hands, gave a little bow, and wished her good night. She heard the carriage clopping away as she opened the door with her own key and went through to the kitchen, which she found was also lighted.

Mr. Trotter was alone in the kitchen, smiling expectantly.

"What you been waiting up for, Mr. Trotter?" Louisa asked, surprised.

"It's my job to wait up," he said, and indicated a decanter of wine and two glasses on a tray. "Fancy a drink, Miss Leyton?"

"Cor, no thanks," she said. "But I'm famished. Haven't eaten anything the whole blessed evening."

She went to the larder and came back with a plate of sausage rolls. She began stuffing them into her mouth while the butler poured himself some wine.

"Went well, then, did it?" he asked.

"Yeh. All right."

She answered in so casual a tone that he looked at her sharply and asked, "Nothing went wrong?"

Chewing hungrily she hooked a finger under the pendant and held it forward for him to see, replying with her mouth full, "Got this to prove it, haven't I?"

He examined it without comment, then stepped back and raised his glass to her.

"I see it did go well. Clever girl. To the future, eh?"

He drank, then added, "With your looks, talent . . ."

"You ain't done so bad yourself, Mr. Trotter. Butler to a lord . . . at your age."

He nodded and said slowly, "That's true. We make rather a good pair, don't we? Oh, Mary tells me you're studying French."

It was true up to a point. Louisa had acquired a French–English dictionary and had been memorizing the meanings of some of the French culinary expressions she had seen on menus and in recipe books.

"Monsieur Alex was very impressed when I told him," he added.

"Oh! I was going to surprise him."

"You did. *Very* impressed."

"So he should be. Daft bloomin' language, anyway." Mr. Trotter put her to a little test of his own.

"Bonjour, Ma'mselle Leyton. Comment allez-vous?"

Louisa frowned and said, "Oh, I can't speak it or understand it. Just some of the names of dishes and things."

This emboldened him to go on, "Ma'mselle, vous êtes tres belle. Je pense que je suis amoureux de vous. Je pense que je vous aime. Voulez-vous m'épouser?"

She had finished the last of the sausage rolls and was now only conscious of the tightness of her boots and of her general tiredness. She yawned.

"Look, stop babblin' all that stuff, Mr. Trotter. I'm goin' to bed. Good night."

She went wearily up the stairs. He remained standing where he was, the glass of wine in his hand. When she had passed out of sight he took a reflective sip, poured some more, and sat down to finish it in a thoughtful mood. It was quite some time before he, too, went to bed.

Later that week Major Farjeon came once again to the house in Charles Street. This time he came by appointment to see Lord Henry Norton. It was noon, and they sipped Madeira together in the library.

"Something of a triumph, then?" Lord Henry commented, after his friend had reported on the success of the dinner party.

"Absolutely, H.R.H. was captivated. So was I, I may say. We all were. By the cooking *and* the cook."

"Really? To think I had a pearl under my own roof and never knew it?"

"Come now, Henry," Farjeon chided him. "Surely you haven't lost your eye for a pretty girl?"

"Damned if I have! Just that I've scarcely seen her. Come to think of it, I believe she is rather good-looking."

Farjeon laughed, then asked with an elaborate casualness which even the vague Lord Henry noted, "She must have a fair number of admirers, I should imagine?"

"Eh? Oh, I haven't the faintest idea. I don't believe we permit followers."

"Even so, an enchanting girl like that . . . I mean to say, there must be someone."

"Well, if there is I don't know." He gave the younger man a sly look and added, "You interested, by any chance?"

Farjeon didn't reply, but persisted, "Your housekeeper would know. They always do."

"I suppose she might."

"Henry, would you mind asking her for me? I'd be most grateful."

Lord Henry stared back at him. "You serious, Johnnie?"

The answer was a nod. Almost reluctantly, Lord Henry walked to the bell beside the fireplace and gave its handle a sharp turn.

The footman who appeared was sent away to fetch Mrs. Catchpole. Meanwhile, Lord Henry poured more wine for them both. Farjeon volunteered no more particulars of his interest in Louisa and his friend was too well-mannered to press him. Inwardly, he was chiding himself for not having taken more notice of this paragon he appeared to be harboring.

When the housekeeper appeared he diplomatically consulted her about arrangements for accommodating a General Murray who would be arriving for an overnight visit. That settled, he allowed Mrs. Catchpole to get halfway to the door before saying, as if from an afterthought, "Oh, by the way . . ."

She stopped and came back a few paces.

"Yes, m'lord?"

"That young cook of ours . . . what's her name? . . ."

"Leyton, m'lord."

"Ah, yes. How's she settling down after all that excitement the other evening?"

"Very well, m'lord. She's a very level-headed sort of girl."

"Good, good. Pleasant nature, I thought."

The housekeeper concealed her surprise that he should be aware of anything about the young woman, except that he paid her wages. She was even more surprised when he continued, "Tell me, you don't happen to know if anyone is . . . interested in her? Romantically, I mean. Any, er, runners in that department?"

"Well . . . ," Mrs. Catchpole managed to reply after a moment's quick thought, "the only person I can think of with . . . that sort of interest in her, since you mention it, m'lord, is . . . is Trotter."

"Trotter? My butler?"

"I have noticed he's been rather attentive to her lately."

"Good lord! And what about her? Feelings . . . reciprocated, are they?"

"Oh, I wouldn't go so far as that, m'lord. I think she quite likes him, but I wouldn't care to say there was any strong interest. Not at the moment, anyway."

"Hm! But from Trotter's side you think there might be . . . something serious?"

"Well, m'lord, if I may put it this way, I'd say he's got his eye on her, certainly."

"I see. Just inquiring, you understand? Like to keep the staff's welfare in mind, you know."

"Thank you, m'lord."

Mrs. Catchpole went away, pondering deeply the certainty that, whatever the truth surrounding this sudden interest, it had no connection with staff welfare. Her aloof employer left that department entirely to her.

In the library, Lord Henry turned to his friend.

"Well, Johnnie," he said with a quizzical upturn of his eyebrows. "You heard. Sorry to disappoint you, old man."

To his surprise, Farjeon was beaming at him. He replied, "But that's splendid, Henry!"

"Eh?"

"Now, this butler of yours. Trotter. Is he reliable? Discreet?"

"Of course he is. You've met him often enough. Dammit, Johnnie, what *is* all this about?"

Major Farjeon tapped the side of his nose. He said, "It, er, would be a great help if they were to get married. Do all you can to push them into it—eh?"

For all of fifteen seconds Lord Norton gaped back at him, his mind churning. At length he said weakly, "You . . . don't mean . . . ?"

Farjeon's only answer was a nod. Lord Henry's response was to pour himself another glass of Madeira and drink it with one swallow. The major grinned at him.

"Not a word, naturally, Henry."

"No, no . . . No, of course not."

"H.R.H. and I leave for Balmoral in the morning. Couple of weeks' shooting. Nice to have some news on our return. Put us all in a good humor for Christmas. Eh?"

He put down his glass and departed. Lord Henry Norton, most imperturbable of men, looked at his own empty one, filled it again, and sat down to drink it slowly, deep in thought.

Six

"*Married!*" Louisa echoed explosively, then sneezed with equal violence. She had come down with a sudden, streaming head cold and had been sent back to bed by Mrs. Catchpole, who now sat in the wicker chair, plying her with handkerchiefs. "What do I want to get married for? I want to be a cook, not a wife. That's the last thing I want."

Mrs. Catchpole had anticipated a difficult task. It was proving to be one.

"Yes," she pretended to agree, "only, you can't be a cook ... I mean, you can't go *out* to cook for important people ... unless you're married. That's the point."

"Who says I can't?"

"Well, Lord Henry, for one. It's not suitable for you to go on like men do, my dear. It's a question of respectability. Of course, if you were married, all doors would be open to you then."

"But I haven't done nothing wrong."

"I know you haven't. But it's generally felt to be better, for all concerned, that you should have a husband."

"But I'm not in *love*, Mrs. Catchpole. And there's nobody in love with me. So that ends it."

She was surprised to see the housekeeper smiling at her, saying, "I think you're mistaken there, you know. I *think* there's someone more than a *little* fond of you."

"Who?"

"Mr. Trotter."

Louisa lapsed into a further paroxysm of sneezing. Mrs. Catchpole unbent so far as to pat the girl's hand and tuck the sheets in beneath her. Then she left the room, to wash and change and find an omnibus that would take her to Wanstead, where she would be expected for afternoon tea, following a letter she had written on Lord Henry's crested notepaper to Mr. and Mrs. Leyton.

At the little house in Camden Road she found Mrs. Leyton in her best, with sandwiches and bought cake and scones set out on the sideboard of the minute parlor. Mr. Leyton was present, too, asserting his independence from the proceedings by continuing to work on the movement of a carriage clock. He kept a watchmaker's glass screwed into one eye, enabling him to appear to be concentrating on what he was doing while leaving his hearing undistracted.

"We couldn't believe it when we heard, could we, dear?" his wife said in his direction. He grunted noncommittally.

"We're all very proud, too," Mrs. Catchpole assured them both, referring to the royal dinner party, whose success she had just recounted.

"I mean," Mrs. Leyton went on, "there's no telling where it might lead, is there? Invitations to cook in all the big houses. She might end up marrying a lord. Way to a man's heart is through his stomach, they always say."

It was the cue Mrs. Catchpole might have prayed for.

"How odd, Mrs. Leyton!" she was able to say. "That's was one of the very reasons why I wanted to come and talk to you myself."

Louisa's mother looked at her blankly. Mrs. Catchpole continued.

"The question of marriage. You see, if your daughter

does want to get on—and I believe she really has every prospect before her now—well, then, it would be much more suitable if she had a husband."

Without raising his head, Mr. Leyton asked, "Why?"

"Because, Mr. Leyton, it is a form of stamp of respectability. Cooks in charge of a household are always known as *Mrs.* as a recognition of their responsible position. But those who go out and about in society do well to be really married. It gives less rise to talk, in any circumstances."

Mrs. Leyton had been considering.

"There's plenty of young men round here always been keen on her. Respectable tradespeople, you know." She addressed her husband's bent head. "That nice young Belling, f'r instance."

"She's got no time for him," he muttered.

Mrs. Catchpole leaned toward Mrs. Leyton.

"What I can tell you," she said, almost as though Mr. Leyton were an eavesdropper there, "is that there's a young man in our own household. I don't know whether she's mentioned him to you in her letters. . . ."

"No. No one."

"Well—it's our butler. Mr. Trotter."

"Butler!"

"A very superior person, if you take my meaning."

"Oh, I'm sure. You hear that, Ernest?"

"It's only my opinion, of course," Mrs. Catchpole went on, trying to reinforce her disclosure, "but I think they'd make a very handsome and capable pair."

Once again Mr. Leyton spoke. "Might I inquire if they love each other?"

"Well . . . they're both quite shy people, Mr. Leyton. But given a little encouragement . . ."

"Our Louisa? Shy!"

But his wife snapped at him, "Why don't you leave Mrs. Catchpole and me to talk this over . . . dear? You could take your cup and your things into the kitchen."

He ignored her. She turned eagerly back to the

housekeeper and resumed. "What . . . sort of encouragement did you have in mind, Mrs. Catchpole?"

"Well, I was thinking it would be quite nice if you asked Mr. Trotter to tea. I'm sure he'd consider it a great pleasure and privilege to meet Louisa's parents."

Mr. Leyton gave one of his rare laughs.

"And what d'you suppose she'd have to say to that?"

His wife replied, "If I ask Mr. Trotter to tea, Ernest, it's no business of Louisa's."

"I reckon it is. You can't force the girl to get married —not if she doesn't want to."

"We're not forcing anything. It's a matter of arranging—for her own good."

"That's quite right," Mrs. Catchpole quickly agreed. "I've already explained to her the difficulties of unmarried cooks working outside. I can assure you, Mr. Leyton, from all my years of experience, it's most advantageous for girls like Louisa to get married as soon as possible. She wants to get on, and this is the best way of helping her. Lord Henry quite agrees, too."

This was a certain clincher where Mrs. Leyton was concerned.

"Lord Henry as well!" she exclaimed. "You see, Ernest? It's very nice of you to be taking so much trouble, Mrs. Catchpole. We'll speak to Louisa ourselves the very next time we see her and make her see it's for the best. And if Mr. Trotter would care to drop us a line about coming to tea, we shall be only too pleased to receive him."

She glared at her husband, ready to crash any defiance. He bent resignedly over his work and said nothing.

"Married?" echoed Monsieur Alex after a much-recovered Louisa had told him what Mrs. Catchpole had said to her. "You are far too young. You take my advice, my child, and concentrate on cooking."

"That's what I want," she said. "But isn't it true that you need to be married if you want to get on?"

"Of course not. It's nonsense. Now, we continue with our lesson. *Crevettes à l'indienne. Salmis d'alouettes.* And you put all that stupid romantic stuff out of your head. Understand?"

"Yes, Monsieur Alex," she promised, feeling much relieved. "It wasn't in my head, anyway. It's in Mrs. Catchpole's."

Unknown to Louisa, though, Mr. Trotter was at that very moment on his way to Wanstead, where Mrs. Leyton was fussing over her tea table yet again. Her arrangements this time were more formal and considerable than on the previous occasion, and Mr. Leyton had been commanded into his best suit.

The youth and dapper appearance of the butler impressed Mrs. Leyton. She thought him positively handsome, and so polite to her, considering that he worked for a lord. Nor did he fail to give Mr. Leyton his share of deferential interest.

"My word," he said, stooping to examine the face of one of the clocks. "Louisa has told me all about your skill with clocks, Mr. Leyton. Is this one of yours?"

Mr. Leyton shook his head. The maker's name was there on the face. Evidently the visitor hadn't noticed it.

"No," he admitted. "That's by a very famous French maker. This is one of mine. And this."

Mr. Trotter stooped again to examine these two. He looked from one to the other, and then back at the first he had commented upon, and said, "To be honest, Mr. Leyton, I prefer your work—if I may say so."

Louisa's father was not impervious to flattery.

"It's very good of you to say so, Mr. Trotter. I'm hardly in the same class, though."

"Well, of course, I'm no judge. But as a man in the street, so to speak, I'd say your work was . . . less fussy. I always think the best taste is the simplest."

When Mrs. Leyton brought in the teapot she was agreeably surprised to find the two men chatting freely.

"I was just telling your husband how fine I think his work is, Mrs. Leyton," their visitor said.

"Oh, yes. I'm so glad you think so, Mr. Trotter."

"This face here is very, very similar to one in Lord Bouverie's house in Eccleston Square. I understand it's by a most celebrated maker, but I'd be hard put to tell it from this."

"There, Ernest! That's a compliment for you."

"Yes, it is."

"Now, come along, both of you. You sit there, Mr. Trotter, please."

"Thank you, Mrs. Leyton. What a grand sight indeed! You wouldn't see many teas like this in Mayfair, I can tell you."

"Oh! Wouldn't you?"

"No, you wouldn't."

"Well . . . it's nothing really. Do take a scone. They're fresh homemade."

"I can see that at a glance, Mrs. Leyton."

Mr. Trotter proceeded to do justice to everything set before him, praising the baking, the brewing of the tea, even the slicing of the bread for the sandwiches. As they all ate, he submitted himself willingly to their interrogation.

"Now then, tell us all about yourself, Mr. Trotter," Mrs. Leyton began. "You seem quite young to be a butler in a lord's house, if you don't mind my saying so."

"Ah, well, there's a story behind that," he answered with an enigmatic smile.

"Oh! I hope you'll tell us it, then."

"Well . . . you see, I never knew my mother and father . . . not for certain, that is. I and my sister were brought up on a big estate in Yorkshire by a lodgekeeper and his wife. They were childless, so it was an arrangement that suited us all. My mother, too,

I presume. I was given to understand later—you know how people talk in a village—that my mother was the daughter of the titled lady of the big house, and she'd formed an attachment with one of the young grooms. Yes, and ran off to Italy with him. I was born in Naples. And then *her* mother went out and brought her back, just in time for my sister to be born. And that was that."

Mrs. Leyton was clearly riveted by this romantic narrative. Her husband asked, "What happened to your father, then?"

"I'm led to believe he met an untimely end. Drink, they say, pining for his lost love. Who can be sure, though?"

Much moved, Mrs. Leyton asked, "And your mother, Mr. Trotter? Did you never see her?"

"It's a strange thing, Mrs. Leyton, but I remember vividly an incident on my twelfth birthday. I was playing in the park with Norah, my sister, and we saw a lady on horseback, quite close by, just watching us. I remember clearly she was wearing a . . . a pale-pink dress. Very beautiful. Then she rode away, and we thought no more of it at the time. But, looking back, I think *she* was my mother."

"And that was the last time you saw her?"

He sighed. "That's right. But ever since then, pink's been my favorite color."

Mrs. Leyton glanced down at her own pink dress and thought how many happy coincidences you got in life.

"Do have another scone, Mr. Trotter," she said. He accepted readily.

"How did you get up to London, then?" Mr. Leyton was asking.

"Soon after that time I was put into service as a hall-boy at a colonel's house nearby. Then he came to London and I was footman with him. Then footman to Lord Henry. Then, some years later, I was made his butler." He gave them a conspiratorial smile. "I seem

to have received some . . . hidden hand in my ad-
vancement."

Mrs. Leyton said, "Well, I'm sure you've fully de-
served to have got where you have, Mr. Trotter."

"It's very kind of you to say so, Mrs. Leyton."

"Not at all. And it's a great comfort to us, meeting
you, isn't it, Ernest?"

Her husband agreed sincerely. Mrs. Leyton went
on. "You hear such stories about young girls like Louisa
all alone in big London houses. It's nice to know she's
got you watching over her."

"Oh, we're all devoted to her, Mrs. Leyton. She's
such a willing and pleasant girl. I'm sure she'll get on
extremely well if she wishes."

There was an awkward little pause, the Leytons
hesitating to raise the matter Mrs. Catchpole had come
to see them about; he, apparently, wanting to say
something which he was finding it hard to bring out.
Eventually, he looked Mrs. Leyton fully in the eye
and said, "As a matter of fact, Mrs. Leyton, with, er,
your permission, that is . . . in the not too distant future . . ."

"Yes, Mr. Trotter?"

"I . . . I wish to propose marriage to her."

"Marriage!" Mrs. Leyton said, succeeding in hiding
her pleasure under the feigned surprise.

"I'm extremely fond of Louisa, Mrs. Leyton. I understood that Mrs. Catchpole had said something about it
to you?"

"Oh, not in so many words, Mr. Trotter. She just
said it would be a good thing for Louisa to be married,
and she dropped a hint about yourself."

"Ah. Well, there is that practical consideration to it,
of course. But it's a more personal matter with me. I
. . . I'm devoted to Louisa for herself."

Mr. Leyton cleared his throat and asked parentally,
"Have you spoken to her at all?"

The butler shook his head. "Not yet . . . sir. I

thought it more proper to speak to her parents first. I can assure you I'll do everything in my power to make her happy. But I may have trouble convincing her of that, if you understand me." He gave a little nervous-sounding laugh.

"She'd be a fool to turn *you* down, Mr. Trotter," Mrs. Leyton said emphatically.

"Well, it all depends whether my feelings for her are reciprocated. If I might have your permission to ask her, Mr. Leyton?"

Urged on by the concentration of his wife's gaze, Mr. Leyton replied, "Well, she's always reckoned she wasn't the marrying kind. But speak to her, by all means. I'm sure her mother and I wish you the best of luck."

Mr. Trotter got to his feet and went around the table to shake his host and hostess gravely by the hand in turn. Mrs. Leyton was tempted to draw him down and give him a kiss, but thought it might be a little forward and premature.

Shortly afterward he took out his watch, made a joke about the ridiculousness of having done so in a room containing so many clocks, and declared that he must be getting back to London. Mr. Leyton walked with him to the omnibus stop and shook hands warmly with him again before he boarded. When he got back home he found the tea table uncleared, except for enough space to enable Mrs. Leyton to work busily on a letter she was writing.

The letter reached Louisa the following day. Recognizing her mother's hand, she didn't trouble to read it until her day's work was over. When she did, she flushed angrily and seized her hat and coat.

"You going out, Miss Leyton?" Mary asked, surprised.

"You bet I am."

"But it's not your night off."

"Who cares? I've had a letter, and it needs answering—in person."

"But what shall I tell them? . . ."

"You can tell 'em there's a conspiracy goin' on!"

She slammed out of the area door. Mr. Trotter heard the crash as he came down the kitchen steps.

"Was that Miss Leyton?" he asked Mary.

"Yes, Mr. Trotter. She seems very vexed. She's had a letter."

"A letter? Who from?"

"She didn't say. Just something about a conspiracy going on."

Mr. Trotter cursed inwardly that he had been putting off until this evening the carefully planned speech he proposed making to Louisa in the privacy of his pantry.

At Wanstead, an hour later, Louisa railed furiously at her parents. She had not taken off her coat and hat in the urgency of her fury.

"Bloomin' cheek! Askin' him here behind my back. What's goin' on, that's what I want to know."

"There's nothing going on," her mother protested. She had fully expected some stubbornness on Louisa's part, which was why she had thought fit to prepare the young man's way for him by writing the letter, but this was pure fury.

"What was he doin' here, then?" Louisa was demanding. "The sneaky devil!"

"Now! That's not a very nice way to speak of your future husband."

"Future husband? Over my dead body!"

Her father ventured, "Listen, Louisa. He told us he wants to marry you, and we think it's a very good idea."

She sat defiantly, keeping her back very stiff.

"Do you? Well, he ain't said nothin' to me about it."

"Because he knows the proper behavior, that's why. He wanted to know our feelings first."

"Your feelings. His feelings. The whole world's bloody feelings, except mine. Nobody asks about *them*, do they?"

She turned to her mother. Her tone changed to one of appeal.

"Look, Mum, he's all right. I don't *mind* him. But I don't love him, and I certainly don't want to marry him. I want to be a cook. I'm good at it. Just a cook, that's all."

"But it'll help you at that," Mrs. Leyton said. "Mrs. Catchpole explained . . ."

Louisa shook her head hard. "That's all bunkum. I asked Monsieur Alex."

"Well, be that as it may, Mr. Trotter's not just an ordinary butler, you know. He's a gentleman. His mother was a titled lady. He'll go far in the world, and if you've got any sense you'll go with him."

"Oh, come off it, Mum. He's not all that cop."

"You tell me someone better, then. You should count yourself very lucky, catching his eye. If you keep him waiting he'll look elsewhere. There's plenty of girls better placed than you who'd queue up to marry somebody like him."

"Let 'em, then. I don't need him."

Louisa got up and went to the door.

"I'm not marryin' him, or anybody—and that's final."

For the second time that evening a door slammed in her wake.

The butler was waiting for her when she got back, but Mary and Ivy were also in the kitchen. Before he could contrive to be alone with her she had bidden them all good night and gone upstairs. It gave him just the chance he needed.

"Louisa," he called quietly from outside her bedroom door a few minutes later. There had been no answer to his knock.

He heard her muffled voice. "Go away."

"Louisa, we ought to have a talk," he said. "We really ought. Please."

He was relieved to hear movement, after which the door opened. She looked agitated, but there was no flush of anger in her cheeks.

"I suppose you'd better come in," she agreed, then turned from closing the door to ask him, "Look, hasn't my mother, or Mrs. Catchpole, or anyone else who's been pushing you at me told you the answer is no? No, no, *no*."

"I just wanted to explain," he said. "I hadn't planned it to happen this way at all. It's . . . just that I do have sincere feelings toward you, Louisa, and I think we could be happy together. Happy and successful."

The latter word perhaps made more impression on her than any of the others. She couldn't help being pleased that he seemed to feel something genuine for her. He was certainly a nice-natured man, superior in every way to any other who had ever wanted to marry her.

But she answered quietly, "I don't love you. So just let's forget all about it."

He merely nodded, the disappointment in his eyes quite touching her. To her relief, he made no attempt to persuade or argue, but left her room.

Two days later one of the footmen came to Louisa and told her that her presence was required in the library. This was, for her, unexplored territory. She had had no direct dealings with Lord Henry. Instructions from him were given to her superiors, and sometimes delegated to her. Anything she was ordered to prepare for him to eat—even a mere plate of sandwiches—was served by a footman. She had not been summoned to the library before, and it seemed portentous.

To her surprise, she found the only occupant of the musty, bookcrammed room to be Major Farjeon, dressed in morning clothes. He seemed pleased to meet her again.

"Come in, my dear," he greeted her. "How are you?"

"Very well, thank you, sir."

"You're still enjoying your cooking? Y'know, the Prince of Wales continues to talk about your accomplishments. I can tell you, he holds you in very high regard."

"Thank you, sir," Louisa said again. The compliment delighted her in a way that few others would have done.

"So much so," Major Farjeon went on, "that I'm sure he'll be asking for you again, in the near future."

"Very pleased to oblige, sir."

He walked around a few paces, then clasped his hands behind his back and inflated his chest in military fashion.

"Yes," he said. "Now, er, we, er, come up against a problem which I'm sure we can overcome between us. Sit down, won't you?"

She obeyed this seemingly impulsive invitation. He himself remained standing as he continued.

"You see, in cases of this kind, there are certain . . . how shall I put it? . . . certain rules we have to observe. I'm sure you appreciate that. The Prince feels . . . and I must say I absolutely agree with him . . . that it would be in everyone's best interest if you were not to remain a single lady. Now, I understand that the butler in this household . . ."

Louisa interrupted him, leaping to her feet agitatedly.

"Oh! Not you as well!"

He seemed mystified. She explained, "Everyone's trying to marry me off to him."

The tall equerry seemed to her to be less than enthusiastic about his errand. He had to make a visible effort to continue.

"My dear Louisa . . . if I may call you by your first name. We know each other well enough, I think . . . I hope . . . for me to be absolutely frank with you. You see, the fact is . . . the Prince's interest in you is not confined to your cooking."

He fell silent and looked at her, as if hoping for her help. But she didn't understand, and he had to go on.

"It extends to you *personally*. Do you follow?"

She thought she was beginning to; though it was unbelievable.

"To . . . *me?*"

He smiled reassurance. "Well, you can't be so surprised, can you? You're an extremely pretty young woman. That's no secret. And the Prince has let it be known to me that he'd . . . well, very much like to get to know you better."

It was lucky for Louisa that she had not moved away from the vicinity of the chair on which she had previously sat, for she now sank back onto it automatically.

"Oh, no!" The room seemed to be going around.

She heard Major Farjeon's voice. "It doesn't alarm you, does it? It's a very great honor, you know. When you consider that he's had the pick of the most beautiful women of European society. To have singled you out . . . However, he is above all things a gentleman, so he has entrusted me with the delicate task—for which I apologize sincerely, my dear Louisa—of finding out your feelings on the matter. Now, most importantly, I do hope that I have your *trust*, as well?"

"Yes, sir," she answered numbly. "But . . . I don't think I could. Honest . . ."

"Yes, yes, I know how you must be feeling. It must seem like some fairy tale come true."

"No!" she retorted, to his surprise. "I mean, I don't *know* him."

"My dear . . . I can assure you that he's the most charming and courteous of men. You've met him . . ."

"I'm sure he is," Louisa assented readily. "But I . . . I just want to be a cook. I'll *cook* for him anytime."

Major Farjeon looked even more unhappy. He said,

as if having to force himself, "I'm afraid that wouldn't be possible."

Louisa shrugged. "There's other people to cook for, then. I've already been asked . . ."

"My dear," he interrupted her gently, "you don't understand. If you were to . . . fall from favor with the Prince, you could hardly expect further invitations from his circle of friends. On the other hand, if you were to . . . consent, your future as a cook—as anything you might wish to be—is assured."

"I see," she said flatly, as the whole notion sank in. "Have I got any choice?"

"Of course you have! Good lord, I haven't come here to threaten you. If you refuse, I'm sure the Prince will understand. There will be no further word spoken on the matter. I'm perfectly sure you will find someone else to employ you on very favorable terms." .

He sighed. "But, if you want my private opinion, it would be a sad waste of talents indeed."

Louisa sat unhappily silent for some minutes, while he stared out of the window, thankful to leave her to her thoughts. He did not turn around when she whispered at last, "Why do I have to get married, though?"

"Because, my dear, the Prince would never compromise a single lady."

She retorted more spiritedly. "Only married ones!"

He turned to her again.

"After the . . . interlude is over they can return to the security of their family lives."

Louisa suddenly began to laugh. She shook with mirth, and leaned forward, putting her hands to her sides. Farjeon watched her with an uncertain grin.

"That's how society carries on, then, is it?" she was able to ask at last.

"Most successfully," he said. "I promise you. Look, Louisa, Trotter's not a bad chap, is he? He seems awfully fond of you."

She asked sharply, "Does he know about all this?"

He swallowed, and answered, "Lord Henry is telling him at this very moment. No one is attempting to deceive anyone."

"I see," she said, as a further sensation of numbness swept through her.

Major Farjeon came over to her. He stood looking down at her as she studied the carpet. There had been a moment, in the carriage returning from the royal dinner party, when she had suddenly wondered if he was going to put his arm around her and kiss her. If he had, so suddenly, at such a moment of anticlimax after the drama of that evening, she would probably have yielded. She didn't know that that very impulse had stirred in him, but he had made himself hold back because he had recognized the all too familiar look in his royal master's eye as he had held the curtsying girl's hand.

"My dear Louisa," he said sincerely, "we're all very fond of you. I give you my word that no harm will come to you. It . . . can only be to your advantage."

She raised her eyes to his. There was no contempt in hers. There were no tears. If there was anything he thought he could read in them, it was sheer wonderment.

She nodded slowly.

Seven

"Here we are," Major Farjeon told Louisa, who was sitting between him and Mr. Trotter in the carriage.

They were pulling up in front of an unassuming little house in a pleasant Chelsea terrace, perhaps seventy-five or eighty years old. They got out of the carriage to stand on the pavement, looking up at the house. There was an air of unease about them all, which Mr. Trotter tried to break by saying, half jokingly, "We could take in lodgers, eh? Put up a sign over the transom. APARTMENTS TO LET."

Louisa made no answer. Farjeon, taking him seriously, frowned and said, "No, I think for the moment that won't be necessary. Shall we go inside?"

He held up a key and turned to the front door. Trotter glanced anxiously at Louisa, who didn't return his look, but followed, silent and unsmiling, after the equerry.

The house was charming inside, a bijou counterpart of some of the bigger ones they had passed in the previous minutes. It was elegantly decorated, in good feminine taste. To any eye, its carpets, curtains, wallpapers, furniture, and ornaments were expensive, and there was in the atmosphere a sniff of new paint and paste and polish.

"Well?" Farjeon asked in the parlor, after showing

them all around the house. It was Louisa whom he addressed, but her features remained unmoved.

Trotter said, "It's lovely, sir. Thank you very much."

"Good," the Major said. "Well now, I, er . . . I'll leave you two together. I'm, er, sure you have a lot to talk about."

"Thank you, sir," Trotter repeated. Louisa still said nothing. She sat down, ignoring Farjeon entirely. He gave Mr. Trotter a last apologetic glance and went briskly out. They heard the front door close.

Louisa roused herself at last.

"How dare they?" she demanded. "How dare they do it to us—that's what I want to know. Pushing and shoving us around like we was sacks of bloody coal."

He made no answer. She looked up at him challengingly.

"Well? Knowing what's behind it all, are you prepared to go through with it?"

He replied carefully, "It's nothing to do with us, really, is it? That . . . side of it. It won't last forever."

She stared contemptuously at him and echoed angrily, "Nothing to do with us? Don't you mind? About me?"

"Of course I mind," he assured her. "I wouldn't be human if I didn't mind very much indeed. But look at it another way, and there's honor attached to it. I mean, my wife . . . the envy of . . ."

"Oh, come off it! Don't give me that guff. That was his line."

But he had detected some sign of resignation in her eyes, sufficient to embolden him to urge her, "Let's play their game, Louisa. We haven't any other choice, have we?"

He let her reflect in silence for some minutes. Then she said slowly, "As long as it's their game, we'll make it our game."

A relieved smile spread across Augustus Trotter's face. He knelt down to bring his face level with hers, though he didn't dare try to touch her.

"That's the spirit, Louisa!" he said. "I . . . I am very fond of you for yourself . . . you know. And to prove it, I'm going straight round to the registrar's office to get a marriage license."

He was surprised to hear her say indignantly, "Registrar's office? I'm not gettin' married in no registrar's office."

"But . . . I thought . . . quick and simple."

"Did you? Well you can bloody well think again. If I'm going to get married, I'm going to get married proper."

"The Church of St. Saviour, Pimlico, m'lord," Mrs. Catchpole was able to report to Lord Henry Norton in his library two mornings later.

"Good," he told her. "No last-minute snags?"

"Oh, no, m'lord. I think Leyton lost all her doubts, once she'd seen round that house."

"Ah, yes. Marvelous opportunity for a young couple, you know. I'll be sorry to lose Trotter, though. Good fellow."

"Will your lordship be going to the wedding?"

"What? No! Must I? I'm fishing on Saturday. Tell you what, Mrs. er . . . Champagne downstairs. That'll excuse me, won't it?"

Mrs. Catchpole beamed. She was fond of a drop of champagne.

"I'm sure that will be much appreciated, m'lord."

She turned to go, but he remembered something and called her back to his desk. After a little moving of objects and feeling under papers he at last located a small box. He handed it to her.

"Small token . . . for your part in all this. From all of us."

She opened it. Inside lay a small but obviously costly brooch, a diamond set exquisitely in a double knot of gold. She snapped the little box shut.

"Thank you, m'lord," was all she thought it proper to say before leaving him.

Mary was ironing a plain cotton frock for Louisa, who was sorting through her cupboard and drawers, discarding some things and packing others. It was the evening before the wedding.

"Are you getting married in *this*, Miss Leyton?" Mary asked, indicating the cheap garment.

Louisa answered defiantly, "What's wrong with it? It's white, isn't it? Do for a wedding dress."

She took it from Mary and tossed it with deliberate carelessness onto a chair. The astonished Mary managed to say, "I'm sorry you're going. This house won't be the same without you. Or Mr. Trotter."

"It's not what I want, Mary," Louisa said quietly. "It's other people."

"But you do love Mr. Trotter, don't you?"

"He's . . . all right. He's kind and he's done well for himself. It's not him. I just don't fancy marrying, that's all."

"But it gets you out of service."

Louisa laughed. "That what you think?"

"Well, I wouldn't mind a nice, kind man looking after me. Having his children."

Louisa made a noise of disgust.

"Cor, I don't want any of *them*. Haven't got time for 'em. Too much I want to do. Anyway, they always disappoint you."

"But . . . you're sure to have them, aren't you?"

Almost to herself Louisa answered, "Not if I can help it."

Aloud to Mary she said, "Why couldn't they just have called me Mrs. Leyton, and have done with it?"

The wedding was over. Louisa had gone through it with the least possible fuss. Tears had come to her eyes as she kissed her father, but that was her only evidence of emotion during the entire ceremony. Now, back in the kitchen of Lord Henry's house, the newlyweds gathered with the servants and Mr. and Mrs. Leyton. Champagne and beer were present in

ample quantities, and plates of delicacies prepared
by Monsieur Alex's own hands occupied every surface
in the big room. Even Louisa, who had been quiet
and pale beforehand, was now pink and animated
from the effects of the wine.

"Just admiring your brooch, Mrs. Catchpole," said
Mrs. Leyton, also pink-faced and overjoyed. "Looks
new. Special for the occasion?"

"That's right," the housekeeper replied, smiling out
wardly and inwardly.

"Very becoming," Mrs. Leyton said. "Oh, I can't
tell you how glad I am—Mr. Leyton and me—that our
Louisa suddenly decided to accept Mr. Trotter—Augustus."

"A nice man, Mrs. Leyton. Such a wise decision."

"I'd have thought, though, that his lordship would
have wanted to keep him on here. And Louisa, too, I
mean."

"Oh, no, that wouldn't quite do. In some households
nowadays butlers are allowed to be married. His lordship is one for the old traditions."

"I see." Mrs. Leyton still looked worried. "What I'm
wondering, though, with such a nice house to go to,
is what they'll live off."

Mrs. Catchpole was careful not even to hint. Mr.
and Mrs. Leyton had, of course, been told nothing of
the truth.

"Don't worry about that for one moment, Mrs.
Leyton," she said in her most disarming way. "As I told
you before, Louisa's best future is going out cooking
in society. Much more chance for her than staying
in employment here, or in any other one household. Now that she's married, she'll be free to accept
any engagement offered her—even by bachelor gentlemen—with complete propriety. And Mr. Trotter,
with his manners and skill, he'll make a perfect partner for her at functions. You mark my words, before
long they'll be in demand all over London."

Mrs. Leyton's face cleared. "Oh, well, that's all right,

then," she said, and turned toward a new commotion attending Ivy, who was entering, a trifle unsteadily, with a modest-sized but beautifully piped wedding cake bearing a single candle.

Applause and enthusiastic shouts greeted it as it was laid carefully on the big table. Monsieur Alex, imposing in his black coat and gray trousers, held up a hand for silence.

"Today," he began to address them all, "is a happy day. Also, it is a sad day. Louisa . . ."—his voice trembled slightly now—"Louisa, my little *protégée* who is like a daughter to me . . . today is she taken into the holy state of matrimony. A most solemn state. Lucky is the man who has wooed her and won her heart. Lucky is our friend Mr. Augustus Trotter."

This produced renewed applause and cries. Glasses were poised ready to drink the toast, but he was going on.

"Louisa is a beautiful young woman, no one can dispute that. She is also a princess of the culinary arts, born with a rare and delicate touch for a cabbage, a chicken—for what you will. I know this because I, too, possess these gifts. But rarely have I seen them in one so young, and a woman, too."

He smiled at Louisa, who gave him a little smile back, but who also thought of the time he had tried his best to dissuade her from her career.

You see, girl! she told herself. You always knew you could do it. And, by God, you will, too, when this lot of nonsense is over.

Monsieur Alex was coming to his peroration.

"She can, if she wishes, become *une reine de cuisine*—a queen among cooks. And now, I bestow on her and her husband my most tender and deeply felt blessings for a long and fruitful life together. I ask you all to drink to Mr. and Mrs. Trotter."

"Mr. and Mrs. Trotter!" The cry went up from all around her, and Louisa thought how ugly the name was, when you came to listen to it properly.

Monsieur Alex was blowing his nose emotionally. Louisa went to him and said genuinely, "That's very kind of you, Monsieur Alex."

Ivy turned her head around to her to say, "'E 'ad to bake it secret. Didn't yer, Missyer Alex?"

He made a deprecatory gesture.

"Though I do say it myself, it is a cake fit for a princess . . . and a prince, of course."

"Thank you very much, Monsieur Alex," said Mr. Trotter, who had come forward to stand beside his bride. "Much appreciated."

"Now," the chef instructed. "First you blow out the candle together."

They bent their heads and blew. The flame wavered, recovered, then went out.

"*Bravo!* Now you take the knife together. No, you must hold it together," he said to Louisa, who was trying to get away with just placing a finger on it. "So . . . and cut, while all of us wish."

As she felt the knife going in Louisa looked around almost desperately for her father. He was standing near her, watching with what she read correctly as a mixture of sadness and concern.

"Wish for me, Dad," she almost begged. He gave her a little smile of encouragement and closed his eyes. Louisa closed her own, and wished fervently.

There was more clapping after the cake had been cut. Monsieur Alex then took the knife and swiftly carved half the cake into perfect slices of exact uniformity, which were passed around by Mary and Ivy while more drink was poured. Mr. Trotter made a short speech, which was much applauded, and Mr. Leyton, pressed from all sides, mumbled a few words which hardly anyone could distinguish. When his fainter applause had subsided, Louisa suddenly said loudly, "Right, that's done. Got to go now, I'm afraid. Cookin' dinner for Lady Margaret Duff."

The hubbub diminished into the silence of surprise.

Monsieur Alex said, "But . . . tonight is your wedding night."

Louisa was putting on her coat. Augustus Trotter, not liking the prospect either, grinned at the others and tried to make a joke of it in his wife's support.

"Keeping her at it, you see, Monsieur Alex. Not letting your teaching go to waste."

"That's right," Louisa said. "Plenty of other nights for us. Whole bloody lifetime. 'Bye all. Thanks for everything."

Without pausing to make any individual farewells she strode out, followed by her husband. The silence they left behind them continued until the door was heard to close. Then excited conversation broke out.

Monsieur Alex looked at Mr. and Mrs. Leyton.

"But . . . plenty of other nights to cook," he said, shaking his head uncomprehendingly.

And there were plenty of other nights to cook, indeed. To Augustus Trotter's frustration Louisa accepted almost every engagement she or they were offered. The only ones she declined were those which clashed with ones already accepted or those which she declared were not up to her standard. Every night saw them out making and serving. The dinner parties invariably ended late, and there were things to be done in the visited kitchens after them, so that it was the small hours of the morning before they returned to the pleasant little house, which was to Trotter starting to seem more like an office or an employment agency than a home.

Louisa would share a few minutes with him in their kitchen while he had a nightcap and she sometimes sipped a hot drink. Then she would get up, give him a little peck on his forehead, and go yawning off to bed. He took the hint and did not trouble her or try to persuade her that he was, after all, her newly wed husband.

Louisa's name, as a cook, had spread in London society with what seemed to be almost magical rapidity. It was only a matter of months since she had been reluctantly taken under Monsieur Alex's tutelage, yet she was now acknowledged a mistress of her art. He had not exaggerated in his farewell speech. She had an inspired feeling for cooking which surpassed anything she learned from anyone else, or out of books; and she read books, dutifully—the cook's bible (Mrs. Beeton's *Book of Household Management* in its most recent edition) and the great Soyer's *Gastronomic Regenerator*—and took their advice sometimes with respect, sometimes with skepticism. She had the born cook's invaluable faculty for knowing how the result of a recipe would taste. And, like Isabella Beeton, she had an instinct for the dietetic value of food, the balance of starch against other substances, the importance to digestion of the perfect sauce, the eye appeal of varied colors in the dishes offered. Of herbs, spices, quantities, and blends Monsieur Alex had taught her all he knew. Her own imagination supplied the rest. Though she had been reared on the plainest of food, no dish was too extravagant or exotic for her to undertake now. *Dindon rôti aux truffes à l'espagnole, pierre grillé au vin de champagne*—she took a sensuous delight in turning such grand titles into glorious-tasting realities. Engage Louisa for your dinner party, and you were sure of outshining Lady Jones and charming the gastronomes of your acquaintance.

Her memory was perfect. She had only to be shown something once for every detail of it to implant itself in her mind. Having learned the classic way of preparing and garnishing a dish of which she might never have heard before, she could thereafter do it exactly right herself, without recourse to notes. And she would add to its preparation some indefinable touch which transcended her employers' expectations.

Hostesses told one another. Pleased diners-out gossiped about this exciting new discovery. And, unbeknown to Louisa or her husband, she was quietly recommended to one or two people in very high places, in part-payment for the extraculinary services she had committed herself to render.

Those services were not commanded immediately. Several weeks passed without any message reaching her. She gradually began to lose the fear, on waking each morning, that this would perhaps be the day. She relaxed and concentrated on her work, hoping against hope that she would be totally reprieved to get on with it in peace.

She was also able to get on with training her own cook, Mrs. Wellkin, a pleasant-looking woman in her late thirties. From the moment of entering the house as resident, Louisa had made it clear that she was not going to do any cooking for Trotter and herself. She would cook like a queen for other people in the evenings, but she would live like a lady during the days, waited upon by a general maid, Ethel, and a younger one named Dolly. Mrs. Wellkin cringed under the lash of Louisa's blunt criticisms, but improved rapidly and almost heroine-worshiped her teacher.

For his part, Augustus found the daytime an increasing bore. Deprived of his employment, except as a sort of temporary footman in the evenings, he had nothing else to fall back upon. He also felt acutely the loss of dignity. His career seemed to him to have gone into reverse, rather than to have taken the leap forward he had expected. And he couldn't prevent himself feeling a growing jealousy toward Louisa and her mounting fame.

One morning he wandered idly into the parlor, to find her at her small desk, carefully writing out a menu in her beautiful hand. The French words no longer troubled her. She knew their spelling and meaning better than most of her clients did.

"Going to be long?" Augustus asked pleasantly.

She didn't trouble to look up, but replied offhand-edly, "Don't expect so."

"Nice day," he tried again. "Thought we might take a walk by the Serpentine. Maybe a music hall this afternoon."

"All right," she answered, still writing. "Don't mind."

He stood watching her for some minutes, longing for her to throw her pen down and spring into his arms. She seemed to have forgotten he was in the room with her.

"Louisa . . ." he ventured at last, moving a step toward her. "Dearest . . ."

He was about to touch her hair, but her sudden movement made him draw back swiftly.

"There!" she said, putting down the pen and getting up. "Finished." She gave him her charming smile. "Get me coat, shall I?"

Before he could reply the door had opened and the little maid had entered.

"Excuse me, madam," she said, "but there's a gentle-man at the door. To see Mr. Trotter."

Annoyed at the girl's having addressed this to Louisa, as though he were not to be entrusted with it direct, Augustus snapped back, "Well, who is it, then?"

"A Major Farjeon, sir."

He and Louisa exchanged glances. He could read plainly in her look that she was thinking the same as he—that the time had come.

He told the maid, "Show him into the sitting room, Dolly. I'll see him there."

The girl gave a little bob and went out. Louisa and Augustus regarded one another in silence for some moments. Then she shrugged, sat down at her desk again, and drew up a blank menu card, to resume writing.

They had not been wrong in their surmise. After the briefest of pleasantries the equerry came to the point. He named a date on which Augustus knew for certain

Louisa had a dinner-party booking. There could be no question of putting this to the equerry. Augustus didn't even try. He merely assented on his wife's behalf, and the go-between went away.

Augustus braced himself to pass the news on to Louisa. She heard it without stopping. When he mentioned the necessity of canceling the booking she only shrugged again.

Four evenings later she sat before her dressing table, carefully making up her face. She was fully dressed in an evening gown she had had specially made and had been saving several weeks for this occasion. Her hair had been done at a salon that afternoon. Much as she liked to play the lady at home, Louisa refused to let any maid dress her, or even touch her.

She was conscious of the fact that her husband was downstairs, in his butler's garb, waiting to open the front door to her royal visitor. It was the greatest irony she could imagine in life. At least the Prince of Wales had made a point of sparing her having to give him a meal. She had often imagined that sort of an evening: herself in her cook's garb, hot-faced in the kitchen until all was nearly ready; then rushing upstairs to change into finery; then going to join him in the parlor, where her own servants—her own husband, even—would gravely serve them the meal she had cooked, while they sipped champagne.

She knew, of course, about the Prince's penchant for ladies, and had occasionally wondered how it was all managed. She had always imagined that he took his choice from among high society, where things could move straightforwardly, watched only by the blindest of eyes. But why her? Well, it had been said often enough to her that a man's heart was to be won by way of his stomach. She didn't believe for a second that she had won this man's heart; but it had certainly been his stomach that had introduced her to his attention.

As to what she would be expected to do for him, she had tried not to think about it. He would know and she would obey. It had to be as simple as that. She felt no more or less revulsion than she did in regard to Augustus Trotter's advances—except that Augustus was certainly a more agreeable figure of a man. She would have preferred to be left alone by both of them. Plenty of other women had the talent, and no doubt the eagerness, to do for them what she was so reluctant to do; but how many women could match her as a cook? None, she reckoned, and thought miserably about the unfairness of life.

She had finished making up. She inserted the earrings through her recently pierced ears. Then she sat up and looked at the overall result in the mirror.

"God, girl," she told her reflection aloud. "Why'd you have to be born a good-looker as well. Cooking'd be more than enough."

And then she heard the doorbell down below, and knew she was on duty.

A duty it was, in fact; certainly not a pleasure. Louisa had grown up basically ignorant of the mysteries of sex, like the other women of her generation, and Edward had been reared in the school of thought which maintained that only prostitutes enjoyed it. Unlike many men of his time, he was neither sadistic nor perverted, in which Louisa was lucky; but, though faintly surprised by her virginity (one had rather thought that women of her class were bound to be experienced), he took no trouble to lessen the pain of her initiation. She was thankful for the self-control that held back her tears, as she had been thankful for having resisted the impulse to hysterical laughter as Edward, without the aid of a valet, removed layer after layer of clothing, including braces, long woolen combinations, and a flannel body-belt.

At least it was soon over. He was old, his taste was jaded. She escaped with relief to the bathroom to change into the loose peignoir she had been advised to have in readiness, and rejoined the Prince for a sedate tea, as though nothing had happened.

He paid her the compliment of staying more than an hour longer, just talking to her. Again, she was surprised. Without saying as much, but through his manner, he gave her the impression that he wanted friendship more than anything else; and even, it struck her, the kind of friendship a mother would give freely to a loved son. Everyone knew how coldly Queen Victoria and the late Prince Consort had behaved toward him. Perhaps he had to spend his days trying in vain to make up for it by eating himself into ill health and searching for the woman who possessed some quality which he had obviously never found in his lovely wife, the Princess Alexandra.

When he had gone, she took off the peignoir, bathed, and put on a favorite old nightdress. Then she went to bed, knowing that Augustus would not want to come hanging around her that night.

She lay in the dark and thought about it all. If that was what it was like, they could keep it, so far as Louisa Trotter was concerned. She was quite sure now that Augustus was never going to get his marital rights, however he might beg, plead, and engage her in undignified struggles on landings. Whatever they said, she felt that her marriage had been an unnecessary farce, just as her present situation was a farce. How absurd it was, a girl of her independence letting herself be hooked into it.

"It can't be for long," she assured herself again, thinking, with a little pity for him, of the Prince's corpulent figure and his hacking cough.

"Stick it out, girl, and you never know but what it'll all be for the best in the end."

Before she fell asleep, her last thought was a regretful one. If she'd only played her cards right, she could have had a house equal to this one, and servants and money and all the trimmings. And she could have had the charming and handsome Charlie Tyrrell, too. At least she'd have known just where she stood then.

Ah, well. . . .

Eight

Having survived her initiation, Louisa settled down happily into the process of furthering her real career. On at least five nights a week, and sometimes seven, she would be booked to cook dinner in some noble or rich household, with luncheon engagements in between. It became apparent to her how few inspired cooks there were in London. Good, reliable ones still abounded, but their employers seemed to be only too eager to give them an evening off and engage Louisa for the most important functions.

Inevitably, she cooked on a number of occasions for the Prince of Wales, though never in her own house. Whenever he was the guest of people for whom she was cooking he would send for her to be congratulated. With an extra pressure of his soft hand around hers and a significant look into her eyes he affirmed his pleasure at their special relationship. On a number of occasions she was told by her employer that in accepting the invitation His Royal Highness had stipulated that she be engaged.

His visits to her house were infrequent, at intervals of several weeks. They amounted to only half a dozen in all. He was unfailingly kind and courteous to her. Her affection for him grew. She made the effort to be more ladylike in her speech for him, but he noticed it, laughed, and told her he liked her as she was. They

laughed a lot together. He encouraged her to call him
Edward, though she was careful to do so sparingly.
She had heard tales of people of higher rank than she
being misled by his cordiality into taking liberties with
him, and how he had promptly put them in their place.

He kept a few belongings at her house—mostly
items of bedroom attire and toilet things. She thought
he felt a special pleasure about this little token of
permanence. And whenever he visited her he
brought a gift.

So she had become reconciled to the arrangement:
pleased that so few demands were made on her, but
not resentful when they were; and glad of this opportunity to establish herself on the highest plane of
her true profession.

Augustus Trotter remained less happy. True, they
were prospering under the arrangement, but that was
all he could say for it. Egged on increasingly by his
acidulated spinster sister, Norah, who had taken to
seeing much more of him—and borrowing regularly
from him—he nurtured his resentment at the way
things had worked out.

The century ended. And three weeks after this
symbolic turning point the longest reign in British history finished, when, on January 22, 1901, Queen Victoria died at Osborne House, on the Isle of Wight,
after a brief illness.

It did occur to Louisa to wonder what it might mean
to her personally, if anything. But she was so busy
catering for the more raffish hostesses, who saw the
ending of the era as a blessed relief and hastily organized dinner parties in secret celebration, that she
had little time to concern herself. Culinary matters
were the only ones which raised her emotions.

"Call this a bleedin' mayonnaise?" she demanded of
Mrs. Wellkin in her own kitchen, one rare evening at
home.

She had been dining alone with Augustus—Gus, as
she had come to call him. Ethel had served the fish

and offered the mayonnaise. Louisa had taken one look, flung down her napkin, seized the sauceboat, and stormed downstairs.

"It's curdled!" she accused her cowering cook.

Mrs. Wellkin faltered. "I . . . I followed the recipe you gave me exactly, madam."

"In a pig's ear you did. I'll tell you just what went wrong. The oil you used was cold. Straight from the pantry."

She had had no doubt of that, though her cook's expression was confirmation enough of it.

"When it got too thick, you bunged in some vinegar, and then more oil, and you beat it all up at once. Right?"

"I was in a hurry . . . madam. I thought it would save time."

Louisa banged the sauceboat down on the table. The mayonnaise was too solid even to quiver.

"You can save time on most things," she said. "But not when you're making a mayonnaise."

"I did my best, madam," the humbled cook muttered. But her mistress was relentless.

"No you didn't. That's the whole point. Your mind wasn't on it."

"I'm sorry," the miserable woman replied, wondering whether a quick death might not be preferable. "I'll be more careful in future. I'll pour it away."

"Hold on, hold on," Louisa told her, the quick anger gone just as speedily. "Waste not, want not. Fetch us an egg."

Mrs. Wellkin obeyed. Watched by her and the awe-struck Ethel, Louisa cracked the egg, separated it into bowls, then proceeded to drip the curdled mayonnaise into the yolk, drop by drop, beating the mixture vigorously with the wooden spoon she had seized in her other hand.

"Slow and steady does it," she intoned, her eyes never leaving her task. "And you can't beat it too hard."

In the ensuing silence, Ethel took the chance to ask something which had been preoccupying her for some days.

"Excuse me, mum . . ."

"What, Ethel?"

"We was wond'rin' if we could go and watch the funeral procession at Windsor? There's ever so many kings and princes and such to be there."

Louisa went on beating concentratedly. It had not passed her thoughts that the man who would be walking immediately behind the Queen's coffin, at the head of an entire Empire's mourning, would be the same one who kept a pair of his slippers in her wardrobe.

She knew that she herself could easily ask for a privileged place to watch the unique procession. But she answered Ethel, "You go and gawk if you want to. See the old girl off."

"Won't you be going to watch, madam?"

"I take no pleasure in funerals."

She threshed the mayonnaise harder.

"See how much beating it needs, Mrs. Wellkin? Oh, go and answer that, Ethel. It's Dolly's night out."

The front-door bell had rung. Ethel hurried up the steps. Louisa beat the mixture for some time longer, then handed it over to her cook, wiping her hands dismissively on a cloth.

"Right," she instructed. "Now, keep beating. Add the rest, drop by drop. And let's have it livened up with a bit of tarragon, eh?"

Hitching up her evening gown, she went back up to the dining room. It was empty. She heard voices in the parlor and went in. Major Farjeon, in evening dress and retaining his hat and cane as a sign that he did not intend to linger, was chatting with Augustus. As soon as she entered the room, Louisa could sense an uneasiness in the air.

"Ah, my dear," her husband said. "Here's Major Farjeon. I'll leave you together." He went out.

"Just passing," the equerry explained to Louisa, shaking hands with her and looking at her searchingly. "I've apologized to Mr. Trotter for not having come by appointment. Only, I have to go to Windsor tonight. His . . . Majesty wants me to oversee some of the funeral arrangements."

"Always pleased to see you at any time, Johnnie," said Louisa, who had come to be on semicomradely terms with him. "Ooh!" she corrected herself, with a hand to her mouth. "Sorry. It's *Sir* John since the New Year, isn't it?"

He smiled. "Johnnie will still do," he said.

"I thought you'd be in the Isle of Wight."

"I just crossed today. My word, there are tremendous arrangements going on. Can you imagine ten miles of warships, Louisa? The pride of the British Fleet. They'll be lining the whole of the way across the Solent when the royal yacht passes with the coffin."

"Phew! Takes your breath away a bit, doesn't it? Takes a bit of getting used to. How is . . . His . . . Majesty?"

"He's stood up to it surprisingly well. He's not a . . . young man, and he's waited longer in history than anyone to become king."

She smiled. "I've heard him say he'd got used to the waiting. Some days he hoped it would never come."

"So did many others, I'm afraid," Farjeon said.

He was quite surprised by the indignation with which she retorted. "They'd better not say that near me, then! Who are they? Who thinks like that?"

"Many in society—and the government. They see him only as a man of pleasure."

"Huh! Blind asses!"

"Exactly. They don't realize how devoted he is to his people and country. He's waited so long to serve them, and never been allowed to."

"What's he going to call himself? King Edward, or King Albert?"

"Edward, I'm glad to say. It will be the more popular choice."

"I'm glad. Couldn't think of him as Albert. It'd seem like . . . someone else. Well, I suppose they'll all have their telescopes trained on him from now on."

Farjeon met her look fully. "Every minute of the day. He must be extremely careful from now onward not to give ammunition to those who expect him to prove unworthy of his high position. That . . . that is really why I'm here."

Louisa realized at once and replied, "So he won't be calling for a while?"

He shook his head and his gaze slipped away.

"Not for the . . . foreseeable future."

She could not have failed to recognize his embarrassment.

"Come on, Johnnie," she said softly. "You don't have to go all round the houses with me. Let's have it straight, eh?"

"Louisa, he asked me to say that he will always cherish the fondest memories of your kindness—your friendship. But in the new circumstances, I'm afraid that the . . . special relationship between you must regretfully be considered as over."

Louisa was too sharp not to have sensed from his manner that something of this sort had caused him to be "just passing" her house in the middle of dinnertime. Her feelings were a bewildering mixture of relief and regret. She might have preferred that the liaison she had not welcomed, but had learned to accept with some pleasure, should have ended less abruptly.

"I just won't see him again?" she asked.

"I'm sorry, Louisa. He hopes you will still meet as friends—in society. The lease of this house is yours, of course, and all the furniture and movables. If in the future you are ever in financial difficulties . . ."

She stopped him with a shake of her head.

"He's been kind enough already. I don't want to sponge off him."

"All the same, times change. In case of need, remember you can always call on him. And now, I really must be on my way. Don't bother to see me out. Thank you for making my mission so painless . . . Mrs. Trotter."

She smiled reassurance at him.

"Louisa will do fine still. I hope we're going on being friends?"

He smiled back. "You know, Louisa, after two weeks of full mourning it's a blessed relief to spend a moment or two with someone as refreshing as you."

She laughed at his solemn compliment. "Go on! You've been taking lessons from him, Johnnie."

"Well—if you'll kindly collect his things together, I'll send one of the valets round to collect them in the morning."

He bowed and went out. The interrupted dinner forgotten, Louisa remained in the parlor. She wandered over to the mantelpiece. Among a profusion of ornaments and a gilded clock, flanked at each end by a colored cut-glass luster, there stood a pair of photographs in matching silver frames. One was of Edward, looking masterful and assured. The other was of his late mother, old, sharp-nosed, and disapproving of everything.

Louisa addressed the latter aloud.

"Well, old girl. You tried all your life to change him. The only way you could do it was by poppin' off."

She turned sharply when she heard her husband's voice behind her.

"So it's all over then? You're free."

He stood a few paces inside the room. His smile annoyed her.

"How d'you mean, 'free'?"

"You know. I can't tell you how I've prayed for it, Louisa."

A retort was on the tip of her tongue, but she bit it back.

"I don't want to talk about it now, Gus," she said. "Some other time, eh? Just . . . leave me alone, and I'll see you in the morning."

He went out disappointedly. She turned back to the mantelpiece, regarding the other portrait with the heavily lidded eyes and the jauntily held head. For a few moments she felt more emotional than she could remember ever having done in her life. Then she picked up the photograph in its frame and carried it to the middle drawer of her little desk. She locked it in there and took away the key.

A few days before the Queen's death Louisa had had "words" with Augustus's sister. The women had little in common. Louisa's forthright and open manner was in complete contrast to Norah's deviousness. Their different ways of looking at any subject often brought them into dispute, with Augustus nervously occupying the middle ground and trying to restore a pretense of amity. On this occasion he had failed and Norah had swept out of Louisa's house, declaring that she would never be seen there again, even if wild horses dragged her.

Nonetheless, early one evening, two days after Major Farjeon's visit, she was around again. She had known about her brother's and Louisa's circumstances all along—it would have been impossible to have kept them from her prying mind. Ever since the news of the royal death had reached her she had been speculating with increasing curiosity about its significance for the household in Chelsea. Now she could no longer restrain herself from calling there.

To her relief, Augustus, as she always called him in her stiff manner, was alone, already changed for dinner. She demanded point-blank to know what was going to happen. Reluctantly, he told her half the truth and had the rest bullied out of him. When she asked what financial provision had been made in recognition of the couple's services, and he admitted, after some hedging, that Louisa had refused to accept anything, Norah treated him to some abusive observations.

He kept defending himself. "It was up to Louisa. She didn't want anything more from him."

"Then what about you? How much did you get?"

"N . . . nothing."

"*Nothing!* You're too soft by half, Augustus. Always have been, that's your trouble. You're the man. It should have been you dealt with it, not her. You should have made sure you got something out of it—to make up for the humiliation. But, oh no, can't stand up for yourself—as usual."

He dared to almost shout back. "Listen, Norah. Listen! All I can feel is that I'm glad it's over . . . that I have Louisa to myself at last. . . ."

"Huh!"

Louisa walked in at that moment, in a plum-colored gown and some of her jewelry. At the sight of Norah she struck an astonished pose and said with coarse provocation, "Wotcher, Nore?"

Norah drew herself up and turned down her mouth.

"Good evening, Louisa," she nevertheless managed to say.

"And what brings you round here?"

"Surely I can visit my own brother?"

"Ooh! Seems to me the last words I heard you say were something about never darkening this doorstep again."

"That's just Norah's way, my dear," Augustus intervened hastily, earning a disdainful look from his sister and a pitying one from his wife. "It doesn't mean anything, really. She just has to speak her mind."

"Oh, I see," Louisa said mildly. "Well, let bygones be bygones. I've no objection to people speakin' their minds. I've been known to do it meself."

She delighted in roughening her way of speaking in

the presence of Norah, who never failed to react with a contemptuous stare, which made her lean features even more sour and amused Louisa greatly.

"The, er, news from the Cape seems better," Augustus resumed hopefully. "Kitchener's pushed De Wet and his army right back across the Orange River."

"Hoo-ray," Louisa responded flatly.

"You must be longing for your brother to come home, my dear," he plowed on.

"Not much. No doubt he'll turn up one of these days, though. Looking for a handout."

This was excuse enough for Norah.

"Yes, Louisa," she said, with an attempt at cordiality. "I was wondering what you were going to live on now."

"Now?" Louisa said sharply. A glance at her husband told her that the matter had been under discussion before she had come in.

"After all," Norah was saying, "this must be an expensive house to run."

"We'll manage."

"But how? If you ask my advice . . ."

"I never ask, when I know I'll get given it anyway. You mind your business, Norah. We'll mind ours. Sorry we can't ask you to dinner. They're only cookin' for us two."

Louisa marched out of the room.

"Well!" Norah fumed.

"Please, Norah," Augustus begged. "Don't go on."

She turned on him furiously.

"You married beneath you! You were one of the youngest butlers in the country. You were highly thought of—in a fine position, with a great future. She put an end to that. She dragged you down."

He tried to speak, but she was relentless.

"You were always too trusting. Well, if you're to have any hope of leading a normal married life with her you must put your foot down."

And to his intense relief she, too, left him. He went

to the brandy decanter and poured himself a good measure. When he had finished it he poured another.

Louisa knew that he had been drinking heavily by the way he walked into dinner soon afterward. He quickly made inroads into the sherry and the wine, only playing with his food.

She tried to rally him in a friendly tone. "Come on, Gus. Eat up. Mrs. Wellkin'll be walking out in a huff if we send all that back."

"I'm not hungry," he said.

She was trying her best for him.

"Look, I'm sorry if I upset Norah," she said, with rare apology. "You know how she gets my goat!"

"She means all right," he replied. "She's . . . she's a good girl. She's only concerned for our welfare."

"Welfare my Aunt Fanny! She wants to know you're still good for a touch."

"How did you . . . ?" he began to blurt out, then checked himself. He had never told Louisa that he was giving his sister money.

"Think I'm blind and deaf? *And* I can add up accounts."

He turned on a wheedling tone.

"She is part of my obligations, dear. My mother would expect it."

This was trying Louisa's sympathy too far. She ordered Ethel out of the dining room before resuming.

"Your mother! I'm sick and tired of hearing you and Norah going on about your great connections. You can't even put a name to them."

He took some more wine and after a few moments' silence made the effort he had been working himself up to ever since the effects of the predinner brandies had begun to make themselves felt.

"Louisa . . . love," he said, a trifle thickly now. "I've been meaning to say . . . that we're just starting all over again now. Everything's starting again. The past —it's over. I . . . I draw a veil over it."

She raised her eyebrows. "What d'you expect me to say to that? 'How decent—how generous'?"

"I'm prepared to forget."

"You're offering forgiveness. *You're* prepared to forgive *me?*"

"I married you and . . . and turned a blind eye."

"You knew perfectly well what was going to happen. I was married off to you to make me available to him."

"But I wanted you, Louisa. I'd have done anything. Anything to get you."

She replied more gently, "You knew how it would be, Gus. I did fight against it."

He was becoming maudlin. "I kept waiting. Hoping. No one would believe what it's been like for me. Never knowing when it would end. I hoped once he'd let you go we'd have a chance, together."

"Well, we are together."

"Really together, I mean. Man and wife. I thought, all this time, maybe you'd get to like me a bit. Be ready to settle down. Maybe realize I could make you happy. And I could. I know I could."

He drained his glass and filled it again. She looked at him anxiously. It was not like him to drink to excess.

She tried to console him. "We get along fine. Nothing's changed."

"I don't *mean* it like that. I want you, Louisa."

She sighed heavily. It was a confrontation she had been fearing for a long time.

"We had a bargain, Gus," she answered. "I told you straight, I didn't love you. I still don't. I'm fond of you, but I don't belong to you, or to anyone. So, as to anything else, I can't promise, Gus."

He shook his head in despair. His eyes were glazing now.

"There's no chance, unless you stay at home. If you're going to go on working out in other houses I won't be able to stand it. Wondering . . ."

"What do you mean?" she asked tensely.

"I'm not having you going to other people's houses. Meeting other men. They take advantage. The women are fair game. I know what goes on. I know what happens."

He was starting to rave now and it annoyed her. Also, she could feel no respect for men who couldn't hold their drink.

"For God's sake!" she hissed. "You always go with me. I'm always busy in the kitchen. What d'you think could happen to me? And get this straight. There won't be no one else. Ever again."

"Only me, then," he shouted across the table. "It's my right. I've waited. I'm your husband."

The growing redness of his face suddenly turned to near-purple. He lurched to his feet, knocking over his chair, and stood swaying, holding on to the edge of the table.

"I'm your husband," he threatened, "and it's my right to make you."

A cold wave of revulsion swept through Louisa. She sat still and regarded him steadily.

"You're stronger than me, Gus," she said quietly. "You can force me. But if you do, it'll be the only time. And you'll never see me again."

She got up quickly and walked straight out of the room and down to the kitchen, where she felt sure he would not so demean himself as to follow in his state. She heard the front door shut with a crash.

Nine

When Louisa reached the kitchen, Ethel, sensing displeasure, said nervously, "There's a person been waiting to see you, mum."

"What kind of person?" Louisa snapped back.

"Young. A servant girl, sort of."

"Where is she, then?"

"Walkin' up and down in the street, mum. She wouldn't come in."

"Why didn't you tell me before, then? In this cold! Fetch her now, before she's perished."

The maid hurried out by the area door and returned some minutes later with a girl wearing a thin cape over her dress. She was shaking with the cold from head to foot. Louisa recognized her at once as her little Welsh friend Mary, from Lord Henry Norton's.

"Mary!" she cried, taking her by the shoulders. "Here. Come over to the fire. Why didn't you say who you were? Why didn't you come in?"

"I . . . I didn't like, Miss L . . . Mrs. Trotter," the girl answered through chattering teeth. "They said you and the master was busy."

She swayed in Louisa's arms and burst into tears. Louisa jerked her head at Mrs. Wellkin and Ethel, looking on intrigued. They caught her message and

113

began bustling about heating up the remains of the soup and fetching a bowl and spoon.

Louisa forced Mary into a chair beside the fire and knelt to chafe her hands.

"You're frozen to the bone, girl. And so thin! What's happened? Here—you're not in the family way?"

The crying girl could only shake her head.

"What, then? Did you get the push from Lord Henry's?"

Mary rubbed at her eyes. "No," she sniffled. "I ran away. Two days ago."

"Two days? Where've you been sleeping?"

"Under the railway arches. But there's awful people there. I was afraid to go back."

"Why didn't you come straight here?"

"I did. I walked past . . . Hoped you'd see me. I was afraid to come in."

"You daft ha'porth," Louisa said, taking the bowl of steaming soup from Mrs. Wellkin. "Bet you haven't eaten for two days, neither."

The girl shook her head.

"Then get yourself round this. Mind—it's hot as a jockey's breeches. Take it slow. Cor, I can't for the life of me think why you didn't just knock at the door."

Mary raised the spoon in a shaking hand, but had, indeed, to recoil from the scalding heat of the soup. She answered, "Ivy said you was all different. You wouldn't want to see anyone you'd . . . been in service with."

She cast a furtive glance at the listening servants.

"She said you was a grand lady and wouldn't want to be reminded."

"Did she, now? Well, there's some people I don't want to be reminded of, and she's one of 'em."

"It . . . it was because of her I ran away."

"Did she bully you?"

"It never stopped. It's never been the same since

you left—you and Mr. Trotter. And Monsieur Alex's gone, too. Couldn't stand the atmosphere anymore, he said. They made me do everything—cleaning, washing, and fetching and carrying. Ivy hit me for being slow. And I got so tired . . ."

Louisa gently guided the spoon to the girl's mouth. This time she managed to swallow.

"Why didn't you tell the housekeeper?" Louisa asked.

"Oh, I wouldn't dare do that," Mary answered, looking fearful.

"Wouldn't you, indeed?" Louisa said, her face hardening.

Next morning she was around at Lord Henry Norton's. She swept a protesting Ivy aside and marched into Mrs. Catchpole's room with only a token rap at the door. She found the housekeeper markedly frailer than she had last seen her, on the wedding day. She noted a wheeze in the older woman's breathing when she spoke.

"I'm so glad she came to you," Mrs. Catchpole said, when Louisa had told her what had happened. "Poor girl. I couldn't think what had become of her."

"Your Poison Ivy's been up to her tricks again, that's what," Louisa answered.

"Oh, dear!"

"Yes. But what're you going to do about it?"

The housekeeper replied mournfully, "What can I do? I've not been well. The house has been so difficult to run since you and Mr. Trotter left—and then Monsieur Alex. We've had a whole series of cooks on a month's trial each. Two of them were quite good, but only competent, really. . . ."

She made an effort and pulled herself together, even managing a little smile.

"But never mind my worries. I'm so happy things have worked out well for you, Louisa. I expect you were . . . provided for."

Louisa shrugged. "I've a house in one of the best parts of town. Servants to look after me. A bit in the bank . . ."

"And a devoted husband."

Louisa merely nodded.

"Most women would envy you," Mrs. Catchpole said warmly. Louisa shook her head this time.

"They'd be wrong," she answered, to the older woman's surprise. "I knew it at the time. From the minute I realized what was behind all the attention—all the special kindness I had from . . . the Prince. Not that I wasn't flattered, mind. Quite cocky for a while. But the price was too high."

"Too high? But knowing the Prince must have . . . well, helped you . . . professionally."

"In a way. Only, now's he's gone—and he *has* gone, Mrs. Catchpole—I'm beginning to wonder where it'll leave me. Too exclusive, maybe? 'By Royal Appointment,' sort of?"

"I don't think you need fear about that."

"Well, I can't help it. It's not only the big success that makes your name, you know. It's going on building up your reputation. *Keeping* it up, all on your own. Everything perfect all the time. It's a lot to ask, and no doubt there's plenty in the know who'd be only too pleased to see me make a slip."

Mrs. Catchpole smiled and seized an opportunity which Louisa's unexpected visit seemed to have sent miraculously her way.

"Lord Henry's giving dinner to the King of Portugal next Tuesday," she tried to say casually. "He's in town incognito."

Louisa grinned. "Oh, Carlos is no problem. He likes good no-frills English cooking—and lots of it. Give him oxtail or oyster soup, halibut, lark pudding, venison patty, and three kinds of roast, and he's happy."

"You see!" Mrs. Catchpole cried excitedly. "Who else would have known that?"

"Lord Henry'll probably get a decoration out of it," Louisa said.

The housekeeper leaned forward and looked hard at her. "And so might you, my dear, if you were to come back and cook dinner for him—just that once."

Louisa had not seen this coming. She considered, then asked, "How many for?"

"Twenty."

"Tuesday's not much notice. Anyway, we're forgetting why I came to see you. What about Mary?"

A cunning gleam shone in Mrs. Catchpole's eyes.

"Say yes, Louisa, and I'll make sure she's taken back," she cajoled.

This time, Louisa was ahead of her. She smiled back.

"Don't worry. I'll keep her myself. If I'm going to go on cooking I'll need someone to help me—won't I?"

With a civil nod to her old ally she got up and left. When she got home she reported her news to Augustus. Having had nothing to drink herself she immediately detected the spirits on his breath. She made no comment about it, though.

"You'd never believe the change in the place," she said of the house in Charles Street. "They've only learned to appreciate you in your absence."

To her disappointment he only grunted ungratefully.

"It'll seem funny to be back where it all started," she added.

He roused himself sharply. "I don't want you going there again," he said.

"Whyever not?"

"I won't have my wife in a menial position in that house—that's why. I mean it, Louisa. I won't have it."

"But Gus, Mrs. Catchpole was only asking me to do her a favor," she explained gently.

"Then she should ask me. Must I keep reminding you that you're my wife?"

Disconcerted by this new and worrying facet of Augustus's character, Louisa got up to leave the parlor. He said in a hard voice, "I haven't finished talking to you. We have to discuss our future."

"Not now, Gus."

"*Now!* We keep putting it off, but it can't be put off any longer."

"All right," she submitted, sitting down again. "Let's hear what you've to say. You and Norah, I expect. I knew I'd get it sooner or later."

He ignored the gibe and assumed a businesslike tone.

"We have to take stock. We live in a house that's much too grand for us. Everything we make—almost —goes to keeping it up."

"You want to sell it, then?"

"Of course not. It's our only asset. All we got out of . . . We should use it."

"How?"

"In the most sensible way. Let the spare rooms." Louisa gaped at him. "Open a boarding house!"

"No, no. *Private* rooms—with service. For gentlemen."

She tried to make a joke out of it. "Oho! You get all huffy about me occupying a menial position, and you want to give up our house to strangers, with me skivvying after 'em."

He scowled. "We have servants to do that. Don't you see? It will give us independence. A chance to keep up our station in life."

"St. Pancras or Waterloo?" she quipped again; but he was clearly in no mood for attempted wit. She became serious.

"All right, let's be practical, then. How much would we make out of letting three or four rooms? Precious little. There's no money in it, Gus."

"There could be, if we budget carefully. And we wouldn't need Mrs. Wellkin if you did the cooking."

"Over my dead body! Locked up in this place all day and night, catering for a handful of moldy lodgers who wouldn't know what they was eating? Just one booking like Lord Henry's, thirty guineas, and I'd earn more than out of ten lodgers for a month."

"But you don't know you'll go on getting bookings."

She opened her mouth to retort, but had to reflect that this was what she herself had said to Mrs. Catchpole that very morning. Would the King ask for her cooking in the way that the Prince had done? If not, would it be noticed in society, that narrow world in which every snub or imagined fall from favor was so quickly seized upon and voiced about? To what extent had her popularity been due to the knowledge that she cooked "By Royal Appointment," as she had put it? It cost far more to hire her for an evening than to pay a resident cook a little extra to buy some special materials, and until her advent society hostesses had managed their entertaining perfectly well.

All the same, she answered Augustus, "All right, love, so we have to be practical. I know it's difficult for you. You're a butler by profession, and you can't very well keep it up and live in your own home. But letting lodgings wouldn't help that, would it? And it's different for me. I'm a cook who can go anywhere. So long as I'm wanted I'm prepared to work hard—all the hours . . ."

"You're my wife," he reminded her weakly, and then spoiled his case completely by adding, "anyway, Norah says . . ."

Louisa jumped up.

"Norah can go and . . ."

She just managed to restrain herself because Ethel had come into the room.

"Anyway," she added low to Augustus, "I'm taking Lord Henry's booking, and we'll see how things go after that."

In fact, things went splendidly. The next afternoon Louisa had to call on Mrs. Catchpole to collect her fee.

She found the housekeeper much happier than at their last interview.

"It was a triumph, thanks to you, Louisa," she beamed. "His lordship was too ill to get out of bed this morning."

"Ill!" Louisa echoed. "You don't mean food poisoning?"

"Oh, no. Evidently the King of Portugal had so many helpings, and his lordship had to match him plate for plate, that he nearly passed out."

They laughed together.

"Still," Mrs. Catchpole said, "he said to thank you most particularly." She opened her drawer and brought out the envelope in which the money lay. She didn't hand it over at once, but looked at Louisa, sitting at the other side of her desk, and said, "I won't beat about the bush with you, Louisa. He was overjoyed to hear that you're available again—if you won't misunderstand me. He's asked me to offer you the position as cook here, at the same salary we paid Monsieur Alex."

She sensed what Louisa's reply was going to be and added hastily, "Don't refuse till you've thought about it, my dear. He'd expect you to work for him only during the Season. The rest of the year you'd be free to take any work you liked. And he's prepared to take Mr. Trotter back as his London butler on the same terms—living out."

"Blimey O'Reilly!" Louisa murmured. It was a handsome offer indeed.

"Talk it over with Mr. Trotter," the housekeeper was urging her.

"No," she replied decisively. "I can make up my own mind. It's a generous—more than generous offer, and I'm tempted. But you see, Mrs. Catchpole, if I'm ever to make a real go of my career I can't work for just one person—even for only part of the year. It would lose me my word-of-mouth, and it wouldn't be me, anyway. I'd be Lord Henry Norton's cook, not

Mrs. Louisa Trotter, special cook to all the best households. I can't go backwards, you see."

Mrs. Catchpole sighed and handed over the envelope.

"I was afraid you'd say that," she said.

"Ta," Louisa smiled, putting the envelope into her bag. "Course, I don't know that anyone else is going to want me anymore."

Mrs. Catchpole smiled sympathetically and produced another piece of paper.

"If I had told you that was so you might have accepted his lordship's offer," she said. "As a matter of fact, though, I had inquiries about you from several of the other evening's guests. I made a list."

She passed it over. Louisa stared and read out, "Lady Paget. Sir Ernest Cassell *Admiral Fisher*. Crikey! Half *Debrett!*"

She went home excitedly, having to suppress a childlike desire to skip. Only when she reached her own gate did her high spirits plummet, to be replaced by anger. On the front door was secured a long white piece of cardboard bearing the words ROOMS FOR GENTLEMEN.

Louisa ripped it off savagely and stormed into the parlor. Augustus was in his fireside chair, a glass of brandy on a small table near him.

"What the 'ell's this?" she demanded, flourishing the notice.

He had been anticipating this reaction and fortifying himself against it, though not to excess.

"It's obvious, isn't it?" he countered. "I've decided to go ahead."

"Go ahead?"

"It makes sense. Our savings won't last forever. We have to have a regular income to keep our heads above water."

"Just now, Gus Trotter, you could do with your head *under* water. We've already discussed this idea and decided against it."

"*You* decided, Louisa. I say every little helps. From four rooms we could net, maybe, twenty pounds a month."

" 'Rooms for Gentlemen' indeed!"

"Discreet, Louisa. Only for the best people."

Ethel made one of her untimely entrances just then, bearing the tea tray.

"Out!" Louisa ordered her. "Out you get. We'll ring when you're wanted."

The girl backed out hastily.

"Now, you see here . . ." Augustus protested to his wife.

"Don't you 'see here' me," she snapped back.

"I . . . I don't understand what you're objecting to," he said, less assuredly.

"That's what worries me, Gus," she said without heat. "You're always on about your dignity, your position in life. When you start putting signs like this up you're throwing it away."

"I want us to be independent."

"You were ready to work. Ambitious. Now you won't lift a finger. This whole idea is a way for you to sit at home and do nothing—except that." She gestured toward the brandy glass. Her speculation had been made impulsively, but it flashed into her mind now that there might be some truth in it, whether he realized it or not. She suddenly felt sorry for him and wanted to help him.

"Gus, I told you I'm keeping my business on. I need you to help me run it. That way we can be independent. We can be together, as you want."

He looked into the fire and muttered, "I'm not a kitchen hand."

"There's plenty of other ways you can help. And prospects *are* looking up. Honest."

He returned to his old theme. "You're a good cook, Louisa. None better. But it's time you learnt how to be a housewife."

She flared up again.

"I'm not a housewife! Or a housekeeper! Or a house-anything! And don't keep trying to turn me into one. Let me tell you, when my business really gets organized—busier than now—it'll bring in fifty or sixty quid a week. That'll go into a bank account for both of·us."

The figures had shaken him.

"Sixty pounds!"

"So, you see, we don't need to let rooms—because I deal with the *real* best people. And some of them will come here to consult me—to make bookings. Which is another reason I don't want this starin' them in the face!"

Louisa bent the cardboard notice and snapped it in two. She tossed the pieces onto the small table, nearly hitting the glass.

She grinned at Augustus. "An' you can put that where the monkey puts the nuts," she said with finality.

With the addition of the willing Mary, being trained as Mrs. Wellkin's assistant and ready to work herself to exhaustion if need be in her gratitude to Louisa, she had a strong and capable team. Mrs. Wellkin was by now able to do all the basic cooking to Louisa's own high standard, leaving her free to add the special touches and do the organizing.

She had devised a system by which as many dishes as could be prepared in advance in her own kitchen were cooked during the daytime preceding a dinner party, or the day before if the engagement was a luncheon. Then she and Mrs. Wellkin would go by cab to the house concerned, conveying it all in hampers and containers, thereby saving much time and flurry on the spot and enabling Louisa and her helper to concentrate on the hot cooking, assisted, with varying degrees of cooperation or surliness, by the resident staff.

Some of the kitchens and their equipment were already familiar to her. She knew of their deficiencies, too, so she would also take in the cab any necessary implements she would not find awaiting her. Whenever they worked in a house for the first time she took no chances and armed herself with a whole selection of her own knives, mixing spoons, molds, and even pans and an assortment of spices.

In counterpart to these positive changes in her arrangements there had been a major negative one. That was the defection of Augustus.

After Louisa's flat refusal to accept his scheme he had helped her on two or three more occasions. But he had put on so miserable a face, and been so gloomy an influence on everyone, that she had told him candidly that he had better either make the best of things or stay at home. Genuinely unable any longer to play second fiddle to his wife and sustain the role of her servingman, he had opted for this alternative—except that "at home" in her absence now usually meant the Grenadier public house around the corner from their road.

"Come on, come on," Louisa chivied her helpers as they prepared to set off on one of these occasions. "The cab'll be here any minute."

"The sauce is nearly ready, Mrs. Trotter," Mrs. Wellkin said.

"It'd better be. Mary, you sure you put everything in that box?"

"Yes, madam."

"Good. Crikey, look at all these things! We'll start needin' two cabs if we go on at this rate."

"You need a bigger kitchen, madam," Mrs. Wellkin said. It was only in proportion to the small house, although equipped with every necessity.

"Yes, we do," Louisa agreed.

"Oh, what about the master?" Mrs. Wellkin remembered to ask.

"There's something cold he can get if he wants it,

isn't there?" Louisa asked offhandedly. "Oh, hang it! We've forgotten the pâtés. Ethel, get 'em, quick."

"I have, mum," Ethel said, indicating another cardboard box.

"Good girl."

Ethel seized on this congratulation to make a bid she had been preparing for some days.

"Please, mum—please, I could do more. I been watchin' how you do things . . . An' now that the master doesn't go no more, I could help with the servin' and . . ."

"Hold on, hold on!" Louisa laughed. "Let's take a look at you. Turn round . . . slowly. Mm! You're not bad looking, Ethel, I'll say that for you. Quite presentable. If you can pick up a bit of style I might be able to use you."

"Oh, mum!" the ecstatic girl gasped. "Oh, ta. Ta ever so, mum!"

While the others, except Louisa, who merely smiled, giggled at her delight, she glanced hopefully down at herself and said, "Will I do like this, if I run and get a clean apron?"

Her pleasure faded as Louisa shook her head.

"No, dear. You won't be coming with us tonight. When you work in other people's kitchens they watch you—extra critical—and I don't want any of my girls showing herself up. You'll start with the basics, like Mary, tomorrow morning at six sharp."

"Yes . . . mum."

And so Ethel, who despite this initial disappointment could hardly get to sleep for excitement that night, joined Mary in the kitchen in the chill dark next morning and began following her about, watching and copying every move in her routine.

With so many busy late nights to keep, Louisa had got into the habit of staying in bed until midmorning, when she would be served her light breakfast with the newspaper. Then she got up, put on a decent enough dress in which to receive any chance callers, though not so good that it might be spoiled in the kitchen, and went down to that part of the house, where her clean, crisply laundered apron would be awaiting her in its appointed place.

Since she and Augustus had separate bedrooms, and he followed no set pattern of life, she didn't know whether he was in the house or out of it, unless she asked the servants or chanced to meet him. It mattered little. He had almost no contact with the business side of things anymore. She had asked him at least to deal with the bookings and other paperwork for her, but he had made no move to do so.

When Louisa came into the kitchen on this morning at eleven, Mrs. Wellkin was standing, preparing a mixture for an egg custard, while keeping an eye on Ethel, chopping parsley on a board. Mary occupied the end of the long table, sorting through, with her limited reading ability, a pile of correspondence and consulting the engagements book. The two girls got up at Louisa's appearance. She waved them down.

"I've been going through the bookings, mum," Mary said. "There's one for the fourteenth. Could you please quote for a dinner party for thirty-six, wines included. Lady ... Lady Beeo ... Byoo ..."

Louisa took the letter from her.

"Beauchamp," she explained. "Got it?"

"Beauchamp. Thank you, mum."

"Who else?"

"The Markis ... Marquis of Thorne."

"That randy old beggar!"

The girls giggled and Mrs. Wellkin flushed slightly.

"What's he want this time?"

"He's willing to pay up to three hundred guineas for a private supper for two. He says ... Ooh!"

Mary had realized that she was running headlong into a gaffe. She handed that letter also to Louisa, who scanned it scornfully.

"I might have expected. He wants me to be the

other one—and at his own apartment. Six delicious courses, with a *bombe surprise* to follow. I'd give 'im a *bombe surprise*, all right. Nothin' doin'!"

The front-door bell rang.

"Who can that be?" she mused. "Is Dolly up there?"

"She's doing the bedrooms, mum," Mrs. Wellkin said.

"I'd better go, then," said Louisa, who had not yet put her apron on. "Where's Mr. Trotter?"

Ethel said, a little apprehensively, "He's at the Grenadier, mum."

This early? Louisa thought as she went up the kitchen stairs.

The caller was a surprise to her, and a pleasant one. He was Major Sir John Farjeon.

"How nice to see you, Johnnie!" Louisa exclaimed. "Come on in. The maid's working upstairs."

She made to take his hat and stick, but he held on to them.

"Just passing, Louisa," he said.

She led the way into the parlor.

"Whenever you say that I get a very funny feelin'," she said, making him smile.

"It's a great pleasure to see you, my dear," he said. "As lovely as ever, too."

"Thank you, kind sir. Well, sit down. Something to drink?"

"No thank you."

He appeared to be rather less than his usual easy self. A thought struck her suddenly.

"What's up?" she asked. "Not another visit?"

"No, no. Nothing like that. I, er, wonder if . . . if Mr. Trotter is at home?"

"Matter of fact, he isn't. He's out this morning."

"Ah. Most mornings, I gather. And evenings."

"Johnnie," she said meaningfully. "Come on. Out with it."

"Well, I'm sorry to say this, Louisa, but word has reached the Palace that your husband spends much of the day in a public house near here. And that when he's had a few drinks he starts talking . . . about things he shouldn't."

"Oh, no!" She had never suspected this.

"Apparently it's nothing malicious," the equerry hastened to reassure her. "It's partly boasting—partly feeling sorry for himself. He tells anyone who'll listen how his life has been ruined. Oh, I don't mean he gives the details, but there are . . . hints, you know. Enough to be dangerous, especially if they get stronger."

Louisa sat in silent horror.

"So far the King hasn't heard," Farjeon said. "But if he does . . . His Majesty is completely discreet himself and demands discretion from others."

She managed to say, with dry lips, "He knows I wouldn't do anything to hurt him. Neither would Gus . . . Not meaning to."

"I'm sure. I admit I have a certain sympathy for Mr. Trotter, and I realize this puts you in a very difficult position. But if the greatest possible damage is not to be done you must find a way to stop him."

Louisa reached a decision there and then.

"Don't you worry, Johnnie," she promised, getting up. "I will."

She saw him out. Then she went to the pass door and shouted down to the kitchen that she was leaving and would be back in an hour or so. She quickly got her coat and hat and went out into the cold February morning, shouting for a hansom in a voice which caused a number of well-dressed passersby to look at her with curiosity.

"Charles Street," she called up to the cabby through the little square hatch. "I'll tell you just where."

Not long afterward she was again seated across the desk from Mrs. Catchpole in the housekeeper's room. But her manner this time was less self-assured than on the previous occasion. Mrs. Catchpole was shaking her head seriously.

"No, I'm afraid it's out of the question, my dear," she said.

Louisa said, "But you told me Lord Henry was keen to take him back."

"Yes, but not without you. It was really you he wanted. A good butler's easier to find than a first-class cook, you know."

Louisa's shoulders sagged a little. "I'll be honest with you, Mrs. Catchpole. I'm desperate," she confessed.

"I'm sure it must be dreadful for you, my dear. I wish I could help."

"I mean, *I* don't matter so much. It's the Palace. Think what some of them scandal sheets could make of it."

"I tell you, you must speak to Mr. Trotter. Warn him."

"I know. Only I don't seem able to talk to him anymore. He gets on his dignity. If you try to lay down the law to him it only makes it worse."

"He's been hurt very badly," Mrs. Catchpole explained. "The fact that since you both left here he's not really worked at anything . . . I mean, been living off you, so to speak . . . He must have lost all belief in himself."

"I asked him to take over running all my business for me. He wouldn't hear of it."

"Because that would make you his employer. He'd be all the more convinced he was a failure."

Louisa flapped her gloves exasperatedly.

"I'm fond of him, and I'm sorry for him," she said. "But it's no use if he won't even try."

"I think you know the answer," Mrs. Catchpole said, rising. "He has to be given back his self-respect and pride. My dear, I only wish I could help."

Louisa made her way back to Chelsea on foot, wanting to think, scarcely noticing the people and vehicles about her, the incessant rumble of many wheels, the smell of horses, the abusive exchanges of their drivers.

What did penetrate to her consciousness, though, was the shrill cries of the newsboys. There had been some particularly sordid murder in Camden Town and they were making the most of it to boost the sales of their halfpenny editions.

She went into a shop where a whole range of morning and evening newspapers was laid out on the counter and selected almost a dozen different ones, as well as some weekly journals specializing in small advertisements. Then she went on her way more briskly and soon reached home.

There was no cooking engagement that evening. She told Mrs. Wellkin she would take the chance to get a good rest and ordered lunch to be sent up to her room at half-past one. Then she locked her door, pulled up a chair to the bedside, and spread the first newspaper open on the counterpane. She turned to the "Situations Vacant" columns and perused the likely entries with care. She spent the entire afternoon doing the same with all the other daily papers and periodicals, making separate piles of those containing nothing to interest her and those others—the majority —in which she had made pencil markings.

Then she went through the latter again, reconsidering and eliminating. It was evening before she had narrowed down the possibilities to just a few.

"Partner in dairy—capital investment and share of profits."

"High-class grocery requires manager with prospects of partnership."

"Gentlemen's club seeks a head steward. Highest testimonials essential."

There were a handful of others. As she compared them yet again, wondering which she might have the best chance of persuading Gus to consider, her eye strayed quite by chance to an adjoining column in one of them. The advertisement stood out because it was boxed for prominence.

Louisa read, "HOTEL FOR SALE. Long-established

family hotel for sale. Excellent position in center of West End. Permanent residents. Small, experienced staff. Present owner retiring. Lease and contents subject to negotiation. EXTENSIVE, FULLY EQUIPPED KITCHENS."

Her heart began to pound with strange excitement. She read the advertisement again, and then again. Then she took up her pencil and made on the paper the boldest of all the marks she had made that day.

Ten

"Well?" Louisa asked Gus. "What d'you think of it?"
He didn't answer at once.

They were standing on one of the pavements of Duke Street, gazing across the roadway at the mid-Victorian buildings opposite. The lower parts of some were shops; the upper, offices or apartments. But it was on one building in particular—the one immediately opposite where they were standing—that their concentration was focused. It was of modest appearance and a little dingy. It had no shop front and its function would have been difficult to determine had it not been for the small sign above its door: BENTINCK HOTEL.

It was the day after Louisa's search through the newspapers. She had gone out early in the morning on an unexplained errand, leaving word with the servants that they were to request Mr. Trotter to stay in for her, as she might be wanting an important word with him when she got back. He had waited accordingly, a little apprehensive about what might be in store for him. But she had come in again all smiles and told him to get his coat and hat and come somewhere with her. She wouldn't say where, or give any sort of explanation. He had thought it best to obey, and a few minutes later a cab had dropped them outside the hotel.

132

They had gone in—Augustus thoroughly mystified by then—and Louisa had given the porter a letter which she had produced from her bag, asking him to take it to the proprietor. A few minutes later that person himself had appeared. He was a stout, aging man who looked unwell. He had greeted Louisa and Gus courteously and then asked them to follow him. To Gus's stupefaction the man had proceeded to show them all over the place.

The Bentinck had seen better days, that was for sure. The carpets on its stairs and landings were worn, the paintwork dingy with age, the plaster cracked and flaking in places. The sitting room looked as though it were never used, and curiously enough, there was no dining room. There were few bedrooms, and only two bathrooms, but a surprisingly large number of suites, each consisting of a sitting room, bedroom, and in most cases a small extra room, which the owner explained was usually occupied by a guest's own servant.

All the suites they were shown into were unoccupied. The others—about half the total—had permanent or semipermanent residents, or were retained by gentlemen or married couples who kept their own furniture and possessions in them, ready for use at any time. They kept to their own quarters and had all meals served to them in their sitting rooms.

Starting the tour of inspection from the top of the building, which was much larger than its frontage suggested, the party finally reached the belowstairs region. Louisa gave Gus's arm a squeeze of excitement when they set eyes on the kitchen. It was large and light and well equipped. A servants' hall adjoined it, and leading off it were a scullery, a larder, and several small wine cellars, all well stocked. Like the rest of the premises, though, there was a rundown air even here.

"Well, Gus?" Louisa said again, and he turned to look at her eager face.

"A good class of premises," he admitted. "Bit gone to the dogs."

"You'd be the boss," she told him. "I'd stick to the kitchen side."

"It'd need a deal of modernizing."

"We could do that bit by bit. It can go on as it is for a while. Seems to be doing well enough."

"He's asking a good price, I'll say that. Four or five thou' for sixty years' lease *and* contents."

"Poor old fellow," Louisa said. "I reckon he's not long for this world. Maybe the money doesn't matter all that much anyway."

Gus stared back at the hotel.

"It's still a lot for us to raise," he said.

"It'd be worth the effort, though, wouldn't it? What I can get for my house, plus the bit we've got put by. And it'll start giving us an income right away, and I can run my cookery from there. Anyway, Gus, it'll give you something to do—that's what matters. I don't like to see you moping so."

He swallowed and said, "If . . . I do agree . . . there'd be a condition."

"What?"

"I'd need a housekeeper to assist. I'd want Norah."

Louisa didn't answer. She stood looking across at the hotel, wrestling with her thoughts.

At length she said, "All right, then."

He hailed a cab and they went home, by way of the estate agency from whom Louisa had obtained the letter of introduction that morning. A partner of the agency accompanied them back to the house in Chelsea. He was visibly impressed by its appearance and location, not having seen this couple as the kind of people likely to be living so stylishly. The interior of the house impressed him even more. He quoted a better final price than Louisa had hoped even in her most optimistic moments—between three and four thousand pounds.

When he had gone she and Gus sat down in the parlor with pencils and paper and worked out the sums. They found that the price for the house and the amount they had in savings would, as Louisa had hoped, just cover the cost of the hotel. But only just.

"Lucky he isn't asking more," she said. "We couldn't have managed then."

He reminded her, "They did promise you . . . if at any time you needed . . ."

"No!" she replied emphatically. "I'd never accept that."

He shrugged. "Well, it's up to you."

"No, Gus. I want you to make the decisions. That's half what it's about."

"Well . . ."

He stared about the comfortable, elegantly furnished parlor. His thoughts traveled uneasily back to the shabby contrast of the hotel. And then he saw himself, important and busy, a man of property dealing on almost equal terms with gentlemen, instead of idling his days away with other servants in the Grenadier.

"All right," he said at last. "Done."

The period of transition was not a long one. As Louisa had suspected, the owner of the hotel was mortally ill. She discovered subsequently that he could have asked, and probably got, twice the price if he had chosen to. London at the turn of the century had relatively few hotels. Needing a base in town, most gentlemen from the country, alone or with their families, had a London apartment, or even a house, of their own. Those whose principal homes were in London had their secondary houses in the country, chiefly in the hunting and sporting shires or in Scotland. The diners-out tended toward places where they could meet *en masse;* where there was coming and going of both sexes and clamor and noise.

The unaccompanied male residents of the Bentinck were mostly the kind who preferred privacy, or indolence, and would tolerate slow service and shabby surroundings more than disturbing restlessness and efficient bustle.

Although Augustus was nominally in charge of the establishment once it had changed hands, Louisa determined that it should retain its present character. She made a point of introducing herself to those actually on the premises. They proved reticent and aloof; but gradually, by talking them around to the subject of food, she managed to draw them out, evidently to their own surprise. It seemed that the cuisine at the hotel in the past had been of about the standard to be found at any gentleman's club—baked, boiled, roasted, and grilled. Once she and her imported staff had thoroughly cleaned and reequipped the kitchens, Louisa began to cater for her clientele in a way to which they had plainly not been accustomed. She started a menu book, with a variety of favored dishes against each name, and submitted a list of suggestions to each every day.

This new regime was obviously appreciated, but it depended very much upon Louisa's own presence, as she discovered one afternoon on her return from cooking for a house party outside London. She found Mrs. Wellkin in tears and mumbling threats of leaving. Louisa stormed up to the general office and confronted Augustus and Norah.

"I go away for only two days, and I come back and find Mrs. Wellkin upset and ready to leave," she shouted. "Why?"

"All I did was send back her menus," Norah answered, with a lift of her chin.

"You *what?*"

"It seemed to me that with only sixteen people staying in the hotel they were needlessly extravagant."

"The hell you did! That was none of your concern, and you know it. Besides, she'd got my approval for everything."

Norah smiled her chill smile. "I should have thought

that even you would have seen the need to economize."

"No! The last thing we ought to economize on is the service we give. That's just where we can make our name."

"You will go on playing the great cook, won't you? All you seem to be concerned with is your precious kitchen. I thought it was agreed that general decisions regarding this hotel should be made by Augustus— and that I am the housekeeper."

Louisa controlled herself with a great effort.

"All right," she said, before stamping out. "But I'll have no more interference with the kitchen arrangements."

On her way down to the kitchen, Louisa gathered up the porter, Jessop, an ingratiating man in his forties whom she instinctively didn't like, and Merriman, the waiter, lanky and antique, and herded them down with her.

"Trouble brewing," Merriman muttered to Jessop. "Knew it all along."

"What trouble?" Louisa demanded, rounding on him.

"Couple more guests left this morning," he told her. "If many more go the shutters'll be up and we'll all be out on the street."

Louisa stamped ahead into the kitchen. She picked up a rolling pin and banged on the tabletop, freezing everyone into attention.

"Now listen, the lot of you!" she commanded. "This 'otel is goin' to be a success. And it's goin' to make its reputation on its cuisine. Whether there's ten guests, or a hundred, they'll get the best meals in London. In six months we'll be turnin' bookin's away. As for my own business outside, it's goin' to go on growin'. So whatever happens, no one's goin' to be idle. Everyone'll be treated fair, and there'll be no sackin'. So carry on. And Mrs. Wellkin . . ."

"Yes, mum."

"The menus stay the same as we arranged."

"Yes, madam."

"Right." Louisa jerked her head toward Jessop and Merriman, the gesture taking in the stairs back to the hall. "Get on with it."

They shambled away. Louisa turned to her female helpers.

"Ethel, you'll take over the preparations for the German Embassy dinner."

"Yes, mum. Only . . . I . . . I wanted to say that the kitchen at the Embassy's so small. Last time we had ever so much trouble keepin' things hot. And when there's fifty or more places . . ."

Louisa had to agree.

"It's a problem we keep running into. I've been thinking about it. We'll use hay boxes."

"A boxes?" asked Ethel, who had never heard of such things.

"H—*hay*. When I was a little girl my grandma used to put the porridge overnight into hay boxes," Louisa explained.

"But we don't make porridge, mum."

"You daft ha'porth! It's the process. You start the food in a big iron pot, then put it into a box packed with straw on the bottom and sides. It goes on cookin' in its own heat and in twenty-four hours it's done to a turn. For bouillons and fricassees and things it'd be perfect."

"If you say so, mum," Ethel responded doubtfully.

"At any rate, we'll try it out on the Kaiser's nephew."

They did; and it worked perfectly. Louisa kept the hay boxes in use after that and was able to cut down further on the amount of cooking needed to be done *in situ*, often under unfamiliar and inadequate conditions. Her freelance business survived the change of headquarters easily and began to pick up as Mrs. Wellkin, Ethel, and Mary became more profi-

cient. The same could not be said for the prosperity of
the Bentinck Hotel, however.

Perhaps self-deluded by the nobly mysterious background he had created for himself, Augustus had assumed a most superior air. He spoke familiarly to the
residents; and while a few of the more raffish of them
appreciated this, and enjoyed exchanging betting tips
and risqué sallies with him, others resented it extremely. The two residents whose departure had caused
Merriman's forebodings had gone because they regarded Augustus as a bounder and Norah, now dressing like a lady of fashion and trying to talk like one,
as a jumped-up snob.

Louisa forced herself not to interfere in the running
of the hotel. She had begun to fear that the arrangement had not had the beneficial effect on Gus she
had intended, and Norah's airs incensed her almost to
the screaming point. She concentrated all the harder
on her cookery, and told herself that it was all that
really mattered.

Inevitably, she sometimes had to be away from London for several days at a time, to cater for house
parties in the country. After one such engagement, she
and Mary, who had gone with her as assistant, came
back a day earlier than expected. It was evening
when they arrived. They went straight down into the
kitchen and found Mrs. Wellkin and Merriman seated
on either side of the range, their expressions reflecting
each other's gloom.

"Evening!" Louisa greeted them cheerily, as they
got to their feet.

"Good evening, ma'am," Merriman said. After an
initial period of suspicion of Louisa he had become
quite attached to her. Unlike Norah she never up-
braided him for his slowness and hardness of hearing.

"We weren't expecting you back till tomorrow, madam," Mrs. Wellkin said.

"We found we could catch the afternoon train,"

Louisa answered, taking off her coat. Her glance fell upon a tray on the dresser containing two small chickens. She went over and looked critically at them, giving them a contemptuous prod with a forefinger.

"What are these?" she demanded of Mrs. Wellkin. "I told you never to buy anything but the best poultry. Anything else is a waste of money in the long run."

"They were . . . the best I could get, madam," her assistant said.

"Rubbish! Mather & Rudd's don't even keep stuff of this quality."

"We don't buy from them anymore, madam. They . . . won't give us any more credit."

Louisa stared, astounded.

"No more credit? Why?"

"I went round to see Mr. Mather himself," Mrs. Wellkin explained unhappily. "He said our bills haven't been paid for ever so long."

"*What?*"

"He said he and the other tradesmen have only been supplying us on your reputation, madam. But they can't anymore. At least, not for the hotel side of things."

Merriman said, "There's only two guests left in the hotel, ma'am." Louisa was rendered speechless by the news. He went on, "Begging your pardon, ma'am, but it's ruination, that's what it is. Staff gone 'cause they've not been paid. Guests gone, 'cause there's no one to look after 'em. There's only Jessop and me upstairs."

"Where's Ethel, and the girls we took over with the place?"

"All gone, ma'am. Ethel was turned out last week. Miss Trotter told her she'd have to go back to being a general maid and stop helping you. She said she wouldn't, so she was put off."

Alternate waves of fire and ice had been passing through Louisa's veins in these last few moments. Her face paled. Mary watched her anxiously as she heard her ask, "Where is Miss Trotter now?"

"Lying down with her novel, I shouldn't wonder," Merriman replied. "It's what she usually is—begging your pardon, ma'am."

"And Mr. Trotter?"

"Café Royal, I suppose. He dines there most evenings."

"Does he, now," Louisa said grimly. "Mary . . ."

"Yes'm?"

"You come with me."

She led the way to the stairs. Mrs. Wellkin and Merriman exchanged glances. They had identified the battle signal.

Louisa, with Mary in tow, emerged from the pass door and made for the office bearing the label MANAGER. There was a stirring from behind the hall desk and the bleary, red-blotched face of Jessop peered over it. His eyes seemed not to be focusing properly.

"Where you goin'?" he challenged Louisa rudely, as she put her hand on the doorknob. "No one's allowed in there."

"Is that so?" she asked, and her tone caused him to make the effort to pull himself together.

"Mr. Trotter said no one was to go in . . . mum. I'm supposed to take his orders and Miss Trotter's only."

"Well, you just try and stop me," Louisa told him. She jerked the office door open and beckoned Mary to follow her in. Jessop scrambled to his feet and made his unsteady way in the direction of Norah's room.

In the office Louisa and Mary stood aghast. The once-neat, comfortable room was a shambles. Papers were strewn everywhere, including the floor. Empty bottles and glasses were on every surface. Cigar butts filled ashtrays and saucers, and the air was thick with the fumes of a taproom. It looked as if several drinking parties had been held there in succession, with no one making any effort to clean up between them.

"Find the cashbox, Mary," Louisa ordered. She herself went to the desk and began pulling open drawers.

It was not long before she located the leather-bound ledger in which the day-to-day accounts were kept. She turned to the most recent entries and her mouth fell open with dismay.

"It's not possible!" she exclaimed.

"I've got the box, ma'am," Mary said. "It was in the safe. Neither of them's even locked."

"Count how much there is," Louisa said. She picked up some bills from the desk top and checked them against the ledger. None had been paid.

"Seven pounds six shillings and fourpence, mum," Mary said at last.

"Then that's all we've left in the world," Louisa said quietly, to Mary's astonishment. "Here." She thrust the ledger at the girl. "Take this downstairs and hide it in one of the ovens. Then clear off to bed."

Mary had only just passed through the hall when Norah and Jessop came hurrying down the stairs. At that same moment the street door opened and Augustus came in with another man. Both were smoking large cigars and were grinning foolishly.

"Hello, Norah!" Gus called out.

She went to him urgently. "Louisa's back," she told him. "She's in your office."

His expression changed dramatically. Leaving his friend standing swaying he hurried into the office. Norah went after him and closed the door behind her.

"I . . . I didn't think you'd be back so soon," he said to Louisa, with an attempt at ingratiation.

"Obviously," was the cold response.

"I . . . had a few friends in."

"Drinking some of our best wines, too," she answered, flourishing a champagne bottle. "And according to the accounts you've signed half the bar bills for weeks, and given free meals to every sponger in London."

"Hospitality, Louisa," he said in a wheedling tone. "Good contacts for the future."

"You mean you wanted to act the big man."

Norah stepped toward Louisa and said, "You've no right to speak to him like that."

"Right?" Louisa flared at her. "You talk to me about rights when this hotel . . . Not a bill's been paid in . . . Everything we made—every penny I slaved for and handed over to be put into the bank has been spent. Why, Gus, why?"

"I had to . . . learn. It's not been easy, you know."

"Oh? Not easy to pour it down your throat and theirs?"

"I tried, love. I tried. If only you'd been closer to me . . ."

"I should have known," she said. "I should've known you'd try to put the blame on me somehow."

"Well, why not?" Norah intervened again. "You've ruined his life. He gave up everything for you."

"Thass right!" Gus said, emboldened by this support. "Everything."

"You've never appreciated my brother, Louisa. How could you expect him to succeed as a common hotel manager. D'you call that a profession for a gentleman?"

"Gentleman!" Louisa echoed scornfully. "He's little better than a thief."

"Don't you dare say that about him. That money was as much his as yours. He is the owner of this hotel."

"Owner be damned! I put him in here to run it—and with your help he's run it into the ground."

Norah demanded of her brother, "Are you going to let her speak to your sister like that?"

"Louisa," he tried feebly, "if only you'd stood by me. We . . ."

Her response was to fling the bottle she was holding to shatter against the wall between them. Norah shrieked and frantically dragged the door open. Louisa was picking up another bottle.

"Out!" she was crying. "Get out of my sight, Augustus Trotter." She followed them menacingly into the hall. "Take your bitch of a sister with you. And him." She pointed at the bemused drinking companion. "Yes," pointing at the cowering Jessop. "And him as well. Clear out, the lot of you."

"Louisa," Augustus tried once more, "how can you run the hotel without us?"

"The 'otel can go to 'ell! If either of you two shows your face in 'ere again I'll smash it for you."

She accompanied her threat by flinging the second bottle. It smashed against the doorframe. Glass flew everywhere. It took no further words to send the four hurrying out into the night.

Louisa stood for some moments looking at the door through which they had fled. Then her shoulders sagged and she went slowly back into the office. The contemplation of the mess there caused her face to crumple and a tear to start into each eye. But she banged her fist against her thigh, gave an angry brush at her eyes with the back of a hand, and sat down at the desk to start sorting things out.

Eleven

After she had worked for a time Louisa got up from the desk, gathered a pile of papers, and went down to the kitchen. Mrs. Wellkin, Mary, and Merriman were there, looking heavily apprehensive.

"Thought I told you to go to bed," she said to Mary.

"I . . . I didn't like, mum. With all the noise and that. I was frightened."

"Oh. You heard it, then. All of you?"

"We couldn't help it, madam," Mrs. Wellkin answered.

"Well, you might have heard far worse if they hadn't slung their hooks when I told them to," Louisa said grimly. "Anyway, that part of it's over and done with. What we've got to concern ourselves with is tomorrow and every day after."

She addressed her assistant cook.

"That offer you had from Lady Croxley—did you turn it down flat?"

Lady Croxley was only the latest of the titled people who had approached Louisa to become their permanent cook. When she had refused, several of them had made alternative bids for Mrs. Wellkin's services. She had admitted to Louisa that she was tempted. The late nights' working didn't suit her and, much as she admired Louisa as a mentor, she was finding the pressure of work too much.

"I said I'd make up my mind, madam," she answered.

"Make it up and take it," Louisa told her candidly. "You'd be in sole charge. It's a first-class kitchen and they're nice people. The fact is, I'm closing this hotel."

They all goggled. She held up the papers she had brought down with her.

"See these? Bills. Two thousand eight hundred and nineteen pounds' worth. Run up by my husband—*former* husband, as he's going to be—and his cow of a sister. You wouldn't think it was humanly possible, would you?"

"No, ma'am," old Merriman said.

"Well, it seems it is. So now you know part of the reason for all that shouting. And, Mrs. Wellkin, that's why I'm advising you to take Lady Croxley's offer. I'm afraid I can't afford to keep you on. I've got to pay this lot off. Every penny."

"I'm sorry, madam," Mrs. Wellkin said. "I'd offer to stay on for my keep, but it just wouldn't be possible."

"Don't worry, dear. I know you'll be well placed, and that's all that concerns me."

"Nearly three thousand pounds!" Mary said incredulously. "But if you're closing the hotel, how can we hope to pay it back?"

Louisa looked at her sharply.

"'We'? Look, it's nothing to do with you, Mary. It's not your worry. I'm sure you'll have no trouble finding a good place. You, too, Merriman."

The old man cleared his throat.

"If it's all the same to you, ma'am," he said, "I'd like to stay on here. Thirty-five years my room here's been my home. If I was to try to start again somewhere else, apart from that no one would take me, it'd kill me off. I know it would."

Before Louisa could answer him Mary said eagerly, "I'll stay with you, too, mum. I've nowhere else to go. If you're going on cooking you'll have to have help."

"What do you mean 'if' I'm going on cooking?"
Louisa snorted. "I'm going to cook all the hours God
sends. For anyone who wants me and who'll pay the
right price. If they want a French banquet, then
they'll get a French banquet. If they want sausage
and mash, they can have that. Still want to stay?" she
challenged.

"Yes, mum."

"Good girl. You Merriman?"

"Please, ma'am."

Louisa grinned at him.

"Who else'd be barmy enough to take you on?" she
said.

And so the Bentinck ceased to trade as a hotel. The
remaining residents were not sorry to leave. The place
had never seemed the same since it had changed
hands. The food had improved markedly, they conceded to one another, but the new proprietor, and especially his sister, had become the cause of growing
dissatisfaction.

Mrs. Wellkin accepted Lady Croxley's offer and departed. Louisa, Merriman, and Mary were left the sole
occupants of the uncannily silent building. To the
astonishment of the others, Louisa ordered her bed to
be brought from upstairs and placed against a wall of
her sitting room, off the hall.

"And the wardrobe and the tallboy," she commanded. Seeing Merriman shaking his head in baffle-
ment she explained, "If I sleep downstairs I can
spend more time in the kitchen, can't I? And the
more time I spend in the kitchen, the sooner I can
go back to sleeping in my bedroom. Got it? Sunk in,
has it?"

He went away shaking his head.

This little economy in timekeeping characterized
Louisa's determined approach to her mammoth task.
She slept only a few hours each night and worked
ceaselessly the rest of the time, helped loyally by

Mary. The one thing on which she refused to let herself skimp was the quality of her ingredients. There was another way to economize on that, however.

Every morning at four o'clock she made her way on foot to Covent Garden market. The streets of London at this hour were in that transitional period where nightlife ends and daylife begins, with some degree of overlapping. Occasional noisy groups of top-hatted revelers wove their way homeward or clustered around workmen's breakfast stalls, bandying good-natured chaff with men in aprons and smocks. Scarlet-painted mail carts, milk carts laden with full churns, high-piled country carts bringing produce, and newspaper carts with their string-tied bundles of the early editions, dodged, trundled, and raced along streets mostly devoid of pedestrians. Destitute men and women lay or crouched oblivious in doorways from where they would soon be moved on to no-where.

Covent Garden market, in Bow Street, was a bustle of carts, porters, warehousemen, and buyers. Louisa could smell, long before she reached it, the fragrance of its massed blooms and the fresh scent of newly harvested vegetables, set out on trestles occupying almost every foot of space in the great hall and the streets surrounding.

It was to the food stalls that she made her brisk way in the early hours, exchanging grins and winks with the porters who scurried about with piled baskets on their heads, sometimes so many of them that their carriers had to have boys to guide them carefully between obstacles.

A poultry-stall keeper arranging his wares saw her coming and broke off his whistling. He nudged his boy assistant.

"Thought I was tempting bleeding providence whistling. Here we go again."

Louisa had come up to the stall now and was already prodding the chickens.

"Have mercy on the merchandise, Mrs. Trotter, love," he pleaded. "It's done you no harm. Now I ask you, what harm's that poor bloody chicken done you?"

"Morning, Mr. Smythe," was all Louisa answered, continuing to prod.

" 'Morning,' she says! Like butter would melt in her mouth. Mrs. Trotter, why don't you ever go and torment any of the other traders? Why's poor Ben Smythe got to be singled out?"

"Because you give me the best prices," Louisa grinned back.

"More fool me. Thank Gawd I get other customers who'll pay what they're really worth." He gave her a leer, leaning forward a little. "You like a bargain. How about a quick kiss and cuddle round the back of the next stall? And while we're there I'll nick you the finest cauliflower this side of Bermondsey Flower Show."

Louisa picked up a quail and looked at it from all angles.

"No one kisses and cuddles me," she replied. "Least of all for bloomin' cauliflower. How much are the quail?"

"Oho! That's different, eh?"

"Gerron! How much?"

He sighed. "A tanner. Cheapest in the market."

"Tanner for two?"

"For one."

"I'll give you fourpence."

"*Four*pence?"

"And I'll take half a dozen."

"Mrs. Trotter," the stallkeeper moaned in mock desperation, "I got a wife an' Gawd knows how many kids to keep. Oh, hell. Wrap 'em up, Jamie. She's got that look on her face."

Louisa granted him her smile.

"Thanks, Ben. And don't forget the finest cauliflower this side of Bermondsey Flower Show. And I'll wait here while you slip and get it."

The man obeyed and Louisa moved on to make a few more purchases before returning through the increasing London bustle to the gloomy, silent Bentinck.

Later that day she had another bargaining encounter. This time it was in much more fashionable surroundings—Mather & Rudd's shop, where the best game, poultry, hams, pies, and other foodstuffs were delicately arrayed in parsleyed surroundings.

"Have you gone barmy, Mrs. Trotter?" asked Mr. Mather, who had quite different voices for the gentry and for the rest, especially those trying to sell him something, as Louisa was now. "You want *me* to buy from *you,* when you're already up to the eyebrows in debt for what *you've* bought from *me!*"

"I know I am," Louisa said again patiently. "That's why I'm suggesting . . ."

The shopkeeper seized a ledger and began riffling through its pages.

"I'll tell you exactly how much you're in debt," he grumbled. "Just to prove I'm not the soft touch you take me for."

"I can tell you how much," she answered simply. "Twenty-eight pounds seven shillings."

He had found the entry at that exact moment and stared across the counter at her.

"Right," she said. "Thank you. Now, in the absence of an apology, the least you can do is give me a hearing."

He threw the ledger down, spluttering, "Mrs. Trotter! It's *you* owe *me!*"

"All I'm suggesting," she went on, "is a way to pay it off—since I can't with money. My way, no money'll change hands. You just keep knocking it off my bill."

Mr. Mather regarded her suspiciously. Louisa read his thoughts and grinned.

"No wonder you got gout, if you get excited like that," she said. "Now then—how much do you charge for cooked quail?"

"Half a crown."

"Right, then. How's this for a proposition from me to you? Two bob cooked."

"Two shillings cooked?" he repeated, more interestedly. "By you?"

"With my own clever hands. Taste better than yours, won't they? And even if you sell 'em for only two and a penny you're still making a profit. All you have to do is hand 'em over the counter and rake it in."

He searched her eyes for a few seconds. Her reputation as a cook was well known to him.

"How many can I have?" he asked.

"Half a dozen today. By teatime. Many as you want to order, other days."

Before any deal could be concluded the shop was invaded by a fierce woman in bombazine. Louisa recognized her as Mrs. Carradine, housekeeper to Lord Ealing. She turned away to examine some foodstuffs intently. In any case, the housekeeper had made straight for Mr. Mather without looking at her.

"Veal and ham pies," she snapped. "I'll take two."

"Sorry, Mrs. Carradine," the shopkeeper said. "I'm afraid we've sold the last today."

"What! This is getting ridiculous. It's every day the same."

"Perhaps if you could call a little earlier, madam . . ."

"Perhaps if you could save me some."

"Well, if I knew in advance how many . . ."

"Really! I am a regular customer, Mr. Mather."

"I do apologize, Mrs. Carradine, but . . ."

"There's nothing more to be said, then."

The black-clad figure swept out of the shop, sniffing loudly. Louisa turned back to Mr. Mather, who was holding on to the edge of his counter so hard that the white of his knucklebones showed through his skin.

"Not the most satisfied of customers," she remarked wryly.

"I'm in the wrong trade, far as she's concerned," he said. "Need to be a bloomin' magician."

Louisa eyed him. "Why not be, then?"

"Eh?"

"You could have veal and ham pies coming out of Mrs. Carradine's hat. Or her bloomers, too, by way of an encore."

"What are you talking about now, Mrs. Trotter?"

"Veal and ham pies, pork pies—any sort of pies you like."

"You're not selling them, too?" he asked eagerly.

She nodded. "As many as you'll take. I'll buy the pork, the veal, and the ham, and I'll make the pies. All you do, Mr. Mather, is smile at your customers and knock it off my bill."

He asked cautiously, "How much a pie?"

"What weight?"

"Say, a pound. Veal and ham."

"Elevenpence-halfpenny," Louisa answered without hesitation.

"Ninepence," he countered. "I can't go a farthing over that."

"And I can't go a farthing under elevenpence-halfpenny."

"I'd need a lot," he said. "Dozens of each."

"All the more profit for you, then."

"Tenpence-farthing," he said suddenly.

"Done! Tenpence-halfpenny it is."

"You said 'done,'" he accused her.

"And they will be. Very well done, Mr. Mather. Remember, we're talking about pies made by Louisa Trotter."

Mr. Mather suddenly held up his palms and smiled in capitulation.

The Bentinck-based pie industry went into immediate production. Louisa bought her materials that very afternoon. Soon, every gas ring in her kitchen was occupied by a steaming pan, the ovens were heating, and the big table was piled with beautifully wrought pie cases. When Mr. Mather received his first consignment promptly at eight o'clock next morning he sighed at the aroma, doubled the order, and carried off one of the pies into the back of his shop for a second breakfast.

So Mr. Mather happily paid his price, and kept increasing the order as his customers' taste for the pies grew. But a different sort of price was exacted from Louisa herself. She was young, she was healthy, and there was no more physically and mentally resilient young woman in all London. But the strain on her was tremendous. Little by little the amounts owing on her bills went down; but new expenses inevitably cropped up. At times, when lack of sleep and excess of work and worry combined to press her spirits down to their lowest level, it seemed to her that she was merely managing to survive, and that new debts were replacing old ones. She juggled with her accounts desperately, following the tried principle of settling with small traders first and letting the bigger ones, who could afford to, wait. She knew that some big shops gave more respect to a customer with a longstanding bill than to those who paid cash. All the same, it was a wearying period for her.

"Yes?" she called tiredly from her desk, early one spring evening, in answer to Mary's tap at the door.

The little Welsh maid came in. Glancing up, Louisa noticed that she, too, seemed gaunt.

"What is it, love?" she asked gently.

"I came to see if you'd finished your tea and toast, mum," Mary said, approaching the desk. "Oh, look! You haven't touched either of them. It's stone-cold."

"Is it?" Louisa responded vaguely. "Never mind. I didn't want anything, anyway."

"You never *have* anything," the maid retorted spiritedly.

"That'll do, Mary," Louisa said in a less kindly tone. "I'm not in the mood for arguing."

When Mary had gone with the cup of cold tea and the rack of untouched toast, she went back to her accounts. But after a time her eyelids drooped and she was soon asleep at her desk.

One afternoon Merriman opened the Bentinck's locked front door to a middle-aged couple, respectably dressed.

"Sorry," he said in his brusque, deaf manner. "The hotel's closed till further notice."

The man said something to him. Merriman leaned closer, cupping a hand to his ear. The man repeated, "We're Mr. and Mrs. Leyton. Mrs. Trotter's mum and dad."

"Mother and father," Mrs. Leyton corrected him.

Merriman stepped back and motioned them into the musty hall. "If you'll wait here a moment," he said, "I'll see if she can see you."

Mrs. Leyton flicked distastefully at the dust on a chair before lowering herself onto it. She and her husband eyed one another with a look of unease.

Feeling like a child suddenly, Louisa threw on a clean apron and ordered tea to be served in her room. She went up and greeted her parents, whom she had not seen for a long time, and took them off into her overcrowded room. After some conversational skirmishing she learned that Augustus Trotter, back in service as a butler, had been to see her parents. Her mouth tightened as she listened to her mother's account of the interview.

"He adores you, Louisa. He really does," Mrs. Leyton concluded.

Louisa sighed. "Yes. Makes it all the worse, doesn't it? He should never have come sniveling to you, though."

"I think it was his sister's idea," her father said.

"Everything's his sister's idea. Did she tell him to tell you what a bitch I am?"

"He just seemed to apologize mostly. Look, Louisa, girl. You can't pay it all off. Not on your own. You can't do the impossible."

"I'm not on my own," she retorted, making a stubborn chin.

"We don't count servants, dear," her mother said.

"Well, I do."

Mrs. Leyton asked carefully, "Hasn't . . . hasn't *he* offered to help?"

"Who?"

"You know, Louisa. Your . . . friend."

Louisa stared. "Here!" she demanded. "What's that bloody Trotter been telling you?"

"Language, girl!" her father admonished. Her mother said uncomfortably, "He didn't tell us anything. Sort of hinted that there was someone . . ."

"All right, Mum," Louisa said. "If there was someone . . . and I'm not going to say if there was or there wasn't . . . and that someone offered to help, I wouldn't accept. I'll be beholden to no one. Is that plain enough?"

"We'd help you ourselves," her father said hastily. "Only, you know how things are with us."

Louisa looked at him keenly and understood with regret why they had come visiting her. She had not been writing home lately, and the contributions she had been in the habit of making toward their living costs had been discontinued. It wounded her much to recognize that even though they could see what difficulties she was in they could still bring themselves to sponge.

She opened a drawer and took out her cashbox.

"By the way," she said, as casually as she could. "I've been putting a bit by for you. I meant to send it on sooner."

The glance which passed between her parents confirmed her suspicion.

"We couldn't take anything from you, Louisa," her mother said, but she did not look her daughter in the eyes.

"No," Mr. Leyton said. "I mean, it wouldn't be fair."

Louisa held out the notes. She saw his hand twich before he restrained himself from putting it out.

"No," he said again. But she leaned over and put the money into his hand. He nodded silently.

"Well, since you insist," her mother said. "You're a good girl."

"Thoughtful," her father put in huskily.

There was a knock at the door and Mary came in.

"Excuse me, ma'am," she said, "the veal's done now, and . . ."

Louisa got up.

"Thanks, Mary," she said. "I'll come straight down." She turned to her parents. "Have to go now. Thanks for coming. See you sometime."

She went off to the kitchen, glad that the visit was over. But it had taken its toll. On top of the labor and stress of the past few months, not to mention the uncertainty about what Augustus might take it into his head to do one of these days, she felt suddenly vulnerable and alone in the face of the crippling debt. She had thought more than once of selling the lease of the hotel; but she would have to pass a share of the proceeds on to him, and she would still not have anything near enough to clear her debt. Besides, she would be depriving herself of her kitchen headquarters. Nothing smaller would suffice. She seemed to be trapped, hemmed in from all sides.

Autumn passed. The approach of the Christmas season brought an increased flood of catering engagements.

"Three more inquiries, madam," Merriman said, referring to a piece of paper. "The Duchess of Launde on January the second, luncheon for twelve. Lady Blackwater, also on the second, supper for four. Mrs. Lionel Watson, fifth, dinner for . . ."

"Accept," she interrupted, going on working at the kitchen table.

"Which?" he asked.

"All of them. All three."

The old man protested. "I don't see how you can. On the fifth you're already doing a luncheon for twelve at the . . ."

"Accept them. We'll manage."

She turned at an unmistakable sound and saw that Mary had slumped into a chair in tears.

"All right, Merriman," Louisa said with a jerk of her head. He went off back to the hall. She wiped her hands and went to comfort the girl.

"Go and rest, love," she said when the worst of the crying was over.

"I can't, ma'am," the girl muttered desperately. "There's the pans to scour, the fish to clean, the vegetables to do, and we've . . ."

"Go and rest. Go on. Forty winks. Well, thirty-nine."

"You don't rest. You never rest."

"Even just ten minutes' lie-down will do you good."

"I could have cleaned the fish in that time."

"You're a good girl, Mary," Louisa said, touched and a little emotional. "I don't know what I'd do without your help. I don't truly. And it's all for my benefit. It's *me* we're working for. What'll you ever get out of it?"

A large pan began to boil over. Louisa went to the stove and grasped the handle. To her dismay she found that she couldn't lift the pan. Suddenly panicky, she turned appealingly to Mary. The girl jumped up and hurried to perform the task for her. Then she guided Louisa to a chair. She sank down, and shook and shook.

Twelve

"How long has this suicidal business been going on?"

The question was put sharply to Mary by the elderly doctor she had called Merriman to fetch when Louisa had crumpled down to the floor from the kitchen chair in a complete faint. She herself had carried her mistress to her bed, undressed her, and tucked her in. Mary was anything but Amazonian in strength, but she had found Louisa surprisingly easy to carry. She felt like nothing more than a bundle of skin and bone, and Mary saw, when she had got her clothes off, that that was about all she was.

"All winter, sir," she told the doctor. They were talking outside the closed door. "Working herself day and night, hardly eating, hardly sleeping. Is she . . . very poorly?"

"Completely exhausted," he answered. "By the looks of you, child, the same isn't far off for you. Come on, get that blouse unbuttoned and let's have a listen."

He had taken the stethoscope out again. He sounded Mary and grunted. He took her pulse, and grunted again.

"Well, you're not so bad," he admitted, putting the instrument away.

"Oh, I get more rest than she does," Mary explained. "She makes me. Besides, she's got all the books to do and the early-morning buying and that."

"I see. You'll have to watch yourself, though. You may be more tired then you feel. Living off your nerves. How are you going to manage while she's in bed?"

"How long will that be, sir?"

"She shouldn't get up for two days at the very least. Preferably, I'd keep her there for a week, but from what you tell me I doubt whether I'd succeed."

He scribbled on a prescription pad.

"I'll call again tomorrow. Get this made up at a chemist's and make her take it three times a day. And above all, make sure she rests and eats properly from now on. Those are strict orders, you understand? She might not be so lucky another time."

Mary answered doubtfully, "I'll try sir. I can't imagine trying to give Mrs. Trotter orders."

They heard Louisa's voice calling weakly from within the room, "Mary! Mary!"

The doctor lingered outside while Mary went in, leaving the door ajar.

He heard Louisa say, "Mary, with all this palaver we forgot to put brandy in the chicken liver pâté. Bring me the livers and a cheap bottle. I'll mix it in here."

There was a moment's silence before Mary answered resolutely, "No, ma'am."

"What the hell do you mean 'no'?"

"I mean no, mum. The doctor says you're to have complete rest and that I'm to see you get it. So I'd like that to be understood, please."

"Well done, nurse," the doctor said to himself as he went away.

Louisa found herself too weak to resist Mary's ministrations. Through eating so little over a long period she had lost the capacity for it, but Mary managed to force some game-soup into her and a slice of toast. Merriman got the bottle of tonic made up and Mary administered the doses. She was pleased to hear

Louisa say drowsily that she thought she would have "just a little nap." This was at eight o'clock in the evening—fortunately, one without any engagement. Mary left her and went down to the kitchen to carry on making the pâté and Mr. Mather's pies. He would just have to go a bit short for the time being, she decided.

It was getting toward midnight before she was free to go to her own bed. She crept into Louisa's room and was relieved to see that she had not moved in the bed and to hear the steady drone of her relaxed breathing.

As usual, Mary was up at five o'clock next morning. She thought of going straight in to see Louisa. She put her ear to the door and listened hard. She could hear nothing. She decided it would be best to let her mistress sleep on as long as possible. She would probably be enough of a handful, once she woke up feeling a bit rested.

By six o'clock, though, Mary was beginning to worry.

"Mr. Merriman," she said to the old man, who was reading the morning paper over a cup of tea.

"I'm reading the paper," he said, without lifting his eyes from it. "When I read, I read. I don't talk as well."

She had long since learned to be persistent with him.

"What is it that I'm in sometimes? When I don't know what to do, and you say I'm in a something? It's a word."

"Quandary," he answered, still not looking up.

"That's it. Well I'm in one again."

"Good," he murmured.

"It's gone six o'clock," she went on. "Before she took poorly Mrs. Trotter would have been up and about by now. But the doctor said she's to stay in bed all day. Well, my . . . quandary is, if I don't take her her morning pot of tea in soon, she might get up and come looking for it. And then what chance would I have of ever getting her back to bed again?"

Merriman turned a page without answering, so she extended the question.

"Only, if she's still asleep and I take it in to her, I might wake her up. And that'd be a pity."

A new thought struck the little Welsh girl.

"Mr. Merriman . . . if she rests and does less cooking and earns less money, it's all over, isn't it? Everything. For all of us. It'll all have been for nothing."

The old man spoke at last, though without looking at her.

"One of the attributes of old age is wisdom," he pronounced. "In my wisdom, I've always said it was a mad idea. And I'm right."

"You said no such thing in my hearing!"

"I thought it, then."

He gave his paper a dismissive shake. Mary got up and went to get the tea caddy.

"I'll take her the tea in quietly," she decided. "If she's asleep I'll slip out quietly."

When she entered Louisa's room a few minutes later she found with a shock that her ruminations had been over nothing. Louisa wasn't there.

She was, in fact, in a lamplit street on the route between the Bentinck and Covent Garden market, returning from her morning marketing. She was pushing the small barrow she used for her purchases. It was laden with produce. Every step she took was an effort and she tottered occasionally. She was willing herself on by counting her steps.

"Two thousand one hundred and twelve, one hundred and thirteen, one hundred and fourteen . . ."

A tall, handsome young man in evening dress came out of a house she was nearing. He stood on the pavement and waved to a young woman peeping from a corner of a bedroom curtain. The woman smiled, blew him a quick kiss, then ducked back out of sight.

The young man started to walk briskly up the street in Louisa's direction. He saw Louisa, but in the semi-darkness merely registered a pale, undernourished woman heaving at a burden that was obviously beyond her strength. It was not an uncommon sight. What he did realize was uncommon about it, a few seconds later, was that the woman looked extremely like a worn Louisa.

He went and stood in her path. She raised her eyes from the roadway and looked at him dully.

"I know you, don't I?" he said.

"I shouldn't think so," she replied and prepared to push the barrow again. He stood his ground and said, "It's Louisa . . ."

"Is it, now?" she responded with some of her characteristic sharpness, and the tone confirmed his belief. "Well, I don't know you from Adam or Eve or the serpent, so shift your carcass and let me . . ."

His face had grown puzzled and serious.

"Louisa, stop it. You know me perfectly well. Charles Tyrrell."

In her bemused state she hadn't recognized him, but she did now.

He tried to lighten things by asking, "Any chance of a lift to Piccadilly Circus?" But she said coldly, "Mr. Tyrrell, please. Just get on your way and let me go mine."

" 'Mr. Tyrrell'?" he echoed her. "It was 'Mr. Charlie' when we first met."

"Not the first time, it wasn't. If I remember right it was rogue, vagabond, rake, and seducer of innocent young kitchen maids."

"*Attempted* seducer. *Failed* seducer. It was the *second* time you called me 'Mr. Charlie.' Anyway, how are you, Louisa?"

"I'm well. Now, can I please go about my business."

"And your husband?"

"No longer my husband."

"You mean you're divorced—so soon?"

"As good as."

He looked even more curious and concerned.

"Louisa, what on earth are you doing at this time in the morning, pushing a barrow, of all things?"

"Well, in the first place I'm minding my own business. And in the second place, whatever I'm doing is a damn sight more respectable than *you*—still in your evening suit at this time of the morning."

"I don't think you are well, actually," he said. "You don't look well."

Louisa decided that the conversation had gone on long enough. She felt the great need to get back to her kitchen and her work. She took up the shafts once more and pushed the barrow forward.

"Where can I call on you?" he asked as he stepped aside to let her pass.

"At the Bentinck Hotel, if you want to," she said indifferently, moving on. "There's no guests anymore. It isn't a hotel anymore. You can please yourself."

He walked beside her.

"You wouldn't object?"

"Suit yourself."

"We *are* old friends. . . ."

"Good morning, Mr. Tyrrell."

But the last color swiftly drained from her cheeks. Her eyes widened with sudden alarm and then glazed. She slumped forward between the barrow shafts and then to the ground.

Louisa had fallen into a complete faint. Charles Tyrrell looked around, but no one else was in sight. For a few moments he stood feeling helpless, wondering what to do. He looked back at the house he had recently left, but knew that he could not take her there. At last he picked her up, surprised, as Mary had been, at her light weight, placed her on the barrow and took the shafts himself. He turned the barrow around and wheeled it off in the opposite direction to that Louisa had been taking.

At any other time the thought of herself being trundled through the streets of London on top of a barrowload of vegetables by a man in evening dress, complete with top hat, would have amused Louisa vastly. But no feelings of amusement came to her when the realization of her new surroundings, and tho recollection of what had caused her to be in them, dawned on her later that morning. She was in bed in a stark, old-fashioned hospital ward, aware of the coughing, hawking, and moaning of several dozen other women patients, whose commonest feature, when she was able to take stock of them, seemed to be that they were toothless, whatever their age. The almosphere was heavy with antiseptic and human smells.

A middle-aged nurse saw her stirring and came over. She explained how Louisa had been brought in and answered with a firm refusal her weak demand to be allowed to go home. There could be no question of it for several days, it seemed.

"And don't you try getting up and doing a flit, young woman," the nurse warned her. "Or you'll end up one of those."

She nodded toward a sheet-covered figure being wheeled out of the ward. The sheet extended over the face, Louisa noticed with a chill of fear. She had never seen a corpse before.

She was given nourishment and sleeping-drafts alternately. After the initial impulse to resist the latter, she surrendered to the drowsiness and sank into deep sleep. Over the next few days this was the pattern of her existence. She thought sometimes of the Bentinck and wondered what was happening about her bookings and her supplies to Mr. Mather; but, strangely, although she wanted to worry about them, she was unable to do so.

After four days the sleeping-drafts were discontinued. She still spent most of her time asleep, though. Her doctor had achieved what he had intended.

Fastidious and innately snobbish, despite her earthiness, Louisa shrank from contact with any of her fellow patients, most of whom were ignorant and coarse of speech and habits. It was a relief to her at length to see the trim and tidy figure of Mary approaching her bed. She carried a small parcel. After a hesitation she ventured to give Louisa a kiss. She held out the parcel.

"I couldn't think what to bring you . . . without spending money," she said. "I was in a quandary. So I brought quail in aspic."

She went on to tell Louisa how a policeman had called at the Bentinck with the news of her collapse and admission to the hospital. She had tried several times before this to visit her, but had not been allowed.

"Mr. Tyrrell said it was horrible," Mary went on. "You collapsing in the street like that. He thought you was dying."

"Mr. Tyrrell?" Louisa asked, surprised. She was sitting up and looking, to Mary's relief, more rested and healthy than she could remember her. "When did you see Mr. Tyrrell?"

"He's called at the hotel every day since it happened, to tell us how you was. Oh, and I've managed to keep the pies going, mum. Mr. Merriman helped as best he could. Only I had to send word to Viscount Stanley and the Honorable George Campbell that they'll have to whistle for their dinners."

"They can all whistle in future," Louisa said. "The kitchen can blow itself up, for all I care. I'm going to chuck the whole thing in. To hell with my debts."

"But ma'am, if we don't pay the debts they'll take the hotel away from you. You'll have nowhere to live."

"Then I'll just die, so the problem won't arise, will it?"

"You're not to talk like that!" Mary scolded her; but Louisa, now sufficiently withdrawn from the influence of the sedatives to be able to recognize the extent of her problems, rambled on into a wholly uncharacteristic vein of self-pity.

"Two patients died in here the other night. One was consumption. The other just didn't want to live anymore. She was younger than me, and prettier. I shouldn't think she'd even heard of quails in aspic. Rotten, isn't it, how parents are always right in the end? If I'd just got decently married, the way they wanted, instead of wanting to play at being a cook, none of this bloody mess would ever have happened."

"But you're the best cook in London," Mary tried to reassure her.

Louisa shook her head fiercely. "What's it all about, anyway? Banquets? Some people don't even get bread. Because I got above my station and stopped thinking about people like that I suppose I didn't believe they existed anymore. Well, look at 'em in those beds. And that's only a bloody handful."

Try as she did, Mary couldn't talk her around. She had no comforting news to build persuasion onto. Feeling she was going to cry, and that this would upset her mistress even more, she said she would come back next day, and left. Immediately outside the ward door she met Charles Tyrrell. He was carrying a bouquet of mixed flowers.

"Hello, Mary," he greeted her. "Merriman said you'd been allowed to visit, so I came straight here. How is she? Does she seem any stronger?"

Mary fought back the tears.

"She's never been like this," she answered miserably. "Ever. Talking about wanting to die . . ."

She shook her head and hurried away, with her handkerchief out. Charles Tyrrell stared after her, then went briskly into the ward. He saw Louisa immediately. She was still sitting up, but her eyes were closed.

"Louisa," he whispered to her, thinking she might have dozed off. But she opened her eyes at once and he was pleased to see her give a little smile.

"Hello, Charlie," she said. Her tone was dull, though.

He put the flowers into her hands.

"Who'd you buy them for?" she asked.

"The first pretty woman I bumped into. And I must say she's looking a great deal healthier than the last time I saw her. How are you, Louisa?"

"Sleeping my life away."

"Well, it'll be time to wake up before long." He sat on the edge of her bed and went on. "Listen, I've been doing some thinking. I think you were right to make yourself responsible for those debts. It would have gone against your nature not to."

She looked at him in some surprise.

"You seem to know a lot about me all of a sudden."

"I've been talking to Mary about you, round at the hotel. She's a bright girl. She can recognize things."

"Well, I hope she can recognize I've been a bloody fool, then."

"She's devoted to you. But she does see—anyone with half an eye could see—that if you go on in this way you'd be dead before half your debts were paid. I can see it for certain, so I want you to listen to a proposition . . ."

"If it's money, the answer's no. I want no one's money."

"Don't you think Mary's told me that? She repeated it over and over again."

"Well then, you know how things stand." She changed the subject abruptly. "How's Lord Haslemere these days?"

He replied a trifle impatiently, "Oh, Father's all right. Keeping as fit as he can because he think's I'm waiting for him to die. Now, listen . . ."

"And are you?"

"Of course not. Anyway, he'll live forever. Now this idea of mine . . ."

"Still living the same sort of life yourself, are you, then?"

"'Fraid so. Like a fairground Johnny, wandering from one friend's house to another's."

"Not changed have you, Charlie?"

"Not in one single respect," he answered with a new earnestness, and plunged on through her diversionary defenses. "Louisa, how much would the lease cost on your hotel?"

"Why?"

"How *much?*"

She replied suspiciously, "About fifteen hundred quid."

"I'll buy it."

"I told you, Charlie . . ."

"Just listen, please. You know I wanted a home of my own in town. Well, I still do. The Bentinck could be it."

"A whole bloody hotel! Don't be daft."

"Not the whole place at all. A suite of its rooms, furnished to my own taste, that I could regard as home. Where I can invite my friends instead of always having to visit them."

She said crossly, "I can smell charity a mile off, and I don't want it."

He responded equally firmly, "It isn't charity, for God's sake! If you don't want to sell, all right. I'll buy somewhere else. But I'm determined to have a place of my own."

"You do that, then. My answer's no."

"Please yourself."

"I always do."

"Louisa, you're stupid as well as stubborn, aren't you? That's one thing I'd never have thought of you."

"Yes, I am stupid," she agreed passionately. "This past day or two I've come to see just how much. I've been stupid all the way along. But I'm not stupid to refuse help. It was being 'helped' that got me where I am now. Death's door."

The strength of his feelings surprised her. He struck the bedcover with a fist and retorted, "'Death's door,' my foot! You'll live as long as my father. As far as anyone being helped is concerned, I'm asking *you* to help *me*. I'm asking you to sell me the best cook in London, kitchen and all."

There followed a long silence while she took this in. At length she asked, "You mean . . . you want me to be your cook?"

"If you're agreeable."

"I told you, the only one I'll be cooking for'll be St. Peter."

"Blockhead! Look, you'd have no debts left. It'd be less work and a damn sight more money."

With less conviction she said, "No one buys a hotel just to get a cook."

"*The* cook, Louisa."

A longer silence followed. He could see her struggling with herself, and kept silent. It was fully two minutes before she said slowly, "Rum sort of hotel. Just one guest and one suite of rooms."

And then his heart leaped, because he knew she had succumbed.

Thirteen

A hooded leather hall-porter's chair stood beside the dais of the auction rooms, with a man in a dustcoat leaning one hand against it. His thoughts were on a horse race and he took no notice of who was bidding.

That was the auctioneer's job. His eyes searched among the gentlemen and ladies seated before him. He saw no significant movement.

"Eighteen guineas, then?" the auctioneer repeated. "Do I hear nineteen? Nineteen anywhere, please?"

In the third row Louisa leaned a little toward her companion and half whispered, "Does he, Charlie?"

"Up to you," Charles Tyrrell answered, but conveyed his opinion with a wink.

"It's terribly extravagant, isn't it?" she asked. "I can't remember the last time I spent tuppence, except on food."

"Going for eighteen guineas, then." The auctioneer raised his gavel.

"Nineteen," Louisa said clearly. Then she told Charles, "That's my limit, honestly. I can't go higher."

"Twenty," a man's voice called from far behind.

"Twenty-one," Louisa said automatically. "And that's definitely it."

Luckily for her, it was. She gave Charles an excited grin as the auctioneer terminated the bidding in her favor.

"Come on," she said. "We'd better go. I've got eight chairs, a dining table, a hall table, pictures . . . Not to mention a hotelful of old junk already."

She started to get up but he restrained her with a hand on her arm.

"Just a moment," he said.

The porter had removed the chair from the dais and three of his colleagues were pushing forward an inlaid rosewood grand piano. The auctioneer was announcing, "And now, ladies and gentlemen, we come to lot number twenty-four—a drawing-room grand piano, handwork of Messrs. Bechstein. Beautiful to look upon, and I've no doubt beautiful to listen to. Messrs. Bechstein, ladies and gentlemen, makers to the late Franz Liszt, Richard Wagner, Anton Rubinstein, to mention but a few eminent names. This particular model would cost approximately one hundred and fifty guineas new. Now, who will start me at, say, fifty?"

There was no response, but Louisa felt Charles stirring. She looked at him in surprise.

"I don't want a piano," she warned him.

"I do."

"You! You don't even play—do you?"

"I could always learn," he said and called, "Fifty."

It was a month since Louisa's release from the hospital. Mary had tried to persuade her to go and stay with her parents at Wanstead for a while, until she got her strength back, but the notion had been rejected. A new excitement seemed to have infected Louisa. Mary and Mr. Merriman had been informed that the lease of the Bentinck Hotel was now the property of the Honorable Charles Tyrrell, who would shortly be moving into apartments there. She herself would still be in charge. She would cook for him, and continue to use the kitchens for her freelance activities although on nothing like the previous hectic scale. Mrs. Wellkin had been invited to return as her assistant and had accepted. Mary and Merriman were welcome to stay on, if they wished. They did.

Charles had done more than completely refurbish the upstairs suite he had chosen for himself. He had insisted on the main hall being redecorated and its new, brighter wallpaper hung with pictures. Carpets, furniture, and decorations elsewhere in the building had been renewed, to his satisfaction.

"I couldn't have lived with all that musty gloom around me," he explained to Louisa, who had protested against his extravagance.

"Charlie," she said tentatively. "Since you've gone to all this trouble . . . I mean, I must be barmy to suggest it, but why don't I open the whole bloomin' hotel again?"

"That's not barmy," he grinned. "I was wondering how long you'd take to come round to it."

"You mean, you did it deliberate?"

"Not actually. It seemed absurd to do up just a part of it and let the rest go to rot. Now that I look at it, I doubt if there's a more comfortable hotel in London."

"What if it fails, Charlie?"

"It won't."

"It might. And I'd be right back at the beginning again, slaving and sweating to pay off a new load of debts."

"You won't let it fail, Louisa," he tried to convince her. "You've got what you wanted in life now, haven't you?"

"I suppose I have," she admitted. "I thought just cooking would be enough, but all this too . . ."

She glanced delightedly around the transformed hall.

"*Is* it all you want in life?" he asked.

She didn't fail to catch the deeper meaning.

"Tell you what I've got for your dinner tonight," she said lightly. "Melon, followed by turbot, followed by roast beef, followed by cherries in brandy. That tempt you?"

She gave him one of her more exasperating grins and went quickly off to the kitchen.

Later that day Merriman answered the front door to a man a good deal smaller than himself. He wore a carelessly brushed bowler hat with a curly brim and a suit whose shine showed its age. Squatting beside him, on a lead, was a mongrel dog of mixed terrier ancestry.

"Starr," the man announced. "Two *r*'s. And this is Fred. We've come in answer to the advertisement. Hall porter."

Merriman looked from the man to the dog, which gazed expectantly up into his eyes, as if anticipating a doorstep interview. Instead, Merriman addressed the man.

"The . . . dog's with you, is it? I mean, wherever you go?"

"Day and night," Starr answered resolutely.

"Well, you'd best come in," Merriman said dubiously. He led them into the hall and left them there while he went to Louisa's parlor to tell her that there were a man and a dog to see her. Even she was a little nonplussed when the dog appeared, towing the man by the lead.

"Do, er, sit down," she said, nearly adding, "both of you."

"Thank you, Mrs. Trotter," Starr said civilly. "Sit, boy. Sit. And no arguments, mind."

"Now then," Louisa said, "where do I start? I'm not all that used to interviewing hall porters."

"That's perfectly all right, madam," Starr said. "We are. I think we might begin by establishing exactly what remuneration you have in mind?"

"Thirty pounds a year, all found."

He looked at Fred, as if for approval. Fred looked at Louisa.

"Plus tips, of course," she added hastily.

"Of course, madam," said Starr. "You would, of course, be looking for a man of experience? A man with excellent references?"

"Yes, that's right. Have you, er . . . ?"

"The very best, Mrs. Trotter. I *am* my references. Yes, Fred? Isn't that so?"

Louisa was by now quite expecting the dog to speak out in his master's praise. She had never been interested in animals, but there was something oddly engaging in the relationship between this self-assured, inscrutable man and the dumb animal which seemed to serve as his companion, confidant, and, for all she knew, adviser.

Since Starr made no move to produce any written references she tried asking, "Where have you worked previously?"

"Here and there, madam."

His gaze met hers frankly as he gave her such answers as his laconic manner permitted.

"I see," she said, not seeing at all. "What doing?"

"This and that."

"Oh. Did you fight in the war?"

"Very possibly," was his remarkable reply. Then, to her surprise, he reversed the roles and almost loquaciously took over the interview.

"Well, now, madam, Fred and I would be grateful if you'd be as frank with us as we have with you, madam. What we'd like to know are: one, the number of guests to whom we are to be of service; two, whether Fred, of course, would be welcome (correct, Fred?); three, the number and character of the remainder of the staff; four . . ."

The one thing he didn't request was a separate wage for the dog. It wouldn't have surprised Louisa if he had. She hired Starr, and, by implication, Fred, too.

While this conversation was going on Merriman and Mary were engaged in one of a very different sort in the hall. Without bothering to ring, two over-dressed and overpainted girls had entered. Merriman recognized what they were immediately.

"Here! Who invited you in?" he demanded. Mary, emerging at that moment from the pass door, paused to look on curiously.

"This is the new 'otel, isn't it?" one of the girls asked in a cheeky, East End voice.

"We're not open yet," Merriman replied. "In any case . . ."

"We was hoping there might be a bit of trade for us," the other girl said. "Any single gentlemen staying . . ."

Mary stepped forward, flushing angrily.

"Out!" she cried. "Go on, both of you!"

The first girl said, "Who the 'ell are you talking to, little bloody skivvy?"

The other, milder-mannered, asked with what seemed to be genuine surprise, "It *is* going to be a hotel, isn't it?"

"Not your kind," Mary replied.

The first girl smirked superciliously.

"They're all our kind, dear. How long you been down from them mountains?"

Ignoring Merriman, Mary bundled the pair off the premises and slammed the door after them. She turned around from it to find Louisa at the door of her room. A man and a dog were behind her.

"What's going on out here?" Louisa demanded.

Mary's face was already red, but she blushed as well.

"It was two . . . two . . . um . . ."

"Tarts, ma'am." Merriman finished the sentence for her.

"They had the effrontery to . . . I chucked them out, ma'am," Mary explained. She was surprised not to receive any congratulations for it.

"No bones broken, then?" Louisa asked instead.

"No, ma'am."

"That's all right, then. Mary, this is Mr. Starr. Mr. Starr's to join us as hall porter."

"And Fred," Starr said, indicating the dog.

"And Fred," Louisa corrected herself, with a smile. Starr gave Mary a little bow, which pleased her.

Merriman was formally introduced and Starr and Fred left. When the door was closed again Merriman asked, "He's . . . what you had in mind, would you say, madam?"

Louisa smiled. "He interviewed me," she admitted. "I don't know anything about him. I think that's why I engaged him. I like mysteries."

She stopped Mary, who was about to go.

"One little thing, Mary . . ."

"Yes, mum?"

"When you chuck ladies out in future, do it gently. Eh?"

"But they were *streetwalkers,* madam."

"Which is another word for working girls, Mary. There's not everyone able to keep a secure job in a nice situation. Never forget that, and don't be a snob."

She terminated the admonition with a smile, though, leaving Mary baffled but relieved.

A few days later, by which time Starr and Fred had joined the establishment and taken up their joint duty in the hall, Louisa displayed yet another side of her remarkably varied attitude toward strangers.

A middle-aged man, well dressed and with a commanding air, marched through the front door and up to the desk. Starr had his back to him, working out some dates on a wall calendar. The man slapped the palm of his hand hard on the desk top and barked, "You there! Some attention."

"Yes, sir," Starr said, turning. "Sorry, sir." He had genuinely not heard the man enter.

Louisa, coming down the stairs, was just in time to hear the stranger reply, in a provincial accent, "Never mind the 'yes, sirs.' I've a cabful of luggage out there. Get it in here, and sharpish."

"Yes, sir. At once," said Starr, assuming the arrival to have been expected. But Louisa stepped forward. She was fashionably dressed and ladylike and could be mistaken for nothing less than the housekeeper, if not the proprietress.

"Just a moment, Starr," she checked him, then turned to the other man. "For what purpose, Mr. er ... ?"

He crimsoned. "For what purpose? It's a hotel, isn't it? I want a room, woman. The biggest and the best, and a damn sight less impudence. 'For what purpose' indeed!"

Louisa said calmly, "I don't think I caught your name."

"Well, in that case, I suggest 'sir' will do."

"Is 'sir' your title?" she inquired, with deceptive innocence.

"No, it isn't. 'Sir' just happens to be the custom when dealing with people who're prepared to give you their good money. My name is Atkinson, Josiah Atkinson, proprietor of the Atkinson Coal-mining Company, Northamptonshire, and I want a room befitting that position."

Louisa raised her eyebrows, "Oh, yes, sir. We have a very good coal cellar."

"You ... you *what?*"

"Otherwise, I'm afraid we have no rooms available. At least, not for the likes of jumped-up snottynoses like you. Try some common lodging house. One of them might condescend to let you a back room."

Mr. Atkinson swayed and it seemed for a moment that he might be about to slap Louisa's face. Starr came quickly out from behind the desk, followed by Fred, who began to bark.

"Scarper! Sling your hooks!" Louisa ordered the startled industrialist. Fred advanced to snarl at his ankles and Starr ominously eased his wrists free of the cuffs of his jacket sleeves. Mr. Atkinson turned about and left swiftly, without another word.

"Lovely!" Louisa exclaimed. She actually patted Fred, who licked her hand.

Starr said, "He was a wealthy man, though, madam. And we've got all those rooms empty."

"I'm just starting as I mean to go on," she replied. "My standards are mine, and everyone'll have to like 'em, or lump 'em."

A still further example of what those standards could embrace was demonstrated that afternoon. Starr entered Louisa's room and informed her that a Major Smith-Barton, D.S.O., requested an interview with her with a view to becoming a long-term resident. She sent him to invite the Major in. He proved to be the archetype retired army officer of modest rank: elderly, rather blotchy about the cheeks and nose, sidewhiskered, and sporting an eyeglass.

"Just back from the East," he explained in a bluff voice after courtesies had been exchanged. "Looking for somewhere to put up, don't you know? Been down in Suffolk, shooting with my cousin, Lord Dedham. Said he'd heard the old Bentinck had opened again, run by a damned fine woman who really knew how to cook. Asked me to stay on down there, don't you know, but the Dedhams live in a drafty old barrack of a house and my blood's a bit thin after so many years in the sun, so I upped sticks and made for London."

"Were you thinking of a complete set of rooms, Major?" asked Louisa, gratified to know that a word-of-mouth was already spreading in good circles.

"Oh Lord, no," he responded. "I'm an old campaigner. Don't like a lot of fuss. If you've got a boot cupboard somewhere, that'll do me."

She liked him. "I think we can do better than that for you," she said and led him back into the hall.

"Starr," she ordered, "let them bring Major Smith-Barton's things in. I'm putting him in Number Eleven."

"Very good, madam."

"I say," the Major said to Starr. "Wonder if I might have a loan of that *Sporting Life* of yours."

"Certainly, sir," said Starr, handing the newspaper over.

"Sure you've finished with it?"

"He's better off without it," Louisa said. "If you'll just follow me, Major?"

"You're very kind, ma'am," the Major said as he went up the stairs after Louisa. "Nicest bit of London, this, too, I always think. Like an old armchair, don't you know?"

Merriman approached them, carrying a tray. Louisa stopped him and introduced them. The Major said, "I wonder if I might have dinner in my room? Cold pheasant and a bottle of claret—something like that?"

"Did you hear that, Merriman?" Louisa asked.

"I did," was the laconic reply as Merriman passed on.

"Poor old fossil's as deaf as a post unless he chooses not to be," Louisa told the Major. "Only keep him out of kindness."

Down in the hall Merriman paused to survey the newcomer's possessions, a mixture of shabby, much-traveled cases, a black metal trunk bearing many dents and scrape marks, a hatbox, two fishing rods, and other odds and ends, bearing many worn labels.

"He's the sort," Starr replied sagely. "Seen plenty of 'em. We'll never get rid of him, now he's here."

Merriman launched into one of his rare monologues, usually precipitated by gloom or crisis.

"He'll want every meal carried up to his room, I suppose. Breakfast, luncheon, tea, dinner. I've seen 'em before, too. There was a day not so long ago when no gentleman would have had his luncheon at his hotel. What does he think his club's for?"

He sighed and went his way, thinking how different everything was becoming since the old Queen's going. Starr picked up some of the baggage and began carrying it upstairs. Fred moved to follow him.

"No, you stay there and mind the desk, Fred," his master instructed. "Getting as busy as Charing Cross round here, all of a sudden."

When they next encountered one another, Charles Tyrrell said to Louisa, "I bet you by the summer you'll be turning people away. Personal recommendation, that's how it's done. I'm doing my best. Every party I go to I become a positive bore about the virtues of the Bentinck Hotel. By the way, the Mastersons say they'll definitely be coming. They're people worth having."

"Well, we get plenty of inquiries, but apart from one old Major . . ." Louisa said. Today she was in a subdued mood; almost edgy. She had been like that since waking, and she knew why. The reason irked her. She considered it beneath her to let it, but there it remained.

Charles had informed her the day before that he would be wanting a special dinner *à deux* served in his room.

"She's an awfully topping girl," he had added. "Met her at a hunt ball in Hampshire last week. Dances divinely."

"Married, I suppose, knowing you."

"I should say so. Husband in the army, conveniently on a mission to Egypt. Said she was coming to London this week to do some shopping, so I asked her to dine. She agreed just like that, keen as mustard."

Louisa grunted. Jealousy over a man was something new to her. She knew that Charlie was a considerable man-about-town where the girls were concerned, and she had had no doubt why he had thought it convenient to set up his own quarters—a lair, almost. But this was the first time that he had invited one of his ladies to visit him. Louisa felt a little as she had when Johnnie Farjeon had brought her her first summons from the Prince of Wales.

But she had no grounds for objecting, and was cross with herself for even wishing she could. She handed him a slip of paper now.

"I've done all the shopping for your little party tonight," she said.

"Rather an occasion," he said. "My first at the Bentinck." He read the penciled draft of the menu. "*Pâté de foie gras, sole bonne femme, croûte de cailles Bentinck . . . bombe surprise.* Oh, by the way, no garlic in anything, please."

Louisa said, "I'll see to it. I'm going to cook it all myself, anyway."

"Thank you. Oh, by the way, she likes roses . . ."

"Does she? Well she can go on liking them. She won't get none here, none at this time of year." It was February, 1902. "I'll get some other flowers." An edge of sarcasm sharpened her tone. "Something nice and virginal."

Charlie laughed, not noticing the little cut.

"And I'll go out now and buy a new waistcoat to impress her," he said, and went gaily away.

That evening she supervised Merriman laying the round dining table she and Charlie had bought for his room. It was set back into an alcove off the sitting room. Louisa had arranged a centerpiece of early flowers.

"While they're eating the soup, put a light under the sole, but not before," she ordered. "And let me know in good time when they come to the quail pudding. I'll bring it up myself."

He made no comment.

"Did you hear me?" she asked loudly.

"Yes."

"Respect, please, Merriman."

"Yes, madam."

"That's better. And don't light them candles till Mr.

Tyrrell rings and says he's ready for dinner. And get done quick when it's over. He won't want you hanging around like a drunk at a wedding."

"No, madam."

Louisa stood back to admire the table setting. Well, he'd been good to her, so it was up to her to do him proud in return.

Even so . . .

Fourteen

Major Smith-Barton and Starr stood beside the porter's chair in the hall that evening, commiserating over the racing pages of a newspaper. Fred paid them no attention. Dogs have more sense than to back race-horses.

"Fell at the third fence," Starr said.

"Probably brought down or interfered with," the Major said gloomily. "Not the horse's fault, sure of that. Real good 'un. Oh, well, sorry, don't you know, but you can't always win."

Starr, who had lost a small amount as a result of the Major's "certain" tip, asked cautiously, "What's your fancy for tomorrow, Major?"

The old soldier's eyes sparkled again. "Sultan's Kiss in the two-fifteen at Sandown," he said emphatically. "Can't go wrong. Had it from a feller who . . ."

He broke off as the hotel door opened and a young woman came through and glanced about. She was about thirty, well and tastefully dressed, and good-looking. The Major, who had removed his eyeglass to emphasize with a gesture his certainty about Sultan's Kiss, replaced it and looked at her appreciatively.

"Yes, ma'am?" Starr inquired, stepping forward.

"Mr. Tyrrell's party, please," the lady said in a somewhat affected voice with a slight lisp. "Mrs. Travers."

"Ah, yes, ma'am. Good evening. Will you follow me, madam?"

He led the way up the stairs. The Major looked down at Fred, who had decided not to bother to follow.

"Nice looking filly, that, Fred. Bit of blood there. Highly strung, I shouldn't wonder. Be all right with the right jockey up, eh?"

The dog wagged his tail.

Merriman disposed of Mrs. Travers's coat and wrap in the small anteroom to Charlie's sitting room and announced her before retiring.

"My dear Belinda," Charlie said, shaking her hand. "How very nice to see you again."

He was, he had just assured himself before his mirror in the bedroom, appearing at his very best, his fashionably cut new waistcoat giving a fresh look to his perfectly pressed evening suit.

"Good evening, Charles," she said, not failing to notice how dashing he was looking. "Ooh, it's cold out. Horribilino."

"Champagne too cold, then?" he asked, indicating a bottle standing in a bucket of ice. "What about some Madeira instead, perhaps?"

"Champagne, please," she said. "But don't open it specially for me."

"Good heavens no," he grinned. "It's mother's milk to me."

He opened the bottle expertly, the cork coming out with the merest sigh, and poured glasses for them both.

"What an unusual place this is," she said, glancing about. "Not a bit like an hotel, really."

He gave her her glass and they drank together, raising the glasses in unspoken salute.

"That's the idea," Charlie explained. "You see, Mrs. Trotter, who runs it, wanted it to be more like a country house."

"How quaint," Belinda said. Charlie could sense that she was becoming puzzled and changed the subject quickly.

"Great fun, last weekend."

"Oh, yes. Really quite deevy."

"Tubby Vernon dressing up as a footman and spilling the soup over old Admiral Squeezy Dick's shirt . . ."

"Yes. Quite a lark, wasn't it?" she agreed.

"I bet the old devil was playing footy-footy with you under the table."

"Yes he did, actually. It was most awfully embarrassing."

Belinda took a quick sip of her champagne. Charles said, "I can't say I'd blame him. What did you do?"

"Oh, my mother taught me always to have a fork ready," Belinda answered, sipping again.

"To repel invaders, eh?" Charles laughed. "I must be careful."

He picked up the bottle out of the ice bucket and advanced it toward his guest's glass, but she placed the palm of her hand over the mouth.

"Please. You'll have me tiddly, you know," she said, the lisp already rather more pronounced.

"Nonsense," he insisted, pouring her a little more. "But there's some rather nice claret ahead. Don't want to spoil our palates. I say, that's the most awfully nice dress you're wearing."

"I'm so glad you like it," she answered, talking more rapidly. "It was part of my trousseau. My sister said she thought it was rather risqué. I'm staying with her in Paddington, you know. I always seem to be cuckooing with some friend or relation or other when Basil's away."

An apt reply, pleasingly so to him, offered itself promptly to Charlie.

"I'm sure you're very welcome in any nest. That's . . . what's so nice about this place. One is so completely undisturbed. Private . . . if you know what I mean. One's own little nest."

He added quickly, "I hope you're hungry?"

"Famished, actually."

Charles went to ring the bell. From behind him he heard Belinda ask, "Was I boringly early . . . or is everyone else boringly late?" Without turning, he answered as casually as he could, "There isn't anyone else."

He turned to face her and indicated the alcove with its table laid for two. Merriman entered and began lighting the candles on it. But Belinda had turned to Charles and was saying, "I'd no idea, Charles. You asked me to a dinner party in an hotel. I couldn't possibly dine with you alone. It would cause an absolute scandalare. I mean, it simply isn't done in Basil's regiment."

Charles looked around, to see Merriman drifting tactfully out of their presence. Of course, long experience had taught Charles that machinations such as his, which had involved an invitation that had not been a lie but had left out the essential truth, could sometimes be rewarded with disappointment. But on more than one occasion he had managed to overcome the initial setback by the application of his considerable charm, if necessary aided by liberal dispensation of champagne.

"My dearest Belinda," he smiled now, picking up the bottle yet again, "you *are* teasing me, aren't you? It's awfully unkind to play at tease, you know."

She put her glass down on the table.

"No, Charles, I'm not. Really, really I'm not."

"But there can't be any scandal if nobody knows. Nobody's going to know. Just one evening. Look, it's all ready . . . and even cuckoos have to eat."

He had replaced the bottle and now tried to take her hand instead. She drew back abruptly and said sharply, "Please don't touch me, Charles. I never took you for . . . for a cad. If Basil knew, he'd shoot you."

"Shoot me!"

"He shot a man in Durban for less."

"What—killed him?"

"He only grazed his finger, actually. But that was because the man moved. You don't know Basil's temper."

It was not so much the threat of retribution from Basil that told Charlie he was wasting his time. It was the expression on Basil's wife's face, and the rigid set of her body, and the glance she had thrown in the direction of the anteroom where her outdoor things lay. He gave in gracefully.

"Do forgive me," he smiled with contrived wistfulness. "It was a silly mistake on my part. You'd like to go home?"

"Yes, I would," she said thankfully. But as he was helping her on with her wrap a sudden thought came to her. "My carriage wasn't ordered until ten-thirty!"

Fresh hope glowed in Charlie. Perhaps she was a better and more teasing tactician than he had suspected.

"Then you'll stay! I knew you would."

Her cheeks went pink. "No, I will not."

"I'll find you a cab, then."

"I couldn't go home in a hackney cab! Not at night."

Even Charles's suavity was melted by a sudden flush of impatience. This was not tactics. It was female obtuseness.

He almost rammed her coat on to her and said, "I'm sure dear Basil wouldn't shoot you for that!"

They went coldly down to the hall. The Major and Starr were still there, so for appearance' sake Charlie said to Belinda, "I'm sorry you couldn't stay longer, Mrs. Travers. Sure you wouldn't like me to see you home?"

"No," she responded in kind. "Thank you, I'll be quite safe by myself."

"Then I'll just take you down to the cabstand," he said, and ushered her out.

"Well, I'll be damned," said the Major to Starr. "Didn't even get her to the post."

When he got back a few minutes later Charlie went straight up to his room. He finished the bottle of champagne in large gulps and opened another which had been chilling in readiness. He had failed similarly before, in other surroundings, but it was always a letdown and a bore when it turned out like this; and more especially on this evening when he had hoped to use for its truest purpose the apartment he had so carefully prepared and had even bought an entire hotel to obtain.

There was a soft knock at the door and Louisa came in.

"Stood up proper, were you?" she asked, not sarcastically, but with less than sympathy.

"Stupid woman!" he growled. "Typical, stuffy, middle-class army . . ."

Louisa raised an eyebrow.

"Retreated in the face of the enemy's advance, did she?"

"I didn't so much as lay a finger on her, damn it!"

"No, but you was going to, wasn't you? 'No garlic'! Thank heavens there's some honest decent women in the world that are prepared to be faithful to their husbands and behave themselves."

He said bitterly, "Thank you for those comforting and consoling words. What are you laughing at? I don't think it's very funny."

She stopped giggling and said, "No, it isn't . . . Rather sad, really."

He indicated the bottle.

"Have a spot of bubbly with me, Louisa."

"Well . . . ta. Just a little."

He poured some for her and another full glass for himself.

"Louisa, I do want to apologize after all the trouble you've taken. I really am most awfully sorry about the waste."

"Cheers, love. Look, don't worry. You just forget the ladies for one night and sit down and eat my nice dinner."

The idea had not occurred to him. Before she had come in he had been contemplating whether to go down and take his pick from the promenade at the Empire, or somewhere more exclusive. He smiled his gratitude.

"Just like you to take it on the chin without moaning," he said. "Thanks. You're a tonic...."

He stopped suddenly and she saw a curious look come into his eyes.

"What?" she asked.

"Louisa ... will you dine with me?"

It came out with an impetuous rush. The silence afterward seemed a long one.

"Me?"

"Yes. Do me the honor of dining with me."

She flushed as she said, "No, Charlie. I couldn't manage it. Not possible. I got another fifty pies almost due out of the oven ..."

"Mrs. Wellkin can manage that, for heaven's sake!"

"... And I got all the bits and pieces to get ready for Lady Manton's dinner tomorrow night ..."

Charlie gave her his most appealing smile, though it was sincerely done.

"That's tomorrow night, not tonight. Just relax for once. Enjoy yourself. Take a night off. No one's worked harder or deserves it more."

She tried to joke it off. "Eat me own poison? That'd be a laugh!"

"It would give me a lot of pleasure if you'd dine with me, Louisa," he said earnestly. "I need cheering up badly. Anyway, I'm your resident. What the guest orders he's entitled to get."

He was pleased to see her grin and hear her say, "All right, Mister the Honorable Misery, sir. I should be pleased to accept your kind invitation to dinner.

I suppose I'll manage. Just give me a few minutes to tart meself up a bit."

She went quickly. Charles picked up his glass of champagne again. But this time he merely sipped it, savoring it. Then he rang for Merriman and told him to go down as quickly as he could and fetch a bottle of the Cliquot Rosé 'Ninety-three to be chilled.

In Louisa's bedroom, Mary finished lacing her mistress's corsets.

"Wish I had a nice tiny waist like yours, ma'am," she said wonderingly. "Can't be more than eighteen inches."

"Comes of eating nothing but tea and toast for so long." Louisa got up. "Right, let's have the dress."

Mary lifted it from the bed, where she had laid it out. It was the one Louisa had worn for her last visit from the Prince of Wales. It had never been out of the wardrobe since. As Mary helped her into it Louisa said, "Haven't worn this for over a . . . Well, not since we came to this place. It was made by a royal dressmaker, you know."

"Will you wear your gold necklace with it, too, ma'am?"

"No. It's the jet one tonight. It's got to be."

"Why, ma'am?"

"Proper brought up lady's maids don't ask that sort of question, Mary. But since you have, Mr. Tyrrell gave me it a long time ago . . . so it'd be only polite for him."

When the dress was fully fastened, and the necklace in place, and the last adjustment made to Louisa's hair, which Mary had already swept up for her with combs and pins, revealing the perfect slender white neck, Louisa held her fan and gloves and twirled in front of her long mirror. The little Welsh maid could almost have cried in her admiration.

"You look beautiful, madam. You look like a real duchess—you do really."

The compliment pleased Louisa, but she replied, "I'm glad I'm not one. What a life. Nothing to do all day, 'cept change your clothes, eat too much, sleep too much, talk too much . . . Still, it feels nice as make-believe."

Picking up the skirt of the gown, she made her way back to Charlie's rooms.

"Pink champagne!" Louisa exclaimed when Charlie drew the bottle of Cliquot from the ice bucket and uncorked it. "That's pushing the boat out a bit, isn't it?"

"It's a special occasion. A launching ceremony."

"Didn't even know we had any in the cellar."

"Ah, but Merriman and I knew, didn't we?" Charles said to the aged waiter, who was assiduously maintaining his deaf pose and made no response.

"Well, here's to a first-rate secondhand evening," Louisa said as she and Charlie clinked glasses and drank.

"Merriman," Charlie said so loudly that there could be no excuse for not being heard.

"Sir?"

"We will now taste this good lady's cooking."

Merriman bowed slightly and moved to help Louisa into her place at the table. He did it gravely, with as much respect as he would have accorded a real duchess.

The *pâté de foie gras* was already set out. Merriman proffered a napkin containing toast he had been warming. It occurred to Louisa how long it had been since she had sat down to a formal meal, and been waited on, and in what unique circumstances and company those last occasions had been. A little of the mood she had felt then crept back to her now. Charlie's starched shirtfront and pearl studs glistened in the light of candles and subdued electricity. The perfectly arranged cutlery gleamed. The various glasses twinkled.

Charlie was staring at her as she started to eat. "You look absolutely ravishing," he said sincerely.

A little nervously she changed the subject. "What would you talk about to your lady if she was sitting here?"

"With the first course, the weather."

"The weather? That don't sound very romantic to me."

"It's a sort of way of breaking the ice. You know, how the fog stopped the pheasants flying well at Mentmore. That's if she likes shooting. At any rate, her husband seems to," he remembered to himself.

"What if she doesn't?"

"Hunting, perhaps. We might consider together how many days the Belvoir has been stopped by frost this season. Then go through every yard of that splendid run we had with the Warwickshire in November. Never missed a fence. Or consider the merits of the big bay gelding . . ."

"What if she likes tiddlywinks?"

"Then we'd play tiddlywinks together—later. Just now, though, it is essential to return to the weather."

"Why?"

"Because just when I am about to suggest that we should go skating on the Serpentine a thought strikes me. I am immediately all attention and apprehension. I must find out if the lady's tiny hand is frozen."

He reached across and took Louisa's hand.

"Here—stop it!" she rebuked him, and withdrew it. But she laughed.

Over the quail pie Charles announced, "At this stage the time is ripe to embark on rather more serious subjects. Such important matters as where the lady is staying for Ascot."

"That's easy," Louisa said, putting on a "posh" accent. "Windsor Castle. If the Queen'll weather it," she added in her own voice.

"Louisa, I said 'serious,'" he mock-chided her.

"Such as what horribilino plays she has been to, and what deevy house parties, and where she has been dinared before dansareing with that divine partnerino . . ."

She chortled at the society slang.

"And who's been poppying into beddies with who, I bet," she suggested.

He was surprised. "Put rather crudely—yes."

They had finished their delicious main course. Louisa got up, saying, "Well, if you'll excusare me?"

She went away behind the curtained-off serving alcove, from which Merriman emerged to clear away the plates and lay smaller fresh ones. Charles was surprised to see him switch off the remaining electric lights, leaving the table illuminated by the candles only, and then leave the apartment altogether. A moment later Louisa came back through the curtain. On a small silver tray she was carrying a perfect sculpture of a swan, fashioned from solid-white ice cream and resting on a nest of creamy meringue. In the middle of the swan's back the blue flame of burning brandy flickered. It was a superb creation.

Louisa laid it in the center of the table.

"And what do you think your lady would say to that?"

"She'd be enchanted—as I am, Louisa."

"She'd say it seems a shame to eat it. They always do . . ."

"She would say that she'd heard this Mrs. Trotter wasn't only the best cook in London, but a most beautiful woman, to boot."

He had spoken without the preceding flippancy and had looked at her very intently while doing so. He took her hand again, but she withdrew it again to enable her to serve them portions of the confection.

"Here, Mr. Dishonorable Tyrrell," she said, concentrating on what she was doing. "You want to watch it, or you'll get a clip on your lughole."

The strains of the song "And Her Golden Hair Was Hanging Down Her Back" drifted downward as far as the hall. The voices were Charlie's and Louisa's, and the uncertain, fumbling piano accompaniment, lagging several notes behind, was his.

Starr raised his eyes from the sporting form.

"High jinks up there, Mr. Merriman," he said, as the old waiter tottered to the foot of the stairs.

"High jinks it is, and no mistake, Mr. Starr," he replied.

He sniffed disapprovingly and went through the pass door. Starr lowered the paper to address his dog, at his feet.

"Bit perky tonight, our Mrs. Trotter. Eh, Fred?"

Fred yawned and snuggled his muzzle again between his paws.

The song ended and Louisa, brandy glass in hand, left the piano and slightly stumbled into a chair.

"I think," she said, speaking carefully, "I think it's about time that lady of yours went back to her pots and pans."

She sipped the brandy and held the glass up before her eyes. It had acquired two rims, and two levels of the spirit.

Two Charlies arose from the piano stool and came toward her, melting into one as they moved into closer focus. He took the glass from her hand and then held both her hands in his.

"No. Not quite," he said. "Not till I have told her that her hair is like the finest gossamer seen at dewy dawn. That her eyes are like twin pools of rare delight. Her cheeks like blushing clouds."

Louisa roused herself.

"What about her Hampsteads, then?"

"What? Oh, her teeth. A . . . a ring of precious pearls, culled from an Eastern crown."

"Not bad," she conceded, and hiccuped.

"Where was I?" he asked. His eyes, even to hers, were a shade glassy.

She pointed to her lips, with a wavering finger.

"Lips . . . like twin rosebuds, new . . . newly opened in June," he managed. "Neck like a column of the finest alabaster."

They stayed there, he kneeling before her, for some minutes, just looking at one another. Then she realized that his eyes had become less blurred, both to her and to him. The double outline of his shoulders had merged into a single one. There was this one man, and this one man only, here with her. She licked her lips.

"That's . . . about far enough, isn't it?" she suggested.

"Yes," he said, looking down, and then up again into her eyes. "Then . . . then I tell her that I love her."

There were some seconds of silence.

"And the magic spell always works?" she asked.

"Lord, no. It's like . . . hooking a salmon. That's the real sport of the thing."

She was not offended by his frankness.

"Just a sport, is it?"

"I suppose it is—usually."

"And you always win in the end."

Another lengthy silence fell. Then he shook his head and said, "No. Sometimes the lady says her carriage is waiting . . ."

The candles behind them flickered. The piano keyboard stretched white and black behind him. The glowing embers in the fireplace rustled as a coal disintegrated into ash and fell.

"I haven't got a carriage," Louisa said, very quietly.

Charlie raised himself from his knees, took her arm, lifted her from her chair, and guided her toward the dark room beyond those in which she had spent the evening with him.

Fifteen

"You want to watch it this morning, Mr. Merriman," Starr remarked next morning in the hall. "Don't he, Fred? Proper tantrum she's in this morning, ain't she?"

Even Merriman was inclined to believe that Fred nodded agreement. The waiter paused with his tray, watching the porter assiduously getting rid of some paw marks on the floor.

"I spoke to her quite civil," Starr went on. "'Your mail, Mrs. Trotter,' I said, and she bit my head off. 'Why isn't it on my desk?' she said. 'And what are all them dirty paw marks all over this floor? This is meant to be a hotel, not a dogs' home,' she says. We don't stand for that sort of talk where we serve, do we, Fred? Seems she's got out of bed the wrong side, and no mistake."

Merriman leaned across and imparted a rare confidence.

"Not her own bed, neither."

Starr gaped and even Fred cocked an ear.

"Is that what you think, Mr. Merriman?" the porter asked.

"More than *think*, Mr. Starr. Sshl"

Mary was coming downstairs.

"Old Major Whiskers is still in bed," she told them brightly. "As I was making up his fire he was telling

197

me about how he fought the fierce Pythons of the
Northwest Frontier of India."

"Pathans," Starr corrected her.

"That's what I said. He said if they didn't have us
to fight, they'd fight each other for the fun of it."

"Just like the Welsh," Starr commented. Mary put
out her tongue at him.

"Anyway," she told Merriman, "he'd like some biscuits and a glass of light port at eleven. Oh, and the
loan of your sporting paper, Mr. Starr, if you'd be so
obliging."

She went through the pass door. The two men
turned to each other and made gestures as if drinking
and tugging on horses' reins.

Charles Tyrrell breezed in through the front door.
"Morning!" he greeted them.

"Morning!" he also greeted Louisa in her parlor
moments later.

"Hullo," she said flatly, not looking up from her
desk, at which she was attending to papers.

"Will you come out to lunch with me?" he asked.

Unexpectedly snappily, she responded, "How can I?
I'm meant to be running a hotel, not waltzing round
the West End with you."

Astonished to find her in such a mood so few hours
after what had happened between them he perched
on her desk and tried to put his hand against her
cheek. She drew back, but let him hold her hand instead.

"Oh, Charlie," she said. "What have we gone and
done? What will people say? What will they think?"

" 'They'? They won't know."

"Course they will. Servants always find out everything. You wouldn't understand things like that.
They'll find out, then everyone'll know."

"Well, does it matter, anyway?"

"Oh? 'Have you heard about that Mrs. Trotter at
the Bentinck? Tucks up with her customers.' It's my
own fault, I expect. I oughtn't to drink."

A hurt look came into his eyes.

"You mean . . . it was just that—and to be kind to me?"

Her grip tightened on his.

"No, Charlie, I don't mean that at all. You know very well I don't. Your . . . magic spell wouldn't have worked unless I'd wanted it to. It's just that . . . I feel in my bones it's dangerous."

"We can't go back now, Louisa. What's done's done —and it was wonderful. Truly wonderful, my dear."

"I know. But we can take a pull back. A real pull."

"You mean, stop?"

"Yes."

"Is that what you really want?"

She cried out, "No, of course it's not what I want. But you can't always have what you want in life. It hardly ever comes to that. I don't know, I don't know. Hell, I got all the accounts to do, and the dinner at Lady Manton's for twenty-four tonight . . ."

Charles Tyrrell had found himself in many situations with many women in the course of his young life. There was a formula solution to most of them, sometimes facile, sometimes painful, sometimes costly in emotional or financial terms. This, though, was something new. No unwritten textbook solution presented itself. Louisa Trotter was unique, and his feeling for her, so newly conceived, seemed to fit none of the familiar patterns.

She released his hand and picked up her pen and an invoice. He quietly left the room.

When she returned to that room, long after midnight, tired but victorious again after a surpassing banquet at Lady Manton's, she saw in the center of her blotting pad a cut-glass vase containing red roses. A white rectangular card leaned against it.

Even without picking it up she could read the handwritten message, *I love you.*

In his sitting room, Charles Tyrrell drew on his pipe, but produced no smoke. He glanced into the bowl and leaned forward to knock out the last shreds of dottle into the waning fire. He glanced up at the mantelpiece clock. It showed half-past one. He considered whether to refill the pipe and the brandy glass beside him. The temptation was strong, but his mouth was sour and dry and he contented himself with draining the last quarter-inch of spirit.

Rare for him, he had stayed in all evening. He had eaten the cold supper Merriman had served, had begun to dress to go out, then had thrown his evening things aside and put on instead his dark-blue silken dressing gown with the quilted collar and lapels. He had glanced through two evening newspapers, without edification, and started reading a novel, which he had given up after two pages. Nothing outside his own life seemed meaningful or real anymore. The hedonistic Charles Tyrrell, wealthy, popular, handsome man-about-town suddenly felt himself to be some sort of hermit in a well-appointed cell in the cavernous depths of this half-empty hotel.

He made the effort to get up and place his pipe on the mantelpiece. He wound the clock, a habit he preferred to reserve for himself, and replaced the key behind it. He turned toward his bedroom door.

Louisa was standing between it and him. She had entered his apartment soundlessly, barefoot and wearing nightdress and dressing gown. Her superb hair hung abandonedly loose about her shoulders and down her back.

They stared at one another for a full five seconds. Then, with a little ecstatic cry, she ran across the carpet to him and pulled his face into the depths of her.

The word-of-mouth advertisement for the Bentinck's accommodation, as well as for Louisa's cookery, was by now widespread about London and as far away as the shires. More apartments had been let. It was well known that Louisa had no objection to what her male residents chose to do in their own quarters, in the matter of the opposite sex; but their carefully scrutinized visitors had to be ladies in the true sense (single or married made no difference), or at least so fashionably regarded in the theater, the opera, or other such spheres as to be acceptable in the best society. Professional ladies of the town, however elegantly got up and pleadingly vouched for by their patrons, got no further than the scrutiny of those watchdogs of the hallway, Starr and Fred.

A few mornings after Louisa's willing surrender to Charlie she returned to the hotel in high good humor, smartly dressed and accompanied by her lover, who carried a big cardboard hatbox. She held out the lilac-gloved little finger of her right hand to Starr, indicating that he should unloop from it an expensively wrapped small parcel.

"Little something for Fred," she smiled.

"Oh, thank you, Mrs. Trotter," the porter said. "Say 'Thank you,' Fred."

The dog indicated gratitude to the best of his ability.

"Er, Merriman's wanting to see you urgent, ma'am," Starr said. "Oh, here he is now."

Louisa jerked her head toward her room. Charlie went on upstairs with the hatbox.

"Excuse me, madam," the old porter said, "but there's a message come round from the German Embassy. Can you do dinner for thirty, Thursday night?"

"No, I can't," she answered, to his surprise. "Not an earthly. Mrs. Wellkin can."

"It wasn't Mrs. Wellkin they asked for . . . madam," Merriman ventured to correct her.

"I dare say it wasn't. Only, I'm going to the theater that night to *The Country Girl*. So you can tell 'em it's no good. It's Mrs. Wellkin, or nothing."

"Very good, madam."

"Thirty for Thursday!" Mrs. Wellkin echoed some

minutes later in the kitchen. "She's gone barmy, and no mistake. I suppose she's forgotten there's people staying in this hotel who have to be cooked for as well. And more due. She's gone barmy, Mr. Merriman. I mean, there's no one I ever worked for who looked after their servants better than Mrs. Trotter. Really thoughtful, she's always been. Granted, her temper's never been good, but what's an argy-bargy every so often? But this business of going all spoony over *him!* I dunno. I really don't."

And she proceeded to take out her anguish upon the dough she was kneading—with the result that when the German Embassy did, of course, get its dinner provided two days later, the pastry was commented upon by all for its exquisite lightness.

The perplexity belowstairs at the Bentinck did not diminish, however. Even Mary had caught its germ.

"Mr. Merriman," she said to him, in one of his more receptive moods, "this . . . passion Mrs. Trotter has . . . it's changed her. I mean, she seems to have gone all flighty. I suppose it's marvelous for her being in love, and all that, but . . ."

"It may be a marvel for her," the old man grumbled, "but it's not for us. More like sitting on a powder keg."

"You mean . . . some sort of explosion's coming, Mr. Merriman?"

"Any second of any day, mark my words. Order and sense out of the window. Confusion reigns. *The Country Girl* instead of the German Embassy, if you get my drift."

"Not entirely, Mr. Merriman."

He sighed. "There was once a chef in a hotel where I worked once. A real touch with fish, he had. Could make a common piece of hake taste like turbot. But when he had a passion on him—and, being a Spaniard, he had one a week—well then, and I tell you the truth, he could make sole taste worse than skate. That's what it can do to a normal sane human being."

Mary regarded the shaking head fearfully.

"She's really took bad, then?"

He replied sepulchrally, "I had hoped to die peaceful in my bed, and it will be a thankful release when it comes. But not in the ruins of the Bentinck Hotel."

Mary shivered.

In the hall Major Smith-Barton was as usual communing with Starr on the matter of horseflesh, while a disapproving specimen of dogflesh looked on. To Fred, a good run in the park would have been more to the point, even on so cold a February afternoon.

"Mrs. Trotter not about?" the Major asked, when matters of priority had been dealt with.

"No, sir. Out all morning."

"Mm! Out most of yesterday, too, wasn't she?"

"Yes, sir. Good deal lately."

Each knew what the other was thinking, but neither could have brought himself to discuss Louisa's private life in fuller detail.

They turned to look at a well-dressed middle-aged man who had just come through the front door.

"Good afternoon, sir," Starr greeted him. The Major went off up to his room for more extended perusal of the racing pages.

"Morning," the gentleman responded. He was very straight-backed and well groomed, and his tone was that of a man accustomed to being obeyed. "I should like to see some apartments. Sitting room, bedroom, bathroom, et cetera. I gather you have such arrangements."

"Yes, sir. Only . . ."

"Good. If you'll kindly lead the way."

"I'm sorry, sir," Starr told him, "but I can't take on any new guest without the proprietor's permission."

"Then I'll see the proprietor."

"Mrs. Trotter's not here just now, I'm afraid, sir."

The gentleman frowned. He was clearly not a man who liked his wishes to be thwarted in any way. He looked at his watch.

"When will she be back?"

"I . . . I've no idea, sir. She didn't say."

"Didn't say? Well, really . . . Look here, there's surely no reason why I should not at least inspect some of the vacant accommodation in the meantime."

Starr swallowed but answered resolutely, "Not without Mrs. Trotter being here. She's very particular, you see."

At the word *particular* the gentleman positively scowled.

"What exactly do you mean to imply by that?"

"Nothing at all, sir. Nothing personal, I mean . . ."

The gentleman had taken out a silver card-case. He opened it and extracted a visiting card.

"In that case," he said, "I should be obliged to you if you would give Mrs. Trotter my card and tell her that I shall not be troubling her after all. There are plenty of hotels in London."

He turned and marched swiftly out of the door. Starr examined the card. It bore a noble name and title.

He looked down at Fred.

"What a way to run a hotel, old son," he said miserably.

In casual conversation one morning not long after Major Smith-Barton's arrival, he and Charles Tyrrell had discovered they had some things in common, the principal being that Charlie's father, the Earl of Haslemere, had been a senior contemporary of Smith-Barton's at Eton. There was enough in this to warrant an evening together with cigars and port in Charlie's apartment. Louisa was out supervising a banquet. Despite her sudden infatuation and preference for Charlie's company, she remained practical enough not to treat all her clients as cavalierly as she had done the German Embassy.

"Very nice drop of port, this," the Major said.

"Croft's 'Seventy-two," Charlie answered. "I brought

it up from home. My father's been forbidden to drink the stuff, to his fury."

"I was given a pipe of port as a christening present by a very generous godfather," the Major recalled. "Sad to say, I never touched a drop of it."

"How was that?"

"When I was twenty-one it was just ready to drink. Unfortunately, my debts were just ready to be paid. I had to sell the lot to raise the booty. Oh well, probably saved me from chronic gout."

Charlie smiled. He liked the man. He himself might end up something like this someday. He poured the Major another glass.

"Thanks, old boy. You know, your father was the best fagmaster I ever had at Eton. Always gave me a tip for everything I did—a half-penny, or a sausage. Something like that. How is your father, anyway? Heard lately?"

"Not awfully good, actually. You know that bad fall I told you he had out hunting in December. Mama wrote yesterday to say it still hasn't got right, and since none of the doctors seems able to do anything new they're just off to New York to see a quack over there."

"Sorry about that. Yes, awfully nice chap. Not like that other brute who messed with him. Duckworth, don't you know? He was a brute. If his eggs or his toast weren't just right he'd wallop my backside black and blue. I hated his guts."

The Major sipped his port in a reflective silence, then added, "Never thought I should feel sorry for that Duckworth. But I was, in the end. He joined some smart cavalry mob, treated his chaps like he treated me at school. They mutinied and Duckworth was court-martialed. Out in the Sudan, I think. It broke him. Last time I saw him he was an old man of forty-five, drinking himself to death in Boodle's. Gone to pot."

He sighed, and added, to Charlie's surprise, "Rather like this place."

"This place? What do you mean? You're not implying Louisa's bullying the servants?"

"Lord no! Most charming woman. Just . . . well, things seem rather to be going to the dogs. You probably wouldn't notice, but Starr chatters away a bit to me. Shouldn't let him, I suppose, and shouldn't be mentioning it to you."

"No, no. I'd sooner hear."

"Well, he's not too happy himself." The Major chuckled. "Perhaps that dog of his has been complaining. But I can tell you, that other cook . . . What's her name?"

"Mrs. Wellkin?"

"That's it. Definitely thinking of making a move. Reckons she's getting far too much shoved on to her just lately."

Charlie said thoughtfully, "That's bad."

"Miss the place myself if it folds up. A great pity, don't you know, after all they tell me about Mrs. Trotter making such a great effort to get it going in the first place."

"A great pity, indeed," Charlie agreed, and determined to have a bit of a heart-to-heart wtih Louisa at the next opportunity.

He was not able to see her all next day or evening, though. She had another inescapable function to attend to—a grand and long luncheon—and then a banquet involving a member of the royal family. Charles had to meet his parents for dinner at the Hotel Cecil. In those sumptuous surroundings he received some information which altered the tenor of what he had to tell Louisa when at last he did get her alone in her room on the morning after that.

"My dear," he said, having perched himself on the corner of her desk and gently but forcibly pushed aside a pile of papers on which she had been trying, without much success, to concentrate. "My dear, I have to go away."

Her eyes widened and she half started to get up. He leaned forward and kissed her brow, at the same time pressing her back into her chair.

"Not for good, you wide-eyed pigeon," he smiled. "Just to the States for a while. Mama's really worried about the Guv'nor. It's the least I can do to be there along with her."

Louisa relaxed with relief.

"Oh, Charlie, I thought for a minute . . . Course you got to go. Only wish I could, too."

He shrugged.

"Look, old sport," he said. "Don't fly off the old handle, or anything, but it couldn't have happened at a better time."

"What's that supposed to mean?"

"Well, with all respect for poor old Papa, I . . . I think it's about time you concentrated a bit more on the Bentinck again, rather than on its first resident."

Louisa searched his face, but his gaze didn't falter.

"You going off me, or something?" she demanded. He shook his head.

"Anything but. But you're going off it. I'm very much to blame. It was all your life until I . . ."

"I know it was, Charlie. But it wasn't enough. I've only learnt to see that now."

"You're right. But, my dear, the Bentinck and all it stands for isn't any less part of your life, just because I happened to come along. And—no, don't get cross—it . . . isn't quite what it was before, is it?"

"Here! Who's been talking to you, Charlie Tyrrell? What's being said behind my back?"

"Nothing," he lied. "I'll be coming back—you have my word on that. But if you once let your reputation slip—your *real* reputation, I mean, as the best cook in London—you'll find it very hard to get back again."

"What's wrong with my cookin'? You saying I'm slippin', then?"

"I'm saying, as kindly as I can, that I came along and built a slide under your feet. Thank God, your feet haven't gone from under you yet, but you're beginning to lose your balance, Louisa. In the few weeks—I hope—I'll be away, I'd like to think of you getting back to normal, really building this place up to the standard it deserves. When I get back, I'd like to find every apartment taken, by the right sort of people, and a waiting list as long as your arm, and the name Louisa Trotter being bandied round every club in St. James's. Is that too much to ask of the girl who didn't give a fig for her beauty, but wanted to be known as the best cook and bottlewasher in London?"

Louisa jumped up and into his arms.

"Oh, Charlie! But you will come back, though? It's not the same as it was when I first said those things. You know how it's changed."

He kissed her warmly.

"Of course I know," he whispered. "It's never been the same since you carried in that ice-cream swan."

They kissed again, then stood apart.

"I hope your dad gets better," she said. "And it'll give Mary a chance to give your rooms a right doing."

Sixteen

Charlie's departure, more than his strictures, had the desired effect upon Louisa. Rid of the sweet distraction of his attentions, she plunged herself into every department of her work with renewed vigor and enthusiasm. Mrs. Wellkin ceased all talk of leaving. Mary bustled and glowed. Merriman's step up and down the stairs seemed to falter less. Starr was kept alert at the hall desk dispensing assistance, letters, keys, advice. Even Fred's growth of spring fur seemed to have benefited from some percipient stimulus.

Only one permanent resident found himself conversely deflated at this time. He was Major Smith-Barton, D.S.O., who one morning, some two weeks after Charles's going, presented himself apprehensively in the doorway of Louisa's parlor, where she was now working with her old brisk efficiency at the accounts. He requested a few words.

"Course, Major," she said welcomingly. "Come and sit down."

He closed the door carefully and did so. He cleared his throat, made a remark about the weather, then said, "It's, er, rather awkward, Mrs. Trotter . . . but I've a . . . a favor to ask you."

Louisa recognized the symptoms.

"Is it about money?" she asked, neither sympathetically nor hard.

"Well, yes, it is, rather. Shortage of same. That is to say, temporary shortage of same . . ."

He looked at her hopefully, but she offered no easy way out. He was compelled to go on.

"It's been a bit difficult lately, don't you know? Trustees being a bit tiresome—that sort of thing. Won't be long, of course. Just a question of getting things sorted out."

He paused again, but she still kept silent. He concluded wearily, "Course, I realize I can't go on staying here with my bill unpaid."

To his sudden relief Louisa gave him her famous smile.

"Course you can, Major. It's not going to ruin us. The old place wouldn't be the same without you."

The Major felt tears at the back of his eyes.

"I say, that's most awfully civil of you, ma'am. I am most . . . most awfully grateful. . . ."

"Forget it. Let's have a glass of wine to drown our sorrows."

She pressed the electric bell on her desk.

"Had any news from Charlie Tyrrell?" Major Smith-Barton asked, thankful to change the subject.

Louisa indicated a picture postcard on her desk.

"Yes. They had a terrible voyage, poor dears. Sick as cats all the way. And New York's cold as charity."

Merriman came in.

"Bring us a bottle of wine and two glasses, will you?" she told him. "And not that muck you gave me last night. Bottle of the Bollinger 'Ninety-three."

"Yes, madam."

Starr, brushing Fred in the dispense off the hall, saw Merriman getting the bottle and said, "He's short of the cash. That's old Whiskers's trouble."

"How can you tell that, Mr. Starr?" asked Mary, who was ironing.

"Always tell. When guests get specially friendly and

confidential, and then borrow a guinea off you to put on a certainty."

"He's not paying for this wine, I can tell you that," said Merriman, forcing the bottle into the ice in the metal bucket. "She is. Drinking the profits."

"But how can a gentleman not have money?" Mary wondered ingenuously.

Merriman deigned to explain, "It's not that he hasn't got any money. It's just that he hasn't got any available. He'll never have any available. People like him never do and never will. Money just slips through their hands, like a piece of wet soap, it you take my meaning. It wouldn't happen to a servant or a workingman. Only to a gentleman."

"Why is that, Mr. Merriman?"

"It's in the nature of things, and there's nothing can be done about it."

Carrying the bucket, bottle, and glasses on a tray, Merriman creaked away. Starr gave Mary a wink.

"Don't you listen to old gloom, Mary. People like the Major have their ups and downs, that's all. One day soon you'll probably find he'll be so flush he'll be taking a whole set of rooms, 'stead of just one, and buying himself a string of racehorses into the bargain. We've seen 'em, haven't we, Fred?"

As arranged, Charles Tyrrell's entire apartments were given a thorough spring-cleaning in his absence. Mary did most of the work, but Louisa felt impelled to look in often, in her extraproprietorial capacity.

One early May morning, when the sun was shining warmly and birds could be heard plainly above the street noises, Mary entered Charles's sitting room, both arms draped with freshly laundered net curtains. She was surprised to see Mrs. Trotter standing at the piano keyboard, pensively picking out notes with one forefinger. There was a dejected droop to her shoulders, which for weeks now had seemed so resolutely squared.

"Sorry, ma'am," Mary said, conscious of having interrupted a reverie. "I thought I'd get Mr. Tyrrell's curtains back up again."

"All right, Mary," Louisa said. She seemed to come to some decision. "Look, just put them down a minute and come and sit down here."

She indicated the settee. Mary carefully draped the curtains over chair arms and obeyed gingerly.

"I'm going to have a baby," Louisa told her abruptly.

The maid couldn't prevent her lips parting and her mouth opening.

"Oh, Lor' . . . ma'am!"

"I been round the doctor's, and I'm nine weeks gone. Oh, don't look so po-faced, girl. I'm sure even in Wales people make mistakes sometimes."

"But . . . but what are you going to do, ma'am?"

"Have it, of course!"

"But . . ."

"Look, I'm not having anyone doing me in, messing about with dirty knitting needles, and I hope you wasn't going to suggest it. Anyway, I happen to believe if God makes a baby He has a reason, and you have to lump it. It'll be all right for a while yet. Then when it begins to show I'll go off somewhere. I'll cut out all the outside cooking that Mrs. Wellkin can't manage, and you'll just have to run this place."

"Oh, but I couldn't, ma'am. I never could."

"You will, by the time I've finished with you. And no one's ever to know about it 'cept you and me."

Mary stared again. "Not even . . ."

"No. Not even him. You won't tell no one. Swear on it!"

There was such vehemence in the way she said it that Mary, who was no Catholic, fumbled the sign of the cross over her breast and hastily promised, "Cross my heart and hope to die . . . ma'am."

In the days following Louisa proceeded to put Mary through a strict, secret course of management and bookkeeping. What the little Welsh girl lacked—which was a good deal—in education and to a lesser degree in brightness, she made up for in willingness and utter devotion to her mistress.

"The credit's bigger than the debit," Louisa explained again, pointing to figures in an account book, "so you subtract the debit."

Mary struggled mentally for some seconds then said tentatively, "That makes eleven pounds and fivepence three farthings."

"Good girl. That's profit, and not bad for one day." She produced the cashbox from the middle drawer of her parlor desk.

"I keep the cash in here, locked up. Always. When there's enough, take it round to the bank in St. James's Street."

"Excuse me, ma'am. What's 'enough'?"

"When it's so heavy that you need both hands to carry it. Now, next page. Tomorrow's Friday, so we pay all them bills. That lot there. Make a list of 'em, and tick 'em off as paid. As to letters, you want to answer all of 'em the same day they come. That way it's more polite. Especially people inquiring about rooms and that."

Mary looked from the pile of bills on their spike to that morning's mail, comprising at least two dozen envelopes, some of them bearing coats of arms. She blew out her cheeks at the prospect of such responsibility.

"How will I ever tell if they're the right sort of people?" she asked. "I mean, not being a snob like you, ma'am."

Louisa took no offense at the term. She knew it was meant in a complimentary sense.

"There's ways of telling," she said, picking up the first letter on the pile and ripping it open crudely with her thumb. She scanned it briefly.

"A Mister Worthington-Jones," she said. "See that book there—*Who's Who*. You look 'em up in there first. Even if they are in, they mightn't be the right sort, and if they're not in, they might. But it's somewhere to start. Worthington-Jones. Maybe Jones, with the Worthington tacked on for luck. But it's nice paper. Handmade and white. Never trust colored papers. And the address is printed from a plate—engraved. Feel that. Common people wouldn't go for that."

"I see," Mary said, marveling. "But supposing I write back, thanking him for his . . ."

"Esteemed inquiry."

"Yes. But when he turns up I still don't know if he's right or wrong."

"You can always ask Starr or Merriman. They'll have a fair idea. Watch whether the dog's hair bristles. Or, if you're really in trouble, try Major Whiskers."

"He may not be here by then, may he, ma'am?"

"He'll be here all right. I reckon, like the poor, he'll always be with us," Louisa said.

A few more months went by. Charles wrote dutifully from America, but he had little good news to convey. His father was referred to one distinguished medical man after another and resigned himself to beginning yet another new type of treatment at the hands of each. As always, there was optimism at first, hopeful signs, then setback and final capitulation. It became clear that the strain was telling on the old man's general constitution. He was too frail to be brought back to England. Charles had not the heart to leave him and his mother in a strange land, and return home; and as it began to be apparent that the Earl's life itself was becoming endangered his son saw it as his duty, not only out of love, but as heir, to stay on.

Louisa missed him, but understood, and put all her thought and energies into running her dual business and training Mary. Then the time came when she could go on no longer. Letting it be known generally that she was feeling a bit strained and so would go into the country for the long rest she had never had chance to enjoy, she slipped out of London, telling no one but Mary where she was going. It never even occurred to her to confide in her parents. A week later she read in a newspaper of the death in the United States of the Earl of Haslemere. The widow and the new Earl, the report read, would be accompanying the late Earl's coffin to England and the funeral would take place in the parish church of the family estate.

Charlie wrote personally to Louisa to tell her the news, and his letter was forwarded to her by Mary. At least the knowledge that he would be traveling about a good deal, and much preoccupied, gave her the welcome excuse not to write back.

One autumn morning Major Smith-Barton looked up from *The Times* in the hall of the Bentinck, where he liked to sit and watch the coming and going, and saw Charles stride in through the door. He wore mourning and his face showed strain.

"Charlie, my dear fellow!" the Major hailed him. "How splendid to see you again."

Charles's face lit up with genuine pleasure as he came over to shake hands.

"My goodness, we've all missed you," the Major declared.

"Well, thank you. I've missed this place, too. My word, it seems to be fairly buzzing."

The hall was very busy indeed, with several people at the desk being dealt with by Starr and cabmen bringing in and taking out luggage.

"Oh yes, going splendidly. Always full up with an awfully good lot of people," the Major said. "I, er, say, Charlie, I was very sorry to see about your father."

"Yes," Charlie said. "It's been pretty grim. In the end, quite frankly, it was a merciful release. But I'll ask you to excuse me just now, Major. Got rather a lot to do."

He nodded and went away toward the stairs, where he encountered Merriman, coming down with a tray.

full of the debris of a meal and looking rather flustered.

"Hello, Merriman," he greeted him. "You well?"

"Fairish, sir . . . m'lord, I mean. Middling, you might say in the circumstances."

"Well, as soon as circumstances permit, be a good fellow and bring a bottle of wine to Mrs. Trotter's room, will you."

"Mrs. Trotter's, m'lord? But she's not here, you know."

"Not here? No, I didn't."

"Beg pardon, m'lord. I thought you'd have known somehow. Been away a few weeks now."

"Where?"

"Holiday, sir. All the work getting her down at last, you know. Said she didn't want to risk another go like that last one, so she decided to get a good rest."

Charles's surprise and concern changed to relief.

"Well, I'm certainly glad to hear that," he said. "Perhaps her letter missed me. These past weeks have been pretty hectic. Who's running things in the meantime, then?"

"Mrs. Wellkin's keeping up the cookery end—though it's been cut down a lot for the time being—and Miss Philips looks after the hotel."

"Miss Philips?"

"Mary, m'lord. A real little treasure that girl is. If you'll excuse me, m'lord, they'll be getting impatient in Number Eight if I don't get their Madeira."

Charles nodded dismissal and Merriman tottered off toward the dispense. Instead of going on upstairs Charles turned and went into Louisa's parlor. Mary looked up from Louisa's desk, stared for a moment, then pushed herself to her feet by the chair arms.

"Mr. . . . Lord Haslemere!" she gasped. "We wasn't expecting you back. Your . . . your rooms aren't all ready yet. I mean, it'll take a couple of days to air them out properly . . ."

Charles smiled reassuringly. "It's all right, Mary. I'm only passing through London. I called in to . . . What's all this about Mrs. Trotter, then?"

He had read nothing untoward in Merriman's impassive features, but he detected at once the aura of embarrassment about this girl, and noted how she looked away, and fumbled with her fingers.

"It . . . it was all the work, m'lord . . . and her nerves was getting a bit bad . . . and the doctor . . ."

"Doctor? As bad as that?"

Mary bit her lip. The reference had slipped out.

"He said she ought to go away for a while. We . . . was all glad she agreed. We've been managing very well, m'lord."

"Where is she?" he asked casually.

Her difficulty in answering was obvious to him.

"I don't know, m'lord. I mean, not for sure. Somewhere on the coast . . ."

"Which coast?"

"Well . . . she said she might travel about a bit."

Charles said sharply, "Mary—I want to know where Mrs. Trotter is."

His face was hard and his usually smiling eyes had a strange light in them which made her frightened.

"I swore I wouldn't tell anyone," she begged. "She made me swear, m'lord."

He brushed past her to the desk. Among the bills, invoices, and other papers on its top was his own letter to Louisa telling her he would be in London for the day and calling in. The hotel address had been crossed out and beside it had been written in ink, presumably by Mary, "Three Aspen Villas, Weston-super-Mare, Somerset."

"All right," Charles said kindly. "You were doing as you were told."

He picked up the letter, pocketed it, and left the room.

A few hours later he was outside the little private

lodging house in the seaside town. The wind was chilly off the sea and autumn leaves were on the pavements and in the gutters. From the path up to the door he could see her, sitting in a small glassed-in conservatory. A shawl was around her shoulders, which seemed unusually hunched, and she appeared to be staring into space. She didn't see him approach.

The front door was held open by an iron doorstop. Another door led off it to the left into the conservatory, behind Louisa's back. Charles opened this door and stepped inside.

"Is she all right, Betty?" Louisa asked without turning.

"That," said Charlie, "is what I was going to ask."

She jumped violently and twisted around.

"Oh crikey!" she exclaimed. "You didn't half give me a turn!"

He gave her a long, tender kiss, then sat down in a wicker chair beside hers.

"Sorry about your poor old dad," she said. "So you're Lord Haslemere now, eh?"

He ignored both remarks, but said quietly, "So it's a girl, is it?"

She looked defiantly at him for a moment, seeming about to challenge him, but then said flatly, "I'll kill that Mary."

Charles produced the readdressed envelope.

"Not her fault. I found this."

"I see. And then I s'pose you wrung it all out of her about the ... baby?"

He shook his head. "I worked it out for myself. It's three hours in the train down here from town. Plenty of time to think. You left the hotel just when things were getting really busy. That didn't sound like the Louisa Trotter I used to know. She wouldn't have left the place even if she was dying ... unless she had something to hide. That, and counting up how many months it's been since ... Well, it didn't need a Sherlock Holmes to deduce what it was."

"I haven't been too clever, have I," she admitted. "Do they all know now?"

"No one else. You didn't think I would?"

He took her hands in both of his and asked fondly, "Was it a bad time?"

"Bit rough," she nodded.

"But why didn't you tell me, Louisa?"

"Because it's none of your business, that's why," she retorted with a return of her characteristic spirit. "It's my mess and I got to clear it up."

"God, you are pigheaded sometimes. None of my business! How can you say anything so idiotic?"

"For pity's sake, it's *not your fault*. Men were born to chase after women or there wouldn't be no human race, would there? And women have to watch out, or they cop it. I broke me own rules. I knew what I was doing. . . ."

She broke off, looked fondly at him, and suddenly smiled.

"It's a nice little baby," she said. "Very healthy. And no trouble—like her ma."

"You really thought you'd get away with it?" he wondered.

"I nearly did, clean and clever. Another week."

"Then what were you going to do?"

"I've been trying to work it out. Was doing when you crep' in just now. Whatever happens, she'll be looked after proper. Never lack for nothing."

"Except a mother and a father," he reminded her.

"You didn't have to say that, Charlie."

"I think I did. I want you to marry me."

They just sat there for some long seconds, holding hands and searching one another's eyes. Then Louisa said, "You're a real gentleman, Charlie. But you don't have to do the decent thing, not this time."

"I love you, you silly woman."

They heard the baby cry in another room, and a girl's voice making comforting sounds to it. Louisa jerked her head in the direction.

"Would you have asked me to marry you if it hadn't been for her?"

It was a question he couldn't answer honestly without hurting her, and one he knew he must not lie about.

"It's not a fair question," he compromised.

Louisa recognized his dilemma and solved it for him.

"It's the greatest compliment I'm likely to be paid in my little life. I appreciate it, Charlie, I do really. But, you see, you're Lord Haslemere and I'm Louisa Trotter. Oh, I know how many chorus girls has married the nobility and all that. But quite honestly, I'm not cut out to be a wife—anyone's wife. Never have been."

He was going to interrupt, but she went on.

"I mean, that baby . . . It's a nice enough little baby. But I don't love it. It could be anyone's, for all I'm concerned. I don't know why. I can't help the way I am. So, you see, I wouldn't be no good as Lady Haslemere, either. Best left as Louisa Trotter. You do see, Charlie, love? It's best to be honest about things."

He nodded. Against his inclinations, he knew she was right.

"It was a wonderful thing we had together," she said, "and I shan't never forget it. Never. But it's all over, Charlie. So we might as well frame it and then we'll always have it handy to look back on. Cheer us up when things is bad."

"Perhaps you'll change your mind, Louisa. Women get depressed after having babies, don't they?"

She shook her head. "I've not been too depressed. Not really, except the quiet of this place. Like a cemetery with seagulls. All I want is to get back to noisy old London—and my hotel."

He sighed, but smiled and gave a shrug of surrender.

"That sounds like the old Louisa talking," he said in

a relieved tone. "But listen—would you mind, please, if I took charge of the baby? Responsibility for it?"

"You? But how could you? I mean, what'd your ma...?"

"I can arrange everything perfectly discreetly. As a matter of fact, we'd be doing a kindness to someone else into the bargain."

"How? Who?"

"One of the grooms and his wife on the estate have just lost their own baby. They're dreadfully upset, and they're an awfully nice, decent couple. If you'd agree, Louisa..."

Suddenly, she saw the future clear ahead again. It needed no consideration to tell her that this was the heaven-sent solution.

"Yes, Charlie. Yes, I will. Thanks for being so good to me... for it all...."

He kissed her long and hard, then got up, raising her from her own chair by her hands.

"Now take me to see her," he said.

"Morning, Starr. Morning, Fred," Major Smith-Barton greeted the porter and his dog a few days later.

"Morning, sir," Starr responded. "No one's speaking to Fred, though."

He indicated the animal's collar, twined with colored ribbons. "Got him all dolled up ready to greet Mrs. Trotter coming back this morning, and what does he do but go absent without leave. Some lady friend down St. James's Square, you ask me."

"Devil with the ladies, eh, Fred?" the Major asked. "Anyway, she's back at the helm, is she?"

"Yes, sir. And she sends her compliments, and would you be good enough to see her in her room as soon as you came down."

The Major's face fell. He nodded, squared his shoulders, and went off to Louisa's door.

"Poor old Major Whiskers," Starr confided to Fred, when the door had opened and closed. "He hasn't had a bad run for no money, though."

Louisa had thanked the Major for his expression of welcome and asked him to sit down. She had one of the hotel's billheads in front of her and he could see his name at the top. There was much writing on the paper, and many figures, and two more sheets were clipped underneath.

"When I came back to see your bill still unpaid I couldn't hardly believe my eyes," Louisa said. There was no concession to his feelings in her tone of voice.

"I really am most dreadfully sorry, dear lady," he said. "Thought I'd best to wait till you got back and explain, don't you know?"

"Can't live on tick all your life, can you?" she said unrelentingly.

"No, no. Matter of fact, though, I'm expecting a draft any day now. Confounded things always seem to come in arrear. Tell you what, I'll pop down to the bank again this morning. Ask 'em to . . ."

"Come off it, Major," Louisa said, tapping the bill. "Any draft you get goes straight on the ponies. I believe if you had a real win you'd pay up . . ."

"Believe me . . ."

". . . Only it's a mug's game, and you ought to know it. Well, I do, and I'm sorry, but this hotel isn't run as a charitable organization for the bookies. Not no more."

The Major nodded hopelessly.

"You all been so jolly kind to me here. Rather dug in now. I . . . I just wish I could think of some way of . . . of making it up to you."

For the first time Louisa smiled.

"*I* can, Major," she said, getting up.

That afternoon a party of new arrivals entered the hall of the Bentinck. They were an elderly country peer and his middle-aged, grande dame of a wife. A lady's maid followed, bearing a jewel case and her mistress's personal bag. A coachman deposited some luggage in front of the desk.

"Afternoon, m'lord. Afternoon, m'lady," greeted Starr, who was already acquainted with them from one of his previous situations. He turned and beckoned with a raised forefinger. From across the hall, where he had been standing beside the porter's chair, Major Smith-Barton, D.S.O., marched briskly forward and grasped the baggage.

"Hullo, Henry," he greeted the astonished peer. "Anthea. Splendid to see you again. Hope you're both well?"

"Y . . . yes. Very."

"Jolly good. Just follow me, then."

As they proceeded up the stairs, Louisa, who had come to the door of her parlor, heard the Major asking, "Put up here before ever?"

"No, no. Just a short visit to town. Not worth opening up the place in Belgrave Square."

"Quite right. Couldn't do better than here. First-class place. Wonderful cooking. I hear there's a fine lot of partridges in Norfolk this season. . . ."

Louisa smiled. Then she smiled again to see Charlie come through the front door.

"Hello, Starr. Hello, Fred," he said, patting the dog, who gave him a lick of familiarity. "Celebrating Mrs. Trotter's return, I see."

"Yes, m'lord. Fred and I're highly delighted at her recovery."

"And so am I. Ah, Merriman, a bottle of wine in Mrs. Trotter's room, if you please."

"With pleasure, m'lord. Welcome back, m'lord."

Louisa went into the room. Charles followed. They remained standing.

Each could sense the difficulty of the moment.

"I'm glad you've come back," she said at length.

He went over and kissed her, gently and chastely.

"But of course I have," he said. "This is my home."

Part II

The Golden Years

Seventeen

The return of Charlie Tyrrell, now Lord Haslemere, to permanent residence at the Bentinck Hotel commenced a period of stability in Louisa Trotter's life of a kind she had not known since leaving her parents' home to make her independent way in the world.

In the few years since 1900, it seemed to her, on the rare occasions when she thought about it, that she had gone through a range of experience that no other London girl of lower-middle-class origins could have matched. From being an apprentice cook under a *chef de cuisine* who had at first done his best to deter her from that trade, she had become established as the best freelance cook in London. From working in the kitchens of people who employed her to cook, she now employed others to do so in her own kitchen in the Bentinck.

And then, of all things, she'd remind herself with wonder and some distaste, she'd gone and had a baby by Charlie Tyrrell. The infant had never known her, and she had scarcely known it. A twinge of conscience pricked her, but only occasionally; the poor little thing would get a far better bringing-up where it was than in a hotel in the heart of London's West End.

After the offer of marriage from Charlie, there were no more romantic passages between them. It had been a single, unexpected escapade that had left no regrets on either side. He continued to maintain his set of rooms in the Bentinck, living in them when he was in London and referring to them as home. He went about town as much as ever, enjoying bachelorhood as long as he could before duty to his family line would inevitably terminate it. He entertained women of his own class, mostly other men's wives, in his rooms, and Louisa cooked for them. She felt no jealousy. What he did with his life was none of her affair; but she was always glad to have him on the premises: a cheerful, affectionate, handsome friend.

So, with all these intrusions over, she settled down to her avowed task of making the Bentinck the best hotel in London. It wasn't the biggest by far. It wasn't the grandest. But an extensive word-of-mouth had it that it was the most comfortable and easygoing, and that the food was superb.

All the rooms were now occupied. Some were in the form of apartments, large enough for a family and a servant, who might stay for weeks. Some were merely simple single rooms, mostly used by officers, businessmen, and other transitory people, who would often leave a few belongings in the hotel's care for use whenever they might happen to be passing by again. A year or more might elapse between these visitations, but the guest would always find his needs anticipated, his preferences remembered, his aversions avoided. Once Louisa became attached to her guests—individuals or families—she made certain that they lacked nothing they desired. If she took a dislike to anyone, though, that person would assuredly never find a vacancy at the Bentinck again.

She herself made no effort to change. There was no attempt to learn to speak "proper" or acquire any of the many graces she lacked. She could afford to dress well, and did, and to be generous with champagne, which she was, and to be magnanimous toward any of her favorites, who, through brief or prolonged financial setback, could not manage to pay their bills.

But, basically, she was what she was, and people had to accept her as abrasive, impulsive, outspoken, rough-tongued—she would not hesitate to address a titled person in the vernacular she used among the stall-holders at Covent Garden. She had her own set of values and they stood her in good stead. Experience and shrewd observation had taught this sharp-witted, determined, and ever-ambitious girl, still in her twenties, that the quality of people could be judged just as accurately as that of any vegetable or cut of meat, once you knew the points to watch for.

Louisa was not what all men would call beautiful, but she possessed a charisma which made her attractive to many. A few who made approaches, not knowing her, were sharply taken aback as soon as she opened her mouth. Her speech had nothing at all in common with her looks or the expense of her dresses. The few who, aware of this, still fancied their chances, were swiftly disabused. She didn't take offense, except on one or two occasions. More likely, she would turn the proposition into an excuse for some rather coarse ribbing and would then assuage her suitor's embarrassment with the best champagne.

In a way, then, she was an eccentric: a woman unique to most who met her. A few were repelled and passed her hastily by. Many more were amused and attracted, though, and Louisa's personality became to them the chief magnetic force of the Bentinck. They admired her for her lack of assumed airs and graces, reveled in her bouts of outrageousness, and, in time of distress or perplexity, knew that her earthy sympathy and wisdom would be unstintedly at their disposal.

And so, for the couple of years since the new Lord Haslemere had moved back into permanent residence, the Bentinck had continued to prosper. Louisa still undertook outside cooking engagements, though she was able to be more and more selective now, and left most of the work to Mary Philips and the new cook, Mrs. Cochrane, who had replaced Mrs. Wellkin.

Now, in the summer of 1904, Louisa Trotter, *née* Leyton, was a contented young woman. She was still young, though heading for her thirties now, an age at which many women begin to look more searchingly at themselves in mirrors, and, if unattached, feel some symptoms of panic. Not so Louisa. If there was anything else she wanted, she didn't know what it was. From now on she would be content to live from day to day, letting each bring its problems, surprises, amusements, dramas, rewards. There would always be some new excitement to contend with.

Starr came from behind the hall desk to attend to a young man who had just come through the swing doors from the street and was glancing about in obvious unfamiliarity with the surroundings. The newcomer was strikingly handsome with a foreign look to him and his clothing, a gray overcoat with an astrakhan collar. But when he answered Starr's inquiry as to whether he might help him, the gentleman spoke with only the faintest trace of an accent. His English was perfect, almost to the point of overcorrectness.

"Are you Starr, by any chance?"

Starr was surprised. The dog Fred merely looked interested; he had evinced no signs of like or animosity.

"Yes, sir."

"I thought so. I am Baron Oppendorf. Lord Haslemere told me all about you. He said I am to trust you in everything except your advice on horses."

Starr smiled with gratification and Fred wagged his tail.

"If you wouldn't mind waiting here one moment, sir, I'm sure Mrs. Trotter would like to welcome you personally and show you to his lordship's rooms. She's been looking forward to you coming."

The Baron nodded and Starr went away to Louisa's

parlor, returning almost at once, to say, "Excuse me, sir, Mrs. Trotter would very much like to welcome you in her room. If you'd kindly step this way."

In Louisa's parlor the Baron bent over her hand. "My dear Mrs. Trotter," he said, "this is indeed a pleasure."

"It's nice to have you, Baron," she replied warmly. Any friend of Charlie's was automatically an instant friend of hers. "How long will you be staying?"

"Oh, a few days. Perhaps a week. I have come over especially for important conferences—with my tailor and my shirtmaker."

Louisa laughed. This was the kind of free-and-easy talk she liked to hear. Nothing arrogant; merely nonchalant self-assurance. It was a quality Charlie himself possessed. And, like him, this man was agreeable to look at and knew his manners.

"I'll show you to Lord Haslemere's rooms," she said. "How is he?"

"In the very best of health. He sends you his kindest regards. Since he saved the old Marchese Fantucci from drowning, when her carriage went careering into the harbor, he is the toast of Monte Carlo . . ."

He was startled to hear a voice, in a thick American accent, say from apparently nowhere, "Monte Carlo? Who said Monte Carlo?"

From the depths of a wing chair a male figure struggled into sight. It was that of a thickset, middle-aged man, who got to his feet with a little difficulty, burdened as he was with a jeroboam of champagne in one hand and a glass in the other. The vast bottle was half-empty, the Baron noticed—and a jeroboam holds not less than four quarts of wine. He was not surprised that the man swayed a little.

"Don't mind him," Louisa was saying. "He's only a senator. Hey, Senator, meet Baron . . . Baron Oppitoff."

The Baron grinned and didn't trouble to correct her. Charlie Haslemere had told him plenty about Louisa's ways. The Senator, after pausing to consider how to manage things, succeeded in placing the bottle on the carpet and came forward, hand outstretched.

"Honored to make your acquaintance, Baron," he said. "Deeply honored."

"Well?" Louisa admonished him. "Aren't you going to offer the Baron a drink?"

"Indeed, I am! Must have a drink from my very first . . . what's it called, Mrs. Trotter, ma'am?"

"Cherrybum," Louisa answered wickedly.

"That's right," he said gravely. "My first cherrybum. A real live cherrybum for a real live genuine baron."

With difficulty, and a good deal of assistance from the others, he dispensed drinks for them all. They toasted one another and chatted convivially for a quarter of an hour, until Louisa firmly packed the Senator and his jeroboam off to his room, while she showed the new arrival to Lord Haslemere's suite, where he found that Starr had already placed his baggage, fetched from his cab.

Late that night, Starr yawned at the desk and looked at the time. Fred was already asleep in his little basket under the counter. The timeless Merriman came shuffling down the stairs.

"More for Number Three?" Starr anticipated.

The waiter nodded. "Whisky, after all that champagne. The American gent appears to have hollow legs."

"Better his head than mine in the morning," Starr said. "What're he and the Baron doing up there?"

"Playing solo poker. And the American's using marked cards."

Merriman moved off to the dispense. Starr prodded Fred gently with his boot.

"Come on, old son," he said gently to the yawning terrier. "Christen your lamppost for the last time, and then we'll shut up shop and go to bed."

Yawning man and yawning dog went out into the summer warmth of the street, still busy with cabs and carriages, fashionable strollers, noisy young bloods and urgent prostitutes.

Upstairs in the Bentinck, in Lord Haslemere's sitting room, the Senator and the Baron were concentrating seriously on their game. Empty whisky glasses were at their elbows and a half-empty soda siphon was on hand. Paul Oppendorf had quite a stack of banknotes beside him. A smaller pile lay before the Senator. Paul appeared to be having the best of things.

"Raise you ten," he said.

The Senator shot him a glance of apprehension, then frowned over his own hand for some moments before saying hesitantly, "Double you."

Paul said promptly, "I'll see you."

Merriman entered with a fresh bottle of whisky and more soda as the Senator spread out his cards on the green baize tabletop. The Baron peered at them. "Oh, you have a flush. Is that right?"

"No, no, Baron. Three queens and two tens. A full house, queens high."

"Ah, I see," the Baron said, showing his own hand. "Then you are too good for me, I think."

The Senator leaned over to look. "'Fraid so," he said, scooping up the stake money. "About time, though. You had me worried there."

"Beginner's luck, I suppose," the Baron said resignedly. "Thank you, Merriman. I'm sure this is all we shall need tonight."

The old man nodded and withdrew. He recognized perfectly well the real game that was being played. The American had been allowing his opponent to win steadily, giving him confidence to put down higher and higher stakes. Before they were through with that new bottle of whisky, he knew, all that money would be on the Senator's side of the table, and maybe an I.O.U. as well.

"A few hands of bezique and a game of piquet with my old great-aunt, the Princess . . . That's about all the cards that are allowed in my family," the Baron told his guest. "I like this game. It's good of you to teach it to me. Oh, please help yourself, Senator."

The American poured himself neat whisky and passed the bottle over to the other, who poured carefully for himself and added a good deal of soda. The Senator, while far from being drunk, despite having achieved the ambition of finishing off the jeroboam, was in rather less than full control of his tongue. He became confidential.

"I'm not a real senator, you know, Baron. That's just one of Mrs. Trotter's wry little jokes. My name's Croker. Collis C. Croker."

Paul rose to his feet. He lurched as he did and clutched at the table edge to steady himself. Then he stood swaying as they shook hands. If he had not had the best part of a gallon of champagne and more than half a bottle of whisky inside him, the American might have noted that his drinking partner suddenly seemed to have become affected strangely. In truth, Paul was not affected at all. He had sensed a change in the wind of circumstance, and it seemed better to act the part while it continued to blow.

"I am . . . delighted to make your acquaintance, Mr. Crocker . . . Croker," he said thickly.

"Call me Collis, eh?"

"Collis."

"I'm gratified," the Senator said gravely. "I'm just a country boy from Cedar Rapids, Iowa. Made my pile canning beef. Chicago. 'C.C.C., the Best Beef there BE!' Expect you've heard of it."

"Oh, but naturally. All over Europe."

Collis C. Croker beamed. "C.C.C. That's me."

"Very successful."

"Sure. Only one thing wrong with my life, Baron."

"What is that?"

"My wife. She's been took religious. She's took religious and she's took against drink. Nearly ruined my life. Had to invent this trip to Europe just to save my sanity."

The Baron tut-tutted and poured his friend another neat whisky. It went unnoticed that he added nothing to his own glass.

"Say, Baron, you don't mind if I ask what you do?"

"Do?"

"For a living?"

The aristocratic eyebrows were raised high with surprise.

"My dear chap, I do nothing for a living. None of my family has, that I have ever heard of. Not for several hundred years, at any rate. You see, we have always had big estates in Bohemia and Thuringia. Money and commerce are things we never mention at home." He raised a deprecatory hand. "Oh, of course my family must have had to amass money at some time. Everyone who is rich must have had ancestors who made fortunes in the past. Or rather, not so much made them as won them—the gift of kings and emperors for battles fought victoriously, for fleets of ships captured laden with treasure."

The Senator was shaking his head in undisguised wonderment. The Baron took a pull at his glass, contriving, however, not to let any of the whisky actually pass his lips. He continued, "In fact, I can only think of one of my forebears who made money. My great-great-uncle Philip. He did literally make money."

"Well, I guess even in the richest families, there's always one guy who . . ."

"No, no, no, no. I mean, he actually *made* money."

The Senator goggled, as well as his by now impaired vision would allow.

"You mean—he had a . . . a mint, of his own?"

The Baron contrived a grim smile. "I think . . . Collis . . . it's a story better hidden in the mists of time. Not a very creditable chapter in my family's history. I should never have alluded to it."

But the American was totally intrigued by now. He leaned his elbows on the baize.

"Look, Baron. I won't think any worse of you, or of your family. I've sailed pretty close to the wind once or twice myself."

Paul returned the Senator's waveringly intense gaze for some moments. Then he shrugged, took a cigar from his case, pierced it, and lit it carefully. At last he said, "Well, toward the end of the eighteenth century it became clear to my great-great-uncle Philip that the foreman on one of his estates had hired a young man with a genius for invention. My great-great-uncle Philip, being a philanthropic sort of man, sent the boy to study in Vienna, where he quickly astonished his professors with his inventions. One of them was a machine for reproducing paper money. A sort of . . . magic box."

The Senator whistled. "That's a useful kind of toy! I wish people could still make toys like that. Anyway, it probably would seem pretty crude work nowadays."

"Oh no it doesn't."

" 'Doesn't'? You mean . . ."

"The machine still exists," Paul nodded.

"Gee! Somewhere on the Continent?"

"As a matter of fact, no. It's here in London. Safe in a vault. You see, my family acquired it. It passed to me from my late father. On his deathbed he made me promise always to take it with me, wherever I might go. He himself put it into my hands."

Moved by more than one sort of reverence, the Senator said, "What I'd give to see it. You . . . you couldn't . . . No, of course not."

"What?"

"Allow me the very special privilege of just seeing it—once."

The Baron appeared shocked. He shook his head.

"It is a matter of strict principles. You understand what I mean?"

"I guess so. It's just that, well, to see something so historic—unique, in fact—why, that would really cap my trip to Europe. I guess I could even face my wife again after that."

Paul laughed. "Collis, I like you. You're open. I trust you."

"Thanks, Baron. May I say, on my part, I feel a bond of friendship has already been forged between us."

His young companion seemed to reach a sudden decision. "All right. If it would really amuse you so much, I'll bring it here the day after tomorrow."

"To . . . to this very room?"

"Strictly for your eyes alone, you understand."

"I'd be most deeply honored, sir."

The American's eyes looked regretfully at the pile of money on the other side of the table. If they hadn't spent so much time chatting, it would have been added to his own by now. Still, there was bound to be another encounter. Perhaps more than one. And if money was no object to this amiable young fellow . . .

But he merely indicated the whisky bottle. "Mind if I take a little of this along with me? Just a settler for the night."

"Take the bottle, my dear chap. I shan't be requiring any more."

Two mornings later, "Senator" Collis C. Croker went eagerly to Lord Haslemere's suite, where his new friend, the Baron, welcomed him affably. To the Senator's regret, the Baron had not been visible all the previous day and evening. At least one chance to win back his poker losses had passed by; but he had further, greater expectations.

"You've got the machine?" he whispered, although they were behind the closed door now. Paul nodded.

The Senator felt relief. He had half expected that, in a more sober mood, the Baron would have reversed his decision. However, Paul's expression was serious as he said, "I must ask you to give me your word that everything you see or hear in this room in the next few minutes will go no further than these walls."

"Surely I will, sir."

The Baron went to unlock a lacquered chinoiserie cupboard. From one of its many compartments he drew out the magic box. It was quite small and plain, of polished wood, with no obvious gadgetry revealed, apart from some small brass dials and a plunger. There were three little drawers and a keyhole. The Senator did not presume to touch it, but contented himself with peering keenly at it.

"Beautiful piece of work," he said.

"Isn't it? And here is one of the first notes the boy made with it."

The Baron was holding out a beautifully designed old Austrian banknote. The Senator took it and examined it closely. It was flawlessly printed. He handed it back.

"How many of these boxes did that young fellow make?"

"Only this one. Shortly after the boy made it he ... he met with a fatal accident, arranged, some say, by my great-great-uncle. You see, philanthropist though he was, he was also a practical man, who believed that for the good of mankind, there are some people who are better dead than alive. If many of these boxes had been produced and fallen into unscrupulous hands ... Well, you can imagine the fiscal chaos which might have ensued—throughout the whole world, even."

"I guess your uncle had his head screwed on the right way," the Senator nodded.

"Even now," the Baron continued, "the responsibility of its custodianship is a constant worry to me. Wherever I go—and I am a widely traveled man—it must go, too. It only requires me to be careless once and leave a lock unsecured, or suffer some little forgetfulness, and . . ." He shrugged significantly. "I suppose it should be kept in some bank vault, but what is the point of that? If it is never to see the light of day again, it might just as well be destroyed. In fact, I have considered . . ."

"No, no!" the American begged hastily, obviously alarmed. "Not that!"

Paul shrugged again. After a few more moments' contemplation of the intriguing object, the Senator said, "Why not donate it to some scientific museum. So that all the world could admire it, without any danger of its being put to the wrong use?"

He waited for the Baron to consider this. The answer at length was, "No, no. It was entrusted to me, and I feel it my duty to honor that trust, however much trouble it costs me."

"Well, I respect you for that, Baron. In any case, maybe it wouldn't even work anymore, so there's no real risk."

"Oh, but it does. It's in perfect working order. Naturally, I have only used it a very few times, simply to amuse my friends."

The Senator swallowed. "I suppose . . . You wouldn't count me enough of a friend to . . . to give me the great privilege of a demonstration?"

Paul studied him for some moments, not condescendingly, but as if needing to struggle hard with his own judgment. At last he smiled and said, "Why not?"

The Senator barely restrained himself from rubbing his hands with glee. In his most serious tone he said, "I'm deeply honored, Baron. Both to be counted so close a friend, and . . ." Emotion almost overcame him. He managed to add, "I swear solemnly not to reveal this to a living soul."

Paul was opening one of the little drawers in the machine and taking out some blank slips of paper of various sizes.

"Might I trouble you," he asked, "for the loan of a note? Any denomination. Preferably little used."

Collis C. Croker's wallet was out swiftly and a freshly minted ten-pound note handed over. The Baron held it against two or three of the slips of blank paper until he found one which exactly matched its size. Then he handed the note back, saying, "Please be so good as to write down the serial number of your note. I assure you no harm will come to your money."

From opposite sides of the machine he pulled out two more drawers. Into one he placed the banknote; into the other went the blank. He closed the drawers. Then he took out his key chain, selected a small key, inserted it in the keyhole of the machine, and began to wind carefully.

"Of course, the secret of how it works died with its inventor. The mechanism is activated by clockwork. The process takes twelve hours precisely. So . . ."—he carried the machine carefully back to its cupboard—"we will leave it in peace, and I hope you will pay me another visit this evening?"

"Surely! I don't know how I'll stand the waiting."

"Well, we could pass the first half an hour or so of it by having a drink, if it isn't too early for you."

But the Senator, for whom no time was too early for a drink, for once declined. "If you'll pardon me, Baron, I have to be off to a luncheon engagement. Till this evening, though."

Paul locked the door and returned to the cupboard in which his magic box lay. He took it out, slid out one of the drawers, and extracted the ten-pound note. He put the machine away again and carried the note to his desk top. From a drawer of the desk the took out a leather case of a size and shape which might have suited it for carrying surgical instruments. It did, in fact, contain instruments, surgical in appearance but not intended for that purpose. It also held a pair of thin gloves and a jeweler's eyeglass.

Paul took out his own wallet and examined all the

ten-pound notes it contained. Most of them he had won from the American in their poker game. He had noted then that they were a freshly minted batch, obviously just withdrawn from a bank. As he had expected, their numbers belonged to the same series. It did not take him long to find one whose number differed by only one digit from that which Croker had lent him.

Also from his instrument case Paul extracted a piece of ground glass, clipped into its lid. He put this on his desk in front of him and over it, side by side, the two banknotes. Then he donned the gloves, screwed the eyeglass into his right eye, selected one of the instruments, which he dipped into one of several phials of different-colored liquids—and, with infinite care and a rock-steady hand, he proceeded to alter that one digit in the second note's serial number to correspond with its fellow on the other. When he had finished, no one but an expert could have detected the forgery.

Eighteen

Exactly twelve hours after he had left Baron Oppendorf's suite, Collis C. Croker returned to it. He found himself almost trembling with an anticipation which had been mounting all day and which he had endeavored to calm with the aid of generous doses of spirituous liquors.

Paul received him graciously. He locked the door and fetched the box from its cupboard, placing it on his desk. "Now," he said, "this part is rather complicated, so please do not speak for a few moments. I have to concentrate to get it precisely right."

The Senator all but held his breath as he watched the Baron, frowning with concentration, adjust the brass dials in turn. Finally he pressed home the plunger and straightened up. A faint whirring sound was heard.

"Now we wait ten seconds," he said, counting them mentally. A sharp click from the box almost made the Senator jump. Paul quickly drew out the side drawers. A ten-pound note lay in each.

"Please do not touch them," he instructed. "They are still wet. But look closely, and see if they are not identical."

The American obeyed. He took out his pocketbook and checked the slip of paper on which he'd written the serial number of his original note. Both of those now revealed to him bore it. To his eyes, they were identical in every way.

"Well, I'll be doggoned!" he exclaimed. "Which is the false one?"

"Neither is false," Paul told him. "One is an exact copy of the other, that is all. They are equally valid as legal tender." He laughed. "Unless anyone were indiscreet enough to tender them both at once, of course. Even so, not even an expert could identify the copy from the original."

He peered closer at the notes. "They are quite dry now," he said. He picked out one and handed it to the Senator. "There you are—your note returned—or is it?"

They laughed heartily together. Paul said, "I think I had better retain the other. The risk of your accidentally spending two identical notes simultaneously is too great to run. No, on second thought, take the other, too. Having seen the miracle performed, I think you are entitled to put the result to the test. Go to two separate banks. At each of them, show a cashier one—only one—of the notes, saying you have heard rumors that there are forgeries about and you wish to be sure that your note is genuine. I guarantee that in each case the answer will be that it is."

The Senator demurred. "No, no, Baron. I can see with my own eyes. Anyway, why should I doubt your word?"

"Thank you. All the same, I should like you to do as I suggest. I promise you, it will bring you even greater satisfaction."

"Well, I guess that's true. I'll go first thing in the morning."

He placed the notes in separate compartments of his wallet.

"Say, how about that return match of poker meanwhile? So long as I don't let you win either of these notes off me."

Paul shook his head regretfully. "I'm sorry, Collis,

but I really must decline. I have a long and complicated business letter to write which will take me half the night. Tomorrow evening, though? . . ."

"Well, sure. Something else to look forward to."

Paul bowed acknowledgment, unlocked the door, and let him out. As he did so, Merriman approached him, carrying a tray of sandwiches and coffee. Paul stood aside to let him in.

Merriman's gaze fell on the mysterious box on the desk. Paul saw it, but noticed that the rheumy old eyes flickered away again without showing curiosity or interest.

"Porridge and deviled kidneys for breakfast as usual, sir?" the waiter asked.

"Thank you. Is that all, Merriman?"

"Yes, sir. Good night, sir."

Starr looked down at his dog behind the hall desk next morning as a beaming Senator Croker bustled past, making for the stairs.

"Senator's in a hurry today, Fred," he observed. The dog nodded. He, too, had noticed the American hurry out of the hotel a few minutes before bank opening time.

Paul was reading a letter and smoking a cheroot over the remains of his habitually late breakfast. He wore his dressing gown over his tieless shirt and trousers. When he heard the excited knock at the passage door he smiled and tore up the letter, putting the fragments onto one of his plates. "Come in," he called. As he had anticipated, his visitor was Collis C. Croker.

"It's a goddam miracle, Baron!" that gentleman blurted out as he bustled into the room. He closed the door, then hurried over to the table, tugging out his wallet and saying, "I went to the Bank of America and the First National Bank of Chicago. Both chief cashiers said the notes are genuine."

He held them out. Paul said, "Of course." He reached forward and took one of them from the Sena tor's hand and tore it into small fragments, which he scattered among the pieces of letter on the plate.

"Hey!" the American cried. "That's a waste!"

"My dear Collis, I told you how dangerous it would be to risk having two identical notes in circulation. It could set off a needless alarm about widespread forgeries which might even do harm to our national currency. In any case, what are ten pounds to you or me. . . ." He broke off abruptly, then resumed, "Although . . ."

"What is it, Baron?"

"Oh, it merely struck me suddenly that the richest people in the world can sometimes be really the poorest—in terms of ready money."

The Senator regarded him with new interest. "You aren't short of cash yourself, Baron?"

"Certainly not. That is to say . . . Well, perhaps unwisely, I have tied up so much capital in investments which will bear great fruit in the medium term that, at this moment, I am a relatively poor man in the everyday sense."

The Senator grinned. "Well, you're gonna be poorer after we get to that poker game, I promise you." Then, suddenly serious, he added, "If you ever do need money—cash—I'll buy that box off you, at a really handsome price."

Paul shook his head firmly. "Oh no. No question of that. I told you, it's a question of family honor."

"Family honor's a damn tough thing for a man like me to understand, Baron. Cash on the nail isn't."

Paul stood up. "No, I'm sorry, Collis. Now, if you'll excuse me, I have to finish dressing. I have an appointment with my bootmaker."

"And with me tonight," the American grinned again. "Say ten? And this time the whisky's on me."

An hour later, Louisa sat in her parlor contemplating a ten-pound note. Or rather, the ruins of one. It was pieced together on the blotter on her desk. Merriman stood beside her chair.

"Talk about throwing money away!" she exclaimed. "Merriman, for a man that looks like a desiccated old bat, you've got remarkably sharp eyes."

"I was noticing all that paper on the plate when I cleared up," he replied modestly. "If you take my meaning, ma'am, eyes are there to be used." He paused for breath and then, uncharacteristically, prolonged his speech. "There is another aspect of the gentleman in Number Three, if you could spare five minutes, ma'am."

Louisa eyed him critically. "Proper old busybody, you're getting in your dotage, aren't you? All right. Let's have it."

In one of the longest speeches he had achieved in years, Merriman described how, in serving the gentleman his coffee and sandwiches the evening before, he had chanced to observe on the gentleman's desk a box. He described it: polished wood, little drawers, brass dials, plunger thing in the top. He went on to recall how, many, many years before, while working as a steward in the first-class dining saloon of a liner, he had seen just such an object in the cabin of a passenger, a foreign gentleman he remembered distinctly, to whom he had been serving champagne.

". . . And when we reached the River Plate in South America, ma'am, the police came on board and arrested the foreign gentleman and his box. And then they came back and examined every single piece of paper money on the ship, and took some of it away. And when we came that way again, next time round, we was told the man had been given years in jail for forgery, and all something to do with that box of his."

"Sherlock Holmes and all," Louisa mocked him.

"Thank you, ma'am," Merriman said. "So, don't you think there might be something funny about the gentleman in Number Three, too? I mean, perhaps you ought to warn him off, ma'am, or we'll have the police coming here."

Louisa flared ungratefully at him. "Warn him off? Look, Merriman, you're the waiter here, not the bloody manager. What people do or don't do in my hotel is their business—and mine."

All the same, she sent a telegram to Charlie Haslemere in Monte Carlo concerning the gentleman in Number Three.

The return poker game duly took place. To the Senator's consternation, though, the Baron produced an expensive new pack of cards. He said he had seen them while shopping that day and couldn't resist buying them. Regretfully, the Senator had to return his own carefully marked pack to his pocket. He cursed himself for not having turned the tables on his opponent earlier in that first encounter: he had let him go on winning too long.

The beginner's luck seemed to be persisting, too. The Baron won the first three hands, displaying seemingly ingenuous delight each time. In the fourth, the stakes began to mount high as neither player cracked. Just as the Senator was beginning to feel genuinely worried, Paul asked innocently, "May I double again?"

"Well, sure—if you really want to."

"I think so." Paul doubled the stake.

It was too much for the Senator's nerve. "See you," he sighed.

Paul laid out his hand. To his opponent's great relief it was no match for his. Only a novice would have run the stakes so high on the strength of it.

Wistfully, Paul pushed all the money across the table.

"The tide really seems to have turned," he said. "Another loss or two like that, and I shall scarcely be able to pay my bill here. Collis, would it be too ungentlemanly of me to withdraw from the game?"

The American poured whisky for them both and

uncased a fresh cigar. He leaned back expansively.

"Men have been shot for less where I was raised," he grinned. "But it ain't in the nature of Collis C. Croker to take advantage of a greenhorn, at poker or anything else. Sure we'll stop. In any case, Baron, there's something more serious than cards I'd like to talk about with you."

Paul lit his own cigar and waited.

The Senator spoke carefully and seriously. "All the day, I haven't been able to put that box of yours out of my mind. That box is of great historic interest—too great for it to be permanently hidden away from view. Ever since I set foot in Europe I've been greatly impressed at the sense of history and tradition all around me, and I've been thinking today what a shame it would be if so many of those great treasures of your heritage just weren't out there for ordinary folk like me to come along and marvel at. Now, I guess we all would like to leave behind us on this earth a little something to be remembered by. C.C.C. canned beef will live on, of course, but it seems to me there should be something more than that. So I've decided to build a museum. The Collis C. Croker Museum of Science, bang in the middle of one of the greatest cities in the world, Chicago."

"That is a very noble idea," Paul said.

The American nodded. "People are going to come from all over the civilized world to see that museum. And shall I tell you what one of the chief attractions will be? It will be the Oppendorf Room, preserving the name of your noble and illustrious family forever. And bang in the center of that display, for all the world to marvel at, will be that magic little box of yours. Now, Baron, what would you say to twenty thousand dollars—in cash?"

He waited breathlessly as the nobleman pondered, obviously deeply tempted.

"It's a generous offer—thirty thousand dollars," Paul said at length.

The Senator took the hint. "Done, then?"

Paul sighed. "Very well."

They shook hands warmly and toasted one another with whisky.

Late the following evening the Senator was back in Paul's room yet again. This time he brought with him a case containing thirty thousand dollars in notes. He insisted on counting the whole lot out as he piled the mound of paper on the desk. In return, Paul handed over the box.

"I hope I'm doing the right thing," he said hesitantly.

"Sure you are, Baron. The world will thank you. Now, have you the instructions, please?"

Paul replied, "I've written them out, as you requested. But it has occurred to me since that since you will not actually be using the box, and as a safeguard, perhaps it might be better not . . ."

The Senator interrupted quickly. "It will be more interesting, historically and scientifically, to have them framed beside the exhibit itself. You have my word that no other person will get access to the box."

Paul nodded and handed over an envelope. He detached the key from his chain as well.

"Thanks, Baron. When I have the museum built, I'll have you come over and open it, if you will."

Paul gave his little bow. "I shall look forward to that great day. You can always fine me via the Ritz in Paris."

They shook hands again and parted company, each man more than satisfied with his side of the deal. A short while afterward Paul went down to Louisa's parlor. She was just in time to push under her blotter a long telegram she had received from Monte Carlo.

"Hello, Baron," she greeted him cheerfully. "Hope you're enjoying your stay in London?"

"I have indeed, Mrs. Trotter. Very much. Unfortunately, it must now come to an end. I should be grateful for my bill the first thing in the morning, please."

Louisa chuckled. "I'm glad of that."

He raised his eyebrows.

"Save me having to throw you out, that's why."

He stared uncomprehendingly for some moments, then gave her his most winning smile.

"You British. I shall never understand you."

"No, you wouldn't," Louisa said, searching for a piece of paper. "Here's your bill. All ready."

He looked at her quizzically, then at the bill. "Ninety-two guineas! But that is far too much."

"No it ain't. Not considering."

"Considering what, madam?"

"That you're not a baron, no more than I am." She fished out the telegram from Charlie: " 'Baron Oppendorf, alias Count Ginsky, alias Prince Zhanovsky . . .' Highly titled, your family. You see, I wired to your friend and mine, Charlie Haslemere, to make some inquiries. He says he's discovered you're nothing but a common little crook, wanted by the French police for crimes too numerous to recount. He advises me to inform Scotland Yard immediately."

Though shaken, Paul could reply, "Which, being a sensible woman and mindful of the reputation of your hotel, you have not done."

"No."

"And won't do?"

"That depends. I don't promise nothing. Who are you, 'Baron'? Let's have it."

He smiled and shrugged. "A soldier of fortune, fighting the good fight in the battle of life. My father kept a livery stable at Hounslow. I grew up to prefer woman and money to horses. So, much to my father's disdain and anger, I went into service."

Louisa smiled. "We've something in common, then."

"I was taken to Amsterdam by a diplomat as his valet and soon found how easily greedy men are parted from their money. Our dear old 'Senator,' for instance."

"So, you've sold him your rotten old box," Louisa

laughed. "How much? Twenty—thirty thousand dollars? Never mind shrugging your shoulders all innocent like that. 'Ere," she half whispered, "what was in the box really? I won't tell no one."

Paul relaxed at last. "We are two of a kind, aren't we?"

"No. Not quite. We both give 'em what they want, and we make 'em pay for it. But I do it straight, and you cheat 'em. It's a bit different, you know."

"I suppose so. Well, a little joiner in Brussels knocks them up for me quite cheaply. A failed craftsman, I often think, when I look at the quality of his work. A beautiful box, some simple clockwork, a couple of rollers, and some drawers. The skill is mine."

"Profitable sideline, though."

"Exactly," Paul admitted. "I sold five last year. Men who are really greedy for money will buy anything, and when our friend the 'Senator' tried to cheat me at poker—me, of all people!—using marked cards, I thought he needed teaching a lesson."

Louisa grinned and reached down beside her desk. A champagne bottle lay there in a bucket of ice.

"Open it for us, will you, ducks?" she asked.

He obeyed, while she produced two gleaming glasses from a small cupboard beside her.

"Where are you off to this time?" she asked, as the cork came out and the chilled wine was poured.

"Lisbon. From there, who knows? The world is my oyster—or most of it is."

"Have you thought," she asked, as they silently toasted one another, "that the first thing he'll do, now he's got your machine, is try it out? And when it doesn't work, he'll be round to your room like a bat out of hell."

Paul sipped and smiled. "The process takes twelve hours," he said. "Anything less than that would be bound to be a failure. And within twelve hours, with the benefit of an early call and an admirable early breakfast from you, madam, I shall no longer be on the premises to try to explain how he must have made some mistake in the rather complicated operation."

"Cheeky devil!" Louisa said. "Here, let's have that bill back a minute."

He handed it over. She picked up a pen and added a final zero to the total before handing the bill back.

"Nine hundred and twenty guineas!" he exclaimed. "This . . . this is sheer blackmail."

"Yes, dear," Louisa smiled. "Though what a rude word to use to a lady. If it's more convenient, I'll take it in dollars."

Paul regarded her for a long moment. She raised the champagne bottle toward his glass. After the briefest hesitation he advanced the glass and allowed her to pour for him. He raised the glass in salute, sipped, then got out his wallet and counted four thousand dollars from his hoard. When he had placed them before her he took her hand and kissed it.

"Goodbye, Mrs. Trotter," he said. "It has been a pleasure to know you."

"Goodbye, 'Baron,'" Louisa returned. "I hope I never set eyes on you again."

Nineteen

Louisa was proud of her King, although she rarely saw him anymore, since she had reduced her outside catering and he was spending an increasing amount of time abroad. After the long, frustrating years of waiting for the throne, he had confounded his detractors and delighted his friends by demonstrating the natural talent for sovereignty which the former had refused to believe existed and the latter had been certain was latent under the sporty, pleasure-seeking exterior of a man who had nothing to do but be sporty and pleasure-seeking.

In particular, he had carried his country to new popularity on the Continent, where his reclusive late mother's influence had been little felt. Treaties with Germany, Italy, Spain, and Portugal had been concluded largely through his efforts, and the establishment of the Entente Cordiale with Britain's arch-rival, France, had been a personal triumph. "Edward the Peacemaker" he was known as now; and Louisa Trotter recalled with pride that his slippers and dressing gown had once reposed in the wardrobe of her own bedroom.

She took little interest in politics, though. If there had been any such thing as a woman's right to vote at this time, she would probably not have troubled to exercise it. If she had, she instinctively would have put herself down a Tory. Most of the aristocracy with whom she had contact were Tories. As a self-made woman, so to speak, the last thing she would have wished to see would be the Labour Party gaining power.

The Liberals left her indifferent. She had a vague notion that they were a party of nonconformists and teetotalers, worthy, well-meaning, but dull and ineffectual. She discovered otherwise one October evening in 1905 when she was invited to join a party in the suite of one of her semipermanent residents, George Dugdale, a Liberal Member of Parliament.

"What's the rumpus?" Starr asked Merriman, seeing the latter making his way toward the stairs with a tray heavily laden with champagne bottles. Starr had just brought Fred in from his evening sniff around his territory. The babble of noises and laughter from upstairs was considerable.

"Them Liberals," Merriman answered. "Knocking back this stuff like water. Barely time to chill it."

"All over winning a little by-election in Yorkshire?"

"Seems they reckon there's bigger things to come. Anyway, Mrs. Trotter's just gone up. She'd account for half the noise."

"Wouldn't put her down a Liberal, would you, Fred?"

The dog appeared to have no opinion.

Merriman, going on his way, said, "Political impartiality, Mr. Starr. That's what you need in this trade. Lose out on tips, otherwise."

As he went up the stairs the hotel's front door opened and a young woman came through. She was in her late thirties, attractive, and quietly dressed. Fred came out to sniff at the hem of her skirt and then returned to his basket, clearly approving.

"Good evening," she addressed Starr. "I'm supposed to be meeting Sir James Rosslyn here. My name is Mrs. Strickland."

"Yes, madam. You'd be the lady he's lending his rooms to for a few weeks."

A cabby had brought her luggage into the hall. Starr paid him off for her.

"Sir James is up in Mr. Dugdale's suite just now," he said. "They're celebrating their by-election. I expect you can hear."

Diana Strickland smiled. Starr asked, "Would you like me to fetch him, madam, or shall I show you to his rooms? They're all ready for you."

"Let's go up, shall we?" she suggested. He picked up the baggage and led the way.

In George Dugdale's suite, the air was thick with cigar and cigarette smoke. Merriman was striving mightily to keep the glasses of the celebrating men topped up. Louisa, the only woman present, was tossing back champagne as fast as any of them. She had commandeered a bottle for herself and recharged her glass after every sip. She was already slightly flown.

She was talking to Sir James Rosslyn, a fastidious, rather puritanical old gentleman, and their host, George Dugdale. Dugdale was a complete contrast to his senior. He was only just fifty, a lawyer by profession and a comparative newcomer to the Liberal Party. His aggressive self-confidence, happily complemented by great energy and a winning charm, had got him elected to the House of Commons the previous year in a constituency that had been thought to be a Tory stronghold. His had been one of the many successes at that time which were now pointing to a close-run contest at the upcoming General Election.

"What I should like to know," he was asking Louisa flippantly, "is whether you're for us or against us."

She laughed. "It's your wine I'm drinking, Mr. Duggy, so I'd better be for you. Mind you, I prefer Tories. They're gentlemen."

"Wicked snob!" Dugdale accused her with a laugh. Sir James Rosslyn told her seriously, "You'll see a

Liberal Government before Christmas, Mrs. Trotter. We're expecting Balfour to resign within weeks."

She said to Dugdale, "You goin' to be Prime Minister, then?" It was Rosslyn who answered, "Sir Henry Campbell-Bannerman seems the likeliest choice."

Starr had edged his way through the throng. "Excuse me, Sir James," he intervened. "Mrs. Strickland has arrived. I've shown her into your rooms."

"Ah, thank you, Starr. I must go and settle her in. Excuse me, Mrs. Trotter."

"Bring her along here," Louisa called to him as he moved away, ignoring the fact that it was not her party. "I always like to welcome my guests with a glass of wine." She winked at George Dugdale. "And if somebody else is paying for it, so much the better." Merriman was passing. She reached out and took another full bottle from his hand, giving him her empty one in return. She poured for Dugdale and herself.

"Mrs. Trotter," he said, "now you can explain the mystery of this lady. Rosslyn has been fidgeting about all evening. Don't tell me the old fox has got himself a mistress."

"What, Sir Rosy? Not likely, is it? Family friend, he said."

"Hm! From the front row of which chorus, I wonder?"

At that moment Sir James Rosslyn was welcoming Diana Strickland in the most decorous fashion.

"Dear James, this is perfect," she said. "But I feel so dreadful about turning you out of your own rooms."

"Not at all, my dear. I'm round the corner in Albemarle Street, with my brother. So I'm on hand if you need me, though I shall be away, moving around the country a good deal. You've heard of our success at Barkston Ash today? We're on the verge of great things at last."

"Yes, I heard. I'm so glad. Harry sends his best regards."

"Thank you. How is he, Diana?"

"Oh, much the same. He's talking more clearly now and he can move his right arm a little. The doctors are quite hopeful."

"Good. Now, I'm bidden by our redoubtable proprietress, Mrs. Trotter, to take you over to George Dugdale's suite, where we're having a little celebration. Do you feel up to it?"

"Why not? With pleasure."

He led her off in the direction of the noise. "You'll find the staff here friendly, if a trifle eccentric. Don't, ah, be perturbed by Mrs. Trotter. She's what is generally termed a 'character,' but she's first-class beneath it."

A blast of noise and smoke hit Diana when Sir James opened Dugdale's door. Louisa greeted her true to form.

"How d'you do? Sir Rosy, fetch her a glass. You another of these cocky Liberals, Mrs. Strickland?"

"I'm not political at all," Diana replied with equanimity. "Just an old family friend of James's, who's kindly offered to lend me his rooms for a few weeks."

"Brought a maid, have you?"

"Oh, no."

"Well, I'll send Mary up directly to do your unpacking. Nice kid. Welsh. Ah, thanks, Sir Rosy. Now, dear, get this down your throat and meet my friend Mr. Duggy, who'll be Prime Minister in about fifty years. It's his party."

Diana turned to George Dugdale and raised her glass to him before drinking.

"Then it's you I must thank for this," she smiled.

He was regarding her with keen interest. "I'm so pleased to meet you, Mrs. Strickland. Welcome to this gathering of distinguished and inebriate Liberals. May I ask what brings you to this notorious establishment?"

"I've come to work. I'm an artist."

"Oh!" Louisa said. "We had Walter Sickert here in the summer, in Number Eight."

"Heavens, I'm nowhere near that standard, Mrs. Trotter. I do things for children's magazines. And Christmas cards and valentines."

"Do you sell?"

"Not as much as I'd like. But I'm beginning, and I'm ambitious."

"Fascinating," George Dugdale said. "Does your husband encourage you?"

"He's . . . quite amused."

"Only amused. Is that enough?"

"Yes, for me it is."

Louisa could sense the probing nature of Dugdale's questioning. She rebuked him. "Of course it's enough. How many husbands would let their wives come to London alone and get on with what they want to do, without interference?"

"Yes, indeed," he had to concede. "Would you allow me to see your work sometime, Mrs. Strickland?"

"Now, George," Rosslyn broke in, "she's come here to work in peace and quiet. . . ."

"Good Lord, I won't make a nuisance of myself. Just a glance, and I shall be satisfied."

Sir James Rosslyn and Louisa exchanged looks. They knew George Dugdale.

Next morning, Diana, comfortably settled into the Bentinck, went out to buy some painting materials. On her way back she was accosted in the hall by Major Smith-Barton, on his way to Louisa's sanctum.

"Diana Strickland?" he inquired. "Yes, it is. Smith-Barton. I stayed a weekend in your house some time ago."

"Oh, yes, of course. How do you do? Are you staying here?"

The Major produced his ready and literally true answer to this potentially embarrassing inquiry frequently made.

"Yes. Treat it as my London home. Sorry to hear about Harry's misfortunes. How's he getting along?"

"Oh . . . his illness, you mean? He's doing quite well, thank you."

After a few more words she went away to her room. The Major entered Louisa's presence with a puzzled look on his face.

"Extraordinary," he said. "What's Diana Strickland doing here?"

"Oh, you know her, do you, Major?"

"Yes. Charming woman. Walked out on old Harry at last, has she?"

"What?"

"Always on the cards. Don't know what she ever saw in him. Pleasant enough chap to go shooting with. Convivial. But don't ever lend him money. Not that I ever did, of course. Creditors chasing him all over Lincolnshire. They say his stroke was a stroke of luck. Kept the hounds at bay for a while."

"So that's the way the wind blows? I don't like ladies who've left their husbands. They're trouble." Louisa was apt not to remember that she was one herself.

"Don't take my word for it," the Major corrected her hastily. "Just wouldn't entirely surprise me. Oh, talking of money, Mrs. Trotter, I had a bit come through this morning. Thought it only right you should have it, after all your kindness. Help put the record straight a bit."

He handed her an envelope. "Only sorry it can't be more."

Louisa smiled up at him. "It's the thought that counts, Major."

A few mornings later, Mary, clearing Mrs. Strickland's breakfast things from her sitting room, stared with admiration at the watercolor painting Diana was engaged upon at an easel near the window. It was of an extremely prissy-looking cat, in a bonnet and dress, admonishing two naughty kittens in children's frocks.

"Ooh, that's lovely, ma'am!" the Welsh girl declared. "Pussy with her bonnet on. My uncle Bryn was an artist."

"Really?" Diana was absorbed, working very fast.

"Thought of quite highly in the village, he was. He did one of me once. My mam's still got it hanging in her bedroom."

She sensed that Mrs. Strickland didn't wish to be disturbed. "Well, if there's nothing else . . ."

"No thank you, Mary."

The girl was just leaving with the tray when she encountered in the doorway Mr. George Dugdale. He gave her his attractive smile.

"Morning, Mary. Is Mrs. Strickland in?" He could see that she was.

"Yes, sir. Only she's . . ."

He walked in past her, leaving the door open.

"Am I interrupting?" he asked Diana, who looked around at him. "Just say so."

"Not at all, Mr. Dugdale." He closed the door. Diana went on. "Forgive me if I don't stop. I have to do my pieces at one go, or I lose myself. It's rather like painting real animals that just happen to have posed for a moment and might run off before I've got them on paper."

"I quite understand." He came over to look at the painting. "Is the cat our heroine?"

"Yes. Frightful creature, always lecturing everyone on how to behave. Here she's telling the kittens they mustn't chase little birds because they're all God's creatures."

"Hm!"

"Yes. Quite."

"What would you rather be doing?"

"I've got a book in mind about the animals I remember from when I was a little girl in Canada. I was born there. Beavers, wolves, grizzly bears . . . My father used to tell me beautiful stories about them."

"Really? Have you made any drawings of those animals?"

"Yes. Over there, in that folder. Please do have a look, if you like. They're only sketches, but I'm looking forward to working them up and writing the stories, if I can find a publisher who'd be interested."

Dugdale picked up one of the many folders lying about and sat in a chair with it spread open across his knees. He went slowly through the loose leaves. When he had finished he said, "These are very good. Have you shown them to any publishers yet?"

"No. I think I'd have to complete a few first and I haven't had time yet."

He shook his head. "I don't think so. I have a good friend who publishes illustrated books for children. Alfred Hurst. I'm sure he'd be interested to see them just as they are and talk to you about the whole idea."

Diana had finished her picture and cleaned her brushes. She came over to him. He said, "This sorrowful old bear reminds me of a certain Tory politician." She laughed. "To tell you the truth, I always try to give them human features. I base them on people I know."

"So I was right. Enchanting! Now, what time do you stop for luncheon?"

"Oh, I don't. I haven't time."

"You must today. I'm taking you to the Savoy."

"But . . ."

"James Rosslyn isn't here to look after you, so I shall. I'll call back at a quarter to one, shall I?"

Diana looked at the clock. There was ample time to get one more painting done before then. "Very well," she capitulated. "That would be very nice."

At three o'clock they had finished the meal at a discreetly positioned table for two in the Savoy

Grill. They had eaten early pheasant with a superb *nuits St. Georges*. Now they were drinking liqueurs and George Dugdale lit a Havana cigar.

"I found the law too easy—a game, really," he was explaining. "Politics is just another game, of course, but rather more fun. There was a by-election at Rye a year ago and I romped home for the Liberals, to all the local Tories' surprise. Now I'm what is called a marked man with an interesting future. I have an enormous belief in myself, as you may have guessed."

Diana smiled. She had certainly found him self-assured during their luncheon chat, but his charm overrode any sense of arrogance.

"My husband stood as a Tory once," she said. "But he was defeated."

"Tell me about your husband."

"Well, I was twenty-three when I met him. He gave me a very nice home, a lovely daughter, Sophie, a place in society. What more could I want?"

He was watching her shrewdly as he asked, "Tell me—I don't know."

"Nothing. Nothing at all." It was said too brightly to deceive him. He pressed the point. "Well, you want his complete recovery from his illness."

"Naturally. He is recovering."

"Without you beside him?"

"He's . . . well enough for me to leave him now. I have to work. There are distractions with illness in the house. I need to be free of them."

George Dugdale smiled through his cigar smoke, which he wafted away from her. "And instead, you're being distracted by me and my impertinent questions. But you must allow me the simple joy of being intrigued by you. I've always found conjugal loyalty a most appealing quality in women."

"Are you married, Mr. Dugdale?"

"My wife died five years ago. Our son is twenty now. He's at Balliol. Have some more Cointreau?"

"No, thank you. I really think I should be getting back."

Instead of summoning the waiter, he reached over the table and put his hand on one of hers.

"Diana ... If I may call you Diana. Let us return to the Bentinck and discuss our relationship in private."

"Our relationship? Really, Mr. Dugdale, you're rushing ahead of me. I wasn't aware there was any relationship."

"Two people dining alone together at the Savoy usually implies some sort of a relationship."

"Well, you must forgive my innocence. If I'd thought that by accepting your kind offer assumptions were being made ..."

He said earnestly, "Good heavens, not at all. I simply have to tell you that you've captured my heart. It was never assumed. It's happened, and I can't conceal it."

Flustered, Diana protested, "But it's impossible! Excuse me, but I really should like to get back to my painting."

"Pussy and her moralizing," he said without sarcasm, withdrawing his hand. He smiled. "Forgive me. Widowers are prone to idiotic passions, you know. You're quite right to treat them with the utmost circumspection."

"It's not that," she said, not wishing to wound his feelings and feeling genuinely complimented by this well-placed, intelligent, good-looking man. "I'm touched. I'm only sorry that you've misjudged me. I'm truly not accustomed to ... adventures."

"So I sense," he said, signaling for the waiter at last. "But if we aren't to be lovers, will you accept instead my humble and sincere offer of friendship?"

She smiled gratitude and relief. "Yes. That I *would* like, Mr. Dugdale."

"George, please—Diana."

It required only two days for his friendship with

her to take tangible shape. He came into her room in the morning, to find her at her easel as usual. The room was rapidly assuming the appearance of a regular studio. Diana wore her rough, stained working overall. Her position by the brightness of the window rendered her expression hard to discern; in any case, Dugdale was too preoccupied with his news to notice a certain puffiness around her eyes.

"I laid them out on Hurst's table and he expressed immediate approval," he announced triumphantly. "I knew he would. He thinks it will make a splendid book, and he sees a whole series. He wants to meet you. I've arranged for the three of us to lunch at the Savoy on Monday. I take it you won't mind breaking off for that?"

Her voice faltered a little as she said, "No . . . no. That's wonderful." But there was no joy or enthusiasm in her tone.

"I shall act as your lawyer and get you a suitable advance payment," he said. "A few hundred, without a doubt."

To his surprise she suddenly subsided into a chair and burst into tears. He hurried across to crouch beside her and ask soothingly and with real concern what the matter was. Unable to speak, she indicated a letter. He picked it up and read it silently, then frowned over the signature. "Joseph Stewart?"

"Our land agent. He's been dealing with all the bills and correspondence since Harry's illness. He wouldn't have told me if he could have avoided it, I'm sure, but this wretched Coulter means to bring a court case."

"Did you know Harry had gambling debts?"

"Yes. But not the size of them."

"I assume the estate is mortgaged."

Diana nodded miserably. "When we had no son, my husband felt it wouldn't be worth perpetuating, anyway. He said we might as well enjoy it."

"What do you do for income?"

She gestured wildly toward the easel. "This is our income. That's why I'm here, trying to work in peace. But I simply can't work fast enough to pay the household bills."

With a determined effort she stopped herself crying again. George Dugdale was getting out his checkbook and fountain pen. He began to write. Diana saw her name and exclaimed, "No, you mustn't! I couldn't accept anything from you. Four hundred pounds!"

George calmly tore out the check and forced it into her hand, which he covered with his. "See it as my investment in our animal friends," he smiled.

She still protested. "I'd rather ask James Rosslyn for help. He's a family friend. I'll never be able to pay you this much back."

"Yes you will. You'll find your work worth far more than that in the long run. Leave that to Hurst and me. Besides, you could regard it as a seal on our special friendship. I . . . pressed my claim too early, the other day. It's a failing of mine. I see something I want and I go for it. I lack patience. Two days have passed now, and I've had ample time to reflect. Please don't think I'm trying to take advantage of your distress—of what I've learnt—and that I'm breaking our bargain, our pact of friendship. But love grows out of friendship, doesn't it? They spring from the same root. So I want to offer you help, protection . . . and love, for as long as you want them."

Clutching his forgotten check, Diana stared at him long and hard. Then thankfully, willingly, she let herself lean against him and, when his arm stole around her, raised her mouth to meet his.

"It's incredible!" Sir James Rosslyn fumed.

He had come around on Sunday afternoon, hoping to find Diana free for a walk in St. James's Park, and been told by a matter-of-fact Louisa that she was spending the weekend with "Mr. Duggy" at his cottage in the New Forest.

"Oh, come on, Sir James," Louisa said. "Cheer up! It's only a weekend in the country."

"Only . . . !"

"Best thing could've happened, you ask me. Her husband's no use to her. She's working her heart out here to keep things going, and she needs friends. I know. I've been through it all meself, and it's no joke, I can tell you."

But he was in no mood for her cocky banter.

"Mrs. Trotter, I don't think you quite understand the implications of this . . . this affair. We're about to fight a General Election. If there should be any divorce scandal just now . . ."

"Who said anything about a divorce?" she retorted, refusing to be put down. "Just a bit of fun, that's all."

Sir James sighed. "My dear Mrs. Trotter, you don't know the lady at all if you believe that. She's not the sort to indulge in 'fun,' as you call it. If that cunning George Dugdale's made his impression on her, as I feared from the start he was out to do, then there will be no going back after this weekend. I fear the worst."

"Well, if the news does get out, it won't be from behind these walls, I can promise you that," Louisa said.

The couple had scarcely returned from an idyllic stay in the New Forest cottage before Sir James Rosslyn sought out Dugdale and charged him angrily with putting the Liberal Party's reputation at risk. George retorted spiritedly that the election result was a foregone conclusion in their favor, and that it would take a scandal of immense proportions to make the slightest effect on the voters. He scoffed at a warning that he might be compromising his own chance of a Cabinet post. With supreme self-confidence, he insisted that he fully expected "something" at the Board of Trade, come what might.

"Anyway," he went on, "who's going to hear about Diana and me? And if they do, who'll have told them? Not you, I hope, my dear James."

"Of course not. But you can't blame me if Campbell-Bannerman learns of it somehow else."

"Well, that's my risk. Anyway, I'm not the only one who enjoys a little discreet private life, you know. Look at Lloyd George . . . Asquith . . . You don't tell me the Prime Minister will give them the Order of the Boot for it."

"No man," Sir James said primly, "however brilliant he may consider himself to be, is greater than the party he stands for."

"Oh, damn the party and such arrant nonsense. All men are greater than the party, unless they choose to be its lapdog, which I'm afraid you tend to be, James. It's individuals who count in the end—warts and all. Oh, I'm sorry. I don't mean to offend you. Sit down and have a drink. We've known each other far too long for this sort of wrangling."

Sir James accepted sorrowfully. He was sincere in his attitude toward the matter, but he knew himself to be no match for the stubborn determination of George Dugdale in pursuit of something he meant to achieve.

"Anyway," George was saying, as he poured sherry, "she'll be along in a minute. She'll be pleased to find you here. She talked about you a great deal. You've been a steadfast friend, and by God she must have needed one."

"You know, then—about the marriage?"

"Oh yes, it all came tumbling out. I've no doubt she was to blame for some of the problems. She's not an easy woman—too highly strung. But I find her adorable. I'm besotted with her."

The object of his adoration arrived just then. She smiled a little nervously at the sight of Sir James getting to his feet. Dugdale put his arm around her and led her over.

"My darling," he greeted her fearlessly, "come and have a glass of sherry with your old friend, who, incidentally, knows all about us."

Her smile changed to one of relief. She asked Sir James lightly, "What have you two been talking about, then?"

George Dugdale answered, "The insignificance of politics."

The publisher's luncheon at the Savoy had been the success George Dugdale had predicted, and more. Hurst was so enthusiastic about Diana's artistic style and her outline for the book that he commissioned it on the spot, with an option on further ones. But he set a fierce deadline for the initial volume, in order, he explained, to catch the spring market.

"Can you manage it?" George asked her, as they sat side by side on his sofa back at the Bentinck afterward.

"I'll work day and night," she declared. "The only time I shall allow myself off will be the time I give to you. You've changed my life—in more ways than one." She kissed him.

"Yes, well, I shan't trespass too much on your time, anyway," he said. "The election's been set for January. I shall have to spend a lot of time in my constituency. After the shock of last time, the Torics will be putting everything they can into their campaign."

"Oh, I wish I could come with you. How can I work without you near me? With you, I can achieve anything."

He patted her thigh. "Nonsense. You'll work all the harder. And I shall be working, too. We shan't distract one another."

She nodded resignedly. "I've made too many demands on you already. I can't believe my good fortune. You do love me, though?"

"I adore you."

"And you will keep loving me? Life could never be the same again without you."

He held her tenderly and kissed her. "When I'm away," he promised, "I shall write to you every single day. You'll see how quickly the time will pass."

She set herself a rigorous working routine, keeping up with her other commitments while devoting part of each day to the book. When January came and George did go away, she found herself able to achieve even more, working additionally in the evenings that she might otherwise have spent with him. When things were well she often yielded to the temptation to work into the small hours, and one morning Mary came in with her breakfast to find her asleep, fully clothed, on the sofa, with pages of handwritten manuscript strewn around her.

"You haven't been to bed, madam!" she scolded, when Diana opened bleary eyes. "You'll wear yourself out, that you will."

But Diana was quickly wide awake, eager to seize a letter lying on the tray and rip it open.

Mary picked up a sketch. It was a heron, with the unmistakable features of Merriman. She smiled at the likeness and put it down. "Not very nice campaigning weather, madam," she said. "It snowed all night. I'll run you a nice hot bath, shall I?"

Diana didn't answer. She was happily absorbed in George's letter.

She received a scolding from Sir James Rosslyn, too, when he called later in the week to ask after her welfare and she showed him the pile of letters.

"Diana, you must come to your senses. There's no future in it, I tell you. You certainly can't divorce Harry, and if he hears about it and divorces you, then George's career is in ruins and you'll both be outcasts from society."

"He says that's all rubbish."

"That's the man's colossal vanity."

"James," she implored, "will you please stop trying to make me feel guilty. Of course I don't want to hurt Harry. He isn't expected to live long, so if we must, we'll wait."

Rosslyn gave her a pitying look. "You think George will marry you? Has he proposed?"

"Not yet. He must know he can't." She gestured toward the letters. "But he talks about our future on nearly every page."

"He doesn't say much about the past, though, I'll wager."

Diana said coolly, "That's unfair of you, James. He's been a widower for five years. I wouldn't have expected him to have remained celibate all that time."

"My dear, the list of women stretches back to a long time before Isobel's death. And it's a long one. The plain fact is that George Dugdale, for all that he may seem to be charming and brilliant, is nothing more than a cheap opportunist. And that's not just my view. . . ."

"And I thought you were his friend!"

"Diana, before anything else, I am *your* friend."

"Well, you've an extraordinary way of showing it. You're a misery and a Jeremiah, knowing my feelings and trying every trick to take away the happiness I've found. Now will you please leave me. I've a lot of work to do."

He hesitated, then went. Diana threw aside the sketch she had started and began to work savagely on a new one. It was of a stringy-looking buzzard, with the face of Sir James Rosslyn.

One Monday morning shortly afterward she went out to buy more paints, pausing at the hall desk to give Starr a letter to post to George.

"Mary forgot to bring my post up this morning," she said. "May I have it, please?"

Starr folded his newspaper. "I'm afraid there were no letters for you this morning, madam."

Diana frowned. It was the first time. "You're sure?"

"Positive, madam. I'm sorry."

When she had gone out Starr went straight to Louisa's parlor, taking the newspaper with him.

"I thought you ought to see this, madam," he said, pointing out a brief item of gossip. "In view of the person involved, and the possible consequences."

"Yeh," she said thoughtfully. "Go and fetch Merriman and Mary here, straightaway."

When they were assembled, and her parlor door shut, Louisa said, "Now then, Mr. Starr has just shown me a piece of tittle-tattle in this rag of his about Mr. Dugdale being seen in Deauville over the weekend with a certain Mrs. Monroe, a widow, and rumors of a romance between 'em."

"Where's Deauville, mum?" Mary asked.

"In France. Now, I'm sure this isn't the kind of newspaper Mrs. Strickland's likely to read, even by chance. She just has *The Times*, and they don't go in for this sort of thing. But it's a wonder how things like this get passed on by so-called 'well-wishers,' and I just want to warn you lot to do anything you can to make sure she doesn't get to know. Right?"

They agreed, and dispersed. Louisa was worried, though. She summoned her counselor, Major Barton-Smith, separately.

"What do you make of it?" she asked.

"There's no smoke without fire, they say."

"But he couldn't do it to her! They're like turtle-doves when they're together."

The Major said, "Funnily enough, I met one of his colleagues in the club, the other day. I mentioned Dugdale and he asked if there was any truth in a rumor about him and this Mrs. Monroe. Apparently, she's got rather a reputation for this sort of thing. Married two politicians, both of whom died before they reached the Cabinet, and the jokers are saying she's looking for a third-time lucky."

"Oh, blimey!" Louisa groaned. "But it says here she's forty-eight. Makes her sound an old frump, compared with Mrs. Strickland."

"Yes, but she has money—influence."

"Well, he's due back any day. She didn't get a letter from him this morning, so he might be on his way."

The Major said, "According to my friend he's been seen in London once or twice while he's been 'away'— at the theater with Mrs. Monroe. Rye isn't far from here, after all. Easily nip up and back again in an evening."

"Then everyone'll know soon. D'you reckon it's any of my business to warn her? I can't stick seeing women getting hurt by men."

"It's a tricky one," the Major said thoughtfully. "It would soften the blow a bit."

"Yeh. Once old Sir Rosy gets wind of it you can bet he'll be running round here like a shot. I'd better tell her. Kinder in the long run."

She did, taking the newspaper item with her as corroboration. Diana was shocked, and cried at first, but quickly pulled herself together and insisted stubbornly that the whole thing was just scandal mongering, with the election coming up. And even as Louisa was talking to her, Mary came in with a letter by a later post. Diana opened it eagerly. It was from George, saying he would be back at the Bentinck that very evening and was longing to see her again. He asked her to order dinner at eight in her room.

A little before eight he breezed into the hotel, greeting Louisa and Merriman cheerfully in the hall. He ran up to his own room to wash and change, then went straight along to Diana's. He found her looking radiant in her dinner gown and embraced her ardently. Nothing in her manner betrayed the lurking doubt with underlay her delight at his return.

"I've missed you so much," he said, as they drank sherry. "I'll be glad when this damned election's over. How've you been? Have you worked well? I can't wait to see what you've done."

"It's all over there in a folder," she said. "After dinner, though. I've missed you, too, darling. Here, I've bought you a welcome-home present."

She handed over a little leather case. He found in it a pair of silver cufflinks, engraved with his initials.

"They're for good luck at the election, too," she added.

"Oh, but they're splendid! Thank you so much, my angel. I shall wear them on polling day." He kissed her again and said, "I'm sorry, I've nothing for you. There simply wasn't time."

Merriman was in attendance throughout the dinner. At last he was dismissed, with their compliments to Mrs. Trotter for a superb meal.

"Much better," George sighed contentedly. "What a difference from those provincial hotels."

"And Deauville?" asked Diana, who had had to contain herself throughout dinner.

He looked surprised, but didn't lose his smile. "How did you know I'd been to Deauville?"

"It was in a newspaper. I'd have thought you'd have sent me a postcard."

"D'you know, I wrote one and forgot to post the damned thing. I found it in my pocket, back in England."

"Why did you go?" she asked, trying to sound casual.

"I went because I was invited. One of my disgustingly rich constituents has a steam yacht. It was only for two days and it would have been impolitic to refuse. I enjoyed it, actually. A rest from speechifying."

"The newspaper hinted at a romance with a Mrs. Monroe—I suppose she is your 'disgustingly rich' constituent. I paid no attention, of course."

He laughed. "A romance with Dorothy? Good heavens!"

He did not manage it convincingly enough, though.

She knew from his forced laugh that he was putting on an act. Also, no two days had elapsed without a letter from him. He must have written one and left it with someone in England to post while he was away. This calculated deception brought back her worst fears with a rush.

"George," she said, "please don't. You have to tell me something."

His smile gradually faded. After a long pause he said, "Yes, I suppose I do. I can't deceive you, because I'm too fond of you. The newspaper was right in the main, only 'romance' is hardly the word. I've known Dorothy Monroe for years. A romance is something special. Something you and I had."

" 'Had'?"

"Look, believe me, Diana, my feelings for you were genuine. They still are. I'd much rather spend my life with you, but we have to be realistic, don't we? The truth is, we're both victims of circumstance."

"Victims! Yes! You took me like a dog picks up a bone. Didn't you realize that you changed my life? That I could never return . . ."

"Oh, good heavens, that's not true. I helped you back on your feet, that's all. You're strong now. You're independent. You have a book to write, a belief in yourself again."

"I loved you! You opened my eyes to possibilities I'd never dreamed of. You were the finest man I'd met. I worshiped your mind, your body. I trusted you."

"Absurd! I am a man . . . with frailties . . ."

"Yes, you are. That was my mistake."

She was too furious to cry. He made a placatory move toward her, but she shrank away. He floundered. "I'm sorry . . . truly sorry you should feel like this about me. I thought . . . I assumed you realized that sooner or later . . ." He got to his feet. "Well, I shan't forget you." He gave her a farewell smile, and gestured toward her folder. "Or my friends in the forest."

Only when he had gone did she cry—dreadfully.

Next morning a red-eyed Diana told Mary she would be leaving the Bentinck that day and requested her bill to be prepared. Louisa brought it up herself, while Diana was packing.

"So it was true, was it?" she asked. Diana, almost unnaturally calm, simply nodded.

"You'll fight him?" Louisa said.

Diana shook her head. "He's not worth fighting."

"Course he is! He's rotten and the whole world should know what he's done to you. Make him an example to the rest of his kind. Besides, we don't want *him* running the bloomin' country!"

"It was my fault, Mrs. Trotter. I was blind, self-ish . . ."

"Oh, come on! . . ."

"Anyway, I've no weapons to fight him with."

"You've got all those letters, haven't you? Look, Lord Northcliffe comes here. He's a pal of mine. He'll know what to do with 'em."

"Why should I hurt him?" Diana retorted, to Louisa's surprise. "He was right, in a way. He did help me. He found me a publisher. He set me on my feet. I've much to be grateful for."

"What!"

"He lent me money, too."

"For Gawd's sake," Louisa cried, "how much?"

"Four hundred pounds. I shall earn it from my first book and pay him back. But now I must return home, to my husband and my daughter. I've neglected them. I've been disloyal to them . . . and George needs Mrs. Monroe. As for the letters, the last thing I shall do before I leave here, Mrs. Trotter, is burn them all."

She did; and left. That same day George Dugdale left again for Rye, to do his final canvassing before the General Election. To his surprise, Louisa presented him with his bill, fully made up. He raised his eyebrows, but, without comment, felt in his breast pocket for his checkbook.

"You won't need that," she told him.

"I beg your pardon?"

"You've paid already. In fact, I owe you some. Seventy pounds ten shillings, to be precise. The balance on what you lent Mrs. Strickland. I'm relievin' you of that obligation."

"But this is absurd!" he protested. "It was a private matter."

"Yeh, well it's my business now. So's you can wipe the whole slate clean between you."

After a long pause, Dugdale said, "What . . . terrible tales has she been telling you, Mrs. Trotter?"

"She said nothing terrible, Mr. Dugdale. She stuck up for you. You won't have no trouble with her. She's a saint, and you're lucky. There's plenty of others you couldn't have done this to and got away with it."

"I see," he said, with something approaching humility. "Goodbye, Mrs. Trotter. I've been most comfortable here."

"Goodbye. And I'd prefer it if you didn't come here again. Not even if you get to be bleedin' Prime Minister."

The General Election proved a triumph for the Liberal Party. The evening following it, the Bentinck Hotel resounded again to an even greater celebratory roar.

"Hurry up, Mr. Merriman!" cried Mary into the dispense. "They're bellowing out for more champagne."

"As quick as I can," the old hand groaned.

"You'd never believe it," she said to Starr. "That Mr. Dugdale's up there as well, with his fiancée, Mrs. Monroe."

"There'll be a fair old rumpus if Mrs. Trotter finds out, won't there?"

"What? She's there in the thick of it."

"I tell you," Merriman said, emerging with his loaded tray, "hotels are like hospitals. They're all bodies. You do your best for 'em, but once you get your feelings involved . . ."

He staggered on his way.

"You lose out on tips, eh?" Starr said. He looked down at Fred. "Mrs. Trotter's learning, me old son. Isn't she?"

Twenty

A few weeks later, Louisa went away on holiday. As always, she went reluctantly, preferring activity to idleness. She rarely did absent herself, and then only when practically ordered to by Charlie Tyrrell, who would visit town briefly, notice signs of strain in her features and manner, and, after long argument, pack her off to Margate or somewhere, even if only for a few days. He never suggested taking her away himself. Their brief romance was never referred to now; that aspect of their relationship was dead and buried.

This time she had been cajoled farther afield—not by Charlie, whom she had not seen since the beginning of the year, but by a French count with a château in the champagne country. She could sense herself that she needed a rest, and the Count was an elderly charmer who stayed at the Bentinck whenever he visited London. Louisa knew that he had a countess and several sons and daughters at the château. She felt she would at least be left unpestered, so she accepted.

"Wish I hadn't," she grumbled to Mary on the morning of her departure, the Count having gone ahead a week earlier. "Can't stick holidays. I'm all on edge, and worst of all, when I come back, everything's always in a mess."

She was standing on the pavement in front of the hotel.

"That's not fair!" Mary had the spirit to retort. "We look after everything, don't we, Major?"

"Do our best, eh?" Smith-Barton grinned. "Don't worry, Mrs. Trotter. I'll keep an eye on things, don't you know?"

"Well . . . Laundry maid, don't forget. There's two applicants coming tomorrow from that agency. And look after Miss Hayward, the bishop's daughter. She's been a regular for years, but she always fusses."

"I know," Mary said firmly. "We'll be quite all right. Now, you'll miss your train unless . . ."

After a last despairing glance up at her hotel, Louisa allowed herself to be driven away by the Major in the smart new hotel bus. It might have been a tumbrel taking her to execution, to judge from her face. Preoccupied with herself, she had no reason to notice a slightly blowsy, poorly dressed young woman who had been leaning on a bicycle within earshot of the conversation.

Louisa had barely been gone ten minutes before Miss Hayward, a brisk and domineering fifty, and her sour, pious maid, Morgan, came marching down to the hall desk, where Starr was checking advance bookings with Mary.

"I want to see Mrs. Trotter," Miss Hayward demanded.

"She's gone away, madam," Starr explained. "Can I or Miss Philips help?"

"My maid has found a cockroach in her bedroom. Show them, Morgan."

The stringy maid stepped forward and, with an expression accentuating her usual distaste for everything, opened a small box at arm's length and placed it on the counter. Starr peered close.

"It's a big fellow," he said interestedly. "See that, Mary?"

With more tact, Mary said, "I'm very sorry, Miss Hayward."

The bishop's daughter sniffed. "What concerns me is that cockroaches are more usually found in kitchens."

"Oh, not in ours, madam. Our kitchens are spotless. You're welcome to come down and see."

"I don't think so, thank you," Miss Hayward replied loftily, as if she had never deigned to enter a kitchen in her life. "Come along, Morgan. Harrods."

They swept out. Mary went off into Louisa's room. Starr threw the dead cockroach in its box into his wastepaper basket. As he straightened up he found Merriman approaching, carrying a letter.

"For you," the old waiter said. "A young woman left it at the back door just now."

Starr, frowning, opened the letter and read its scrawled message. His frown deepened. Then he asked Merriman to look after the desk and Fred while he just popped out for a few minutes.

His steps took him to a small public house, some fifty yards around the nearest corner, mostly frequented by servants, soldiers, and small tradesmen. It was fairly full and he had to glance around until he saw the person he was seeking. It was the young woman bicyclist who had overheard Louisa's parting words to the Major and Mary. Starr went to where she was sitting at a long table with two glasses of stout in front of her. She smiled up tentatively, but he didn't smile in return.

"Hello, Joey," she greeted him. "Bought you a glass of your old favorite." She indicated the stout. "See—I don't forget. You're lookin' all right. Smart uniform."

He sat down reluctantly, wanting to keep their conversation subdued.

"What you doing here, Lizzie? What d'you want?"

"See you, that's all. No law against it, is there? Hard to find, though, you were. Tramped all over Lon-

don. Still be lookin', if I hadn't met Corporal Philpott
—remember, the one with the big ears? He's a baker's roundsman now and he knew where you was."

He said suspiciously, "I thought we agreed . . . not
to meet again."

"Is that all you can say, Joey? Didn't you never
think of me—if I was alive or dead, even? I've thought
of you."

"Evidently, or you wouldn't be here now. What're
you after, Lizzie?"

She looked at him levelly. She was in her early
thirties, some few years younger than he. Her face
bore vestiges of a wild beauty and her figure was
still good, but her forehead and neck were lined and
her hands were rough, with dirty nails. Her clothing
was far from new and not well tended.

"I want a job," she answered simply.

"A job? Well, I can't give you one."

"You could help. Must be somethin' in that hotel—
cleanin', scrubbin' . . . I'm not proud. Please, Joey. I'm
desperate. It's not been easy . . . on me own."

He hadn't touched the drink she had bought him.
He said flintily, "I don't believe you've been on your
own, Lizzie. Not you."

Her eyes glittered resentfully. "I have! More often
than not, anyway. I'm not a whore."

"All right, calm down, calm down," he urged her,
glancing anxiously around. She insisted, more quietly,
"I'm not askin' for money, Joey. I ain't got none, but
I'm not askin' for it. Just want a job and bit of respect,
like you've got."

"There's other jobs," he pointed out.

"Yeh, I've had some of 'em. Makin' trousers in a
sweatshop. Twelve hours a day for a lousy shillin'. Bar-
maid in Stepney. That wasn't bad, but the landlord
was. Joey, there was a time when you thought I was
worth more'n that sort of thing."

"I don't want to talk about that," he said firmly. "It's

finished. I've got my life settled now and I don't want you barging your way back into it. I'm sorry, Lizzie, but you'll have to look elsewhere."

She looked him full in the eyes and asked, "Do they *know* about you at the Bentinck, Joey? Tell 'em all your past, did you?"

Starr had been more than reticent upon that subject when first interviewed by Louisa. And ever since, he had maintained his inscrutable pose, volunteering nothing about himself to anyone and carefully avoiding answering the occasional probings of Merriman, who sensed a fellow old soldier in Starr, but couldn't win so much as an admission that he had ever been one.

"Bitch!" he said to the watching woman.

"Yeh," she sighed. "That's what life can make you, innit?"

"Do your worst," he replied, trying to call her bluff. "Go and tell 'em, then. It won't get you a job, though. Anyway, there isn't one going."

"There is. I heard that woman, just before she got on the bus. Talkin' about some laundry maids comin' to be seen. I could do that."

"No."

She changed her tone, not to wheedling, but to what Starr thought he sensed was genuine desperation.

"Oh, please, Joey. Just till I get on me feet. Then I'll move on. I won't make you no trouble. Promise."

He looked at her for some moments before replying uncertainly, "You won't breathe a word?"

"Honest."

There was a further pause before he said, "I can't . . . fix it for you. You'd have to get it on merit, against the others."

She smiled again. "You could give me a reference at least. Thanks, Joey. Drink your stout, love."

She placed her hand over his on the table. He gave

her a little smile at last, picked up the glass, and drank.

Mary Philips interviewed the applicants in the laundry room itself, a belowstairs apartment with a stone floor sloping gently toward a gutter and drain, a boiler, a row of tubs, two mangles, an ironing table, and various shelves and cupboards holding piles of folded white linen. The first two women were disappointments: one too old and slow, the other young but clearly not mentally fitted to do more than scrub floors or carry coals. Lizzie, by contrast, made a good impression. She had tidied her hair and cleaned herself up. She spoke respectfully and confidently.

"After me husband died I had to get work where I could," she explained to Mary. "I never worked in a hotel before, but I expect it's the same as washin' and ironin' in your own home, innit? Only, like a bigger family."

"I suppose it is," Mary smiled.

Lizzie went on, "Sort out all the different things into piles, do I? White linen, body linen, collars . . ."

"That's it. How would you remove an ink stain, say?"

"Good rub with soap and water?" Lizzie suggested hopefully, not knowing.

"No. You need salts of sorrel for ink marks."

"Ah, well, soon pick it all up; if you don't mind me askin' questions, miss."

Mary's mind was almost made up. "And you say you're acquainted with Mr. Starr, Mrs. Talbot?"

"Oh, some years. We hadn't bumped into each other for ever such a long time, though. Mr. Starr was my late husband's best friend. Sergeants together. He was with my husband when he was killed. Brought his things back for me. I'm sure he'll speak for me, miss."

"All right," Mary told her. "We'll take that for granted, then. The job's yours."

"I'm ever so grateful, miss. There's . . . no chance of livin' in, is there?"

"I'm afraid not. Have you far to come?"

"From the East End. But I've got me bike."

"Good. Well, the wages are fifteen shillings a week and all meals. Is that satisfactory?"

"Thank you, miss. Want me to start now, as I'm here?"

"If you could I'd be grateful. We are rather behind. There are some aprons over here."

Lizzie took off her coat and hat and hung them up, donned an apron, and began with a will.

A little later Mrs. Cochrane looked around the door and saw Lizzie ironing busily.

"Hello, dear," she smiled. "I'm the cook, Mrs. Cochrane. We're having our tea in a minute. You'll come and join us?"

Lizzie accepted pleasantly. "Ta. Just finish these last things first."

When she went into the servants' hall she found Mrs. Cochrane, her kitchen maid, and Merriman seated at the table, drinking tea and eating bread and jam. Introductions were made and Merriman lapsed into munching silence again. Mrs. Cochrane passed Lizzie her cup and said, "Mary—Miss Philips—says you're a widow, Mrs. Talbot."

"Yeh. Call me Lizzie, please."

"Very well, dear. I'm a widow, too."

"Hard life, eh?"

"Yes. Mr. Cochrane's been gone fourteen years come August. He went in for a bathe at Margate, straight after a big dinner. I told him it would be bad . . . Still, my children've been good to me. You got any children, Lizzie?"

"No. Only married six months."

"Oh, what a shame!"

"Yeh. Tall, handsome, my Jack was. Big shoulders. Lovely man."

"And he was killed fighting with Mr. Starr, I believe."

"Side by side, at the battle of Omdurman."

Starr entered at that moment, in time to hear the reference to him. Even Merriman shed his deafness in the presence of some interesting information at last.

Lizzie smiled at Starr and patted Fred. "That's a nice dog, Mr. Starr," she said. "You always was fond of animals, wasn't you? Remember in Malta, that big white rabbit we had that John looked after?"

"Didn't know you was in Malta, Mr. Starr," Merriman said.

Starr said nothing, but Lizzie prattled on. "Yeh. That's where they were. Rifle Brigade. Second battalion. Before they went to Egypt."

"You was in the Rifle Brigade?" Merriman tried again, impressed.

"Quartermaster Sergeant," Lizzie answered, smiling at Starr, who shot her a warning look.

"Kept that a dark secret," Merriman continued.

Again Lizzie put in, "Well, not all men like to boast about their fightin' days, do they, Mr. Starr?"

He crammed bread into his mouth, and was further saved from having to speak by the entry of Mary, with a list of guests due to leave and talk of arrangements to be made accordingly.

That evening, Starr ushered Fred into their bedroom. The dog barked once and growled. Starr was astonished to see Lizzie in her underclothes, holding her dress.

"What the hell! . . ." he exclaimed, shutting the door hurriedly and silencing Fred, who by now had recognized Lizzie, anyway.

"Just had a bath along the passage," she explained. "Ain't got one where I live. It's all right, I asked Mrs. Cochrane. Smell . . . real soap. I feel human again."

She extended a slender arm. Even in his shocked

state of indignation he could see that her body was attractively molded. He ignored the arm and said, "This is my room. You've no right in here."

"Is it?" Lizzie replied with apparent innocence. "I thought it was a spare."

True, Starr had made little imprint of himself on his surroundings. Most of his belongings were out of sight. But the dog basket beside the bed was obvious enough.

"Well, hurry up and get out," he said curtly. "Hope no one saw you come in."

Lizzie went on dressing. "Don't be hasty with me, Joey," she said. "I've had a hard day. Worked like a slave in that laundry room. Made a good impression, have I?"

"Not on me, you haven't. Too much blabbermouth. You promised . . ."

"Well, how was I to know you'd told 'em nothin' at all? There's *some* bits you're not ashamed of."

"It suited me to tell 'em nothing. Build up again from scratch. A new man. Now you've come and the questions'll start. I'm not as easy a liar as you are. They'll catch me out, and then I'm done for."

She had got her dress fastened now. She looked at herself in his small shaving mirror.

"Sorry, Joey, I won't say another word, even if they ask me." With a coquettish twirl around to face him she said gaily, "Kept me figure, you got to admit. Bloomin' miracle. Fancy takin' me for a drink?"

"Can't. I'm on duty."

"Oh, well, see you tomorrow, then," Lizzie said, clearly disappointed.

"Where are you living?" Starr asked, unbending a little.

"Whitechapel. It's quite quick on me bike, really."

He asked hesitantly, "Lizzie . . . You living on your own, are you?"

She smiled. "Course I'm on me own. One room. Just like this. Good night, Joey."

She went out quickly, closing the door. Starr sat on his bed, absently running his fingers through Fred's coarse fur, lost in thought and memories.

Next morning, he entered the servants' hall to find Mrs. Cochrane clucking over Lizzie, who was seated on a chair, wincing as the cook applied a compress to what was revealed to be a nasty black eye.

"Young thug gave her it on her way to work," Mrs. Cochrane explained.

"Yeh," Lizzie confirmed quite cheerfully. "About fifteen, he was. There was a gang of 'em, pummelin' some poor little runt. Florence Nightingale goes to his rescue and gets this for her pains."

"The sooner you're out of the East End, the better," the cook told her. "Don't you agree, Mr. Starr? No place for a poor young woman on her own."

Lizzie's good eye caught Starr's look. She managed a wink. He didn't return it or answer Mrs. Cochrane's remark; but later in the day he did come down to the laundry room and invite Lizzie to have a drink with him when he came off duty that evening.

They went to the pub of their first encounter. Fred did not accompany them. He had been left in Merriman's care. Lizzie's eye had really blackened by now and was nearly closed. She looked around and giggled.

"Gettin' some funny looks," she said. "They must think you're my old man and it was you done this." She pointed to the eye.

Starr smiled. He was more relaxed in her presence now. She could feel it. She said, "We oughter gone somewhere else, I suppose. Someone you know might come in. Bad for your reputation."

He was genuinely touched that she should have given the matter a thought.

"Anyone who knows me knows I live in and I'm not married," he replied easily. "Does it hurt?"

"No. Wait till I see that coppernob kid again, though. I'll put one on him first."

"Rest of you's all right—what I've seen," he surprised her by saying.

"Thanks, Joey," she said. "That's nice of you."

"I'm taking you home," he said suddenly. "You're not fit to bike with one eye shut. We'll get the bus."

"I'm all right, Joey, thanks," she said hastily. "Really." But he was draining his glass and getting up. "Come on," he ordered. "I'm hungry. We'll get some jellied eels."

He failed to recognize her reluctance as she got up and obediently left the public house with him. As they walked along she said, "I don't want you to see my home. It's not nice."

"I don't care about that."

She had to give in. "Well, if you must. But I warn you . . ." She cheered up. "I've got some halibut, if it hasn't been nicked. How about that, fried?"

Starr licked his lips and grinned. "Quite fancy a bit of that." When they were well clear of the vicinity of the Bentinck he took her arm and held it all the way to the bus terminal at Piccadilly Circus.

The room, in the noisy tenement building, proved to be as unsavory as she had warned him it would. It was a small low-ceilinged little place with a bare floor and stained walls, a rickety table, one plain chair and two fruit boxes, a couch-bed with a ragged coverlet, and very little else save for a hissing gas jet.

Lizzie was frying the halibut on a small old gas cooker. Starr stared about with distaste.

"How long've you been here?" he asked.

"All winter. Lucky to get it."

He wandered about, eyeing the marks where bugs had been squashed and flies swatted. A few pans lay on an open shelf. He spotted something else there, too.

"What's this?" he demanded. His sharp tone made her turn. He was holding up a mug containing a shaving brush and a stick of shaving soap.

Lizzie merely shrugged and turned back to her cooking. Starr looked around more keenly. On instinct, he stooped and looked under the bed. A bundle of clothing lay there. He dragged it out. It was a man's jacket and trousers.

"Might have guessed!" he said bitterly.

Lizzie had looked around again. She said urgently, "No, Joey, it's not that. I don't know whose they are—honest. I have to share the room."

"*Have* to?"

"It's the truth. Ask the landlord. Three bob a week I have to pay for sharin'. Bloody swiz!"

"Who with?" he asked, deeply suspicious.

"Don't ask me. It changes. Sometimes a man, sometimes a woman. We have it in shifts. We don't see each other. It's the rule. Now you know why I come to find you. Sooner I can get out, the better."

"Same *bed?*"

"There ain't another, is there? Anyway," she grinned, "I took me own sheets in to the Bentinck this morning and did 'em with the rest of the wash." She indicated the bundle she had carried on their way home. "At least we got clean sheets tonight." Her grin went and she looked at him seriously. "Will you stay, Joey?" she asked. "Face is a bit of a mess, but the rest of me's all right."

She stepped toward him, holding out her hands. He took them impulsively and pulled her toward him. Their lips met in a long kiss. The halibut sizzled unheeded in its pan.

Merriman took Fred out for his night rounds, then took him along to Starr's room. "There you are, Fred," he said, pointing to the basket on the floor. The animal stood looking questioningly up at him. "He'll not be long now," Merriman said. "Master'll soon be back."

He went to his own room. He was too deaf to be woken an hour or two later, and again as dawn was breaking, by outbursts of whines and a low, keening howling. It was the first time Fred had ever been apart from Starr's presence for a whole night.

"Are you quite sure, Miss Hayward?" Major Smith-Barton was asking.

He was facing the truly irate bishop's daughter in Louisa's parlor, to which Mary had summoned him upon having heard what Miss Hayward had to say. This time it was no mere complaint. It was serious.

"Of course I'm sure," came her answer. "I'm not in the habit of making false accusations of theft. I think it's absolutely disgraceful."

"Won't you sit down, please, madam?" the Major suggested tactfully. "I should like to hear the details for myself, if I may."

She startled Mary by saying, "The police will have to be informed, of course." But to the relief of both of them she accepted the chair and told the Major what she had already told Mary, while he polished his eyeglass vigorously.

"Yesterday morning I left seven pounds on my dressing table. Seven pounds exactly—shopping money. When I came back from my morning walk there was just four pounds."

"Yesterday?" Mary said. "Why didn't you tell us sooner?"

The Major interceded smoothly. "I'm sure Miss Hayward wanted to make quite certain before coming to the conclusion that the money really had been stolen, don't you know?"

"Exactly," Miss Hayward agreed. "I searched high and low. I asked Morgan if she had moved any of the money. Quite naturally, she pointed out that she had had no cause to; and that if she had, she would have moved it all, not simply three pounds of it."

Mary said, "But I did your room myself yesterday. Your chambermaid's away sick."

Miss Hayward favored her with one of her rare smiles. "You had told me you intended to, Miss Philips. That is why I was confident enough to leave the money lying about anyway. Not that, I must say, in all my years of coming to the Bentinck, I have ever had cause to doubt the honesty of any member of the staff. It makes it all the more upsetting."

"Quite, quite," said Major Smith-Barton. "I'm sure that, on Mrs. Trotter's behalf, we are deeply appreciative of your remarks, dear lady. However, if I might suggest it, there is one alternative you may have overlooked. Your room is not locked, I believe. Your maid comes and goes from time to time. So, rather than any member of our staff, it could have been the private servant of a fellow guest who took your money. I wouldn't go so far as to suggest that it was an actual guest . . ."

"I should hope not, Major!"

"We can vouch for everyone in the hotel at present. But in one or two cases their servants are newcomers to us, and the trivial amount of the theft certainly points to someone for whom three pounds would be valuable enough to make the risk worth taking."

Miss Hayward was looking at him with positive admiration.

"How clever!" she cried.

"Not at all," he muttered modestly. "Some experience of this sort of thing in the army, don't you know? My suggestion—if I might, that is . . . ?"

"By all means."

"Thank you—is that you leave the matter in my hands. A few careful inquiries, rather than have police all over the place, asking awkward questions and upsetting people."

"Yes," Mary said. "And the missing money will certainly be deducted from your account, Miss Hayward."

Much mollified, the bishop's daughter thanked them both and went off. After brief consultation with Mary, the Major went out into the hall. Starr was on duty as usual, looking, the Major noticed, unusually pale and peaky for him.

"Spot of bother, Starr," the Major confided. "Some money taken from Miss Hayward's room—so she believes, anyway. Always unpleasant, this sort of thing. Bad feeling all round, don't you know? Then I expect it'll turn up in her handbag. Oh, by the way, Merriman was telling me you were in the Rifle Brigade."

"Yes, sir," Starr admitted defensively.

"Second battalion? Malta? Did you ever serve with an old friend of mine, Captain Mayhew?"

Starr's reply came instantly. "No, Major. Never."

"Ah. Good man. Must bring him round here sometime. You can have a chinwag."

"I'm not much taken with chinwagging, sir," Starr said. "About the past, that is. Foot-forward's my motto."

In the kitchen, Merriman, that retailer of news, said in a low voice to Mrs. Cochrane, "An old romance raised from the embers, d'you reckon? *Her* and Mr. Starr."

"Mrs. Talbot? Whatever makes you say a thing like that, Mr. Merriman?"

"He wasn't in his own bed last night. When I got up at six I found his poor dog whining and scratching at the door, so I went in. Not like Mr. Starr to forget Fred, is it?"

The cook considered, then came down on the side of romance. "Well, what if there is something? She deserves a bit of luck, poor thing. Losing her husband so soon."

Merriman was musing. "Husband Jack. Yes, now where does he fit in? Was Sergeant Starr carrying on with her before or after the Battle of Omdurman, if you get my drift?"

Mrs. Cochrane blushed. "You've got a wicked mind, Mr. Merriman."

He tapped his nose on one side. "A soldier's nose, Mrs. C. There's something fishy going on, mark my words."

His suspicions were deepened when, that evening, Starr asked him if he wouldn't mind giving Fred his late-night walk, adding, though, that he would be back easily by midnight. Merriman made no reference to his complete absence the previous night, and Starr volunteered nothing about it. Merriman agreed, curious to know what might happen next in this new game.

He was even more intrigued that evening to find Lizzie Talbot, dressed for going home, talking to the dog in his basket in the hall.

"Where's Master, then?" she was asking playfully.

Merriman startled her by replying, "Mr. Starr's gone out."

"Out? But . . ." She checked herself just in time from saying that she'd expected Starr to want to take her home again. He hadn't said anything to her during the day, and she had had no chance to chat with him, though they had managed to exchange an affectionate wink or two.

"Has he been gone for long?" she asked.

"All evening," Merriman said. "Didn't say where. Were you wanting to see him about something?"

His hopes that some further clue might be forthcoming were dashed, as, evidently, were her spirits. She just said, "No. It's nothing," and left by the front door, disregarding his reminder that it wasn't for staff use.

The last thing Lizzie suspected as she made her way disappointedly to what she called home was that Starr had left earlier in order to race there ahead of her. When Lizzie tiredly climbed the stairs to her room, Starr was lurking out of sight around the corner of the passage onto which her room opened. When she had gone in he crept to the closed door and listened. His jaw tightened when he heard her ask someone, "What you doin' here? I might have brought *him* back again."

A man's deep voice replied, "We've got our story. I'm a tenant. Sharin'."

"Yeh, but I told him we never ..."

"Shut up. I came for what you've got for me, if you've got it—and you better had."

"Can't wait, can you?" she said contemptuously. "Here you are. Three quid. And it's the last I'm nickin' for you, so make the most of it."

Starr heard the man chuckle. "Three lovely nicker. There you are my darlin'—one for you, two for me. Now come 'ere."

"Get your paws off me. And keep your lousy quid. Keep it and get out. Go back to sea. Anywhere. I'm finished with you, Frank Corelli!"

"Gone soft, have you?" he sneered. "Whose idea was it, anyway? Yer old lover boy. Too much for you, is he?"

Starr heard a sudden movement and an exclamation from the man. Then a loud slap and a cry from Lizzie.

"Stinkin' little whore!" the man shouted, and there was another blow. "Whore from the gutter! ..."

He got no further. Starr burst into the room and flung himself at the man, regardless of the fact that the other was bigger and burlier than he. With the advantage of surprise, Starr bore the man to the floor. But the man began to retaliate strongly. Starr sensed rather than saw Lizzie run from the room as his opponent began to get to his feet. Desperately, knowing himself about to be outclassed, Starr seized the only chair in the wretched room, raised it high, and brought it down on the other's head. It knocked him back to the ground, dazed. Starr, his eyes blazing, raised the chair once more, quite berserk now, ready to smash it down again and again.

But the fearful man on the floor saw him hesitate suddenly. A strange, far-off look had come into this wild intruder's eyes. He lowered the chair slowly and staggered out of the room, like an automaton. Frank Corelli could have rushed him and hurled him downstairs. But his head hurt like hell and things were spinning around. He was content to lie where he was, rubbing his head and swearing.

Merriman was interested to see Starr return much earlier than he had thought he would. He looked somewhat disheveled and had nothing to say as he went straight past to his room.

There he sat on his bed, his happy dog's muzzle on his knee. "Set up, we was, Fred," he said. "Should've learnt my lesson years ago. In Malta, before your time, old son. Should've learnt my bloody lesson then."

There came a tapping at the window, urgent and almost continuous. Starr leaned over and lifted the curtain. Lizzie was outside. He could hear her saying, "Joey! Let me in, please. Let me explain."

"Go away," he told her.

She shook her head. "You've got to. I'll scream the whole place awake if you don't let me in."

Wearily, Starr went out and unlocked the back entrance. Lizzie slipped past him and straight to his room. He glanced around but no one was about.

Behind his closed door she pleaded, "It was his idea, Joey. I swear it wasn't me. He said find you, get a job here, then start nickin'. I didn't want to, but he always makes me do anything he wants. The other morning—this eye—it wasn't kids. It was him. What could I do, Joey? He'd have killed me."

"Maybe he should have."

"I only took up with him because I was broke. I needed somebody, and he was better than nothin'.

Then I met you again, and I knew I wanted shut of him and the whole thing. Joey, it's *you* I want—honest."

"You had me once. You had your chance." He added contemptuously, "Rifleman Williams!"

"He never meant nothin' to me, Joey. You was away —maybe killed. I was scared. He took advantage . . ."

"They always do, don't they? Never your fault. Just a poor little victim. I loved you, Lizzie."

"I know."

"Worshiped you. When I met you again my mind . . . went back."

Hopefully, she smiled. "Yeh—they was good days in Malta, wasn't they? We can still do it, Joey. This hotel—I like it here. I'll go straight. We can be happy. We was the other night."

"Yes," he admitted. "But I've been thinking since. I thought I'd better do some checking up, and it turned out I was right. You bring shame on me—always. You ruined me once, but not again, Lizzie. Not again. Now get out. Get back to your pimp and find somewhere else to start stealing for him."

There was real fear in her eyes. "No, please!" she begged. "He'll be there . . . waitin'."

"Out of my room. Go on."

"I can't, Joey. He's waitin', I tell you. I won't. I'll scream. I'll . . ."

He seized her around the waist with one arm, jerked the door open with his free hand, and almost threw her across the threshold. He shut the door and rammed its bolt home. Fred came across to look up at his panting master, standing listening with his back to the door. The threatened screams never came.

Starr went back to sit on the bed. He stroked the dog, whose inquiring eyes seemed to be trying to read the meaning of it all from him.

"Gone, Fred," was all the explanation he got. "Gone. And good riddance."

Lizzie didn't come to the hotel the next morning. Mary asked the other staff if she had said anything to them. Starr said heavily, "I know all about it, miss. And Fred and me're leaving, too."

"Oh, no!"

"You can't do that, old chap," the Major said. "Anyway, why?"

"Private reasons, Major."

"To do with Mrs. Talbot?" Mrs. Cochrane didn't hesitate to ask.

Starr nodded. "Sorry to inconvenience you, Mary."

The Major said suspiciously, "I think we're entitled to an explanation, Starr. Mrs. Trotter certainly would be."

Starr hesitated briefly, then said, "It was her who took Miss Hayward's money. And since she came here at my recommendation, Fred and me think it's only right and proper that we should take our part of the blame."

"But that's silly!" Mary protested.

"You had no part in it, did you?" the Major demanded.

"No, sir."

"Well, then . . . Now, come on, Starr, you just tell us all about it. We're all . . . friends here."

After a further hesitation, and a doubtful glance at the women, Starr capitulated and told all his many-faceted secret. He addressed himself to the Major. It was easier to confess to an officer.

"I met her in Malta—Lizzie . . . Mrs. Talbot. Lot of 'em were after her. She chose me for some reason. Happy as larks we were."

"But what about her husband?" Mrs. Cochrane put in, preparing to become outraged.

"No such man. Just me she had, or so I thought. Common-law wife. Well, I went to Egypt and fought and came back. I'd had my suspicions of her and this Rifleman Williams before I went, but this time it was

obvious. I lost my temper. The sun, Egypt, the beer
. . . Anyway, I slammed him on the head with a rifle
butt. Cracked his skull. He lived, fortunately, but I
paid my dues. Court-martial. Dishonorable discharge.
Two years in the glasshouse. Lost my pension, *and*
they took my medals away. Your friend Captain Mayhew will tell you, sir. He spoke in my defense."

"Good heavens!" the Major said, and replaced the
eyeglass which had dropped out halfway through this
narrative.

"Yes, sir. Eight years ago, all that was. Reasons
for my reticence in matters military, Mr. Merriman.
And now, I think, Fred and me'll be on our way."

"Whatever for now?" Mary asked.

"Pride, miss. All right while nobody knew. Now
it'll be common gossip . . ."

"It certainly will not!" Mrs. Cochrane said, glaring
at the others for their confirmation. "We've gossiped
enough about you because you kept so secret. Made
up all sorts of things, haven't we, Mr. Merriman?"

The old man nodded and came over to shake
Starr's hand. "As one military man to another, Mr.
Starr, you've my word there'll be nothing said."

"And mine, too," the Major said, also shaking hands.
The women chimed in their support. But Starr said,
"Mrs. Trotter'll never keep us on."

"Mrs. Trotter will never know," the Major answered
firmly. "That's a further promise."

"Well . . ." Starr said doubtfully. He looked down
at Fred. Fred looked up at him, showing the whites
of yearning eyes. "Oh, well, we'll see how it goes, eh?"

They dispersed about their duties. Starr went off to
his room to change back into the uniform he had
taken off when he had resolved to leave. While he
was gone two big men came into the hall. One was a
police constable, but when the Major approached them
it was the other who asked, "Are you by any chance
the proprietor or manager of this hotel, sir?"

"No, no. The actual proprietor's away at the moment. But I have a sort of official, er . . . Can I help you, sir?"

"Chief Inspector Land, sir. Scotland Yard. If there's somewhere we may speak privately, please. Oh, and I should also like to speak to a Mr. Joseph Starr who I believe is employed here."

"He'll be along in a few moments," the Major said. "Just changing into his uniform."

Starr arrived at that moment. The Major ushered the party into Louisa's parlor, where Mary was sitting at the desk, and made the introductions. The Chief Inspector said, "I understand you've recently had a laundry woman working here, by the name of Mrs. Talbot."

"Yes, sir," Mary said. "She hasn't turned up today, though."

"No," the policeman said. He referred to a notebook. "Mrs. Talbot, or Lizzie Starr, or Mrs. Frank Corelli, and"—he turned to Starr—"really named Mrs. Joseph Starr. Your wife."

"Not legally," Starr replied. "Common law. Years ago."

The officer nodded. "I understand you haven't been living together as man and wife. Mr. Starr, could you tell me when you last saw her?"

"Yes, sir. Last night." He paused, then added, "When she finished work. About half-past six."

"Did she go straight home, do you know?" He was watching Starr keenly.

"I couldn't say, sir," Starr lied. "Has . . . something happened?"

"I'm afraid I have to tell you that she's dead. Her body was taken out of the river by Wapping Steps in the early hours of this morning. We've reason to believe she either jumped from a bridge—or was pushed. There was a lot of bruising about her face and body."

Starr said grimly, "The man you want is Frank Corelli, sir."

The policeman said, "We know him of old. I'm

afraid, though, Mr. Starr, I must ask you to come and identify the body, please, and perhaps you would give us your statement at the same time."

"I'll be glad to, sir. Poor Lizzie. A victim to the last."

"Do you know any reason she might have had for taking her own life?"

"A lot of reasons," Starr said, almost inaudibly. "Years of 'em."

He nodded to Mary, who was crying, and the Major, and went away with the policemen. He was back on duty by lunchtime.

"Hello Mary, Starr," Louisa said, as she breezed in through the front door a couple of days later. "Hello, Major. Good to be back. Chased all round the vineyards, I was, the old devil. Anything been happenin' here?"

They were all ready for her. "Nothing to speak of, Mrs. Trotter," the Major answered. "Very quiet, really, don't you know? Miss Hayward has gone. There have been three arrivals."

"Get the new laundry woman all right, Mary?"

Mary swallowed. "Yes—well, we had one for a day or two, but she left."

"Left? What was wrong with her?"

"She . . . wasn't quite suitable, ma'am. But there are two more coming from the agency this afternoon."

"Blimey!" Louisa said. "I can't turn my back without . . . Well, I'll pick one myself, this time."

She bustled off. The three looked at one another in relief.

"Well done," the Major said softly; and they dispersed.

Twenty-One

Merriman pushed open the door of Louisa's parlor and entered. He carried a tray with a decanter of dry sherry and two glasses. The fire was burning brightly in the little grate. It was cold outside—a cold early autumn morning in 1907.

Louisa was at her desk, making up a bill from a pile of service dockets beside her, watched unseeingly by the framed photographs of two men. Lord Haslemere's was signed with his cheerful scrawl: *Louisa, with Fondest Regards, Charlie.* King Edward the Seventh's was tactfully unsigned.

"Fourteen pounds, plus three pounds eight . . ." she muttered aloud before looking up. "Oh, stick it over there," she told Merriman with a vague gesture. "I'm expecting my solicitor, Sir Michael Manning. Tell Starr to show him straight in."

"Yes, madam," he said, setting the tray down on a small table.

"I'm making up Mr. Buckhurst's bill," she said. "There's eight bottles of claret down to him, but you've only charged for six."

"That's right, ma'am. He returned two. He said one was corked and the other was not what he had ordered."

"Did he? You startin' to slip, Merriman?"

"Certainly not, madam. It was a very good year.

301

He said I'd transferred a label from an empty bottle of good claret onto one of an inferior vintage."

"He what! And just who does Mr. Nigel bleedin' Buckhurst think he is?"

"Other members of the staff have opinions about that."

"I see. Well, you can take his bill up to him and the sooner he's off these premises for good, the better."

He took the bill and left. Louisa, flushed with irritation, looked at Charlie's picture and said, "There's not enough like you about anymore, love."

There was a knock at her door. The Major entered.

"Sir Michael Manning, madam," he said. Manning came in, wearing a heavy overcoat and carrying his top hat and cane. He was middle-aged, alert, and distinguished-looking: the archetypal prosperous solicitor.

"My apologies for being late, Louisa," he said. "Some business in Chancery took longer than I expected."

"That's all right. Nice of you to pop round. Oh, Major, say to Starr that we're not to be disturbed. Not for any reason."

"Of course, of course," said the Major, and went out.

Sir Michael removed his coat, accepted some sherry, and after a brief exchange about the weather asked, "Now, what's all this about? Your note had a tone of urgency and alarm."

Louisa found a letter on her desk and passed it to him. "I got this yesterday from Firbank, Bricelow and Firbank. They're solicitors for the people who lease the Bentinck to me. I can't make head nor tail of it."

He scanned it quickly, then said, "It's quite simple, really. They want to renegotiate the lease."

"It doesn't say that. I could have understood that."

He smiled. "Solicitors frequently avoid saying what they mean. That is why, so often, another has to be

engaged to translate. The arrangement allows us to
live in modest comfort."

"Huh! Trust you lot to have it all nicely fixed up
among yourselves. Are you sure that's what they're
after, though?"

"Reading between the lines, I sense that, having
granted you a long lease on a decrepit hotel which
has now become prosperous, they feel they ought to
be getting more ground rent."

"Well, they can feel what they like. It's my blood
and sweat's made the Bentinck what it is. And the
lease still has fifty years to run."

"Fifty-three, to be precise—if you don't break it."
He tapped the letter. "There's just the slightest suggestion here that you may have done so."

"How?"

"By allowing gaming parties to run until all hours
of the morning. And doubtless they have in mind
other things they choose not to commit to paper."

Louisa knew perfectly well what Sir Michael meant.
It was universally known in raffish society that she
willingly turned a blind eye to what she termed "respectable goings-on" in the rooms of solitary gentlemen. "Respectable," that is, according to her own
judgment.

"If they're sayin' I allow street girls to use the place,
they're bloody liars," she said.

The lawyer shook his head. "They're not saying
that. The letter simply refers to that stipulation in the
lease which requires that 'the aforementioned premises shall be used only and solely for the purposes
specified, and not for any purpose which may be
deemed to be of an illegal, immoral, or otherwise
disreputable nature.'"

"Bloomin' cheek! What's it got to do with them,
so long as I pay the ground rent regular? I can't tell
my guests to sing hymns after supper and pack them
off to bed at nine prompt."

"Exactly. I've no doubt that if you agreed to pay

more they would be willing to delete the clause under a new agreement. However, the first move is to find out if they're merely trying it on. There really is no ground for suggesting that the Bentinck could be held in public disrepute. I shall write to these people, informing them, in terms of the utmost legal courtesy, that we don't think their gambit will stand up."

"Oh, thanks, dear," Louisa said, pouring him another sherry. "That's taken a real weight off . . ."

She was interrupted by a commotion outside the door. Men's voices were upraised. She heard one demanding, "Will you get out of the way?" and the Major replying, "I'm sorry, sir—Mrs. Trotter gave strict instructions . . ."

"Excuse me," Louisa said to Sir Michael and went quickly out, closing the door behind her. She found the Major literally barring her doorway against Mr. Nigel Buckhurst, who was holding, she noted, his bill. He was in his twenties, dressed in a dandified style, and very red in the face. Merriman hovered uncertainly in the background.

"Thank you, Major," Louisa said quietly. "What seems to be the trouble, Mr. Buckhurst?"

He sneered. "Where would you like me to begin? Perhaps with the dilatory and discourteous service of the doddering pensioners you employ? Or the apparent inability of the kitchen staff to supply a simple snack without two hours' notice?"

"It had gone midnight, sir," Merriman intervened. "I explained that the kitchen staff had gone to bed, then did my best for you myself."

"That'll do, Merriman," Louisa said, still quietly. "The gentleman hasn't finished."

"Not by a long chalk. I haven't even started on the general surliness and impertinence of the hall porter, who took ten minutes to fetch me an evening paper, and did it with damned ill grace."

Merriman was not to be silenced. "He had four suitcases and a cabin trunk to bring down on the way," he told Louisa.

Still looking at Buckhurst and keeping ominously calm, Louisa suggested, "You haven't complained about your room yet. Must've been something wrong with that."

"As it happens, yes. I quite clearly asked to be moved to a larger one. The suite on the second floor has been vacant since I arrived. It would have suited me excellently."

"It's permanently reserved for . . . a regular patron."

"Huh! I'm surprised such a creature exists, or that anyone should want to stay here twice."

Louisa's face reddened now. She snapped back, "And I'm surprised you've stayed as long as you have. If you'll just settle your bill . . ."

"I have no intention of paying such an exorbitant sum for such inadequate service." He held the bill up and ripped it savagely in two. Starr, coming down the stairs with his luggage, was just in time to see it happen. He paused, to hear Mrs. Trotter tell the irate guest, whose back he, too, was looking forward to seeing, "Very well. Since you've torn it in half, I'll only charge you half. Hand over ten pounds twelve shillings and fourpence—*then clear off my premises!*"

Her control had gone now, and the last words were shouted. When Louisa lost her temper she was a daunting spectacle; but Buckhurst didn't quail. He said triumphantly, "Now, there's an admission that you deliberately tried to overcharge me. Well, you won't get a penny now. That's the price for cheating your guests."

"Starr," Louisa ordered the porter, "get them bags back upstairs. Lock 'em in Mr. Buckhurst's room and see that they stay there till he settles his bill—in full."

Starr turned about and set off back up the stairs. Buckhurst was after him with a bound. Fred, who had been lying obediently in his basket behind the desk, flew out, barking furiously, and went for the man's ankles.

And from the dispense, which led off the hall, appeared a police constable, putting on his helmet as he came. He was one of the men on the local beat, and it was his custom, like the rest of them, to pop into the Bentinck on a cold morning for a cup of something warm in the dispense and a chat with Starr or Merriman, his hosts there.

Sir Michael Manning came out, a few seconds later, from Louisa's room, to witness the extraordinary sight of men and pieces of luggage rolling entangled down the staircase. His startled gaze caught the gleam of uniform buttons and a policeman's helmet rolling unevenly to rest at his feet. Automatically, his mind began to revise the text of the letter he had already envisaged writing to the Bentinck's leaseholders, assuring them primly of the place's respectability.

In a Fleet Street public house, the Vineyard, two young reporters on rival newspapers were enjoying a friendly drink. One of them, whose name was Nelson, of the *Daily Mirror,* was congratulating the other, David Culliford, of the *Morning Banner,* on the prominent by-line his editor have given him on a sensational exposé of life in an East End slum. Culliford, an adventurous and slightly raffish man, had earned his reward the hard way, living in the slum for ten days to gather the sordid material for his article.

"Praise from the competition is especially welcome," he thanked his friend. "Millie—two more Scotches, please."

"Just a small one for me," Nelson said. "I've got to get back to the office."

"Harmsworth riding you hard, is he?"

"Not especially. I want to write up a nice little piece I picked up at Bow Street this morning. A Mr. Nigel Buckhurst was fined for causing a disturbance at the Bentinck Hotel—injuring the hall porter and assaulting a policeman."

"That's pretty small beer for the *Mirror*, isn't it?"

"Amusing, though. The woman who runs the Bentinck, Louisa Trotter—you must have heard of her —she was as good as a music-hall turn in court. Even brought a smile to the beak's thin lips. A real character." He grinned mischievously at Culliford. "And, of course, there's the added spicy little detail that the accused is your publisher's nephew."

Culliford's eyebrows rose. If he knew anything about Gerald Bulstrode, principal proprietor of the *Morning Banner*, the tactless Nigel Buckhurst would receive a harder time out of court than in it.

He did. His retrial took place next day in the office of the *Banner*'s editor, Gordon Lawrie, a cynical Scot in his late forties. Lawrie was not present, though. He had diplomatically removed himself when Nigel Buckhurst had entered, sent for by Bulstrode, who was waiting for him there. Bulstrode's name fitted him well. His pomposity and overbearing manner were his most obvious characteristics. He was in his sixties, gray-haired and frock-coated. On this occasion he was carrying a copy of the *Daily Mirror*, with Nelson's near-hilarious account of the court case angrily ringed in red ink.

Bulstrode bellowed true to form, leaving his nephew little chance to defend himself. There was no defense to offer, anyway. He had sent the policeman sprawling down the stairs, the latter losing his helmet and his dignity. He had sprained Starr's ankle for him, wrestling for possession of his luggage. And he had used disgraceful language. The magistrate had fined him and delivered a stinging rebuke.

When the publisher had finished finding Buckhurst guilty on the additional charges of humiliating his mother, Bulstrode's sister, and getting the family name into disreputable print, Bulstrode dismissed his nephew without troubling to listen to an apology, and sent for the editor, who came in looking a trifle apprehensive himself. To his relief, Bulstrode smiled and threw the rival newspaper into a wastepaper basket.

"Does 'em good to get a dressing down occasionally," he said. "No more than youthful peccadillo, I expect." He paused for a moment, then asked, "Tell me, what do you know of this place in Duke Street?"

Lawrie answered, "The Bentinck? Not much. I attended a private dinner party there once, about a year ago."

Bulstrode frowned. "You surprise me, Lawrie. It hardly sounds the sort of place I'd expect you to frequent. Reading between the lines of that piece, it seems distinctly demimondain—little better than a common house of assignation, patronized by all the riffraff. If I'd known that young man was staying there at all I'd have ordered him out."

Lawrie said, "I think, sir, Mr. Buckhurst's lawyer painted it in the worst possible colors. My one experience gave me the impression of a well-run establishment. The meal was excellent."

"Hm! That's not the impression anyone will get from that piece in the *Mirror*. No smoke without fire, I believe. This woman who runs the place . . ."

"Louisa Trotter."

"Know anything about her?"

"Eccentric. A real character. But a great cook. I'm afraid she's no time for journalists, though. She told me so to my face when we were introduced. That's her way."

Bulstrode was looking thoughtful now. "Might her dislike arise from fear, do you think?"

Lawrie risked a smile. "I don't imagine she's afraid of anything, that one. What should she fear, sir?"

But his employer was not smiling. "The integrity and purpose, the proper inquisitiveness of the Press, Lawrie. Its capacity for exposing matters which others

would prefer concealed. Now, as you are aware,
Lawrie, it is my stated position not to interfere with
the editorial policy of this newspaper. That is your
province. You make the decisions and accept the responsibility. Nevertheless, I reserve the right to make
an occasional suggestion to you—and I have such a
suggestion to make now."

Later that morning the editor sent for his promising
young feature-writer, David Culliford. He had ascertained, in the meantime, that, as he had deduced
and hoped, the porter at the Bentinck was temporar-
ily incapacitated with his sprained ankle and the hotel
was advertising for a stand-in. Passing on their employer's instructions, Lawrie told the young man to
hurry there and try to get the job. The story of the
Bentinck from the inside might make as telling a
piece as the slums exposé and would do its writer
much good in the publisher's eyes.

"Revenge for his nephew's treatment?" Culliford
ventured to suggest. The editor shook his head.

"Nothing so trivial as that. Our principal proprietor
has a very genuine nose for what sells newspapers.
No newspaper ever lost circulation by catering to
the prejudices of its readers. Our readers, I don't
need to tell you, are the new literates; the working-
people of this land, now beginning to flex their political muscles. The *Banner* will assist in that exercise,
and with twenty-two Labour Party members elected
last year there is clearly a horse worth riding."

"Ah, I see."

"You'll also be aware that our principal proprietor
has certain preoccupations of his own at the moment.
Harmsworth's elevation to the peerage has given rise
to certain hopes. The proprietor and guiding spirit
of a crusading newspaper, dedicated to exposing
the injustice of our society, revealing without mercy
the moral cancer rotting the fabric of this, that, and
the other . . ." The editor gave his cynical smile.

"Such a man must surely find his reward in the Honours List. Do you follow me?"

"Perfectly, sir," Culliford grinned. "I'll get round there straight away. Oh, I'd better get a reference first. I know just the place where they'll give me one."

He hurried to the Vineyard, bought the landlord and himself a drink, and explained what he wanted. The landlord grinned, bought him a drink in return, and scribbled something on a sheet of notepaper bearing the pub's name.

A quarter of an hour after that, Culliford, calling himself Jenkins and using a slightly roughened version of his natural speaking voice, presented this testimonial to Starr at the desk of the Bentinck. Starr read it, asked a question or two, then, limping painfully, took it in to Louisa, leaving the young man patting Fred's head.

"Very civil and neat about his person," Starr told Louisa. "Miles beyond that other chap who tried."

"What does Fred make of him?"

"Took to him at once, ma'am. Wagged his tail."

"Sounds promising, then. Wheel him in."

Louisa was impressed, too. Hall porters were seldom given to being young, healthy, neat, and deferential all at the same time. And the landlord of the Vineyard, it seemed, couldn't praise him too highly.

"Why'd you leave there?" she asked.

"To better myself, ma'am. I didn't want to stay a potman all my life. I thought I'd like to make my way in the hotel trade—and this seemed a golden chance to get a bit of experience in the very place to learn."

"Well," she said, successfully flattered, "I can't keep you long. Only till Starr's leg's better. Say a week, guaranteed? It'd be long hours and you'd have to turn your hand to anything that comes up—running errands, helping in the kitchen, seeing the guests' shoes get polished. And I can't pay all that much for a temporary."

"That doesn't matter, madam. I'm only too grateful for the chance."

"Righto. Then you can take it."

"Thank you very much, madam."

Approved of by the formidable Mrs. Trotter and the infallible Fred, Culliford had achieved his object with perfect ease. He proceeded to make himself as useful as possible from the start, going so far as to volunteer for tasks, such as carrying trays for Merriman and saving the disabled Starr the trouble of hobbling out to call cabs for guests. This naturally made a good impression. Though not quite all around. Major Smith-Barton, D.S.O., had been in the army long enough to know that no man but a fool or a scrounger ever volunteered for anything. This young man was clearly no fool; in fact, in the first conversational exchange between him and the Major, he showed himself to be far above the level of intelligence of potmen or temporary hall porters, and much better spoken. Even allowing for the fact that he averred he had merely been starting from the bottom and had much higher ambitions, there was something about him which told the Major's instincts that he was not "quite right." He said nothing, but his manner toward "Jenkins" was noticeably cool and cautious.

One evening the new man was working in the hall, vigorously polishing some brasswork that gleamed already, when he heard the Major tell Starr at the desk, "Oh, by the way, young Mr. Forbes-Maltby is expecting a guest for supper tonight. You're to show her straight up to his rooms."

"I'll do that for you, Mr. Starr," Culliford said. "Save your leg. What name will she give, Major?"

"Any name she fancies," Starr grinned, and winked. "It won't be her real one."

"Anyway, it's none of your business," the Major

snapped at the temporary porter. "I was speaking to Starr." He marched away, showing disapproval in the way he moved.

"I dunno," Culliford said to Starr. "He's took a dislike to me. Been snapping at me since the day I arrived. What've I done?"

"Nothing," Starr consoled him. "He can be a funny old cove at times. Ask Fred. He'll tell you."

"Thanks, Mr. Starr," said the young man. Resuming his polishing, he said casually, "I thought Mrs. Trotter was strict about letting the street girls in."

"She is. But them's tarts. This one's a lady." Starr winked at his assistant. "Just doesn't want to get her husband upset."

A couple of evenings later, Culliford knocked on Louisa's door and went in to get her coal scuttle for refilling. She wasn't there. Keeping his ears pricked sharply, he went quickly to her desk and glanced over its contents. She had left a letter on her pad, not quite completed. He read it with the swiftness of practice. He noticed the two photographs, one of them affectionately inscribed. He seemed to recognize the face, but couldn't immediately put a name to it.

Not daring to risk staying any longer, he got the scuttle and went out.

The Major, in his usual seat near the hall window, thought casually that it had taken a long time just to fetch a coal scuttle. He resolved that when this strange young fellow went back in with it he would make a point of chancing to go in himself. He was saved the trouble, though. Louisa returned at that moment, and when her temporary porter brought back the full scuttle she was addressing an envelope and placing her finished letter into it.

She gave him a friendly smile. "Not had an evening off, have you?" she said.

"Oh, that's all right, Mrs. Trotter. Only too willing."

"Look, things are as quiet as the grave," she said. "The Major's around, if anything crops up." She stamped the envelope and handed it to him. "Just drop that in the post for me, there's a dear, and the rest of the evening's your own."

"Thanks, madam," he said. "If I get a move on I might just be in time for the last showing at the Bioscope."

He hurried out. The Major watched him go, disapproving of porters who read the addresses on letters they were given to post. But now David Culliford knew whose the second portrait was. The name had come back to him, for there it was on the envelope, addressed to "Lord Haslemere, Bishopsleigh, Yorkshire."

The next morning Louisa was arranging a vase of flowers in her parlor. She cared little about flowers herself, but thought they looked proper to any visitors. Her temporary porter came in, aproned, to say, "Excuse me, Mrs. Trotter. Mr. Merriman says to tell you that the new lot from the wine merchant is in the bins now. He's waiting in the cellar to check over the stock list when you're ready."

"Be down in a minute," she replied. "Enjoy the Bioscope last night?"

He hesitated. "I . . . didn't go. Well, to tell the truth, there's a young lady serves behind the bar in the place I used to work . . ."

"Oh, yes?"

"I went along to see if she fancied going with me—it was her night off—but we got talking instead. Serious. In the end I . . . well, I popped the question."

"That was quick, wasn't it?"

"Well, I didn't say anything to you before, madam, but I've been offered a situation up north. Nice little pub for a married couple. I've got to take it up by next Wednesday at the latest, so I had to make up my mind and speak to Millie. She said yes."

"Well, congratulations, I suppose. Sounds like a good beginning."

"I think so, Mrs. Trotter. I was going to ask you today if you could see your way to letting me go? I really ought to go up straightaway and make arrangements."

Louisa nodded. "Starr's just about mended. Between you and me, I reckon he's been putting it on a bit, these last couple of days. Glad of a rest. You'd have had to go on Friday, anyway. Tell you what, I'll make up your wages to Friday for you and you leave as soon as you like."

"That's very kind of you, Mrs. Trotter," he said. Although he was a journalist, and ambitious, he was not entirely thick-skinned. He felt even worse when she added, "And I'll pop a little extra in the envelope as a wedding present." She refused to let him dissuade her.

That lunchtime he was back in the Vineyard, talking to Millie. Nothing was said of matrimony or of pubs in the north, though. She was perfectly happily married already.

Twenty-Two

A week later Louisa was rereading, with mounting horror and fury, a long and prominent article in the *Morning Banner,* illustrated with a photograph of the exterior of her hotel. Major Smith-Barton and Starr, who had brought the newspaper in to her, stood uncomfortably by.

"'In Duke Street, that discreet and fashionable thoroughfare, is to be found the discreet and fashionable Bentinck Hotel. Discretion is its stock-in-trade and the proprietress of this very private hotel, Mrs. Louisa Trotter, guards its clients and their activities from the ever-curious gaze of the outside world with the zeal of a tigress protecting her cubs.

"'Here, in this temple of wealth and privilege, the rich may disport themselves, secure in the knowledge that no prying eyes will disapprove their indulgences, certain that their indiscretions will go no further than its elegant apartment. Here, they may game from sunset to sunrise, if they wish, or meet with the ladies of their choice in amorous dalliance . . .'"

Louisa exploded at last. "Sounds like I'm runnin' a bleedin' whorehouse! Where the 'ell did they get this stuff from? Who's been staying here pretending to be who they wasn't, and then goin' off writing this muck?"

"It's by one David Culliford," the Major pointed

315

out. "I can assure you, madam, we've had no journalists here incognito."

"Well, then, who's been openin' their mouths outside?"

"Your staff are completely loyal to you, Mrs. Trotter."

"Yeh . . . well, whoever it is knows too much. Even at first glance I can see that he's just changed a name or two, but it's obvious who he means. Coming on top of that court business, this is the last straw." She jumped up. "I'm goin' down to the *Banner* now and have it out with that editor. And let 'em try to stop me."

Of course, they did try to stop her, all the way up from the *Banner*'s foyer to the editor's room; but Louisa Trotter, in determined motion, was an irresistible force. She stormed into the astonished Lawrie's presence, flourishing the by now crumpled copy of his newspaper.

"Do you run this scandal sheet?" she demanded, having tracked him down by dashing about looking for a door labeled EDITOR. "Half a mo'," she paused to say, as he got to his feet. "I've met you before."

He had sensed from the moment he had read David Culliford's copy that there would be trouble coming sooner or later, and here it was, in person. He smiled nervously.

"Yes, I'm the editor, Mrs. Trotter. Gordon Lawrie. I had the pleasure of meeting you about a year ago."

"Well, it won't be a pleasure meeting me again. What do you mean by printing all these lies about my hotel?"

He answered carefully, "I am confident that we have printed only the truth."

"Don't tell me what's true and what isn't. No David Culliford's ever been inside its walls."

"The journalist in question is noted for the accuracy of his reporting, madam. He has based the article on extensive inquiries, following your recent case in court."

"Has he, indeed? Well, just you get him in here and I'll give him some real home truths."

The editor shook his head firmly. "Out of the question, Mrs. Trotter. Quite apart from the fact that such a thing is never done, Mr. Culliford is not in the building at present."

Louisa looked around for a chair and went to sit in it. "Then I'll wait till he comes back," she declared. "I shan't budge until I see him. And it's no use thinking of having me carried out, kicking and screaming."

He was eyeing her speculatively. He puzzled her by saying slowly, "No. Not without illustrations."

He strode from his room and a few minutes later came back with a photographer, who proceeded to set up his tripod camera and prepare his flash pan.

The door opened again and Bulstrode came in, carrying a proof. He stared about in surprise at the photographer, the defiantly seated woman, and the editor, also seated, looking on with what seemed to be grim amusement.

"A photographic session, Mr. Bulstrode," Lawrie explained. "May I introduce Mrs. Louisa Trotter, of the Bentinck Hotel. Mr. Bulstrode, our proprietor."

"Madam," Bulstrode greeted her, with an automatic little bow.

Lawrie continued. "Mrs. Trotter declines to leave my office until she has spoken to Culliford. I have, of course, declined to permit the interview."

"Quite correct, I'm afraid, Mrs. Trotter. But . . . why the photograph, Lawrie?"

"It will enhance the page on which our further article on the Bentinck is printed. Indeed, Mrs. Trotter has kindly offered our readers the spectacle of her being carried struggling from the room by the two commissionaires I was just about to summon."

Bulstrode slowly broke into a broad smile. "An excellent notion! I will write the caption for it myself."

"You're not taking my bleedin' picture," Louisa said, beaten. She got up. "You call yourselves men?"

With all the dignity she could muster she swept out, to a bow, mocking this time, from Bulstrode. She heard their laughter behind her. At the pitch of her humiliated fury, she turned the corner of the passage—and walked straight into David Culliford.

There was just one moment's pause for mutual recognition. Then Louisa swung her hand all the way up from her side and gave him a cracking slap across one cheek, before marching on without speaking a word.

Back at the Bentinck she paraded the Major, Starr, and Merriman and told them what she had found out. The Major started to speak but she silenced him.

"Not one word. Not one bloody word!" She turned on Starr. "As for reckonin' to be a judge of character . . . You should 'ave that bloody mongrel of yours put down, too."

She was calmer but unrepentant that evening when she entertained Sir Michael Manning privately to dinner. The interview was at his urgent request.

"My dear Louisa," he told her, "the impulse was understandable, but to call round to see them—even worse to assault one of them physically—a grave mistake. Still, I suppose it can be presented as an instance of innocence outraged. It may not prejudice our case too badly."

"Case? What case?"

He looked surprised. "You can't possibly let matters rest, don't you see? The damage done by that article could be enormous. You must proceed against this newspaper for libel."

"Oh, no! Please, no lawyers. No letters."

"It need never reach court. A printed apology, a retraction, and an agreed sum of damages . . ."

"D'you think they'd wear it?"

"Since you appear to have left the editor and the proprietor uninjured, it is just possible. But if they decline, you must be prepared to go all the way against them."

She shrugged. "I suppose I'll lose a bit of custom. Maybe attract some I don't want. But the Bentinck's reputation will recover. No, I'd sooner forget the whole thing."

The lawyer asked uncomfortably, "Louisa, answer me very carefully. Is there any substance in Culliford's article?"

Her eyes flashed, but she had to say, "Well . . . it's true and it isn't. It's more the way he's written it. That bit that refers to young Forbes-Maltby. It reads like the girl's some tart."

"We could produce Mr. Forbes-Maltby to refute that."

"God, no! There'd be a divorce. Anyway, I told you, I'm not going near a court."

He had to tell her at last, "I'm afraid you have no alternative. A note of hand was delivered to me today, requesting me to call round for a word with Firbank, Bricelow and Firbank. I spoke to the senior partner. It's no longer a simple matter of trying to increase the ground rent. The lessors wish to see the lease terminated as soon as possible. They object to having their premises used as . . . well, in their own words, as a house of ill-fame."

"But . . . they can't do that, can they? Not just because some gossip-monger . . ."

He warned her emphatically, "I'm afraid that if we allow this report to go unchallenged it will be taken as an admission that there is truth in the allegation."

Louisa could only sigh deeply and agree to let him set it all in motion.

Two days later, Gordon Lawrie read out to his chief proprietor a letter which had just come by hand.

"'. . . This being so, unless a full and agreed retraction is published and given equal prominence, and unless compensation is offered for the damage sustained by my client, she will have no alternative but to seek a writ for libel against your newspaper and all those persons connected with the matter. I remain et cetera ... Sir Michael Manning.' "

The editor said anxiously, "Manning. The lady can afford the best."

Bulstrode comforted him. "But we can afford better. So long as you can assure the Board that young Culliford's piece was accurate."

"As I told Mrs. Trotter, I believe we printed the truth."

"In the public interest. Quite so. Then be assured that I shall stand behind you."

With Scottish candor, Lawrie told his employer, "Since the suggestion for the article was your own, I should have thought that beside me would be a more appropriate position."

"Indeed, indeed," Bulstrode said smoothly. "Yes, I recall having made several suggestions, so I can hardly quarrel with the fact that you found one worthy of attention. The manner of its execution is, of course, your responsibility—and you are aware of my feelings on the subject of editorial responsibility."

It was a constantly recurring theme of his, always reiterated at great length. His editor regarded him suspiciously.

"Am I to understand, Mr. Bulstrode, that this threatened libel action is going to be solely my concern?"

"And Culliford's, of course. You will appreciate that I myself can't become involved. Wrong assumptions might be made about why the piece was published."

"Your nephew?"

Bulstrode smiled. "You take my point exactly."

When he had gone, Lawrie made urgent inquiries for David Culliford. The consensus of opinion was that at this time of day—it was lunchtime—he would almost certainly be in the Vineyard. Lawrie was not a drinking man and felt a strong aversion to Fleet Street's pubs. Too much talent, too much potentially good writing, had evaporated in their smoke and fumes, in his opinion. Nevertheless, today he went at once to the Vineyard and was relieved to find Culliford as soon as he entered. He recognized the surprise on his writer's face.

"Yes, yes. The taverns of this street have been the ruination of many good journalists and not a few bad ones," he said. "But I wish to talk to you urgently, where our conversation can be informal and unofficial. I intend, if need be, to deny that it ever took place." To this portentous opening he added, "You may purchase for me a glass of seltzer or something equally innocuous, and join me in the corner there."

When David came back with the soda water and another whisky for himself—a neat one, so that it might appear small to his disapproving editor—Lawrie looked around, then asked in a low tone, "This Bentinck business. You are quite certain of the facts?"

"Of course, sir. I've full notes of who went there during my time, and for what purpose—plus a lot of entries copied from the register."

Lawrie showed little relief. He explained, "When you say 'for what purpose,' have you any proof that those purposes were carried out?"

"Well, no. I couldn't go that far."

"So it can only be speculation—in which case a libel action might well succeed. I don't mind admitting I've feared this all along."

"But we haven't been threatened, have we?"

"This morning. 'Retract or we sue,' they're saying."

"You're not going to print a retraction, are you . . . sir?" Culliford asked, suddenly fearful for his reputation.

"Not at all. Mr. Bulstrode has set his face firmly

against it. Therefore, we must persuade Mrs. Trotter to drop the action or . . ." he looked around again before adding . . . "destroy her character to such an extent that the action will fail. A woman of that sort has a past, and you would do well to set straight about discovering what that past is."

As he had done several times while writing his article and since, Culliford thought unhappily of Louisa's generous gesture toward the supposed temporary hall porter, and felt again a sense of having betrayed her.

"I . . . doubt if there's much to find out," he answered.

"You must have overheard servants' gossip."

"Nothing worth remembering."

The editor said, "I detect a certain lack of enthusiasm."

"Well . . . Why go on persecuting her, sir?"

"To prevent her from *prosecuting* us, Culliford. You and me, as author and editor respectively. Of course, the *Banner* will be sued with us, as printer and publisher. But don't let it escape your notice that we are mere individuals, while it is an organization."

"You mean . . . they wouldn't stand by us?"

"They'd have to—but only up to a point. I've already had some intimation of where that point might be. It could have a calamitous effect on both our careers. Now, where do we start with Louisa Trotter?"

Culliford took a pull at his whisky and said, "I'll need to go to New Yarmouth."

Two evenings later he was back in the Vineyard, this time in the more familiar company of Nelson from the *Mirror*.

"Thought you'd signed the pledge, or something," the latter said, paying for their drinks. "Thought he'd deserted us, didn't we, Millie?"

"Yes, duckie. By the way, Mr. Culliford, there's been a man asking for you. An oldish codger. Been in several times, lunchtime and evenings."

"Did he give you a message, or his name?"

"No. Just kept asking . . . Oh! 'Ere 'e comes now."

Culliford turned to the door and was startled to see Major Smith-Barton advancing toward him. He hurriedly excused himself from Nelson and went to intercept the older man.

"Evening, Major," he said as cheerfully as he could. "Can I get you a drink?"

The Major's expression of affront and contempt answered him.

"You're a rogue and a scoundrel," he said. "If I were a younger man, I'd thrash you."

Culliford was stung to retort, "Tied to the wheel of a gun carriage, I suppose?" But he regretted the insult and looked sheepish.

Major Smith-Barton pulled a piece of paper from his breast pocket. Culliford recognized it as the testimonial he had got the landlord of this pub to write for him as "Jenkins." "If you're wondering how I found you, it was through this," the Major said. "I suspected you from the start. I have come to appeal to any decent feelings you might have left. You have injured a fine woman. Caused her great distress. She hasn't been sleeping for nights. Now, it seems, she's going to lose her hotel."

This really startled the young man. "Mrs. Trotter's going to lose the Bentinck!"

"Something to do with the lease, don't you know? And all because of your lying innuendos."

There was no note of triumph in Culliford's response to this. He said unhappily, "I'm afraid there's worse still to come, Major. I've just returned from New Yarmouth. I got an interview there with Mr. Trotter. Mr. Augustus Trotter."

Louisa groaned when the Major reported this to her, half an hour later. "That does it, then. The fat's in the fire, and no mistake. One bottle of brandy and my dear husband'll talk for a week—and throw in a song for good measure."

Although she spoke flippantly, she was deeply worried and disturbed. Once more, it seemed that all she had built up was collapsing on top of her. She sensed that even her resilient spirit might be crushed incurably this time.

The Major went on, "He declined to reveal what Mr. Trotter told him. I thought he might tell you, though. I formed the impression that he was quite anxious to come and see you, so I, er, prevailed upon him to return with me, don't you know?"

"Culliford's here!"

"In the hall. And Starr's having to keep a tight hold on his dog's collar—though I fancy he'd sooner let him loose."

"Better show him in, then."

"Would you like me to stay, too?"

"No thanks. I can manage Master bloody Culliford on me own."

The journalist was duly ushered in and the door closed. Louisa had seated herself magisterially. She kept him standing.

"I suppose you're proud and pleased with yourself?" she said icily.

"Pride doesn't come into it, Mrs. Trotter. I do my job as best I can, and I think it's worth doing."

"Call it a job? There's girls on the street outside got jobs more worth doing. Some job, worming your way in here with lies and then printing more lies in your rotten newspaper."

"I reported what I saw and heard," he answered resolutely.

"What you wanted to see, you mean."

"Mrs. Trotter, a few weeks ago I wrote about what it was like to live in an East End slum—the squalor, the hunger, the hopelessness. The sheer brutality of

the fight to survive. Then I come to a place like this.
A place where the worst tragedy that can happen is
a soufflé going flat."

"Oh, Gawd, where've I heard all this before? Anyway, what's wrong with helping other people have a
bit of fun and pleasure?"

"Possibly the girls on the street might give the same
answer."

Instinctively, he took a step backward as Louisa's
eyes flared and she looked wildly around. One of the
many things her husband had told him under the
influence of brandy was of the last time he had seen
his wife, as he and his sister had retreated before her
hail of bottles.

"I'm sorry, Mrs. Trotter," he said earnestly. "Don't
hit me again, please. We have an important matter
to discuss."

"Yes. What Gus told you."

"He was . . . very forthcoming."

"You mean, he was drunk."

"Drunk and bitter, Mrs. Trotter. He seems to think
he's been treated very badly. But he'll be sober
enough in the witness-box, if it comes to it, and I'm
afraid what he has to say won't do your reputation
any good. Mrs. Trotter, if you drop this action, I've
good reason to believe my employers are prepared to
forget the whole matter."

"If I drop this action, I'll lose the lease on my hotel.
Look, couldn't you say you made a mistake—that
you'd got it all wrong? I wouldn't want damages. If
you just printed that . . ."

"Then the *Banner* would be made to look foolish—
and I'd lose my job."

"What about my hotel?" she said, knowing that she
had lost the initiative.

Culliford didn't like one bit having to apply so
relentlessly what he had come to recognize as moral
blackmail. He felt sincerely sorry for her. But if she

was in a corner, he was in one opposite her. One or
the other of them had to lose, and he would fight,
rather than let it be himself.

"You have a difficult decision to make, Mrs. Trotter,"
he lectured her. "When I said that your husband was
forthcoming, I meant it. He instanced several things
..."

His gaze had left hers. She saw where he was
looking—at the photographs of Lord Haslemere and
His Majesty the King—and she no longer doubted
that her world was about to crash.

For once in her life, Louisa pleaded with someone.
She begged him to keep to himself matters that would
bring great hurt and grievance to other people. Matters that lay in the past and had no bearing on her
conduct of the Bentinck Hotel. Despite his feelings, he
was adamant. He left soon afterward with no concession made; and she immediately penned a note to Sir
Michael Manning, instructing him to drop all plans
for a libel action.

When he reported back to his office, Culliford went
at once to see his editor. Lawrie listened unhappily, then shrugged his shoulders and told him to get
on and write the second article. His last hope seemed
to be that if Culliford could contrive to let Mrs. Trotter see it, before it went into print, she might just
be shocked into surrender.

"Put it all in," he instructed. "The worse it reads,
the better; but nothing but fact, though. Either way,
we've got to make sure of winning."

Culliford went away and began to write. As his article grew he realized what a sensational scoop it rep-
resented for his paper, and his mind's eye pictured
his by-line on it and the congratulatory smiles of his
superiors. And then he paused, suddenly remembering
something the editor had said to him that morning.
He thought for a while, wrestling with his inclinations this way and that. Then he began to write again,

this time with a grim smile set almost permanently on his countenance.

When he had finished he took his copy to the editor, and watched with some amusement the appalled expression on his face as he read. Finally Lawrie looked up.

"For God's sake, take it and show her it," he ordered. "There'll be repercussions all over the world if this gets into print. She wouldn't dare let us run it."

But Culliford had a countersuggestion ready. He put it. Lawrie looked at first startled, then intrigued. At length he nodded agreement.

That evening, with Sir Michael Manning already present, Louisa coolly but politely greeted the *Morning Banner's* principal proprietor in her parlor. His secretary had telephoned an hour earlier to request the honor of an urgent appointment.

Louisa had had sherry laid out. Bulstrode accepted his glass with a determinedly conciliatory smile.

"Your very good health, Mrs. Trotter," he said, somewhat surprisingly. "Ah! Excellent! To come straight to the point, now. I have read young Culliford's further article about you. Some of its contents shocked me considerably, but I obtained the boy's assurance that they represent the truth, as obtained from your husband. I have brought the article with me, and if you would care to read it for yourself before I continue? . . ."

"No, thanks," Louisa said bitterly. "I know what it'll be. I don't want to see it spelled out."

"Exactly. Now, when I myself came to the passages concerning your, ah, conjugal difficulties, I paused to consider the matter very carefully. My heart is not of stone, Mrs. Trotter, and I have no wish to drive you to the wall. While your attitude has scarcely been conciliatory . . ."

"It was your rotten paper that started it!" she burst out. Sir Michael touched her restrainingly and said, "Please, Louisa. I think Mr. Bulstrode has a proposition to put."

The other man nodded. "I have. I have never been a man to bear a grudge, and I have certainly no desire to injure an . . . an innocent child; nor, for that matter, to cause unnecessary distress to its mother. In other words, I have decided that if you are prepared to abandon this ill-advised suit, it is possible that I might be able to meet you halfway."

The lawyer asked, "Plainly, Mr. Bulstrode—will you print a retraction?"

"I am willing to consider—no more than consider —the possibility that our writer, Mr. Culliford, may have overstated certain facts in the original article. I say 'may have,' Sir Michael. I admit to nothing."

"Then, what form would the retraction take?"

Bulstrode drew himself up and in his most pompous manner replied, "The *Banner* will not grovel, let that be clear. I have in mind a brief but dignified expression of regret that the wrong impression may have been conveyed. That the *Banner* now accepts that the Bentinck Hotel is an establishment of the utmost respectability. That its proprietress is a lady of impeccable reputation . . ." Suddenly, he could keep up the excessive dignity no longer. He relaxed visibly and smiled at Louisa. "Oh, you know the sort of thing, Mrs. Trotter. We can leave the precise wording to the lawyer johnnies. No offense, Sir Michael."

"I accept," Louisa said promptly.

"Now, Louisa, don't be hasty!" Sir Michael cautioned her, but she insisted, "I accept, I accept, I accept!"

Bulstrode smiled again and told the lawyer, "Sir Michael, you would appear to have your client's instructions."

Louisa poured more sherry for them all.

"What do you want?" Starr growled suspiciously that same night when David Culliford presented himself at the reception desk. Fred was growling steadily, too.

The journalist held up a copy of the first edition of next morning's *Banner,* which he had snatched straight from the printing press and brought around by cab. "She'll want to see this," he answered.

Reluctantly, Starr admitted him to Louisa's parlor. Despite the release of tension she had experienced only a few hours earlier, she was still at her desk, drinking wine, smoking a cigarette, and fiddling distractedly with this piece of paper and that.

"Be careful," Culliford warned her. "The ink's still wet."

"Never mind that," she said, unheeding, and dirtied her fingers in her haste to read the promised notice of retraction.

"Well," she said at last, throwing the newspaper into her wastepaper basket, "it'll do. And now I've seen it, you can push off and rake around for some dirt elsewhere."

He smiled. "I am clearing off—well out of harm's way. Tomorrow, as it happens. I've been appointed the *Banner*'s correspondent in New York. Quite a step up."

"Well, I hope you're seasick all the way."

"Thank you. It ought to be a relief to know that your secrets are three thousand miles away."

"It's no thanks to you they're still secrets at all!"

"You'd be surprised," he said. His steady smile puzzled her. "You see, I wrote the whole thing in as lurid a manner as the facts would allow. When I ran out of facts I invented some. It made the paper curl."

"Then I take back what I said about being seasick. I hope you fall off the dock at Southampton."

"Mr. Bulstrode was very impressed. But, of course, he decided not to print it."

"Shows there's some gentlemen left."

"Oh, his ambitions run higher than being a gentleman. He's even got his title chosen for the Honours List. So he's not likely to offend the one man who can see that his name doesn't appear in it, is he?"

Louisa stared uncomprehendingly. For once, her quick mind was not up to the pace of what seemed to be going on about her. The young journalist was pausing aggravatingly, leaving the implications to fall into place. Eventually, Louisa said slowly, "He . . . said it was for the sake of my . . . kid. And she's got . . . nothing to do with . . . a certain personage."

Culliford grinned. "Somehow or other, Mr. Bulstrode got the notion that she had."

She spelled it out frankly. "The King isn't her father."

He shrugged. "Must've been the way I wrote it, then."

There was a very long silence. Then Louisa said, "Have a glass of wine before you go."

"Thanks, Mrs. Trotter."

While she was pouring it he was fishing out his wallet and extracting two pound notes. He placed them on her desk.

"I owe you a couple of quid," he said. "Return of unused wedding present."

Twenty-Three

Ascot Week, in June, was always one of Louisa's periods of peak activity. The Bentinck was full of people up from the country who had made reservations long in advance. There were nightly parties in most of the suites, with much coming and going of guests' guests. On top of it, her services were in hectic demand for outside catering; and there were still the accounts to keep up to date, never Louisa's favorite activity.

On the morning of the day before the end of Ascot, 1908, she sat at her desk desperately adding: ". . . and four is nineteen, twenty-one, twenty-seven, thirty-five . . . two carry four . . . Come in," she said automatically in response to a knock on the door. She didn't raise her head.

"Hello, Louisa," said a voice from the past which caused her to look up quickly. She smiled real pleasure to see her old friend Major Sir John Farjeon, former equerry to the King and go-between in his relationship with her.

"Johnnie!" she cried. "Well I'm blowed!"

"It's been a long time," he agreed, pleased, too.

"How are you?" she asked. "I seen you got married. Seems to suit you. Put on a bit of weight, haven't you?"

"That's a secret between me and my tailor."

"And I seen in the *Gazette* you gave up the equerry lark. Couldn't stand the pace, eh?"

"Not that and marriage. I'm back with the battalion now. Second-in-command."

"Good for you. So what're you doing here?"

"Phillida—my wife—she's, well, a bit raw, but fearfully keen to do things properly. So we took a small house down at Ascot, just for the week. A small house party—six of us. Should have been ideal, but it's turned out an unmitigated disaster."

"Guests not get on?"

"That's only one of the problems. The staff we've inherited defy description. And the cooking . . . Louisa, I was hoping you'd help me take the curse off the whole thing by organizing a really good dinner party for tomorrow—the last day?"

"Tomorrow! I've got too many dinners already, never mind about running the hotel."

"Yes, I imagined you'd be pushed. I wouldn't have asked if . . . Charlie hadn't said you'd help if you possibly could. He's one of the houseguests," he added, trying to sound casual.

Louisa saw through it. "And he put you up to it, did he? I might have known. You crafty couple of . . ."

Major Farjeon interrupted quickly, "Actually, it all started because the Palace has offered me a sturgeon. I've been on the list a long time. It seemed providential for a very special dinner, only the cook we've got couldn't even do sardines on toast. Besides, it's the royal fish, and Charlie rightly pointed out that it needs the Queen of Cooks to do justice to it."

Flattery on such lines influenced the snob in Louisa a great deal, as Farjeon and Haslemere were aware. She protested again, but agreed.

"How many will you be?" she asked.

"Ten, all told."

"How's your cellar down there?"

"Deplorable."

"Sounds like you ought to ask for your money back. You'll want me to do the wines as well, then?"

"Everything, please, Louisa."

"How big's this sturgeon? And have I got to have it picked up, or will they send it over?"

"I've no idea," he said vaguely, vastly relieved to relinquish all responsibility.

"Oh, run along!" she scolded. "I'll telephone the bloomin' Palace myself."

When he had gone she summoned Major Smith-Barton, her adviser on fine wines.

"What would you serve with sturgeon?" she asked.

"Well, a Rhône, I'd say. The 'Ninety-nine Hermitage, perhaps? Or, of course, the Puligny-Montrachet 'Oh-two, if you really want to spoil 'em, don't you know?"

"That'll do," she said, writing it down.

"When is this for?"

"Tomorrow. An extra client."

"But I thought . . ."

"Yes, I know we're booked right up. But this is an extra *special* client—a friend of Charlie's. I'll have to ask you to help out, if you can."

"With pleasure, madam," the Major said. "And speaking of Charles, I was meaning to ask you how well he knows Desmond Elleston."

"Why?"

"He owns Vital Spark—the racehorse, don't you know? Well fancied for the Alexandra Plate tomorrow. I've got one surefire tip—Bembo, for the Hardwicke Stakes. I was thinking about making Vital Spark the second leg of a double. Wondered whether Charles would have any inside advice."

Louisa got up. "I'll give you mine for nothing. Save your money. With your luck, the odds on them both dropping down dead is the only ones you'll double. Do yourself a favor, Major. As far as Ascot goes, you stick to driving the bus for me tomorrow."

They returned to the subject of wines. Eventually, Louisa had her menu complete:

Consommé

Esturgeon Farci

Soufflé de Cailles

Pièces de Boeuf à la Gelée en Bellevue

Asperges en Branches

Fraises Natures

Le Café   *Les Petits Fours*

They agreed on the Montrachet with the sturgeon and a 'Ninety-four claret with the beef. The Major also recommended three bottles of Madeira, three of Imperial Tokay, a Quinta de Noval 'Sixty-eight port, and a fifteen-year-old Exshaw brandy.

All these things were duly assembled the following day and delivery arranged for the sturgeon, that mighty fish which, though rarely caught in British waters, automatically became the property of the Sovereign, to eat or give to some favored applicant.

As usual when going to cook in a kitchen strange to her, Louisa took no chances with the equipment. Where she had once had to hire one or even two cabs to carry her own, she now had the gleaming hotel bus. Into it went the ingredients for the meal, the wines, the condiments even, and all manner of accessories, including, on this occasion, a huge fish kettle. Mrs. Cochrane accompanied Louisa, who had to leave behind her kitchen staff to help Mary run the packed hotel.

"Did you have a word with the couple in Number Seven?" Mary asked Louisa through the bus window.

"Oh, yes, I almost forgot. You were dead right. They couldn't begin to pay their bill."

"I knew it all along," the Welsh girl said. "Told you, I did, ma'am."

"I know. Should've asked them sooner. But the way he came out with admitting it, I couldn't help but laugh. They've got style, those two, and there's not so much of it about as there was."

Mary knew her employer's prejudices and methods by now. "What are you going to do about the money, then?"

"I stuck it on Sir George's bill. Clerical error if he finds out, which he won't. He just pays up."

It was a long-standing custom of Louisa's to rob the rich to pay the poor, so long as the latter amused her, or had her sympathy for some reason or other, or innocently appealed to her eccentric standards.

Mary smiled resignedly and waved as the Major engaged the gear and drove the bus away down Duke Street, to turn into Oxford Street.

A pleasant drive took them into Surrey. Eventually the Major turned the vehicle in at the gates of what proved to be a large, ugly, red-brick Victorian house.

"Ugh!" Louisa exclaimed. "No wonder they need a decent meal."

"Nothing much to feast the eyes on, what?" the Major agreed, instinctively preparing to drive to the front door. Louisa had to remind him quickly that they were there as servants, not houseguests.

"Sorry. One forgets, don't you know?" he said, and took the bus around the back.

The back door was opened to them by a tweeny, so young-looking that she might have been a child. She was unsmiling and appeared tired beyond her years. A gloomy passageway stretched behind her.

"Who are you?" Louisa asked kindly.

"Kath, ma'am."

"Well, I'm Mrs. Trotter. I'm here to do the dinner."

The unmistakable figure of a butler was approaching, lofty and in late middle age. His manner was civil enough, though, and noticeably worried. He introduced himself as Mr. Sterling, and began to apologize at once.

"The kitchen staff's in uproar, Mrs. Trotter. When he let the house for the races the master sent the regular staff on holiday, excepting myself and young Kath here. This lot are from an agency and they've been nothing but trouble from start to finish."

"Come on," Louisa said grimly, and marched in, calling over her shoulder to the Major and Mrs. Cochrane to start unloading.

She made her instinctive way to the kitchen, took one glance around it, and recognized that it was ill-equipped, grubby, and untidy. The description might have applied also to the cook, her two assistants, and the footman, who were ranged up in stony assembly.

Mr. Sterling made introductions. No one moved or smiled.

"What's the matter?" Louisa asked him, in mock surprise. "All deaf and dumb?"

"We've been insulted, that's what's the matter," the cook retorted. "Bringing you down 'ere. This is my kitchen."

"Looks like it," Louisa retorted pointedly. The irony was lost on the woman.

"You touch one thing in here, and we all gives our notice."

The Major and Mrs. Cochrane entered with the first load.

"Give in your notice?" Louisa said. "I can't wait that long. Touch *one* thing, was it? Well, how'll this do, then?" She picked up a large knife and brandished it. "There. And you'd better get out before I'm tempted to use it on you. I've come here to do a friend an especial favor, and I'm not having it spoiled by a crew like you. So make up your minds—either knuckle down to it as I tell you, or get out."

With a glance at one another they shuffled silently away.

"Good riddance!" Louisa said loudly after them; but Mrs. Cochrane was looking aghast.

"We're going to be ever so shorthanded, ma'am," she pointed out.

"You don't, er, feel her ladyship should have been consulted first?" the butler ventured to suggest.

"She's at the races, isn't she?" Louisa replied. "Then if we'd stood here arguin' till she got back there wouldn't have been any dinner at all, would there? Now, what other staff have you got?"

"Only outdoor."

"Visiting valets? Lady's maids?"

"There's Sir John Farjeon's soldier servant, Guardsman Wilson, and Lady Farjeon's maid, Miss Jennett. We've been looking after the others between us."

"Fetch them in here," Louisa ordered unhesitatingly.

"It's . . . most irregular. . . ."

"It's all hands to a sinkin' ship. Don't you see?"

He did, and without further protest went to fetch the other two servants and explain the situation to them. Fortunately, neither objected to helping serve the dinner, though Jennett, a pleasant girl, rightly pointed out, "The trouble is, you'll lose us when they're dressing for dinner. Just when you need us most."

"Can't be in two places at once," agreed Guardsman Wilson, who hadn't been able to suppress an instinct to snap to attention when introduced to Major Smith-Barton, and kept calling him "Sir!" while wondering what on earth this sporty-looking old gent could be doing in a kitchen.

Louisa replied, "We'll all have to be quick on our feet, that's all. Major, you'll have to be acting-unpaid dogsbody."

"With pleasure, Mrs. Trotter," he said, to Wilson's incredulity.

Louisa turned to Kath. "Going to risk it, love?" she asked, with her warmest smile. The girl smiled back, for the first time. "Good girl. Well, you're kitchen maid, so that's one problem solved. Now, first off, we've all got to clean this kitchen from top to bottom, or we're liable to poison the lot of 'em. Mr. Sterling, perhaps you could stretch a point and help the Major finish unloading the bus."

The butler was thoroughly into the spirit of it now. He gave a little bow and went to do as she had asked.

For the rest of the morning and all the afternoon they toiled, with only the briefest respite for a quick lunch at staggered intervals. As soon as the sink area had been thoroughly scoured and the preparing table scrubbed, Kath was given the vegetables and told how to prepare them. Her willingness made up for her lack of experience. After a few minutes' supervision, Louisa was confident to leave her to it.

When the old-fashioned range had been degrimed and degreased, Mrs. Cochrane was able to start the beef and turn her attention to boning and stuffing the fish. Again, Louisa had to supervise. Mrs. Cochrane had never handled sturgeon before. In fact, though everyone worked with a will, it was Louisa who was here, there, and everywhere, ordering, advising, supervising, checking, while at the same time performing a myriad of tasks of her own.

"Beef?" she demanded of Mrs. Cochrane, who opened the oven door for inspection.

"Baste it regular, and turn the pan round in about half an hour." Louisa turned to Kath. "Veg?" The girl displayed the asparagus, waiting in a basin of cold water. Louisa said, "Keep changing the water until they're actually put on. Strawberries, Jennett." They were ready, in a big dish under a damp cloth. Wilson was also on parade with filled bowls of cream and sugar.

At length, Louisa was able to announce that they had won the battle so far. They were wilting, but she, who had done twice or thrice as much as any of them, showed no tiredness, and they copied her example.

"Thank you, one and all," she said. "Now there's time for a nice drop of wine before they get back from the races."

To her surprise, Sterling produced a bottle of champagne at once.

"You're catching on," she said admiringly.

"The Major gave me the hint."

"Trust him!"

They all laughed and enjoyed a drink together. Sterling and poor Kath both felt, in their different ways, that this was the only happy time they had known all that week.

Much less happy was the newly wed Lady Farjeon, when she returned that evening to find her staff all gone, except for Sterling and Kath, and her own and her husband's personal servants laying the dining table.

"Mrs. Trotter," she complained, with the outraged dignity of a young wife who is conscious of her authority but out of her depth in exercising it, "I find that you haven't been five minutes in the house before half the staff have given notice—simply walked out."

"You're better off without them," Louisa said, carrying on with what she was doing in the dining room, though at least having had the tact to shoo away the others who had been assisting her there. "I know just how you feel, dear, but if I'd had that lot of weary willies under my feet you'd never have got your dinner."

Lady Farjeon goggled at this roughly and bluntly spoken woman.

"You don't seem to realize. We have a house party."

"Finish tomorrow, don't you?" Louisa said, straightening spoons.

"I know. But someone has to give them breakfast."

"Oh, if that's all that's worrying you, I'll see to it. Leave it all so's Kath and Sterling have only to heat it up and serve it."

"Can you . . . really. . . ?"

"I'll have it done by the time dinner's been washed up. Now, how d'you like the flowers?"

"They're . . . lovely."

"I like to do me own flowers. Seen the menu, have you?"

She shoved one into Lady Farjeon's hand. The latter could only stammer, "I don't . . . see how it could be bettered."

"No, it couldn't. But it's really nice of you to say so, dear. I heard you'd had a bad week, one way and another. We had to try and do something a bit special for you. You've not been married long, have you?"

"N-no."

"Lovely fellow you got there—Johnnie. I reckon he hasn't done so bad, either."

"You're an amazing woman, Mrs. Trotter," conceded Lady Farjeon, overwhelmed and disarmed.

"Thanks, dear. Just so long as you have an amazing evening."

"Oh, I think we shall. I *really* think we shall."

They laughed together suddenly, and the sound penetrated to the smoking room, where the men were sitting over their predinner drinks. Charles Tyrrell, Lord Haslemere, had insisted on his father's ex-fag from Eton days, Major Smith-Barton, joining them. The only absentee was Lady Farjeon's godfather, George Ross. Upon entering the house in a foul mood he had gone straight off to his room to bathe.

"Peace reigns supreme in the dining room, it seems," Farjeon remarked with relief, having raised his head to listen to the two women's laughter.

"But not throughout the household," Charlie Haslemere said, breathing into his whisky. "Look, Johnnie, Phillida's godfather or not, if he makes one more accusation about Vital Spark, I'm warning you there'll be trouble."

The Major, who had pricked up his ears, said, "Oh, ah, Vital Spark? Second favorite and widely fancied. I almost made him the second leg of a double, don't you know?"

"Count your blessings," Charlie told him.

"Oh? What, er, happened?"

"He simply faded. Don't understand it."

"No," said Sir John Farjeon grimly. "Nor did Phillida's godfather."

"Well, he's as rich as Croesus," Charlie said. "He can afford to lose a packet."

"That doesn't mean to say he likes to. It's how he stays rich. He keeps hinting that there was something funny about it," Farjeon explained to the Major, who, despite his equivocal position in Louisa's hotel, was clearly her confidant, and could therefore safely be taken to be an honest man.

"Ah!" was all the Major said, though he was looking thoughtful. He got up and screwed his eyeglass into place. "If you'll excuse me, gentlemen. The second gong will be going soon. Better send your soldier servant up to you, Major Farjeon, sir, hadn't I?"

"Yes," said Sir John, with a concealed wink at Charles. "If you would, sir."

In the kitchen, Kath watched openmouthed as Louisa delicately spooned gelatine over the *pièces de boeuf*, transforming what had been a platter of plain garnished sliced beef into a subject worthy of a master of still-life painting. Without realizing it she had been holding her breath in wonder. Now she let it all out in one great sigh of relief and admiration.

"It's like a picture!" she declared.

"That's how it should be," Louisa nodded, satisfied. "The first job I ever had, d'you know what the *chef de cuisine* told me there?" She achieved a passable imitation of the accent of her mentor, Monsieur Alex: "The most important things, they are, first, ze smell . . ." She tapped her nose, in the way she had never forgotten he had done. "After ze smell, ze taste —ze tongue. And then—ze *eyes!*"

Louisa was surprised to see the pale little girl's eyes

gleaming animatedly in her tired face, and the head nodding as if the knowledge had been there already. It stirred further recollections of her own past.

"You . . . fancy bein' a cook, do you?" she asked.

Kath nodded hard, then startled Louisa by saying passionately, "I want to be the best cook in England. I want it more than anything else in the world."

There followed a long pause, while Louisa collected herself enough from hearing this almost exact echo of her own words to say, "Well, wanting's half of it." She roused herself. "Back to the sink now."

"Yes'm."

The girl went, with Louisa's eyes on her. The distant ring of the front-door bell jerked her back into animation again.

"That will be the first of the outside guests," said Sterling, hurriedly donning his tailcoat.

"We're ready when you are," Louisa replied.

Her confidence underwent a considerable setback some time later, though. The order to begin serving up had not yet come. All were poised and ready for it, from Louisa and the Major and Mrs. Cochrane to their temporary helpers, Kath and Jennett and Guardsman Wilson. Mr. Sterling alone was absent; and now he came hurrying down the stairs to tell Louisa, "Her ladyship's compliments, Mrs. Trotter, but would you put back dinner half an hour, please?"

"It can't be done," was her emphatic answer. "Everything's right to the point."

Unhappily, he explained, "There's a terrible row going on in the smoking room. It's . . . Mr. Ross, Lady Farjeon's godfather, and Sir John himself and Lord Haslemere. Lady Farjeon has the other guests in the drawing room, but they can hear the noise from there. She sounded quite distracted."

"Right," Louisa said. "Mrs. Cochrane, you time my soufflé—to the second, mind you. Kath, dish up the consommé. The rest of you, carry on like I told you."

She hitched up her long skirt and ran up the stairs from the kitchen.

"What will she do, Major?" the butler asked Major Smith-Barton.

"Murder—if her dinner's spoiled."

In the smoking room Charlie was threatening Ross, an aggressive, commanding elderly man, "You repeat that to a living soul and I'll take you through the courts!"

"For God's sake, Charlie!" hissed an almost distraught Major Sir John Farjeon.

"Thank you," Ross told him smoothly, "but I'm quite capable of taking care of myself."

Louisa burst in without knocking, just in time to catch the last words.

"Doesn't sound to me as if any of you's capable of anything," she snapped, less to the surprise of Haslemere and Farjeon, who knew her of old, than of Ross, who had never set eyes on her.

"Stupid slanging match!" she was going on. "Can't you hear yourselves?"

"May I ask who you are, madam?" Ross demanded. Farjeon explained, grim-faced, "This is Mrs. Trotter, of the Bentinck Hotel."

Ross smiled and rose to his feet. "A considerable personality and a distinctive hostelry, or so I'm told. Under other circumstances I'd be pleased to meet you, Mrs. Trotter."

"Yes," she said, "and I'm here to do the dinner. Any minute now it's going to spoil. And, having put meself out, I don't intend that it should happen on account of a crowd of men stood there shoutin' the odds. Come on," she said in a suddenly changed tone, which, again, Haslemere and Farjeon were familiar with, "you're all grown up. Behave like it. What's it all about?"

Charlie said, as though answering his mother or his nannie, "Ross accused a friend of mine called Desmond Elleston of cheating."

Ross was stung into defending himself before this female interloper. "I had it from a racing journalist, who knows."

"Oh, crikey, newspapers again!" she cried. "What did he say?"

Charlie answered. "That Desmond gave orders that his horse shouldn't win the Alexandra Plate this afternoon. The big race."

"Whyever not? What's he want to chuck that away for?"

"To lengthen the odds for the next race he has the horse entered for—at Goodwood. I say it's unthinkable. Desmond's a gentleman. I've known him all my life."

But Ross, despite his manner, was arguing from what sounded to Louisa an acceptable standpoint.

"Charles, I'm not complaining because I lost a lot of money I can afford to lose. We're not talking about someone who's diddled one of his rich friends at cards. If I'm right, Elleston's cheated a lot of poor hopefuls today in order to cheat a lot more at Goodwood. I confess I didn't realize he was such a pal of yours. But if he's done what I say he's done, he doesn't deserve to be."

"What was this horse called?" asked Louisa, on a sudden instinct.

"Vital Spark," Farjeon told her. "What's that to do with it, Louisa?"

She didn't tell him that it had to do with a "poor hopeful" who dwelt under her own wing, and who was at this moment waiting in the kitchen for the signal to help serve these squabblers from his own class.

"Look," she told Charlie and Ross. "You're neither of you goin' to give up till you know the truth, are you."

"No," they replied in unison.

"Then, find out. Have an unofficial inquiry. Get him here."

"Desmond would never agree," Charlie said, aghast at the idea.

"Is he down here?" she persisted.

"Of course. Staying with the Westmacotts."

"Then, invite him over after dinner."

There was silence for some moments. Then Ross said, "We'd need an independent arbiter."

"There's one in this house," Louisa said. "Major Smith-Barton, D.S.O. One-time honorary steward to Calcutta Racecourse. Now, what d'you say? Or do I chuck the bleedin' sturgeon in the dustbin and tell the Major to drive me 'ome?"

Sir John Farjeon looked at Ross and Charlie. They nodded. He said, "I'll telephone."

Lady Farjeon's despairing voice could be heard approaching, pleading for them to come in.

"All right," he told Louisa. "I'm sorry. Please start to serve up."

The dinner went smoothly and all the dishes were well eaten; but those who did the actual serving reported that there was a conspicuous absence of jollity about what had been intended to be a little festivity. At last it was over and word came down that the men, intsead of remaining in the dining room alone, had gone into the smoking room, where a caller, Mr. Desmond Elleston, had joined them. To little Kath's surprise, Major Smith-Barton, who a few minutes before had been drying dishes as she washed them, was invited to go up and join them. There was report of more raised voices from behind the door.

"Ma'am," Kath said tentatively to Louisa, who was setting out things for her to heat up for next morning's breakfast, "what's Mr. Elleston doin' here, and all the shoutin'?"

"What do you know about him?" Louisa asked.

"My brother Fred works for him, ma'am. In his stables."

Louisa was suddenly interested. "Where Vital Spark's trained?"

"Oh, yes ma'am. He's goin' to win everythin' sooner or later, Fred says."

"Well, he doesn't seem to have won today. Between you and me and the gatepost, the row's about some-one accusing Mr. Elleston of holding the horse back, or whatever they call it, so's he'll get better odds at Goodwood. Daft sport, I reckon."

But Kath was even more worried now. She was fumbling in her apron pocket for a crumpled letter, which she handed to Louisa.

"Fred sent me this, ma'am. Not that I gamble much . . . Can't afford more than once or twice a year. But he gives me a good tip now and then, and he sent me this letter. Said to save my money on Vital Spark today, but have a real go on 'im at Goodwood."

Louisa read the letter, then turned toward the stairs.

"You're not goin' to take it to 'em!" the girl cried in alarm. "I don't want to get Fred into trouble."

"Neither do I, love. I just want to get a pal of mine out of it."

Her quick ear had detected movement upstairs, and male laughter. There was a convivial note to the men's conversation which reached her as she went up the stairs. The "inquiry" had just broken up in complete amity. Desmond Elleston had explained what he could only conclude had gone wrong with Vital Spark that day: he blamed himself entirely for instructing his jockey to take up the lead early in the race. Once Vital Spark had done so, and found noth-ing in front of him to race against, the horse had lost interest and it had been beyond the jockey's abilities to pull him together again.

"Mr. Ross's point," Major Smith-Barton had put it to him finally, "is that you now stand to make a for-tune if Vital Spark wins at Goodwood."

"I might just be that farsighted," Elleston had

agreed. "Regrettably, though, my creditors aren't, sir. I shall be sold up by then."

Such candor had proved finally disarming. There had been apologies all around, a final, wholly amicable drink, and now Elleston was leaving, Sir John Farjeon and his guests were about to rejoin the long-suffering ladies, and Major Smith-Barton was on his way back to help tidying up the kitchen.

"Thank you, Mrs. Trotter," Ross said, as he encountered her in the hall. "Your suggestion was an admirable one. Saved us all a scandal. I'm very grateful."

"That's handsome of you," she smiled. He added, "I'm sure Mr. Elleston would wish to thank you, too."

He gestured toward that gentleman, who was taking his leave of Charlie Haslemere alone, then bowed and went on his way to the drawing room, where Farjeon had already gone to make their apologies. Louisa went to where the two men were chatting and was introduced by Charlie.

"Liked your tame Major immensely," Desmond Elleston told her. "Delightful old chap. Tell me, what is he, er, exactly? . . ."

Her expression surprised him. "I'll tell you what he is," she said, in a harsh, low tone. "He's one of them poor little people you might have took this afternoon, if I hadn't warned him off bettin'. He was one of the lucky ones. I can't make you pay the others back, and if it wouldn't make Charlie here look a proper fool, and upset the Farjeons, then I'd show Mr. Ross this letter here that proves exactly what you meant to do. But you run Vital Spark at Goodwood, and try to take a lot more little people, and I swear I will."

"You . . . you're bluffing," Elleston said. But he had paled, and Charlie was looking at him curiously. "Let me see that letter."

"If you see it, the other men do. You know what I'm talkin' about, don't you?"

"You realize I shall go bankrupt," Elleston said defeatedly.

"That could be the least of your worries. You'll be kicked out of society, the other way, and you'll never get back. And if you want to know, my nice little Major *is* bankrupt, or as good as, and could've been worse in it today because of you."

Without another word Elleston nodded and walked out of the house. Charlie tried to take the crumpled letter from Louisa, but she wouldn't let him have it.

"A bargain's a bargain," she said.

He replied, stricken, "I would have gone on oath that that man ..."

She smiled. "You always was a lousy judge of character, love."

Back in the kitchen she secretly gave the letter back to Kath. "Burn it," she said. "Now. No one's read it, and they'll never know what it was. But it did the trick, thanks."

The girl hastened to stuff it into the glowing embers of the old range.

"I don't go poachin'," Louisa told her as she did so, "but if you ever decide to chance your arm up in London, look me up and we'll see what we can do. Eh?"

"Oh, thank you, ma'am!"

"Don't let it go to your head, meantime, though. You make sure they get a nice breakfast. Gawd knows they deserve it."

She turned to her assistants. Everything was packed up in the bus outside.

"Hope we haven't ruined your hands, Miss Jennett," she told Lady Farjeon's maid. "And you'd make quite a good footman, if you didn't keep jumpin' to attention," she chaffed Guardsman Wilson, who grinned back at her and did it again.

"I won't say it's been fun, but we had our moments, didn't we?" Louisa said finally to Mr. Sterling as they shook hands. "Give my respects to Sir John and Lady Farjeon, will you. I expect he'll be in touch."

She led her own troops off into the night.

Twenty-Four

"What d'you know about Cowes?" Louisa asked Merriman abruptly in her parlor one morning in the summer of 1909.

Taken somewhat aback, he ventured, "Cows, ma'am, are large vegetarian mammals. Female—of the bovine species."

"Oh blimey! I'm talkin' about rudders, not udders. Tillers and spinnakers and ruddy great yachts. *Cowes* —the sailin' place."

"I see, ma'am. Well, Lord Haslemere's a member of the Royal Yacht Club there. He's the man to ask about Cowes, I should say."

"Obviously no use asking you," Louisa snarled and turned dismissively back to the page of newspaper on which she had scrawled a circle around an advertisement for a house.

She not only asked Charlie about Cowes; she surprised him by asking him to take her there in his car. He was the newest member of the committee of that august club and he had to go down for a meeting. She gave no reason for wanting to go, other than a sudden fancy for a day out and a breath of sea air. Charlie, only too pleased to have her company, didn't think to question this uncharacteristic notion.

As they approached the gates of the Royal Yacht

Club grounds, a certain discomfort which had been growing in him welled up. He swallowed and said nervously, "I'm awfully sorry, Louisa. I'm not allowed to take you inside." Louisa, he knew, was not one for being made to seem inferior or obeying anyone's rules but her own. "Look," he added hastily. "I'll see you back here at one o'clock, shall I, and take you for a jolly good luncheon?"

To his surprise and relief, as he stopped the car at the gates bearing the notice STRICTLY PRIVATE—MEMBERS ONLY, Louisa smiled and said, "That'll be fine. I'll stroll down the prom, or something."

She got out and shut the car door. "Go on. You're late already, aren't you?"

He drove in, saluted by the burly gatekeeper, an ex-Signaller R.N. named Wilkins. Louisa loitered a moment, surveying the trim premises. Two expensively dressed ladies swept past her without a glance. The gatekeeper saluted again and greeted them deferentially. Wanting to get a better view of the celebrated club, Louisa moved forward to just within the gates. The custodian stepped quickly toward her, frowning aggressively.

"You can't come in here, lady," he told her, looking her up and down.

"Blimey!" she retorted, her accent confirming his estimate of her class, "I was only havin' a look."

"Yeh. Well, do your looking from outside," he ordered.

Pausing only to regard him in the way she would have looked at a piece of moldy cheese, Louisa walked away. She did not go far, though. Just next door, in fact, to stand regarding a small house named Rock Cottage. It was the one she had found advertised in the newspaper. After several minutes she smiled and walked briskly away into the town, to seek out an address she carried with her.

Charlie Haslemere found that the meeting had

started without him. His fellow committee members were Major Gutch, the secretary, a pleasant but anxious man in his late forties; Sir Reginald Blenkiron, a jovial man some years older whose face was sometimes seen at the Bentinck Hotel; Colonel Sibley, another Bentinck habitué, who, with Blenkiron, had put up Charlie for the committee; and George Oscroft, a Rear Admiral in his sixties, of a gruff disposition. The meeting was chaired by the Royal Yacht Squadron's Commodore, Sir Evelyn Grant-Wortley, a crusty old woman-hater. He regarded the latecomer sourly and refused the secretary's suggestion that he read the minutes again for Lord Haslemere's benefit.

"The item under discussion," the Commodore condescended to explain, "is the desirability or otherwise of purchasing Rock Cottage, the house adjoining these premises, for the benefit of our lady members." The contempt with which he referred to them left no doubt of his opinion.

Major Gutch told Charlie, "I put forward an offer at our last meeting, which you couldn't attend. Unfortunately, it was short of the asking price. The question is, do we increase it?"

"Waste of money," Admiral Oscroft barked.

"But the ladies do have a problem," Gutch pointed out. "Nowhere to go if it rains."

"The marquee," Oscroft retorted.

"It's only up in regatta week," Sibley reminded him, and Blenkiron put in, "It's not just the weather. I mean, they're rather stuck on the lawn . . . for other emergencies."

Oscroft countered, "They can use the Strangers' lavatory."

"Complaints about that. They have to queue up."

The Commodore spoke up. "We're not having them in the clubhouse, come what may. It's about the last place on earth you can escape from your damn wife *and* your mistress."

"Then we've got to get Rock Cottage for them," Blenkiron said. "You agree, don't you, Arthur?" he asked Sibley, who nodded vigorously, saying, "Mutiny otherwise—from my wife, anyway."

"And we also have to protect ourselves from the possibility of disagreeable neighbors, now old Mrs. Crisp's gone."

This additional argument clinched the matter at last. The Commodore commanded the secretary, "Offer another couple of hundred. They'll accept that. Now, let's get on with the rest."

While the committee deliberated the problem of a distinguished member and his wife, both in their eighties, who had taken to early morning bathing from the clubhouse steps, and might thereby set a precedent for others, Rock Cottage was being inspected by Louisa in the company of the estate agent she had gone into the town to locate. The quite charming little house was unfurnished and rather run-down, but it had an irresistible terrace with a superb view out over the water.

"Right on the finishing line of the regatta, Mrs. Trotter," the man told her. "In Mrs. Crisp's day there were the most wonderful parties, I gather. Fairy lights hanging from all the bushes and along here . . ."

To his astonishment she said simply, "Right, I'll take it."

"You mean . . . you wish to make an offer, madam?"

"I said I'll take it. Something wrong?"

"No, no. Only . . . we have had another inquiry. I ought not to divulge . . . Well, it's from the Royal Yacht Club next door. We're just waiting for them to come back with a better figure."

Still smarting at her exclusion from that establishment, and the gatekeeper's manner toward her, Louisa said firmly, "Look, I'm offerin' you the full price. Cash."

She opened the large handbag she was carrying and

held it toward him. The estate agent's eyes widened at the sight of tied up bundles of banknotes.

Charlie was horrified when she met him and told him casually what she'd done.

"You can't!" he protested. "We've just decided to buy it."

"Should've been quicker off the mark, then, shouldn't you?"

"You mean you just walked in and . . ."

"No. Saw it advertised in the paper. That's why I asked for a lift down."

"Took advantage of me, and now . . . ! Oh lord, when the committee hear about our . . . connection they'll think I put you up to it."

"So what? Some of my best clients are members of your snobby old club. Reggie Blenkiron, old Saffron Walden . . . They'll be happy to have me near."

"They might but their wives won't. The ladies of the club have set their hearts on the cottage."

"Too bad for 'em. Look, Charlie, whose side are you on? You should be pleased as Punch. Nice little place to come and stay. We'll liven the place up a bit, too. I reckon we'll have a real housewarming, soon as I've got some furniture in."

The furnishing process did not take long. Meanwhile, Louisa gave all the Bentinck's residents and guests notice that she would be taking two months' holiday and that most of her staff would be accompanying her, including Mrs. Cochrane, Merriman, Starr, and the maid, Ethel. Mary Philips and Major Smith-Barton would supervise the hotel and meals would continue to be provided by the kitchen assistants, though not on any elaborate scale.

Then the day came when she and her retainers, together with an amiable but impoverished marquis, Tommy Shepherd, and his red-haired widow friend, Mrs. Delaney, piled into the hotel bus and were driven off by Starr, with Fred sitting up beside him. Champagne was, of course, drunk throughout the journey, and when the party eventually debussed at Cowes their steps were unsteady and their voices loud.

A band on the Yacht Club lawn was playing Gilbert and Sullivan. Teaspoons were tinkling in saucers like extra instruments. The arrival of some noisy persons at Rock Cottage did not go unremarked and there were exchanges of outraged looks between the members' ladies when some raucous singing was heard. Lady Blenkiron, Mrs. Sibley, and one or two others departed from decorum to stand on their wicker chairs and look over the hedge. Louisa saw them and grinned.

"Wotcher, ladies!" she greeted them. At that moment Tommy Shepherd dashed into view, whooping with mock fear as Mrs. Delaney pursued him with a croquet mallet. The watchers' heads disappeared like a row of knocked-down coconuts.

"Who are those dreadful people?" Lady Blenkiron demanded.

Hugo "Saffron" Walden, who was smiling, answered with what sounded like glee, "Louisa Trotter and guests, dear lady. She's taken the cottage."

Lady Blenkiron glared at her husband, who was not openly sharing his bachelor friend's enjoyment of the prospect. She said accusingly, "You informed me categorically that the house would be *ours*."

"My dear, I told you we were outbid. The club funds couldn't enable us to go over the full price."

"I've heard the woman runs a brothel," Mrs. Sibley said, shocked.

"Oh, no," her own husband answered. "It's a jolly nice place."

"You mean to say you've been there!"

"I, er . . . Well, everyone stays there at some time or another. I mean, Members of Parliament . . . the King, in his time . . ."

"Hm!" Mrs. Sibley's suspicions were even deeper now.

"Clergy, too," Blenkiron hastened to say. "Lots of 'em."

Major Gutch, who had been keeping out of it, felt he should make some official utterance. "I assure you, ladies," he said, "we shall be keeping a careful eye on the situation. If we feel a complaint is justified, we shall not hesitate to make one."

"I think there is little doubt that you will be doing so," Lady Blenkiron said. "Great heavens, what next? A dog loose on our lawn!"

Fred, impelled by curiosity, had entered the grounds at a moment when Wilkins, the gatekeeper, had not been looking. Wilkins had seen him now and was advancing fast. Fred looked all around, his shaggy features bearing no sign that he was impressed. He wandered over to a basket chair, cocked a leg up to it, then nonchalantly trotted away back to friendlier territory, calmly eluding Wilkins as he went.

The housewarming party took place two nights later. Colored fairy lights were once more in profusion in the small garden of Rock Cottage and along the terrace, adding to the romantic effect of the riding lights of the moored yachts. Several of Louisa's friends had traveled specially down from London and there was no letup for Merriman in his rounds with the champagne bottles.

Charlie Haslemere was there. So, also, was a very special catch of Louisa's, Irene Baker, the current toast of the West End musical stage.

"How on earth did you get her?" Charlie had asked, when Louisa had told him Irene would be coming to stay with her. "Half of London must be offering her yachts and villas, now that her show's just closed."

"I just asked her," Louisa said casually. "She was in the hotel with someone before we left, and I asked her. Mentioned you might be here, and she seemed to jump at it."

He looked at her suspiciously, but her face gave nothing away.

Now, arriving late at the party after dining on someone's yacht, Charlie found Irene on a sofa, appearing, to judge from their positions, to have been edging unsuccessfully away from "Saffron" Walden.

"Charles, dear boy," Walden greeted him, "I was just saying to Miss Baker that her dance in the second act was like a bright star in a horribly dull season. Wouldn't you agree?"

Charlie took Irene's hand. "I can't remember a more intensely enjoyable evening in the theater," he said sincerely.

"Thank you," she said, "I can't remember a nicer compliment."

Their hands stayed in one another's. Walden sighed and got up.

"See I'm superfluous," he said, and wandered off with his empty glass in pursuit of Merriman.

Charlie sat down next to Irene. She didn't edge away from him. Their thighs touched and stayed. She was very beautiful; beautifully dressed; beautifully perfumed . . .

"I was hoping I might have seen you again . . . after that party at Romano's," she told him candidly.

"You were so surrounded by admirers, I felt my chances were slim, to say the least."

"You should have had more faith."

Charlie felt his heart leap. "How . . . how long are you staying?" he blurted out.

"I've three weeks before my next rehearsals start."

"But that's marvelous! *Will* you stay? Have you ever been sailing?"

She shook her head. "I used to stand on the beach, as a child, and watch the yachts go by, and dream that someday . . . Of course, I've got a lot of offers now, though."

Charlie told her delightedly, "Then I claim the privilege of being the one who fulfills your dream for you. If you'll allow me, that is?"

She gazed into his eyes and nodded slowly.

In the kitchen Merriman told Starr and Mrs. Cochrane, "She's set her compass at his lordship, and no mistake."

"What does Mrs. Trotter seem to think about it?" the cook asked.

"Seems to be encouraging them."

"Waste of time," Starr said. "She'd never make a lady in a hundred years. Her father's a jobbing builder at Bognor."

"Lady or not," Ethel said, coming in and hearing this, "I wish I had a body like hers."

When Merriman got back to the terrace with yet another bottle of champagne he found Lord Haslemere and Irene Baker with their backs to him, taking turns to peer through a long brass telescope on a mounting. It was tilted skyward. There was silence in the house now. All the other guests had gone and Mrs. Trotter had disappeared.

"Uranus, I think," his lordship was saying. "Or is it the Pole Star?"

"I don't believe you know one from another," the beautiful actress giggled. They were shoulder to shoulder and his arm was about her slender waist. Merriman retreated silently behind the curtains and uncorked the bottle there with an unnecessary pop. They had stood apart by the time he went out to them.

"Thank you, Merriman," Lord Haslemere said. "Don't wait up for me. I'll turn out the lights."

Merriman took polite leave of them. When he had gone, Irene was about to move to Charlie again. He stopped her with a gesture.

"Don't move. The moon has caught you perfectly. Onstage, I thought you were the most divine apparition I'd ever seen. Offstage, I find you . . . even more divine. Irene. . . !"

He didn't restrain her this time as she came forward into his arms and met him in a long, passionate kiss, after which she murmured into his shoulder, "And I've imagined somebody like you all my life."

Next morning, Louisa did a rare thing for her: she went for a walk with no more purpose than to enjoy the air. Preferring to chat rather than keep silent, she looked for Charlie to accompany her, but was told he was still asleep. So she commanded Starr to go with her; and, of course, Fred went too, trotting happily a few paces ahead, weaving from side to side and enjoying a whole new range of smells.

"Not so bad, this fresh-air lark," Louisa remarked contentedly.

"The air is surprisingly bracing, madam," Starr answered.

A middle-aged couple approaching them smiled and nodded to Louisa and went on.

"That's Lord Pembroke," she told Starr. "Bit before your time. If his wife knew what I know about him she wouldn't be lookin' so pleased with herself."

Another couple were approaching now. Both were ladies and Louisa recognized them as the pair who had passed her at the Yacht Club gates, and whose faces had been among those peering outraged over the hedge into her garden.

"Mornin', ladies!" she greeted them cheerfully.

They stuck their noses into the air. "Don't answer," the beefier of them said to the other, deliberately loudly.

"I wouldn't presume to," replied the companion.

"Every bit as common as she looks," came floating back to Louisa when the women had gone by. "I can't think what Cowes is coming to. Brothelkeepers now."

Starr, who had also heard, took the liberty of clutching at his employer's arm, just in time to prevent her turning and running after the women to give them an extended sample of Covent Garden argot.

"No, no, ma'am," he pleaded. "I beg you, don't rise to it!"

His persuasion worked; but Louisa's taste for strolling was gone. She stormed back to Rock Cottage with Starr hurrying beside her and Fred no longer allowed to keep pausing on the way. She found Charlie and Irene in the garden.

"What's happened?" Charlie asked, recognizing one of Louisa's furies from well-known signs.

"I've been insulted, that's what's happened. By so-called ladies from your club. Called me a brothel-keeper. Well, I want their names. One's built like a bus—wears a wig and a hat with tomatoes on it . . ."

Charlie took care not to smile. "That sounds like Rose Blenkiron," he said. "She generally goes about with Mrs. Sibley. But I'd ignore them, Louisa."

"No bloody fear! I don't ignore personal injuries—you should know that. It's war!"

The roulette party Louisa proceeded to throw that evening was surpassingly noisy. She encouraged those guests who were not preoccupied with the wheel and the counters to join her in singing lusty choruses of music-hall ditties of the broadest nature. Fuelled by her champagne, they complied willingly, including those of them who were respected members of the club next door, where their wives believed they were playing a quiet game of bridge.

The following day the Commodore of the Royal Yacht Squadron summoned Charlie to his presence in the library. The band was playing something vaguely pastoral on the lawn, where the ladies were mustered as usual.

"This woman friend of yours next door, Haslemere," Sir Evelyn Grant-Wortley began without preamble. "You know her pretty well, they tell me."

"Mrs. Trotter?" Charlie answered coolly. "Yes, I do."

"And you told her to buy that cottage?"

"Certainly not. I'd no idea ..."

"Well, that's not what I've heard. Anyway, she's causing trouble. Complaints from members. Noise."

"Really?" Charlie replied innocently. He had been present the previous evening, though he had spent most of it exclusively in the company of Irene Baker.

"Tell her to pipe down, or get out," the Commodore ordered.

Imagining the outcome of his undertaking any such hazard, Charlie said, "Sir Evelyn, I really don't think it's my business personally."

"What? Dammit, you can hear her now."

They could, indeed. Shrieks and bellows of laughter were coming from across the hedge. Charlie could just imagine what was going on—an unserious croquet game between Tommy Shepherd and Mrs. Delaney, with suggestive promptings from the champagne-bibbers.

As he and the Commodore went to the window to see for themselves, Lady Blenkiron, losing all restraint, got up onto her chair on the lawn again and roared at the Rock Cottage people, "Will you keep quiet over there!"

"You keep your band quiet!" Louisa's voice was heard to yell back.

"Oh, Lor'!" the Commodore moaned at Charlie's side. "More trouble coming from the blasted women. Had enough already."

He and Charlie watched Lady Blenkiron clamber down and march over to the bandmaster. She shouted something forceful up at him. He gave a little bow of acknowledgment, rounded off the number they were playing, gave some instructions to the players, and, raising his baton high, crashed them into a march tune.

Retaliation was not long forthcoming. To Charlie's horrified disbelief an upper window of Rock Cottage

was pushed open a few minutes later and there hurtled out of it a missile which crashed onto the Yacht Club lawn, near Lady Blenkiron's table. It was white in color and fragile in texture, for it smashed into several pieces, which flew about dangerously. It was followed by another and another. Though all shattered where they fell among the cowering ladies there was no difficulty for the men at the library window in identifying them as chamber pots.

Cries of "Outrage!" "Scandalous!" and even "Police!" arose from the ladies as they scattered.

"My God!" the Commodore groaned, and hurried away to hide.

"It was unforgivable!" Charlie scolded Louisa later. He was really annoyed with her. "What on earth possessed you?"

"They asked for it."

"No they didn't. Don't you realize you could have injured someone seriously? Some of those old ladies have matchstick bones."

Louisa was unrepentant. "They're askin' for conveniences, aren't they? Well, I gave 'em some chamber pots."

"It isn't a joke, Louisa. The Commodore's furious now, and with good reason. He wants an immediate apology."

"I'm not apologizin'."

"You *are* apologizing. Your behavior was stupid, dangerous, and damned irresponsible."

He had never spoken to her like this before. The fact registered, despite her own anger. She countered resentfully, "Well, your behavior hasn't been much to write home about, neither, these past few days."

"What's that supposed to mean?"

"Don't look so innocent. You and Miss bloody Baker."

"Louisa, that's extremely unfair. You practically

threw us together—in fact, I think you did deliberately."

"Well, you don't have to make such a meal out of it."

"Oh, for God's sake! . . . Irene and I are just having fun together. I mean, she's awfully sweet, and . . ."

"You goin' to marry her?" Louisa asked with a directness which startled him into pausing before answering.

"Of . . . course I'm not," he said at first; then amended it to "At least, I don't think so." After a further pause he asked in his more familiar schoolboy manner, "Would you mind if I did?"

Louisa shrugged. "It's your life. Do what you like."

He surprised her by saying, "I could never do that . . . never marry anyone . . . without your approval, Louisa. To be quite honest, I was looking on Irene as a sort of blow for freedom."

"What's that supposed to mean?"

"Well, to help separate *us*. It must happen one day —mustn't it? I thought she was a sort of present from you, for that purpose. I was rather touched."

Irene appeared in the doorway at that moment. "Are you coming now?" she asked Charlie. "I'm ready for town."

He looked at Louisa, who hadn't moved. "Just a moment, my angel," he told Irene. "See you in a moment."

The girl hesitated, then went. Charlie told Louisa quietly, "Look, all in all, I think perhaps it's best if I leave here."

"Why?"

"I just do."

She roused herself. "You can't. You can't leave me to the mercy of your old Wart-Grantly, or whatever he calls himself."

"Oh, yes. I'd forgotten that. He wants to see you, and I'm expected to arrange it."

"I said Mrs. Trotter's right. The club wives *are* treated abominably. It's quite like the Middle Ages. What do you propose to do about it, Commodore?"

"My dear Lady Blenkiron . . ."

"No. Sweet words are not going to be enough. Action is what is needed. Mrs. Trotter mentioned give and take on both sides. I for one should be most interested to hear what she has in mind."

"I'll tell you," Louisa answered. "I'm prepared to sell your club the annex to my house—for the ladies only."

"Waste of money," Admiral Oscroft grunted. "Managed for fifty years without."

" 'Managed' is hardly the word, George," Lady Blenkiron rebuked him. "Have you ever been in the Strangers' lavatory?"

The Commodore intervened, clutching at the straw of hope. "Mrs. Trotter, may we take it, then, that you will sell us your annex?"

"Yes," Louisa said. "But only on condition that . . ."

The following afternoon Charlie and Irene stood facing one another in the cottage sitting room.

"Must you really go?" she pouted.

"Yes, really. Estate business to attend to, and so forth."

"But you haven't taken me sailing yet."

"I'll arrange for someone to take you out. There'll be no shortage of volunteers. In any case, I'll try to come back . . . next weekend. And I'll write every day."

His instincts were genuinely pulling him in opposite directions. She sensed that he was experiencing some difficulties.

"You haven't got tired of me?" she asked, watching his eyes closely. He managed not to let his gaze falter.

"No. Oh, no. I adore you."

She pushed herself into his arms and they kissed passionately again, he just as eagerly as she. They were interrupted by a commotion of voices from outside the house and then the hurried entry of Tommy Shepherd.

"Oh, awfully sorry," he exclaimed. "Only . . . there's a most amazing thing happening out there. Do come and look."

Hand in hand, Charlie and Irene followed him on to the lawn. Mrs. Delaney was pointing excitedly out over the water. They shaded their eyes and looked.

The pinnace of the Commodore of the Royal Yacht Squadron was nearing shore. In its bow stood the Commodore. But he occupied a position of deference, a pace behind another figure—Louisa.

Leaving his friends, Charlie dashed from the cottage to the club gates, where, to his astonishment, he found a strip of red carpet, reserved for royal visits, laid. Several of his fellow members, including Sir Reginald Blenkiron, Colonel Sibley, Admiral Oscroft, and "Saffron" Walden were lined up, together with Major Gutch, to form a reception committee. Wilkins came stiffly to attention as the pinnace touched the steps and the Commodore personally handed Louisa ashore.

Charlie, who had, of course, heard the conditions of sale she had laid down, but hadn't expected them to be taken seriously, stepped hastily into line with the rest. From the corner of his eye he saw the ladies rising in amazement from their chairs to get a better view of the incredible proceedings. The band, which had been playing something insipid, struck up "Rule, Britannia!"

Like a queen, the Duchess of Duke Street proceeded along the red carpet, accepting Wilkins's salute with a gracious inclination of her head and bestowing a nod and a smile of greeting to each member in turn. When she found Charlie at the end of the line, she paused, just momentarily, to say, "Blow for freedom, eh, Charlie?"

Then she went on, straight into the clubhouse, to become the first woman ever entertained there to tea.

Twenty-Five

Having waited so long for the throne, and for the authority to rule his people so far as any modern constitutional monarch could do so, Edward VII worked tirelessly to make up for the frustrating inactivity of his first sixty years. But although he achieved much, the chance had come too late. Enforced idleness and luxurious living had undermined his health permanently. For years he had carried a great excess of weight, eating, drinking, and smoking far too much than was good for him. These abuses had inevitably affected his heart and lungs.

The year 1909—his sixty-eighth—proved to be the most stressful of his reign. The triumph of the visit to Germany and the elation at winning the Derby were soon eclipsed by the political crisis engendered by the high-handed new Chancellor of the Exchequer, Lloyd George. His budget was almost calculated to incur the veto of the House of Lords, thus providing the excuse to abolish that House altogether or at least so to pack it with newly created Liberal peers that it would be powerless to oppose the government's measures. In his speech at the opening of Parliament, in which he could only pass on his government's proposals, whatever he felt about them, Edward was careful to say that he was merely expressing the opinion of his advisers. Had he heeded the opinion of those other advisers responsible for his health, the following year, 1910, might have turned out rather differently for him.

In the event, though, he had a further severe attack of bronchitis, followed by a series of heart attacks. On top of the work, the worry, and the overweight, they were enough to kill him. They did, on May sixth.

"That Asquith killed him," declared Louisa of the Prime Minister, who had been booed to that effect in the streets by crowds shattered at the loss of their popular monarch.

Louisa was addressing Starr in the Bentinck's hall. She was dressed all in black. The news of the death had staggered her as much as it had anyone, and more than most. Memories, surprisingly tender memories, had swept over her like a flood tide when she had been told. She had not seen him for the past few years, and their intimate relationship had been brief and long ago. She was not an emotional woman; but time had deepened her affection for him and she had followed his triumphant career with personal pride. The fact that he had been so gravely ill had not been made public, so that his death had had all the more impact. It was as if he had been snuffed out like a candle still only half burned.

Starr wore a black crape armband. Even his dog had his crape mourning collar.

"Lord Henry Norton's come to see you, ma'am," Starr told Louisa, who had just come in. "I took the liberty of putting him in your room."

Louisa was surprised. It was some years, too, since Lord Henry had been in touch with her, although Charlie Haslemere referred to his uncle from time to time. Merriman was crossing the hall. She ordered him, "Bottle of wine in my room—if you please. And four glasses."

"Yes, madam." He had long known better than to ask what sort of wine she desired. It was invariably champagne—the best.

She found Lord Henry examining the many photographs of favorite hotel guests, mostly male, which almost papered the walls of her littered parlor-cum-office: men in uniform of all kinds, in hunting clothes, polo outfits, yachting blazers and caps, and other sporting rig. He, too, wore mourning clothes.

He smiled and shook hands with her. "How are you, Louisa?" She was surprised to hear him use her Christian name. "Sad news, eh? One less for your gallery, I'm afraid." He gestured to the framed photograph of Edward.

She nodded wistfully. "And the most important one. If it hadn't been for him I mightn't be here now. Still your assistant cook, eh, Lord Henry?"

"I often wish you were. But we were both lucky. The King honored us with his friendship. But it's quite extraordinary—how all the people one sees in the street look so sad."

"He was their friend, too," Louisa said. "The finest gentleman I ever ran up against—present company excepted, of course."

She sat down, and rubbed her thighs. "I'm creaking. Been on me knees across at the church in Piccadilly. Bought a black dress, too. I wouldn't have done neither for anyone else."

Merriman knocked and entered with the champagne. When he had opened it she ordered him to call Starr in and come back himself. He did, and poured two glasses, then hesitated.

"Go on," Louisa commanded. "You two take a glass as well."

Merriman poured again. Then Louisa proposed a toast. Her voice quavered slightly.

"Here's to the memory of King Edward the Seventh. May God bless him where he's gone."

The strangely assorted quartet—peer of the realm,

hotel proprietress, hall porter, and ancient waiter—
drank together gravely. Then Louisa jerked her head
and Starr and Merriman retired.

"What's the new bloke like?" she asked Lord Henry, referring, of course, to His Majesty King George the
Fifth.

"I hardly know him," he answered. "Nice, quiet,
respectable married man. Very naval, I gather."

"Not particularly likely to patronize this place,
then," she laughed. "Charlie Haslemere wired. He's
coming up today."

"Yes, I know."

"I haven't seen him for months . . . what with his
huntin' and fishin'."

"Yes," Lord Henry said, seeming to accept this as an
opportunity to say what he had come to say.
"That, er, is what I wanted to talk to you about really, Louisa. You see, I'm not his only surviving relative. Near relative, that is. *In loco parentis* sort of
thing, don't you know? It's a bit of a responsibility—
the estate and, ah, so forth . . ."

Louisa smiled again. "So you think he oughter stop
sowing all them wild oats and start doing a bit of
harvesting? Settle down."

"Exactly," Lord Henry replied, relieved.

"Well, I can do a lot of things for him, but I don't
think I can find him a wife."

"Oh, no, no. But I think . . . I, ah, hope *I* have."

This jolted Louisa somewhat. Charlie might be no
more to her emotionally nowadays than the late King
had been, and she had long since grown accustomed
to cooking for him and his married lady friends,
knowing full well what they would be up to when
the dinner things had been removed. But the thought
of his really marrying had been so remote from her
mind that it came as a little shock.

"Oh . . . Good," was all she could say.

"Very nice girl," Lord Henry went on. "Parents both
dead, sadly. Nice family, though."

"That's good, then. I hope he'll be happy. But it's not my concern, is it?"

"Oh yes it is, Louisa. I'm very fond of Charles, as you know, and I know him pretty well. I also know that there's no one in the world he admires and respects as much as you. You, ah, know what I'm talking about?"

"Yeh, I know," Louisa said, realizing that he was referring to her and Charlie's baby. "Well, I won't do anything to muck it up, don't worry. That is, if I think they're suited."

Lord Henry looked at her with sharp suspicion. "Is he very bitten with her?" she asked.

"Well . . . It's not quite the same as . . ."

He was interrupted before he could make any further allusion, however oblique, to the short-lived relationship between her and his nephew by the entry of the latter himself.

"Caught you at it, by George!" Charlie said accusingly to his uncle, who looked startled. "Drinking at this hour," he added with a grin.

Lord Henry relaxed again, getting up from the chair on which he had been seated.

"Bad luck for you we've finished the bottle," he said. "I must be off. You're dining with me tonight, Charles, and don't you forget. The Keppels and the Farjeons are coming, so it'll be rather gloomy, I'm afraid. All down in the dumps just now. Wish you were doing the dinner, Louisa. Got a temperamental Italian feller as chef nowadays. Can hear him screaming his head off in the library. Poor old Mrs. Catchpole's going into a decline, too."

He shook hands with Louisa and went. She turned to Lord Haslemere and regarded him. He came forward, smiling, and gave her the usual chaste but fond kiss.

"Haven't seen you for a bit," she said, feeling awkward. "Been behavin' yourself, like a good boy?"

"You know me," he said lightly; but she could sense his unease. "Louisa, I've . . . got someone coming to tea."

"That's all right. You just have to ring the bell in your room, same as usual."

"I think it would be better if we had it in the hall."

"Please yourself."

"You see, it's a girl."

"Oooh! Now you do shock me, you really do, Lord Haslemere."

"Louisa, be serious, please. You see, she's a rather quietly brought up sort of girl. She wouldn't understand it if we had tea in my rooms. I mean, without a chaperone."

Louisa persisted with the banter. "Knowing you, she might learn a thing or two."

But he went on seriously, embarrassed. "Will you be . . . I mean, will you be very careful? Er, watch what you say—your language?"

She would have taken instant offense at this, coming from anyone else, and it did sting her, even from him.

"Crikey!" she exclaimed. "If her ears are that delicate, why don't you take her to Gunter's, where she won't be corrupted?"

"Louisa, I particularly want you to meet Mar . . . Miss Wormald. She's . . . a girl I met up in Scotland. She's awfully good at fishing. Likes walking . . . She's an orphan. Actually, Sir James Rosslyn's her guardian."

"Oh, old Rosy!" she exclaimed, recalling the senior Liberal politician, another person she had not encountered for quite some time.

Charlie concluded his pathetic attempt to prepare the ground. "Living down in Dorset most of the year, she's had, well, rather a dull sort of life." Louisa knew perfectly well what he was doing, but spared him any blunt questioning in the light of what Lord

Henry had told her. The girl sounded to her hearty and heavily country, hardly Charlie's usual type at all. "I do hope you'll like her," he added.

"All right. I'll put on me best bib and tucker and mind me *p*'s and *q*'s and a few other letters."

"Thanks. Oh, by the way, she particularly likes chocolate éclairs."

"There's none made."

"Please—Louisa."

"Oh, bleedin' hell. I wish you'd stayed put where you was."

There was more unconscious meaning in that than either of them recognized. He merely thanked her and went away.

That afternoon Louisa looked on as Margaret Wormald tasted her first mouthful of éclair at the table beside the hall fireplace. She was a pretty enough girl, in her early twenties; demure, in an old-fashioned way, which her rather dull clothes complemented exactly.

"I think that's just the best éclair I've ever tasted!" she exclaimed, as soon as her mouth was empty.

"Louisa—Mrs. Trotter—made them herself," Charles Haslemere told her. She looked up at the impassive Louisa with awe.

"You mean . . . *you* cooked them, Mrs. Trotter?"

"With me own fair hands."

"I . . . I didn't know you cooked as well."

"I don't, as much as I used to. Only when it's something special."

The girl seemed surprised to be regarded as "something special." Louisa nodded, by way of confirmation, and said, "Well, if you'll excuse me, I've got the menus to see to." She went off to her room.

"What a funny woman!" Margaret Wormald said to Charlie, pouring him more tea. "Such a common voice."

"Yes," he had to agree. "But a very good cook. A great one."

"And you always stay here when you're in town?"

"That's right. I've got permanent rooms. You must come up and see them sometime."

"Uncle James stayed here once. I think he found it rather ... noisy."

"Oh? Really?"

At that moment Sir James Rosslyn himself came through the front door. He, too, wore mourning. He glanced around and spied the couple at their table.

"Hullo, Haslemere," he greeted Charlie, who rose and shook hands. "Come to take this young lady away from you. Going to a lecture at the Royal Society— on volcanoes."

They heard Louisa's approaching voice. "Hello, Sir Ros! You Liberals not so cocky now, eh? Majority of only two, wasn't it?"

"Not good," he agreed, shaking hands.

"Nobody's fault but your own," she told him bluntly. "That Winston Churchill's a nice boy and appreciates my cooking, but he thinks with his mouth. And as for Lloyd George and this people's budget of his—you'll ruin us all."

"Perfectly sound fiscal measure," he answered. "We'll get it through, once we've scotched those half-baked Conservative peers. Oh, beg pardon, Haslemere."

"Don't mind me," Charlie laughed. "Here you see the most unpolitical Conservative peer in captivity."

"That's where most of 'em should be," Louisa said. "Behind bars at the zoo."

Her opinion of Margaret Wormald rose a little when that young lady said, with sudden spirit, "We could go and feed them all with buns."

"Louisa's éclairs, please," Charlie said. They all laughed. Then Sir James, who had a taxi waiting, took Margaret away, promising to return her safely.

"He don't change much—dry old stick," Louisa said to Charlie.

"He treats her as if she were still about fourteen," he replied. He glanced around the hall, then said, "I say, Louisa, could you spare a minute? In your room?"

"Of course, love," she consented. As they passed the desk she ordered Starr, "Tell old Dundrearyman to fetch a bottle to my room."

"Yes, mum," he answered. "'Old Dundrearyman,'" he repeated to Fred, who trotted after him toward the dispense in search of Merriman. "Shall we tell him she called him that, eh?"

In Louisa's parlor Charlie stammered, uncertain how to say what he wanted to say, so Louisa said it for him.

"You want to know if you should pop the question to your little Miss Wormygold, is that it? Wondering whether she's the right one for you at last."

"How the devil... ?" he gaped.

"Oh, Charlie, love, I can read you like an open book. Always could. But why ask me this one?"

"Well, you're the only person I've ever asked to marry me so far. Isn't that a good enough recommendation?"

"I dunno," she sighed. "I mean, how well d'you know her?"

"Well, we met quite often in Scotland."

"All by yourselves, was you?"

"No. Never." After a pause he added, "She's quite jolly, really. Not half such a mouse as ..."

"You don't have to apologize for her."

"No. The trouble is—it's damn difficult to get to know someone like Margaret. Properly, I mean."

"*We* managed to get to know each other, all right."

"Oh, but that's not possible. I mean, I couldn't ..."

"She bein' a lady," Louisa couldn't help retorting cattily.

"That's unfair!" he protested.

"Yes, it was," Louisa had to agree. "You always

treated me like a lady, though I wasn't one, I'll give you that."

Merriman came in with the champagne. She was able to take her discomfiture out on him.

"Been over to France to get it, 'ave you? Just leave it for 'is lordship to open. You 'op off and die somewhere."

Accustomed and impervious to her insults, the old man put down the tray and ambled out. Charlie opened the bottle and poured for them both. They drank a little private toast, each remembering old times. He gave her one of his light kisses.

"Can't see no stars in your eyes, Charlie," she sighed. "You're not head over heels, that's for sure."

"No, I'm not. But don't you think it better . . . or might be better . . . just to start off liking each other . . . ?"

"And then, as time goes by, getting fonder and fonder? Like it was a piece of furniture, or a dog, or something?"

He shrugged uncertainly. She had to help him as best she could.

"She looks healthy enough, and the big idea's to produce a future little Lord Haslemere, I suppose?"

"Frankly, yes."

"Then, she's a lucky girl, Charlie."

"You think I should, then?"

"Why not? You pays yer money . . ."

"That is, if she'll have me."

"Or if Sir Rosy will have you."

He stared at her. This hadn't entered his mind. But when he went to call on Sir James Rosslyn at the first opportunity for a formal talk, next day, he soon found that Louisa's point had been a cogent one.

"I do want you to see it from my point of view, Haslemere," the fastidious older man said, when the preliminaries were over and Charlie had made his request without receiving a direct answer. "Margaret's parents were my very, very dear friends. She was their only child. I'm not only her guardian, but her trustee. She is my greatest responsibility in the world. I think I feel more responsible for her than her actual parents would—that is to say, if they were alive."

Charlie noted to himself that the man's pomposity certainly hadn't decreased with the years. He decided to cut short the homily.

"And I clearly don't meet with your approval," he said.

"I didn't say that. I didn't say that at all. But we can be frank with each other. In fact, we *must* be frank. You have, er, ah, a reputation. A certain reputation for . . . how shall I put it. . . ?"

"Being a flibbertigibbet."

"A what?"

"No matter."

"Hm. You see, Haslemere, I don't like rumors. But there was at one time something of a rumor that you and . . . and Louisa Trotter . . ."

"Sir James," Charlie interrupted quickly, "I like women and women seem to like me. I'm lucky to have lots of friends and plenty of money. So I've had a very jolly ten years or so enjoying myself."

"That's exactly what I mean. Your character is rather . . . light, if I may say so. You haven't cared to take on any responsibility. Politics. Justice of the Peace . . ." He sighed. "However, I must admit that Margaret seems very fond of you. Only, she's seen very little of life."

"Whose fault is that?" Charlie couldn't help riposting; but Sir James Rosslyn was not one for self-criticism.

"I've done my duty as I've seen fit," he said stiffly. "And, having said my piece, I must tell you that if the marriage-settlement arrangements are suitable, as I am sure they will be, I do not feel I should stand in your way. So you have my blessing."

He stood up abruptly and offered his hand. Astonished by the unexpected consent, Charlie shook it automatically, stammered some thanks, and left, feeling suddenly committed and unsure of himself again.

A few days after the announcement of the forthcoming marriage had appeared in *The Times* and certain other newspapers, Charlie again sought out Louisa for a confidential interview in her parlor. He was looking unusually serious and quickly crushed her banter. From his pocket he drew out a document and placed it on her blotting pad.

"What's this?" she asked, recognizing a legal document.

"It's a writ of Breach of Promise of Marriage, taken out against me by Irene Baker."

"Irene! Crikey!"

"She's obviously seen the announcement in the papers."

"The twisting little bitch! Unless, of course . . ."

"No, Louisa. Absolutely not."

"Well, you must admit you were a bit over the moon, there on the old Isle of Wight."

"We had some fun, yes."

"You sure you didn't get overexcited and drop a little hint? Give her a ring, 'just to remember me by'? Presents?"

"I gave her lobster, if you call that a present."

"What'd you give her that for?"

"To eat, of course."

"Well, she can't bring that up in court. We hope."

"Very funny. But it's not going to court. I've been with my lawyers half the day. They say if they get in touch with Irene's people the whole thing can be settled quietly, without anyone hearing a word of it."

"Pay up, you mean?"

"Yes. They'll have to agree on a sum, of course."

"But that's lettin' her win. Givin' in to bloody

blackmail. Don't you do it, Charlie—or I'll never speak to you again."

He said helplessly, "But I can't face it in public. Think of the papers . . . the distress it'll cause everyone. You, too, Louisa. You and your hotel would be bound to be dragged in."

She railed at him. "All right, let me be dragged in. Let's all get dragged in. Charlie, you've got to face up to things in life. It's no good shoveling 'em under the carpet. Someone always finds 'em in the end. If you hush this up, and pay up, and one day your wife hears of it—which she will—then bang'll go your marriage, matey. She'll imagine all sorts of other things you've been doin' without lettin' on. She'll never trust you again."

Charlie thought silently for some moments. Then he said miserably, "I really don't think I can face Margaret and tell her about it."

"You can face me, so why not her? You want to know how much she loves you—well, then, you'll find out this way."

He considered this, then said with some relief, "Oh hell, you're right as usual, I suppose."

"Course I am. And it'll put old Sir Rosy to the test, too."

It did, indeed, and he made no bones about his reaction.

"I am absolutely horrified by the whole business."

"But James," interceded Lord Henry Norton, in whom his nephew had confided and who had accompanied him to see Sir James, "Charlie had no idea. It came as a complete bolt from the blue. I mean to say, he's completely innocent, and if the marriage announcement hadn't appeared in the press this woman wouldn't have dreamed of trying it on."

"You may think that, my dear Henry. You may indeed think that. But I was at the Bar as a young man, before I became a Member of Parliament, and

I can tell you these cases are very often—not to say usually—settled in an atmosphere of emotion. It is not like a . . . a merchant overcharging for a ton of coal. Not at all. Who is acting for the plaintiff?"

"Some King's Counsellor. Newsom, is it?"

"Newsom! Patrick Newsom? Good lord, he could blacken the character of the Archangel Gabriel and get damages from the Holy Ghost. Especially if the plaintiff were a pretty girl—which Irene Baker is. By the way, have you seen this?"

Sir James produced, with an air of distaste, a copy of that morning's *Daily Banner,* a newspaper that did not enter Lord Henry Norton's household, except to the downstairs region. The front page bore a large photograph of a girl—Charlie recognized Irene Baker immediately—carefully posed, gazing wistfully at a framed photograph of himself.

"Monstrous!" Lord Henry exclaimed.

"You know what they say about love and war," Sir James reminded him. "I don't know whether word of this will have reached Margaret yet, but I intend to get her back to Dorset and do my best to soften the blow."

"I should like to explain it to her myself," Charlie said resolutely. Sir James shook his head.

"You've done enough harm to her for the moment, I think, Haslemere. I am not going to insist on a public announcement that the engagement is being canceled. That would be tantamount to hitting a man when he's down. But if the case goes against you, I think you will know what honorable action to take."

Twenty-Six

Despite Sir James Rosslyn's insistence, Charlie got to Margaret before her guardian could, and told her all. To his intense relief, she responded by expressing complete belief in him.

She knew more of his reputation than he had even begun to suspect. Her guardian, it seemed, had dropped a few heavy hints when he had noticed them spending so much time together in Scotland. But she also had friends who knew Lord Haslemere in society and hadn't spared her the gossip. Her appearance of innocence of the world and its ways masked a good deal of shrewdness and capacity for broadmindedness. She had long since told herself that if Charles should ever propose to her, as she had for some time been expecting him to do, she would accept him, but must take him for what he had been and was. She imagined he would make a good husband for her, and a reliable father to her children, and would be faithful to her in his fashion. For more than that she did not hope. From the example of some of those friends of hers—the ones who were married—she had learned of the difference between willing companionship and the strain upon both parties of a possessive relationship.

So when Sir James at last came to her and requested her to pack her things and return to Dorset forthwith, she declined politely, and, when ordered, simply refused. There was nothing he could do to make her; in fact, he secretly admired her spirit. The one thing he was adamant about, though, was that she should not receive newspaper reporters or attend the court. She consented to the former but argued about the latter. Only after Charles had seen her again, and added his plea to Sir James's, did she agree not to be present.

"But I'll have to sit here, in these wretched rooms, just waiting—not knowing," she protested finally.

"You *do* know—don't you?" Charlie asked her gently. "If you don't believe me, then no one's going to."

"Oh, of course I do, darling!" she cried. "I'm sorry. I know, when you come to tell me the news, it'll be good news. If there's any justice left in the world, that is."

He smiled, and kissed her. "I think you'll find there's a modicum of it about."

But even Charlie's confidence—and he was an optimist in most things—flagged a good deal in the awe-inspiring surroundings of the King's Bench Division of the High Court of Justice, with himself the center of attention of several dozen people—barristers, ushers, policemen, clerks, pressmen, public, and a jury of twelve men who, from the look of them, might have been handpicked as guardians of public morality. The only friendly faces he could discern were his uncle's and Louisa's. Sir James Rosslyn's expression was blank; he was plainly waiting to be convinced. Two or three of Charlie's female acquaintances were in the public seats. He would scarcely term them friends, though—just couriers for any juicy passages which might fail to get into print.

Irene Baker sat near her counsel. She was demurely dressed in a dark frock and hat, and looked wistfully ravishing. She gave Charlie a prolonged sweet smile, which achieved its purpose of being widely noticed.

He returned a briefer one, and a polite little nod of acknowledgment.

When the elderly judge had taken his place and the opening formalities had been concluded, Irene's leading counsel, Newsom, a formidable-looking being in comparison to Charlie's own rather mousy man, Randall, proceeded to outline the plaintiff's case.

"For some years now my client, Miss Irene Baker, has enjoyed an increasingly successful career on the stage as an actress and dancer. She first met Lord Haslemere at a party at the Bentinck Hotel, Duke Street, early last year. Evidently they were mutually attracted, and Lord Haslemere took Miss Baker to supper at Romano's restaurant.

"The two parties continued to see each other from time to time, but their friendship can be said to have blossomed into something more intense during a holiday they both spent as guests of Mrs. Trotter, the proprietress of the Bentinck Hotel, at her house in the Isle of Wight during August of last year.

"During that time Lord Haslemere proposed marriage to Miss Baker on several occasions, and later in London, but it was mutually agreed that no public announcement should be made until Lord Haslemere had had time to discuss the situation with his family and his trustees. Miss Baker also had contractual and other professional affairs to settle.

"At that time Lord Haslemere's ardor was such that he could hardly bear to be parted from Miss Baker for even a day or so, or, in his own words, 'even an hour.' When she was not with him he bombarded her with letters and telegrams."

Newsom picked up a small pile of papers from his desk and looked up at the judge.

"If I might be permitted to read some extracts from these letters, m'lud?"

"If you consider them relevant," the judge assented, to the obvious relief of the press and public.

"Regretfully, I do, m'lud." Newsom selected one and began to read, "'My darling Pally . . .'"

"'Polly'? Who is this 'Polly'?" the judge inquired.

"No, m'lud, 'Pally,'" counsel responded, to an accompaniment of subdued chuckles. "'Pally,' m'lud, is Miss Baker. They called each other by pet names. Miss Baker was 'Pally,' Lord Haslemere 'Ally'—derived, I am told, from the shortened name of a well-known London racecourse."

There was open laughter at this, which an usher quelled. Charlie looked wretchedly down at his feet. Louisa seethed in her place. Irene Baker cast the jury a soulful glance.

Newsom continued to read. "'My darling Pally, I absolutely adore you, my love. Every hour away from you is agony. I am counting every *second* until Wednesday night. You are the most gloriously marvelous girl in the world . . .'"

Without seeming to do so, he was skillfully conveying to the jury the impression that here was a man of breeding and education so besotted with a girl that he had lapsed into the gushy sentiment of the cheapest romantic fiction. The reporters scribbled with a will, as he went on.

"Another is dated August the ninth, 1909. 'You are much the most important thing in my life. . . . In returning my love you have paid me the greatest compliment possible. . . . Every moment of the day and night I see your sweet face before me . . .'

"September twentieth, written from Lord Haslemere's house in Yorkshire: 'How I shall miss you. I shall kiss your photograph every day. Please come back soon.' I should explain, m'lud, gentlemen of the jury, that Miss Baker was about to go away to Europe and South America for most of the winter on professional engagements. There are many more letters in a similar vein, but they tend, I am afraid, to become repetitive. If I might now call Miss Baker?"

With bowed head and shoulders sagging a little, Irene made her slow way to the witness stand. She began to read the oath so quietly that the judge had to request her to speak up. She did so with visible effort, but managed to swear firmly to tell nothing but the truth. Her voice, it was noted, was pleasant, though a trifle uncultivated for an actress.

"You may sit down, Miss Baker," the judge told her in the tone he reserved exclusively for pretty female plaintiffs. She gave him a little bow and gratefully sat. Newsom turned to her, holding up a framed photograph—it was the one in the picture in the *Daily Banner*.

"Miss Baker, did Lord Haslemere send you this photograph of himself?"

"He did. And I sent him one of myself with a similar inscription."

"Will you kindly read that inscription?"

With just the hint of a break in her voice, Irene read out, " 'To my adorable Pally, with my everlasting love.' "

Newsom put down the photograph. "Lord Haslemere suggested marriage to you on a number of occasions?" he asked.

"Yes."

"Can you remember his exact words?"

"N-no. Not now." This time her voice almost did break. "I was . . . so much in love myself . . ."

Newsom consulted one of the letters again. " 'In returning my love you have paid me the greatest compliment possible.' How did you interpret those words, written to you in a letter early in August?"

"Well, I thought they just confirmed what I already knew—that Lord Haslemere wished to marry me."

The judge intervened at this point, addressing Newsom. "I cannot detect any firm proposal of marriage in those words myself, Mr. Newsom. Is there such a proposal in any of the letters before you?"

"Not as such, m'lud. There are many inferences to be drawn, however . . ."

"And it is right and proper that it should be the jury who should draw them, Mr. Newsom."

"As your lordship pleases."

Newsom sat down and Charlie's counsel got up. Charlie did not know him, but he had been highly recommended by Sir James Rosslyn. He was discouragingly unprepossessing.

"Miss Baker," he addressed her in a flat tone, "we have heard that you and Lord Haslemere formed a . . . a warm friendship during a holiday by the seaside last summer. You assert that he offered you his hand in marriage. Did he give you any more tangible tokens of his love? Any presents, for instance?"

The lobster was either forgotten or ignored. Irene replied, "I didn't want any. He was all I wanted."

"And no engagement ring?"

"We decided it would be best for me professionally if he only gave me the ring when we put the engagement in the papers."

"I see," Randall nodded. "So you waited, worried yet patient. You waited, in fact, until the end of May of this year when Lord Haslemere did announce his engagement in the newspapers—but to another lady."

"Yes, sir."

"How did you hear of his engagement to Miss Wormald?"

"I saw it in the papers."

"Ah, of course. Yet . . . you didn't write to him? You just issued him with a writ of Breach of Promise of Marriage?"

"I was too upset. I was really ill. Too ill to work." Irene threw the jury a despairing look. "It . . . it has ruined my life."

"And yet," Randall insisted, with a spark of animation which surprised Charlie and raised a flicker of hope in him, "and yet you were able to give an interview to the press and have your photograph taken holding his photograph—within the same week?"

"Well, they wanted it . . ."

"Don't you think that was rather a cruel thing to do?" he pressed on, ignoring her response. "Cruel not only to him, but to the lady he had become engaged to?"

Irene flushed and retorted, "It was him was being cruel to me. That's all I thought."

"I see. And yet, all through the winter and the early spring of this year you never wrote one word to Lord Haslemere?"

"Well, I was busy . . . traveling round all over the place."

"Weren't you worried that he never wrote to you?"

"Of course I was. But men don't like girls that push. And I had his promise, and his photo. And I knew— well, I thought I knew, he'd be kissing it every day and remembering me, like he'd said he would." Her voice began to go again and there was murmur in court as a tear was seen to glisten on each of her cheeks and she managed to say, "I had his promise— as a gentleman," before she broke down completely.

"Randall didn't sound awfully hopeful afterwards," Charlie told Louisa. They were seated that night in her parlor, sipping the inevitable champagne, which was doing nothing to elevate their spirits.

"He's a bit of a drip, if you ask me," she said. "He didn't put up any sort of fight. As for that girl and her playacting—ugh! Enough to make you sick."

Charlie nodded gloomy agreement. "I'm sure it isn't affecting the jury that way, though. Old Sir James said these cases are often decided on sentiment, or whatever you call it. You know—the wicked young rake and the poor injured actress . . ."

" 'It's the rich wot gets the pleasure . . .' "

Charlie finished his glass and declined a refill. "I'm

afraid Margaret's going to be most dreadfully upset"
were his last words, as he went off to his rooms and a
much-needed sleep.

Louisa sat for a while, deep in thought. Then she
opened the door and bellowed for Merriman. The
waiter came out from the dispense and was pushed
into her room and the door shut behind him.

"You're comin' to court with me tomorrow," Louisa
told him without preamble. "So try to tidy yourself up
a bit. You look like a walkin' scarecrow."

"Oh, not me, ma'am. Not in any court. I . . . I
wouldn't know what to say."

"You'll be asked questions and you'll answer them."

"Mixed up in a court of law!" he was mumbling on.
"No good for a hotel, madam. Nothing turns the guests
away like . . ."

"Shut up when I'm talking! Lord Haslemere's in
the tripe, an' we got to help get him out of it the best
way we can. If it wasn't for him, we wouldn't be here
now, healthy an' happy. There wouldn't even be no
Bentinck, an' you'd have gone to your last rest years
ago. He pulled us out of it when we was in it, so we're
goin' to do the same for him. Right?"

The old man had no option but to consent.

"Lord Haslemere," Newsom addressed Charlie
next morning, "are you in all honesty, and under oath,
prepared to say to this court that you never, at any
time, thought for a moment of proposing marriage to
Miss Baker."

"Yes . . . Or I should say no," Charlie replied with
a confusion which kindled a special sort of gleam in
his antagonist's eye. "I really never seriously gave it a
thought."

"Yet we have heard that, in writing, you several
times pledged your eternal love for Miss Baker,
whom you referred to constantly as adorable, incred-
ibly lovely, et cetera, et cetera."

Charlie shuffled his feet and looked appealingly toward the judge, who was writing notes and ignored him.

"I know I did," he admitted. "It sounds rather silly . . . especially when read out . . . but you see, at the time . . . last summer . . . I was rather struck with her."

Now the judge was looking at him keenly, as Newsom suggested, "Infatuated?"

"Well, yes, I suppose so. We were having a lot of fun together . . . and she was rather keen on me. In fact, she wrote a lot of the same sort of nonsense to me. I burnt her letters. I think that's the best thing to do with, well, private letters."

"That sort of 'nonsense,' as you are pleased to call it so casually, nearly a year later, can be rather serious, Lord Haslemere. Enough to break a girl's heart. Having toyed with Miss Baker's affections, you just casually went away and left her hoping . . . waiting . . ." He emphasized his words with an airy flutter of the fingers of his right hand.

"Oh, not exactly," Charlie protested mildly. "I mean, we had dinner together in London. I think it was in September. She seemed in very good form, chattering about her dancing and all that sort of thing. But things had, well, rather cooled off between us by then—or I thought they had."

"The onset of winter, no doubt," remarked the judge and received his deferential laugh from all around the court. Randall, Sir James, Lord Henry, and Louisa Trotter were not smiling, though. Neither was Merriman, seated at Louisa's side and looking thoroughly apprehensive.

"Quite honestly," Charlie blurted out without having been questioned, "I just wish Irene . . . Miss Baker . . . had written to me. The last thing I'd have wanted would have been to distress her—in any way. If I'd only . . ."

He looked about him desperately. His counsel was looking more mournful than ever, playing with his pencil. Louisa's eyes were blazing at Charlie, telling him to shut his silly mouth. He got the message and obeyed.

Then it was Louisa's turn to take the witness stand, to the keen interest of the onlookers. Since she was a defense witness it was the mousy Randall who questioned her first.

"Mrs. Trotter, you have known Lord Haslemere very well for some considerable time?"

"That's right," she answered confidently. "He's been a resident in my hotel for must be nearly ten years. And he's a great personal friend of mine, as you might say."

"Do you think Lord Haslemere is the sort of person who would propose marriage to a lady and then, er, leave her in the lurch?"

Despite an objection from Newsom to this mode of questioning, Louisa answered and the judge let her do so.

"It isn't what I *think*. I *know* he wouldn't. Lord Haslemere's a gentleman and he knows how to treat ladies. And I don't mean just ladies, I mean women of all sorts. He'd be just as nice and polite and thoughtful to the old girl who sells matches outside in Duke Street as he is to everyone else. He's the most thoughtful, kindhearted, decent man I've ever had the pleasure of meeting. . . . And I know men."

Someone in the public seats guffawed at this and was promptly shut up by a withering stare from Louisa.

"What's more, milord," she told the judge, "Lord Haslemere's just the sort of nice bloke that a certain sort of woman always takes advantage of. And there's one other thing I can tell you. Lord Haslemere wouldn't never ask a girl to marry him—not without consulting me first."

The judge raised his eyebrows. "Lord Haslemere became engaged recently. Did he consult you first in that case?"

"Yes, milord. He certainly did."

"Thank you, Mrs. Trotter," said Randall, and sat down, pleased with the beneficial effect the judge had produced for him. Newsom was quickly to his feet to try to reverse it.

"Mrs. Trotter," he beamed, deceptively amiably, "if I may say so, you seem to be a woman of some considerable character."

Louisa was unimpressed by the flattery, but said, "If that's a compliment, I accept it."

"It is indeed, madam. Now, you also know the plaintiff in this case well, I believe?"

"If you mean Miss Irene Baker, not half as well as I thought I did."

"Lord Haslemere and Miss Baker first met in your hotel—under your auspices?"

"Yes. There was a little party going on, and I introduced them."

"How very pleasant of you. And later you asked Lord Haslemere and Miss Baker to stay with you for a holiday at your house in the Isle of Wight?"

"Well? What's wrong with that?"

"Nothing. Nothing at all. Only, it might seem to some people that perhaps you were deliberately throwing the two together. Matchmaking, possibly."

"They were my friends and I just wanted us all to have a nice bit of a holiday together."

"But it got rather out of hand."

"They fell for each other, if that's what you mean."

Newsom asked, a shade more sharply, looking at the jury as he did so, "You admit that, in your opinion, they fell in love?"

"Boys do fall in love with pretty dancers."

"Lord Haslemere is hardly a boy."

"Well, he is to me. Anyway, it was only a bit of fun."

Newsom turned back to face her. His tone was perceptibly hardening now, and he no longer smiled.

"You have heard some of the contents of Lord Haslemere's letters. I should have thought 'infatuation' would be a better word than 'fun.'"

"All right, then. Use it if you want to," Louisa retorted to some chuckles. "It's the same thing, though, and if people can't write that sort of nonsense to each other, then the world would be a pretty dull old place. Though I do say," she added to the judge, "me own motto is 'No letters, no lawyers, and kiss me baby's bottom.'"

"An admirable sentiment and excellent advice," agreed the judge, who had seen too many men come adrift in his courts through having put pen to paper. As if sensing that Louisa was winning for the defendant the sympathy of the judge and perhaps the jury, Newsom persisted with his questioning.

"As they were staying with you, Mrs. Trotter, no doubt you were in an ideal position to observe their conduct toward one another?"

"Oh, yeh." Louisa leaned across the stand and gave the barrister her winning smile. "Look, sir—you're a nice-looking gentleman. No doubt you've had a cuddle and a kiss with girls in your time . . ."

The court rocked with laughter. The judge found it necessary to blow his nose with a handkerchief, concealing his lips at the same time. An usher restored some semblance of order, but to the delight of the audience, and the obvious embarrassment of Newsom, Louisa was going on imperviously.

"Every time you took a girl in your arms and kissed her, and whispered sweet nothin's in her ear, you didn't think she was thinkin' you was askin' her to marry you, did you?"

When order had been restored again, Louisa concluded, standing up straight now, her smile gone and her face turned toward the jury. "Well, Irene Baker didn't, neither. When she saw that engagement in the papers, she thought she'd have a go, knowing Charlie Haslemere's as soft as butter when it comes to bloody women. She's just out to squeeze a bit of cash out of him, that's all."

"M'lud, I object most strongly," Newsom cried, but Louisa shouted him down.

"Then when Lord Haslemere didn't come up to scratch right away, the poor, lovelorn girl asks a photographer from the papers to come and take a picture of her mopin' over her lost lover. My heart bleeds for her, it does. I tell you this, by the time she saw that engagement notice, she'd got so many other irons in the fire she'd almost forgotten about Lord Haslemere. She . . ."

Something like chaos reigned briefly, with Newsom objecting, Randall bleating to Louisa to be quiet, the judge ordering her to be silent, and the usher vainly trying to control the spectators. At last, under combined efforts, order was restored. The judge, who had given Louisa an inch and regretfully seen her take a yard, told her sternly, "Mrs. Trotter, if you do not stop uttering these unsupported calumnies against the plaintiff, it will be my duty to have you removed from this court by force, or even arrested for contempt."

Louisa answered quietly and respectfully, "I'm sorry, milord. I ain't got contempt for no one in this court—only for her." She nodded toward Irene Baker, who sat pale with fury and alarm.

Newsom was glad to be rid of Louisa, and Randall, desperately needing to silence her before she could undo all the good she seemed to have done, said he had no more questions for her. The judge dismissed her from the stand with some relief, but a certain amount of regret. His court was by no means often so lively.

Her place at the witness stand was taken by an old man, every inch still the Victorian. He agreed with the clerk that his name was Arthur Cornelius Merriman.

Randall asked him, "Are you a waiter employed at the Bentinck Hotel in Duke Street?"

"I am the headwaiter, sir," Merriman answered with dignity. "Have been since . . ."

"Yes, yes. Do you recognize the plaintiff?"

"Who?"

"That lady, sitting there."

"Oh, Miss Baker—yes. Yes, I do indeed."

"Have you seen that lady on the premises of the Bentinck Hotel at any time during the last six months?"

Newsom's head jerked up sharply when he heard this. He frowned and looked across at his client as Merriman replied, "Yes, sir."

The old man took out a pair of spectacles which might have been as old as himself and put them on. He produced a little red exercise book and turned to a marked page.

" 'December twelfth,' " he read out. " 'Spent the night in Number Eleven.' "

The judge said, "I don't understand. You mean she took a room—Number Eleven?"

"No, milord. It was a gentleman who had the room."

A loud murmur quickly died away as the judge went on to ask, "How do you know Miss Baker spent the night in this room with this gentleman?"

"Because, milord, she was there last thing, when I took them their drinks, and she was still there next morning, when I took them their breakfast." Without waiting for any response to this he turned pages of his notebook and read again, " 'January seventh and sixteenth in Number Eight . . .' "

"One moment," the judge interrupted. He turned to address Newsom, who rose to his feet.

"Mr. Newsom, I believe your client said in evidence that she was out of the country during the winter months."

Newsom had a quick, whispered consultation with Irene, then told the judge, "Not all the winter months, m'lud."

"Evidently. Pray proceed, Mr. Randall." But Randall left Merriman to continue with yet another extract from his surprise chronicle.

"On January twenty-fourth the young lady entered the hotel with the Marquis of . . ."

Randall stopped him urgently. "No names, please, Mr. Merriman. It will be sufficient if you will refer to the noble lord as Lord X."

Merriman cupped his ear in his obtuse gesture.

"Lord who?"

"Lord X."

The old head was shaken. "I never heard of any Lord Hexe, sir, and I take pride there's not many I don't . . ."

"Thank you. Thank you, Mr. Merriman. That will be all," Charlie's counsel said, fearing to tread further.

Unseen by any of the principals in the case, a woman had quietly entered the court and slipped into one of the few vacant seats. All eyes were on Newsom as he rose to glare challengingly at Merriman. His voice was acid with sarcasm.

"Mr. Merriman, are your duties as waiter—I beg your pardon, *head*waiter—at the Bentinck Hotel arduous?"

"I should just say so, sir. On me feet all day and half the night . . ."

"Yet you seem to find ample time to play the detective as well."

"Part of the job, I've always reckoned, sir." He flourished the exercise book. "Keep a note of who comes and goes—what they like and don't like. Who shouldn't know who's been with who, if anyone asks, if you get my drift?"

Newsom's voice was louder this time as he turned
to face the jury again, saying to Merriman, "In that
case, Mr. Detective Merriman, I put it to you that
your researches will have served to convince His
Lordship and the jury that the Bentinck Hotel is
nothing more than a common house of assignation."

The court was hushed, with all eyes on Merriman.
Newsom, too, had swiveled around dramatically on
his last words to face him. The old man was not to be
flustered, though. He answered quietly, "Not at all,
sir. Mrs. Trotter won't allow no ladies of the town in
the hotel, sir. No streetwalkers. Very strict rule, that.
She likes her guests to be free and easy, like they
was in their own homes, as you might say."

Newsom hesitated. All the arrogance of complete
confidence had left him. Suddenly, there seemed to
be no line of questioning he could pursue with safety.
He mumbled something and sat down.

A piece of paper, scribbled on by the woman who
had so recently entered the court, had been passed
down to Randall. He turned to look at her, and Louisa
and Charlie followed his surprised gaze. They saw
that she was Margaret Wormald. Randall glanced at
them, then rose.

"My lord," he addressed the judge, who was writing
savagely, "Lord Haslemere's fiancée, Miss Margaret
Wormald, is in court and has expressed her willingness to come forward and give evidence."

The judge tossed his pen down.

"I am sure Miss Wormald's gesture is an admirable
one," he said. "But apart from the fact that she is in
no position to give any evidence which might have
bearing on this matter, and might only succeed unwittingly in inflicting further pain on herself and
Lord Haslemere—quite apart from these considera-
tions, I have had enough of this most impertinent and
disgusting case, which in my opinion should never
have been brought. Gentlemen of the jury, I instruct

you to find for the defendant, Lord Haslemere. The plaintiff will pay all costs."

He got up and, after the most perfunctory of bows, swept out.

"The court is adjourned," the clerk called. "Clear the court."

No one heard him. The hubbub of delight was too great.

Twenty-Seven

The wedding took place several weeks later, on a fine September day. Louisa attended. At first she had wanted to decline the invitation, but then had made herself accept. Merriman, too, had been there, as a reward for his vital part in the court case.

Mary Philips and Starr were left in charge of the hotel, Major Smith-Barton being away. It was a hectic time. The publicity the case had attracted had certainly had no adverse effect on the Bentinck's reputation. Quite the opposite, in fact. Every apartment and room was taken and applicants were having to be turned away. Only one apartment stood vacant, and that, too, had been prepared for the arrival of occupants—Lord and Lady Haslemere, who were to spend the first night of their marriage in Charlie's suite before leaving for the Continent.

"Everything all right, Starr?" Louisa asked the overworked porter when she returned that evening, dressed in her wedding finery. "The Haslemeres' rooms all ready?"

"Yes, madam. Mary attended to them personally."

"Well, I'll just go up and take a look myself."

She went. Merriman, who had shared the wedding car with her, came in looking remarkably dapper and sporting a carnation in his buttonhole.

"Oh, good evening, my lord," Starr greeted him.

"Fred, get out of that basket and give his lordship a bow." Fred merely yawned. "How was the wedding?" Starr asked his colleague.

"Very pleasant. Reception wasn't up to much, though. Food very badly done and wine undrinkable. Should've had it here."

"No thanks! There's enough doing without that. Your temporary's useless, by the way. Half sozzled, I reckon. The sooner you're into your harness, the better."

Merriman groaned resignedly and wandered off to the dispense to change and get back to work.

In Charlie's rooms Louisa automatically checked the flowers, the perfectly laid dining table, the position of the cushions. Mary had done her job with her usual thoroughness.

Louisa's eye fell on the bottle of champagne, already chilling in the ice bucket. It was Cliquot Rosé 'Ninety-three, the very wine she and Charlie had drunk in these same surroundings on the evening they had fallen in love. The sight of it stirred sharp recollection in her: the echo of their abandonedly singing "And Her Golden Hair Was Hanging Down Her Back," to Charlie's inept piano accompaniment; their charged conversation, which had begun with her chaffing him about the amorous approaches he would have made to the girl who should have been dining with him, but whose defection had led to Louisa's taking her place.

Then I tell her I love her.

And the magic spell always works?

Not always. Sometimes the lady says her carriage is waiting.

And, after the long pause, her own words: *I haven't got a carriage.*

She was brought back from this reverie by voices and movement at the door. Charlie and Margaret came in, followed by Starr with Margaret's luggage. Louisa braced herself and greeted them.

"Welcome. Welcome home. I hope you'll be comfortable, Lady Haslemere."

"Margaret, please, Louisa. Unless you're going to start calling Charles 'Lord.'"

"Not likely," was the instant response. "I can think of some other things to call him at times, but Charlie'd be safer."

They both kissed her and she left them to it, going down to her parlor without troubling to change her clothes and busying herself at once with accumulated paperwork. It was quite late when Merriman came in with a tray bearing a bottle of champagne in an ice bucket and two glasses. She saw from the label that it was Cliquot Rosé again.

"Here, what's this?" she demanded. "I never ordered . . ."

"I did," Charlie said, entering past the waiter. "Margaret's having a rest before supper, so I thought perhaps . . ."

"Good idea!" Louisa said, with real pleasure. "Pink champagne. Didn't even know we had any left in the cellar." She suddenly recalled using those same words on that same evening years ago.

Charlie recalled them, too, and repeated his reply: "Merriman and I knew . . . didn't we, Merriman?"

"The last bottle of the 'Ninety-three, madam," the old man answered. He opened it, poured, and withdrew, closing the door.

"Old muddleman," Louisa grinned. "He was tickled pink you asked him to the wedding. I don't reckon he's ever been to one where he was served instead of serving. Poor old Starr's real put out, I reckon."

"Well, I couldn't invite a damn dog as well, could I?"

They laughed, but there was an uneasiness between them. Louisa said, "It was a nice wedding. Your . . . Margaret made a lovely bride. . . ."

"I thought old Sir James's speech was going on forever. . . ."

"Oh, well, he was paying, wasn't he? . . . And he likes the sound of his own voice."

Charlie poured out some more champagne and carried Louisa's glass to where she still sat at her desk. He hesitated, then sat down on his own chair again and said, "Louisa . . . I think probably this will be the last night I shall spend in the Bentinck."

The tension she had been conscious of was released in a bristling retort. "Oh, is it! She's worked pretty quick, hasn't she. I might have guessed. Hardly gets you to the altar before she starts . . ."

He said gently, "It's nothing to do with Margaret. She doesn't even know about it. But, you see, we'll need somewhere to live in London, and a hotel isn't, well, a very suitable place to begin married life."

"I don't see why not. Anyway, Lady . . . Margaret will mostly be in Yorkshire, won't she? I'd have thought she'd have been glad to have no domestic worries for you, and food provided . . . Seems an ideal arrangement to me."

Charlie took a deep breath. He had had to summon up all his resources of courage for this interview.

"Louisa, my darling," he said, "it won't do. You've got to let me go. It's no good trying to hold on."

"I dunno what you're talkin' about," she said; but she spoke automatically, knowing full well.

He explained, "You once said to me that we've got to be honest with ourselves. Not to/ pull the wool. Well, let's be honest now. If my marriage is to have any hope it 's got to be without your help."

"I don't own you."

"You do, really. You have done for the past nine or ten years. I've come to rely on you completely, and you've never let me down. I even had to ask you if I ought to marry Margaret at all. Well, now I've got to learn the lessons you've tried to teach me. Learn to walk on my own two feet—to be responsible for my wife and . . . children . . ."

Louisa sighed. "Yeh," she said after some moments.

"All right." She paused again, then said, "I didn't really ought to ask you this, Charlie . . . but it may be my last chance for a bit. Have you seen our little girl?"

"Oh, yes. I saw her last Christmas. We have a sort of party for all the tenants' children on the estate. She's bright as a bee. The schoolmistress has had to invent a special class for her. And she's going to be a beauty."

"Well, that's not a bad start in life—depending on how things turn out."

"Louisa," Charlie went on, coming to the other difficult part of what he had to say, "I'm going to leave my money in the hotel."

She shook her head, as he had foreseen she would. "You don't have to. It isn't a charity."

"That's nothing to do with it. I happen to regard it as a very good investment. And I want you to have the furniture that's in my rooms, in part payment of a debt which, whatever I did, I could never repay you in full."

"Nonsense!" was her immediate reaction. But then she said, seeing that her refusal would hurt him. "Oh well, thanks."

She stood up. He did, too, and went to stand looking down into her huge blue eyes.

"Whatever happens to us, Louisa darling," he said, "I want you to know that some part of me will always be yours alone."

He drew her to him and kissed her long and tenderly. She responded almost desperately, as if it were the last thing that was going to happen in her life. Then he released her suddenly and went quickly from the room.

Left by herself, in the late evening gloom, Louisa felt lonelier and sadder than she could remember having felt ever. She idly picked up the champagne bottle. It was empty. She upended it and struck it neck-first into the ice bucket.

The finality of the gesture jerked her out of her mood.

"Men!" she said out loud to the room—and went back to her papers.

ABOUT THE AUTHOR

MOLLIE HARDWICK is one half of the charming and creative writing team of Mollie and Michael Hardwick. They live on the outskirts of London in a cozy little nineteenth-century house that is filled with art and antiques, souvenirs of the various historical periods and personages they have written about during their long careers. Both of them are well versed in British history, a fact that gives their historicals and period novels a convincingly authentic tone. They have successfully collaborated on more than fifteen books. Mollie, in addition to writing several historical novels and a biography of Emma Hamilton, has done a great deal of novelization work including books for the very popular BBC series *Upstairs, Downstairs*. She is presently at work on a vast English family saga for Bantam Books.